PRAISE FOR THE FALL AWAY SERIES

"Douglas follows *Bully* with a gritty, racy new adult tale peppered with raw emotions. This smoking-hot, action-packed story is a powerful addition to the edgy side of the genre, and readers will eagerly anticipate the next installment." —*Publishers Weekly*

"*Bully*, the first book in Douglas's new adult romance Fall Away series, was a self-published sensation, and *Rival*, the latest installment, is bound to capture even more readers with its intensely emotional writing, angst-driven plot, and abundance of steamy sex scenes." —*Booklist*

"*Bully* was a wonderfully addictive read that kept my heart racing from start to finish. I could not put it down! 5 stars!!" —Aestas Book Blog

"A heated and passionate novel, full of feeling and intensity that will appeal to the reader seeking an emotional rush." —IndieReader

"I love, love, love, love, love, love, love this book! What a wonderful debut novel by Penelope Douglas! This book had me hooked! So addictive! So witty! So devastating! So amazing!" —Komal Kant, author of *The Jerk Next Door*

"Jaxon Trent was so worth the wait! Penelope has masterfully combined the best of new adult with all of the scorching intensity of erotica to make *Falling Away* the best installment in [the] series." —Autumn Grey, Agents of Romance

T0038714

TITLES BY PENELOPE DOUGLAS

The Fall Away Series

BULLY

UNTIL YOU

RIVAL

FALLING AWAY

THE NEXT FLAME
(includes novellas *Aflame* and *Next to Never*)

Stand-Alones

MISCONDUCT

BIRTHDAY GIRL

PUNK 57

CREDENCE

TRYST SIX VENOM

The Devil's Night Series

CORRUPT

HIDEAWAY

KILL SWITCH

CONCLAVE
(novella)

NIGHTFALL

FIRE NIGHT
(novella)

PENELOPE DOUGLAS

BERKLEY ROMANCE

New York

BERKLEY ROMANCE
Published by Berkley
An imprint of Penguin Random House LLC
penguinrandomhouse.com

Library of Congress Cataloging-in-Publication Data

Names: Douglas, Penelope, 1977– author.
Title: Punk 57 / Penelope Douglas.
Other titles: Punk fifty-seven
Description: First Berkley Romance edition. | New York : Berkley Romance, 2023. |
"Punk 57 was originally self-published, in a different form, in 2016"—Page iv.
Identifiers: LCCN 2023022197 | ISBN 9780593641996 (trade paperback)
Subjects: LCGFT: Romance fiction. | Novels.
Classification: LCC PS3604.O93236 P86 2023 | DDC 813/.6—dc23/eng/20230512
LC record available at https://lccn.loc.gov/2023022197

Punk 57 was originally self-published, in a different form, in 2016.

First Berkley Romance Edition: December 2023

Printed in the United States of America
1st Printing

To Claire and Bender,
and what would've happened Monday morning . . .

Dear Reader,

I remember the day I got the idea for *Punk 57*. I was living in our rental in Las Vegas, lying over the ottoman and staring at the ceiling. I was in the mood to write a stand-alone, and usually, ideas just happen at odd times, but that day, I was *trying* to have an idea. Lol.

And then I actually had one, which was weird! At first, it was going to be a faked-death scenario. Ryen had gotten word that Misha—her pen pal—had passed away, but he's not dead at all. He's hiding right under her nose at school. After a short while, I felt that idea was too ambitious for my skill set at the time, and that's when I decided that it was best if she didn't know what had happened to him.

Then, the story just took off from there. It was my eighth book, and after *Corrupt*, I wanted to go back to my roots and return to angst for a while. The idea blossomed so easily, and it's one of the more fun times I had writing a story.

What I didn't expect was how painful some of the scenes would be to write. I related to Ryen so well—the insecurity, the shame, the need to be heard. . . . I tapped into memories that weren't good places to visit, but if anything, I knew I wasn't alone. Other people had similar thoughts and feelings, even beyond our teenage years. Some of the things Ryen thinks and feels can last a lifetime for some people.

No matter the ages of the characters, I knew most people out there would relate, no matter how old.

Thank you for reading, and thank you for sharing your love for *Punk 57*. I love the library scene. And the drive-in scene, of course. The spice is great. But I hope you also take away the knowledge that life is short and the only thing to fear is regret. You're not alone.

Love,
Pen

Dear Reader,

This book deals with emotionally difficult topics and includes references to rape, homophobia, violent and bullying behavior, sexual blackmail, body-shaming, depression, and off-page death of a sibling. Anyone who believes such content may upset them is encouraged to consider their well-being when choosing whether to continue reading.

PLAYLIST

"Bad Girlfriend" by Theory of a Deadman

"Bleed It Out" by Linkin Park

"Blow Me (One Last Kiss)" by P!nk

"Colors" by Halsey

"Dirty Little Secret" by All-American Rejects

"Do You Know Who You Are?" by Atreyu

"Happy Song" by Bring Me the Horizon

"I Think We're Alone Now" by Tiffany

"Lose Yourself" by Eminem

"Love the Way You Lie" by Eminem

"More Human Than Human" by White Zombie

"Mudshovel" by Staind

"Sk8er Boi" by Avril Lavigne

"So Cold" by Breaking Benjamin

"Square Hammer" by Ghost

"Stupid Girl" by Garbage

"True Friends" by Bring Me the Horizon

"Where'd You Go" by Fort Minor

"Wildest Dreams" by Taylor Swift

1

Misha

Dear Misha,

So, have I ever told you my secret shame?

And no, it's not watching Teen Mom like you. Go ahead and try to deny it. I know you don't have to sit there with your sister, man. She's old enough to watch TV by herself.

No, actually, it's far worse, and I'm a little embarrassed to tell you. But I think negative feelings should be released. Just once, right?

You see, there's a girl at school. You know the kind. Cheerleader, popular, gets everything she wants . . . I hate to admit this, especially to you, but a long time ago I wanted to be her.

Part of me still does.

You would absolutely hate her. She's everything we can't stand. Mean, cavalier, superficial . . . The kind who doesn't have a thought stay in her head too long or else she needs a nap, right? I've always been fascinated with her, though.

And don't roll your eyes at me. I can feel it.

It's just that . . . given all of her detestable attributes, she's never alone. You know?

I kind of envy that. Okay, I really envy that.

It feels like shit to be alone. To be in a place full of people and feel like they don't want you there. To feel like you're at a party you weren't invited to. No one even knows your name. No one wants to. No one cares.

Are they laughing at you? Talking about you? Are they sneering at you like their perfect world would be so much better if you weren't there, messing up their view?

Are they just wishing you'd get the hint already and leave?

I feel like that a lot.

I know it's pathetic to want a place among other people, and I know you'll say it's better to stand alone and be right than stand in a crowd and be wrong, but . . . I still feel that need all the time. Do you ever feel it?

I wonder if the cheerleader feels it. When the music stops and everyone goes home? When the day is gone and she doesn't have anyone to entertain herself with? When she removes her makeup, taking off her brave face for the day, do the demons she keeps buried start playing with her when there's no one else to play with?

I guess not. Narcissists don't have insecurities, right? Must be nice.

My phone buzzes from the center console of my truck, and I look away from Ryen's letter to see another text roll in.

Dammit. I'm so late.

The guys are no doubt wondering where the hell I am, and it's still a twenty-minute drive to the warehouse. Why can't I be the invisible bass player no one cares about?

I stare at her words again, running over the sentence in my head. When she removes her makeup, taking off her brave face for the day . . .

That line really hit me the first time I read this letter a couple years ago. And the hundred times since then. How can she say so little and yet so much?

I go back and finish the last part, already knowing how the letter ends but loving her attitude and the way she makes me smile.

Okay, sorry. I just had a social media break, so I feel better now. Not sure when I turned into such an idiot, but I'm glad you put up with it.

Moving on.

So just to set the record straight from our last argument, Kylo Ren is NOT a baby. You understand? He's young, impulsive, and he's related to Anakin and Luke Skywalker. Of course he whines! How is this a surprise? And he'll redeem himself. I'll bet you on it. Name your price.

All right, I gotta go. But yes, to answer your question, that lyric you sent me last time sounds great. Go with it, and I can't wait to read the whole song.

Good night. Good work. Sleep well.

I'll most likely stop writing you in the morning,
Ryen

I laugh at her *Princess Bride* movie reference. She's been saying that for seven years. The first year, we were required to write each other as part of a fifth-grade project, pairing students in her class with students in mine.

But after the school year ended, we didn't stop. Even though we live less than thirty miles away from each other and have social media now, we continue to communicate this way because it keeps it special.

And I do not watch *Teen Mom*. My seventeen-year-old sister

watches it, and I got sucked in. Once. I'm not sure why I told Ryen. I know better than to give her ammo to tease me, dammit.

I fold the letter back up, the worn creases of the black paper threatening to tear if I unfold and read it even one more time. A lot has changed in our letters over the years. The things we talk about, the subjects we bicker over, her handwriting . . . writing that has gone from the big, unpolished penmanship of a girl who has just learned cursive to the sure, confident strokes of a woman who knows who she is.

But the paper never changes. Not even the silver ink she uses. Seeing her black envelopes in the pile of mail on the kitchen counter always gives me a nice shot of adrenaline.

Slipping the paper into my glove box, among a few other of my favorites of Ryen's letters, I take my pen, hovering it over the notepad that sits on my lap.

"Spread on your bravery, line the eyes and the lips," I say under my breath as I write on the paper, "glue up the cracks and paint over the rips."

I stop and think as I pull my bottom lip in between my teeth, grazing the piercing there. "A little here," I mumble, the lyrics turning in my head, "to cover the bags under your eyes, and some pink on your cheeks to spread the lies."

I quickly jot down the words, my chicken scratch barely visible inside the dark car.

I hear my phone beep again, and I falter. "All right," I growl, willing the damn texts to stop. Can't my bandmates host a party without me for five minutes?

I put the pen to paper again, trying to finish my thought, but I stop, searching my brain. What the hell was next? *A little here to cover the bags under your eyes* . . .

I squeeze my eyes shut, repeating the line over and over again, trying to remember the rest.

I let out a breath. Shit, it's gone.

Dammit.

I cap the pen, tossing that and the notepad onto the passenger seat of my Raptor.

I think about her last sentence. *Name my price, huh?*

Well, how about a phone call, then, Ryen? Let me hear your voice for the first time?

But no. Ryen likes to keep our friendship status quo. It works, after all. Why risk losing it by changing it?

And she's right, I guess. What if I hear her voice and her letters become less special? I get to imagine her personality through her words. That would change if I heard her tone.

But what if I hear her voice and I like it? What if her laughter in my ear or her breathing into the phone haunts me as much as her words, and I want more?

I'm already obsessed enough with her letters. Which is why I'm sitting in my truck in an empty parking lot, rereading one of her old ones, because they inspire my music.

She's my muse, and she has to know it by now. I've been using her as a sounding board for years, sending her lyrics to read.

My phone rings, and I look down to see Dane's name.

I let out a hard sigh and snatch it up. "What?"

"Where are you?"

"I'm on my way." I start the truck and put it in drive.

"No, you're sitting in some parking lot writing lyrics again, aren't you?"

I roll my eyes and end the call, tossing my phone onto the passenger seat.

So driving helps me think. He doesn't need to bust my ass just because I can't help it when ideas hit me.

Pulling onto the street, I lay on the gas and head to the old warehouse outside of town. Our band is hosting a scavenger hunt to raise money for our summer tour in a few months, and even though I thought we should just set up some gigs—maybe team up with a few other local bands—Dane thought something different would draw in a bigger crowd.

I guess we'll see if he's right.

The bitter February chill cuts through my hoodie, and I turn on the heater and flip on my brights; the wide light casts a glow deep into the darkness ahead.

This is the road to Falcon's Well, where Ryen lives. If I keep going, I'll pass the warehouse, the turnoff for the Cove—an abandoned amusement park—and eventually, I'll arrive in her town. Many times since I got my license I've been tempted to drive there, my curiosity overwhelming, but I never did. Like I said, it's not worth the risk of losing what we have. Unless she agrees to it, too.

I lean over to the passenger seat and shove the notepad and other papers away, searching for my watch. I left it in here yesterday when I washed the outside of the truck, and it's one of the only things I'm responsible with. It's a family heirloom.

Kind of.

I find it and hold the steering wheel, fastening the black suede cuff around my wrist with a timepiece inserted between two brackets. It was my grandfather's before he passed it down to my dad at my parents' wedding, to be given to their firstborn son. My father finally gave it up last year, only for me to realize he'd lost the original timepiece in it. An antique Jaeger-LeCoultre watch that's been in the family for eighty years.

And I will find it. But until then, I'm stuck with a piece of crap sitting in its place on my grandfather's cuff.

I finish securing the strap and look up, seeing something on the road ahead.

As I get closer, I make out a form moving along the side of the road, the blond ponytail, the black jacket, and the neon-blue running shoes unmistakable.

You gotta be kidding me. Son of a bitch.

My headlights fall across my sister's back, lighting her up in the dark night. I turn down my music as she jerks her head over her shoulder, finally noticing someone is there.

Her face relaxes when she sees it's me, and she smiles, continuing jogging.

And she has her fucking earbuds in, too. *Awesome safety precautions, Annie.*

I slow the truck, roll down the passenger-side window, and pull up beside her. "You know what you look like?" I bellow, anger curling my fist around the steering wheel. "Serial killer candy!"

Letting out a silent laugh, she shakes her head and speeds up, forcing me to, as well. "And do you know where we are?" she argues. "On the road between Thunder Bay and Falcon's Well. No one's ever on this road. I'm fine." She arches an eyebrow at me. "And you sound like Dad."

I frown in disgust. "A," I say. "*I'm* on this road, so no, it's not empty. And B. Don't shake your head at me just because you're the only one dumb enough to jog in the middle of nowhere at night, and I don't want you to be raped and murdered. And C. That was uncalled-for. I don't sound like Dad, so don't kick me in the nuts like that again. It's not nice." And then I bark, "Now, get in the damn truck."

She shakes her head again. Just like Ryen, she loves to tease me.

Annie is my only sibling, and despite my less-than-stellar relationship with our dad, she and I get along really well.

She continues jogging, breathing hard, and I notice the bags under her eyes and the sunken look of her cheeks. An urge to scold her nips at me, but I hold it back. She works too hard, and she's barely sleeping.

"Come on," I tell her, growing impatient. "Seriously, I don't have time for this."

"Then what are you doing out here?"

I look out to the empty road to make sure I'm not swerving. "It's that scavenger hunt thing tonight. I'm putting in an appearance.

Why aren't you on the well-lit track at the park with the safety of the two dozen other joggers around? Huh?"

"Stop babysitting me."

"Stop doing stupid shit," I retort.

I mean, what the hell is she thinking? It's bad enough being out here alone during the day, but at night?

I'm a year older, graduating this May, but normally she's the responsible one.

And that reminds me. "Hey," I grumble. "Did you take sixty dollars out of my wallet this morning?"

I noticed it missing, and I'd just taken out money yesterday. I didn't spend it, and this is the third time my cash has gone missing.

She puts on the ten-year-old sad face she knows works on me. "I was going shopping for some science project supplies, and you never spend your money. It shouldn't go to waste."

I roll my eyes.

She knows she can just ask our dad for more cash. Annie's his angel, so he'll give her anything she wants.

But how can I be mad at her? She's going places, and she's a happy kid. Anything I can do to make her happier, I guess.

She grins, probably seeing me relent, and lurches over, grabbing onto the window frame and hopping up onto the cab step under the door. "Hey, can you pick me up a root beer?" she asks. "An *ice-cold* root beer on your way home from the warehouse? Because we both know you're only going to stay there for five minutes unless you find a hot girl who entices you to be sociable, right?"

I laugh to myself. Twerp.

"Fine." I nod. "Get in the truck, and you can go to the gas station with me. How about that?"

"And some caramels," she adds, ignoring my request. "Or anything chewy." She then hops off the step, taking off at a faster pace down the street away from me.

"Annie!" I lay on the gas, catching up to her. "Now."

She looks over at me and snickers. "Misha, my car is right there!" She points ahead. "Look."

I shoot my glare farther up the road and see that she's right. Her blue Mini Cooper sits on the right shoulder, waiting for her.

"I'll meet you at the house," she tells me.

"You're done running, then?"

"Yessssss." She bows her head in dramatic nods. "I'll see you when you get home, okay? Go get my root beer and candy."

I give her a joking smile. "I wish I could, but I don't have any money."

"You have money in your center console," she throws back. "Don't act like you don't stuff change everywhere and anywhere instead of putting things in their proper place. I bet you have a hundred bucks all over that truck."

I snort. Yeah, that's me. The bad older brother who doesn't pick up after himself and eats mozzarella sticks for breakfast.

I step on the gas and head down the road, but I hear a yell behind me.

"And some dill potato chips!"

I see her in my rearview mirror, her hands framing her mouth as she shouts. I honk the horn twice, letting her know I heard her, and speed ahead, pulling over in front of her car.

I see her shake her head in the mirror, like I'm so overbearing, because I won't leave until she's in the car.

Sorry, but yeah. I'm not leaving my pretty seventeen-year-old sister on a dark road at ten o'clock at night.

She pulls her keys out of her jacket pocket, unlocks the door, and waves to me before she climbs in. When I see the headlights come on, I put the truck in drive again and finally go.

I lay on the gas and sit back in my seat, heading down the road toward the abandoned warehouse. Her headlights fade from view in my mirror as I go over a small hill, and worry creeps in. She doesn't look right. I don't think she's sick, but she looks pale and tired.

Just go home and get in bed, Annie. Stop getting up at four thirty in the morning, and get a decent night of sleep.

She's the perfect one out of the two of us. A 4.14 GPA, star of our school's volleyball team, coach of a little girls' softball team, not to mention the clubs and extra projects she takes on . . .

My bedroom walls are covered in posters and black marker from writing lyrics everywhere. Her walls are covered with shelves of trophies, medals, and awards.

If only everyone could tap into the energy she seems to have.

I pull onto the gravel road, round a few turns, and see a clearing ahead, surrounded by dark trees. The massive building stands tall and imposing in front of me. Most of the windows are shattered, and I can already make out the lights inside and the shadows of people moving around.

I think they used to produce shoes here or something, but once Thunder Bay became an affluent, wealthy community, production was moved to the city, keeping the noise and pollution far away from the fragile ears and noses of its residents.

But the warehouse, although falling into ruin, still has its uses. Bonfires, parties, Devil's Night . . . It's a space for havoc now, and tonight it's ours.

After parking, I climb out of the truck and lock it, more conscious of protecting Ryen's letters and my wad of notes than my wallet in the console.

I walk for the entrance, but once inside, I don't stop to look around. "Square Hammer" by Ghost plays as I weave through the crowd and make my way for the corner where I know I'll find the rest of the guys. They always snatch up the seats over there when we party here.

"Misha!" someone calls out.

I glance up and nod at a guy standing with his buddies near a pillar. But I keep going. Hands pat my back and a few people say hi, but mostly I see everyone moving about, their laughter rivaling the music as phone screens light the air and pictures snap around me.

I guess Dane was right. Everyone seems to love the event.

The guys are exactly where I knew they'd be, sitting on couches in the corner. Dane works on the iPad, probably managing the event online. He's dressed in cargo shorts and a T-shirt, his usual attire no matter what temperature it is outside. Lotus fastens his black hair into a ponytail as he talks to a couple of chicks, while Malcolm raises his bong to his mouth and lights the stem, his curly brown hair covering his no-doubt bloodshot eyes.

Awesome.

"All right, I'm here." I lean down to the table, pick up the guitar cables one of them left lying in a spilled drink, and fling them to the couch. "Where do you want me?"

"Where do you think?" our drummer, Malcolm, snaps. Smoke pours out of his mouth as he jerks his head to the crowd behind me. "They want you, pretty boy. Go make the rounds."

I shoot a look over my shoulder, grimacing. "Yeah, no." Getting up and singing or playing a guitar is one thing. I have a job then, and I know what to do.

But this? Humoring people I don't know to raise money? We need the cash, and I have my gifts, but conversation is not one of them. I don't mingle.

"I'll do security," I tell them.

"We don't need security." Dane stands up, the ever-present hint of a smile on his face. "Look at this place. Everything's awesome." He walks up to me, and we both turn to look out at the crowd. "Relax and go talk to someone. There's tons of good-looking girls here."

I cross my arms over my chest. *Maybe.* But I'm not staying long tonight. That song is still in my head, and I want to finish it.

Dane and I watch the crowd, and I see people carrying cards around, which they picked up at the door. Each one has various tasks to complete for the scavenger hunt.

Get a picture of a six-person pyramid.

Get a picture of a man with lipstick on.

Get a picture of you kissing a stranger.

And then some of the tasks get a little dirtier.

They have to upload the photos to Instagram, tag our band's page, and we'll pick a random winner to win . . . something. I forget. I wasn't paying attention.

Everyone has to purchase a ticket to get in, but since there's a full bar, it clearly—from the looks of it—wasn't hard to draw a crowd and get people to pay the price. The bartenders are supposed to card everyone, but I know it's bullshit. Everyone drinks and gets away with it in this town.

"So how are you doing?" Dane asks. "Your dad on your case again?"

"I'm fine."

He pauses, and I know he wants to push harder, but he lets it go. "Well, you should've brought Annie. She would've liked this."

"Not a chance." I laugh, the scent of weed drifting into my nostrils. "My sister is off-limits. You got that?"

"Hey, I didn't say anything." He feigns innocence, a cocky smile on his face. "I just think she works hard and could use some fun."

"Fun, yes. Trouble, no," I correct. "Annie's on a good track and doesn't need distractions. She has a future ahead of her."

"And you don't?"

I feel his eyes on me, the challenge lingering in the air. I didn't say that, did I?

Dane stays quiet for a moment, probably wondering if I'll answer, but again he just changes the subject.

"All right, so check this out," he says, leaning in closer and holding the iPad in front of me as he scrolls. "Four hundred and fifty-eight people have checked in already. Videos and photos are being posted, hundreds of tags, and people are even going live on their own profiles . . . This worked better than I could've imagined. The exposure is already paying off. Our YouTube videos have quadrupled in hits tonight."

I glance at the screen, noticing our band's name with a lot of pictures in the feed. Drinks are raised in the air, girls smile, and some videos play as he scrolls, showing the warehouse.

"You did good." I gaze back out at the warehouse. "Looks like the tour is bankrolled."

I have to hand it to him. Everyone's having fun, and we're making money.

"Come by tomorrow," I tell him. "I have some lyrics I want to try out."

"Fine," he answers. "Now do me a favor and go relax, please. You look like you're at a chess tournament."

I shoot him a scowl and grab the iPad out of his hands, letting him walk back to the guys, laughing.

Drifting around the action, I scroll the feed as I walk, recognizing lots of names of friends and classmates who showed up to support us. The small fires from the pits waft through my nostrils, and I study a picture of a guy with the word *Horse* written in Sharpie over his fly. A girl points to it, posing for the camera with her hand over her mouth in surprise. The caption reads, I found a horse!

I laugh. Of course, some of the tasks, like snap a picture of yourself with a horse, can't be done unless you get really creative. Good for her.

There are a zillion pics and videos, and I don't know how Dane's going to sort through all this shit tomorrow. Though, knowing him, the winner won't be random and fair at all. He'll just choose the best-looking girl from the photos.

Scrolling down, I spot a video that starts playing, and I watch as a girl takes a bar gun, faces it upward and away from herself, spraying water. It shoots up and then falls back down like a fountain.

She performs a sexy little dance move and laughs at the camera. "I'm standing in a fountain!" she announces, her breasts barely contained in her tank top.

A tank top she's wearing in the chilly New England February weather.

But then one of the bartenders snatches the gun out of the girl's hand and sets it back in place at the bar, shooting her an annoyed look.

I hear a quiet laugh from the other side of the camera.

The girl in the tank top reaches for the phone. "Okay, that was embarrassing. Give it here. I need to edit it before I post it."

"Uh-uh," the female voice behind the camera taunts as she backs away.

But tank top girl charges her, squealing, "Ryen!" And then I hear laughter, and the video ends.

I stand there, staring at the iPad, my heart slowly starting to pound in my chest.

Ryen?

The girl behind the camera is named Ryen?

No, it's not her. It can't be. There are tons of girls who probably have that name. She wouldn't be here.

But I look at the video, and my gaze is drawn to the names at the top of the post. She'd tagged the band and a few other people, but then I look at the name of the person who posted it.

Ryen Trevarrow.

I straighten my back, my chest rising and falling with shallow breaths.

Oh, my God.

Shit! I instantly look up, unable to stop myself from scanning the crowd, drifting from face to face.

Any one of these girls could be her. She's here? What the fuck?

I look down at the iPad again and hover my finger over her name, hesitating.

Seven years I've known her, but I've never seen her face. If I search her out now, there's no going back.

But she's here. I can't not look for her. Not when I know she could be within arm's reach.

That's too much to ask of anyone.

And we never promised we wouldn't look each other up on social media. We simply said we wouldn't communicate that way. For all I know she's searched for me. She could be looking for me right now, knowing what band I belong to and that this is our event. Maybe that's why she's here.

Fuck it. I tap her name and stand frozen as her profile comes up.

And then I see her.

Her picture appears, my stomach drops, and I stop breathing.

Christ.

Slender shoulders under long, light brown hair. Heart-shaped face with full pink lips and a daring look in her bright blue eyes. Glowing skin and a beautiful body.

From what I can see, anyway.

I let my head fall back and draw in a breath. *Fuck you, Ryen Trevarrow.*

She lied to me.

Well, she didn't lie exactly, but I damn well got the impression from her letters she didn't look like that.

I'd pictured a geek in glasses with purple streaks in her hair dressed in a *Star Wars* T-shirt.

I look back down at her picture, my eyes falling down her back where parts of her skin peek through the design of her sexy shirt as she looks over her shoulder at the camera. My body warms, and I quickly scan her profile, looking for some clue—any clue—that it's not her.

Please don't let it be. Please just be sweet, socially awkward, shy, and everything I've loved for seven years. Don't complicate it by being hot.

But it's all there. Every clue confirming that it's Ryen. My Ryen.

The check-in at Gallo's, her favorite pizza place, the songs she's listening to, the movies she's watching, and everything posted from her latest-version iPhone. Her most favorite possession in the world.

Shit.

I turn off Dane's iPad and start weaving around people as I slip through the crowd. The heaters warm the frigid air, and I pass more fire pits, smelling the roasted marshmallows. Music blares from the speakers all around, and I flex my jaw, trying to calm my heart.

I walk up to the bar and set the iPad down, turning and crossing my arms over my chest. *Just stay put.* If she's here to see me, she'll find me. If not, then . . . What? I'll just let it go?

"Hi."

I dart my eyes up, my heart plummeting into my stomach. The fountain girl from the video stands in front of me, a few feet away.

And next to her . . .

My eyes lock on Ryen, and I know her friend just spoke, but I don't care. Ryen stands quietly at her side, eyes slightly thinned, looking at me hesitantly.

Her hair is long and straight—not curled like in the Instagram photo—and she's wearing a black off-the-shoulder sweater and skinny jeans that are torn to near shreds. I can see bits of her thighs.

Ryen. My Ryen. I tighten my fists under my arms, my muscles tensing.

She isn't saying anything. Does she know who I am?

I hear her friend clear her throat, and I blink, dragging my eyes over to her and finally answering. "Hi."

Fountain girl cocks her head at me. "So, I need a kiss," she says matter-of-factly.

I breathe shallow, so aware of Ryen it hurts.

"Do you, now?" I say, noticing her long, dark hair spilling around a scarf she wears with a gray tank top. It's fucking freezing in here.

She gestures to her card. "Yeah, it's on my scavenger hunt."

And then her eyes fall down my body, a smile playing on her lips. I guess that means she wants a kiss from me?

She steps forward, but before she gets too close, I take her card out of her hand and skim it.

"Funny. I don't see it on here," I say, handing it back.

"I'm doing it for her," she explains, shooting a look to her friend. "She's shy."

"I'm picky," Ryen retorts, and I quickly turn my eyes on her again, her flippant response goading me.

She cocks her head defiantly, staring me full on in the eyes.

So does that mean I'm not worthy? Well, well . . . I hide my smile.

"Lyla!" someone nearby yells. "Oh, my God, come here!"

Ryen's friend turns her head to a group of people to her left and laughs at whatever they're doing. She must be Lyla, then.

She turns back to me. "I'll be right back." *Like I care.* "Just please kiss her. She needs it." And then she notices Ryen shoot her a glare and turns back to me, clarifying, "For her scavenger hunt, I mean."

She walks away, laughing. I almost expect Ryen to follow her, but she doesn't.

It's just us now.

A cool sweat breaks out on the back of my neck, and I look at Ryen, both of us locked in an awkward silence.

Why isn't she saying anything? She has to know who I am. Of course, she doesn't know I formed a band recently, because I wanted to surprise her with an actual old-school demo tape for our graduation in a few months, but it's damn near impossible to be invisible these days. Our names and pictures are on our Instagram page and the rack of cards by the entrance. Is she fucking around with me?

She shifts her stance, and I see her chest rise with a heavy breath, like she's waiting for me to say something. When I don't, she lets out a sigh and looks down at her card. "I also need a picture of eating something *Lady and the Tramp*–style with someone."

I keep my arms crossed and narrow my eyes on her. She's going to keep up with this charade?

"Or . . ." she goes on, sounding annoyed, probably because I haven't responded, "I need a picture of a picture of a picture. Whatever that means."

I remain silent, getting a little pissed she's acting clueless. *Seven years, and this is how you want to meet, Angel?*

She shakes her head, acting like I'm the one being rude. "Okay, never mind." And she turns to walk away.

"Wait!" someone calls.

Dane jogs up behind Ryen, stopping her, and then walks up to me, scolding under his breath, "Dude, why are you looking at her like she slapped your grandma? Damn."

He turns back to Ryen and smiles. "Hey. How are you doing?"

I drop my eyes but only for a moment. Does she really not know who I am?

I guess there would be plenty of people here who haven't heard of us. We're not a big deal, and this is probably the only thing going on in a fifty-mile radius, so why wouldn't she be here, if only because there's nothing else to do?

Maybe she has no fucking clue she's standing in front of Misha

Lare right now. The boy she's been writing letters to since she was eleven.

"What's your name?" Dane asks her.

She turns back, her eyes flashing to me, clearly indicating her guard is up now. Thanks to me.

"Ryen," she answers. "You?"

"Dane." And then he turns to me. "And this is—" But I shoot out my hand, knocking him lightly in the stomach.

No. Not like this.

Ryen sees the exchange and pinches her eyebrows together, probably wondering what my problem is.

"So you live in Falcon's Well?" Dane continues, taking my cue and changing the subject.

"Yeah."

He nods, and they both stand there, falling silent.

"Okay, so . . ." Dane claps his hands together. "I heard you say you needed to eat something *Lady and the Tramp*–style?"

Not waiting for her answer, he reaches over the bar and digs in the garnish containers.

He holds up a lemon wedge, and Ryen winces. "A lemon?"

"I triple-dog dare you," he challenges.

But she shakes her head.

"Okay, wait," he urges, and I keep watching her, unable to tear my eyes away as I try to process that this is fucking Ryen.

Her thin fingers, which have written me five hundred eighty-two letters. The chin where I know she uses makeup to cover up a small scar she got from a fall during ice-skating when she was eight. The hair she told me she ties back every night, because she says there's no hell worse than waking up with hair in your mouth.

I've had half a dozen girlfriends, and all of them I knew ten times less than I know this girl.

And she really has no idea . . .

Dane comes back with a wooden skewer, the tip holding a roasted marshmallow from one of the fire pits.

He walks up and shoves it at me. "Cooperate, please."

And then he turns to her and grabs her phone. "Go for it. I'll take the picture."

Ryen's amused eyes flash to me, immediately turning dark, because she clearly doesn't want to eat anything *Lady and the Tramp*–style with me.

But she doesn't back down or feign shyness. Walking up, she grabs a barstool and steps up on the prongs to raise herself higher. She's not short, but she's definitely shorter than my six feet. Leaning in with her lips parted, she stares into my eyes, and my fucking heart is going wild. It takes everything I have not to unwind my arms and touch her.

But she stops. "I'm coming at you with my mouth open," she points out. "You gotta show me you want it."

And I can't help it. The corner of my mouth lifts in a small smile.

Fuck, she's sexy.

I didn't expect that.

And I fold. I hold up the marshmallow and open my mouth, holding her eyes as we both lean in and take a bite, pausing a moment for Dane to take the picture. Her eyes lock on mine, and I can feel her breath on my lips as her chest rises and falls.

My body is on fire, and when she leans in farther to bite off a bit extra, her lip grazes mine, and I groan.

I pull away, swallowing the goddamn chunk whole. *Damn.*

She chews the bit of marshmallow, licking her lips and stepping down off the stool. "Thank you."

I nod. I can feel Dane's eyes on me, and I'm sure he knows something is wrong. I toss the skewer down on the bar and meet his eyes. He's wearing a coy smile.

Fucktard.

Yeah, okay. I liked the marshmallow, Dane. I'd like to eat a dozen of them with her. Maybe I won't rush home quite yet, okay?

My phone buzzes in my pocket, and I take it out, seeing Annie's name. I hit *Ignore*. She's probably wondering where I am with her snacks. I'll call her back in a minute.

"So . . ." Dane says. "All these pictures you're posting on the page . . . you don't have a boyfriend who's going to come hunting us down, right?"

I tense. Ryen doesn't have a boyfriend. She would've told me.

"Nah," she replies. "He knows I can't be tied down."

Dane laughs, and I stand there, listening.

"No, I don't have a boyfriend," she finally answers seriously.

"I find that hard to believe—"

"And I'm not looking for one, either," she cuts Dane off. "I had one once, and you have to bathe them and feed them and walk them . . ."

"So what happened?" Dane asks.

She shrugs. "I'd lowered my standards. Too low, apparently. After that, I got picky."

"Does any man measure up?"

"One." Her eyes dart to me and then back to Dane. "But I've never met him."

One. Only one guy who measures up. Does she mean me?

My phone vibrates again, and I reach in my pocket, silencing it.

I glance up and see cameras flashing all over and spot people taking a pic in front of the graffiti wall to the right.

I step up and take her phone, surprising her. Walking around behind her, I turn on the camera, changing it to selfie mode, and lean down, capturing our faces on the screen. But I adjust it to also include the guy behind us taking a picture of two girls in front of the graffiti pictures. "A picture"—I speak low in her ear, indicating our selfie—"of a picture"—I point to the guy behind us on the screen taking a pic—"of a picture." And I gesture to the graffiti wall they're standing in front of.

A smile finally breaks out on her face. "That's clever. Thanks."

And I click the pic, saving the moment forever.

Before pulling away and saying goodbye, I inhale her scent, frozen for a moment as I smile to myself.

You're really going to hate me, Angel, when we finally do meet some-day and you put all this together.

Ryen takes the phone and slowly walks away, looking back over her shoulder at me before disappearing in a throng of people.

And already I want her back.

I dig in my pocket and pull out my phone, dialing my sister. How much will she hate me if I ask her to go get her own snacks? I'm not sure I'm ready to leave yet, actually.

But when I call back, there's no answer.

2

Ryen

Three Months Later . . .

Dear Misha,

What. The. Hell?

Yeah, you heard me. I said it. I might also say this will be
my last letter, but I know that's not true. I'm not going to
give up on you. You made me promise I wouldn't, so here I am.
Still Miss Fucking Reliable after three months of no word
from you. Hope you're having fun, wherever you are,
douchebag.

(But seriously, don't be dead, okay?)

You have the notes on the lyrics I sent with my previous
letters. Kind of wishing I made copies now, since I feel like
you're gone for good, but what's the point? Those words are
meant for you and only you, and even if you're not reading
the letters or even getting them anymore, I need to send
them. I like knowing they're in search of you.

On the current news front, I got into college. Well, a few,
actually. It's funny. I've wanted everything in my life to
change for so long, and when it's finally about to, my urge to
escape slows down. I think that's why people stay unhappy

for so long, you know? Miserable or not, it's easier to stick with what's familiar.

Do you notice that, too? How all of us just want to get through life as quickly and as easily as possible? And even though we know that without risk there's no reward, we're still so scared to chance it?

I'm afraid, to be honest. I keep thinking things won't be any different at college. I still don't know what I want to do. I won't be any more confident or sure about my decisions. I'll still pick the wrong friends and date the wrong guys.

So, yeah. I'd love to hear from you. Tell me you're too busy to keep this up or that we're getting too old to be pen pals, but just tell me one last time that you believe in me and that everything's going to be fine. Shit always sounds better coming from you.

I Don't Miss You, Not Even a Little,
Ryen

P.S. If I find out you're ditching me for a car, a girl, or the latest Grand Theft Auto video game, I'm going to troll The Walking Dead message boards under your name.

Capping my silver-inked pen, I take the two pieces of black paper and tap them on my lap desk before folding them in half. Stuffing them in the matching black envelope, I pick up the black sealing wax stick and hold it over the candle sitting on my bedside table, lighting the wick.

Three months.

I frown. He's never been quiet this long before. Misha often needs his space, so I'm used to spells of not hearing from him, but something is going on.

The wax starts to melt, and I hold it over the envelope, letting it drip. After I blow out the flame, I pick up the stamp and press it into the wax, sealing the letter and finding the fancy black skull of the imprint staring back at me.

A gift from Misha. He got tired of me using the one I got when I was eleven with a *Harry Potter* Gryffindor seal on it. His sister, Annie, kept making fun of him, screaming that his Hogwarts letter had arrived.

So he sent me a more "manly" seal, telling me to use that or nothing at all.

I'd laughed. *Fine, then.*

When we first began writing each other years ago, it was a complete mistake. Our fifth-grade teachers tried to pair up our classes as pen pals according to sex to make it more comfortable, but his name is Misha and my name is Ryen, so his teacher thought I was a boy, and my teacher thought he was a girl, et cetera.

We didn't get along at first, but we soon found that we had one thing in common. Both of us have parents who split early on. His mom left when he was two, and I haven't seen or heard from my dad since I was four. Neither of us really remembers them.

And now, after seven years and with high school almost over, he's become my best friend.

Climbing off my bed, I slap a stamp on the letter and set it on my desk to mail in the morning. I walk back, putting my stationery supplies back in my bedside table.

Straightening, I place my hands on my hips and blow out an uneasy breath.

Misha, where the hell are you? I'm drowning here.

I guess I can Google him if I'm that worried. Or search him on social media or go to his house. He's only thirty miles away, and I have his address, after all.

But we promised each other. Or rather I made him promise. Seeing each other, where we live, meeting the people the other one talks about in their letters, it'll ruin the world we created.

Right now, Misha Lare, with all of his imperfections, is perfect in my head. He listens, pumps me up, takes the pressure off, and has no expectations of me. He tells the truth, and he's the one place I never have to hide.

How many people have someone like that?

And as much as I want answers, I just can't give that up yet. We've been writing for seven years. This is a part of me, and I'm not sure what I would do without it. If I search him out, everything will change.

No. I'll wait a little longer.

I look at the clock, seeing that it's almost time. My friends will be here in a few minutes.

Picking up a piece of chalk out of the tray on my desk, I walk to the wall next to my bedroom door and continue drawing little frames around the pictures I taped up. There are four.

Me last fall in cheerleading, surrounded by girls who look exactly like me. Me last summer in my Jeep, with my friends piled in the back. Me in eighth grade celebrating '80s Day, smiling and posing with my whole class.

In every picture, I'm up front. The leader. Looking happy.

And then there's the picture in fourth grade. Years earlier. Sitting alone on a bench on the playground, forcing a half smile for my mom, who brought me to Movie Night at my school. All the other kids are running around, and every time I ran up and tried to join in, they acted like I wasn't there. They always ran off without me and never waited. They wouldn't include me in their conversations.

Tears spring to my eyes, and I reach out and touch the face in the picture. I remember that feeling like it was yesterday. Like I was at a party I wasn't invited to.

God, how I've changed.

"Ryen!" I hear someone call from the hallway.

I sniffle and quickly wipe away a tear as my sister opens my door and waltzes into my room without knocking. I clear my throat, pretending to work on the wall as she peeks around the door.

"Bedtime," she says.

"I'm eighteen," I point out like that should explain everything.

I don't look at her as I color in the same section I finished yesterday. I mean, really? It's ten o'clock, and she's only a year older. I'm more responsible than she is.

I can smell her perfume, and out of the corner of my eye, I see that her blond hair is down. *Great*. That probably means she has some guy coming over and will be well-distracted when I slip out of the house in a bit.

"Mom texted," she tells me. "Did you finish math?"

"Yes."

"Government?"

"I finished my outline," I say. "I'll work on the paper this weekend."

"English?"

"I posted my review for *Brave New World* on Goodreads and sent Mom the link."

"What book did you pick next?" she asks.

I scowl at the wall as white shavings drift to the floor. "*Fahrenheit 451*."

She scoffs. "*The Jungle*, *Brave New World*, *Fahrenheit 451* . . ." She goes on, listing my latest nonschool books Mom gives me extra allowance to read. "God, you have boring taste in books."

"Mom said to choose modern classics," I argue back. "Sinclair, Huxley, Orwell . . ."

"I think she meant like *The Great Gatsby* or something."

I close my eyes and drop my head back, releasing a snore before popping it back up again, mocking her.

She rolls her eyes. "You're such a brat."

"When in Rome . . ."

My sister graduated last year and goes to the local college while living at home. It's a great arrangement for our mom, who's an event coordinator and is frequently out of town for festivals, concerts, and expos. She doesn't want to leave me alone.

But honestly, I have no idea why she puts Carson in charge. I make better grades and stay out of trouble—as far as they're aware—a hell of a lot better than her.

Plus, my sister only wants me in bed and out of the way so she can get it on with whatever guy is on his way over here right now.

Like I'm going to tell our mom.

Like I care.

"I'm just saying," she says, planting a hand on her hip, "those books are a lot to wrap your head around."

"You don't have to tell me that." I play along. "All those big concepts inside my itty-bitty brain. It's enough to make me feel as dumb as a bag of wet hair." And then I assure her, "But don't worry. I'll let you know if I need help. Now can I get my nine hours? Coach is taking us through a circuit in the morning."

She shoots me a little snarl and glances at my wall. "I can't believe Mom let you do this to your room."

And then she spins around and pulls the door closed.

I look at my wall. I decorated it using black chalkboard paint about a year ago and use it to doodle, draw, and write everywhere. Misha's lyrics are scattered over the wide expanse, as are my own thoughts, ideas, and little scribbles.

There are pictures and posters and lots of words, everything meaning something special to me. My whole room is like that, and I love it. It's a place where I don't invite anyone. Especially my friends. They'll just make a joke out of my really bad artwork that I love and Misha's and my words.

I learned a long time ago that you don't need to reveal everything inside of you to the people around you. They like to judge, and I'm happier when they don't. Some things stay hidden.

My phone buzzes on my bed, and I head over to pick it up.

Outside, the text reads.

Tapping my middle finger over the touchscreen, I shoot back, Be out in a minute.

Finally. I have to get out of here.

Tossing the phone down, I peel off my tank top and push my sleep shorts down my legs, letting everything drop to the floor. I dash to my armchair and snatch up my jean shorts.

Pulling them on, I slip a white T-shirt over my head, followed by a gray hoodie.

The phone buzzes again, but I ignore it.

I'm coming. I'm coming.

Stuffing some cash and my cell phone into my pocket, I grab my flip-flops and lift up my window, tossing them out and sending them flying over the roof of the porch, down to the ground.

Scooping up my hair, I fasten it into a ponytail, turn off my light, and climb out the window. I carefully push it down again, leaving my bedroom silent and dark as if I were asleep. Taking careful steps over the roof, I make my way over to the ladder on the side of the house, climb down to the ground, and pick up my sandals, dashing across the lawn to the road ahead, where my ride waits.

I pull open the car door.

"Hey," Lyla greets from the driver's seat as I climb in. I glance back, spotting Ten in the back seat, and toss him a nod.

Slamming the door closed, I bend over and slip into my sandals, shivering. "Shit. I can't believe how chilly it still is. Tomorrow morning's practice is going to suck."

It's late April, so it's warming up during the day, but the early morning and evening temperatures still drop below fifty. I should've worn pants.

"Flip-flops?" Lyla asks, sounding confused.

"Yeah, we're going to the beach."

"Nope," Ten chimes in from the back. "We're going to the Cove. Didn't Trey text you?"

I look over my shoulder at him. *The Cove?* "I thought they posted a caretaker on site to keep people out."

He shrugs, a mischievous look in his eyes.

Oooookay. "Well, if we get caught, you two are the first ones I'm throwing under the bus."

"Not if we throw you first," Lyla singsongs, staring out at the road.

Ten laughs behind me, and I shake my head, not really amused. The thing about being a leader is that someone's always trying to take your job. I was joking with my comment. I don't think she was.

Lyla and Ten—aka Theodore Edward Neilson—are, for all intents and purposes, my friends. We've known each other throughout middle school and high school, Lyla and I cheer together, and they're like my suit of armor.

Yeah, they can be uncomfortable, they make too much noise, and they don't always feel good, but I need them. You don't want to be alone in high school, and if you have friends—good ones or not—you have a little power.

High school is like prison in that way. You can't make it on your own.

"I've got Chucks on the floor back there," Lyla tells Ten. "Get them for her, would you?"

He dips down, rustling through what is probably a mountain of crap on the floor of the nineties BMW Lyla's mom passed down to her.

Ten drops one shoe over the seat and then hands me the other one as soon as he finds it.

"Thanks." I take the shoes, slip off my sandals, and begin putting them on.

I'm grateful for the shoes. The Cove will be filthy and wet.

"I wish I'd known sooner," I say, thinking out loud. "I would've brought my camera."

"Who wants to take pictures?" Lyla shoots back. "Go find some dark little Tilt-A-Whirl car when we get there and show Trey what it means to be a man."

I lean back in my seat, casting a knowing smile. "I think plenty of girls have already done that."

Trey Burrowes isn't my boyfriend, but he definitely wants the perks. I've been keeping him at arm's length for months.

About to graduate like us, Trey has it all. Friends, popularity, the world bowing at his precious feet . . . But unlike me, he loves it. It defines him.

He's an arrogant mouth-breather with a marshmallow for a brain and an ego as big as his man-boobs. Oh, excuse me. They're called *pecs*.

I close my eyes for a second and breathe out. *Misha, where the hell are you?* He's the only one I can vent to.

"Well." Lyla speaks slowly, staring out the window. "He hasn't had you, and that's what he wants. But he's only going to chase for so long, Ryen. It won't take him long to move on to someone else."

Is that a warning? I peer at her out of the corner of my eye, feeling my heart start to race.

What are you going to do, Lyla? Sweep in and take him from under me if I don't put out? Delight in my loss when he gets tired of waiting and screws someone else? Is he doing someone else right now? Maybe you?

I fold my arms over my chest. "Don't be concerned about me," I say, toying right back. "When I'm ready, he'll come running. No matter whom he's killing time with."

Ten laughs quietly from the back seat, always in my corner and having no idea I'm talking about Lyla.

Not that I care if Trey comes running or not. But she's trying to bait me, and she knows better.

Lyla and I are both brats, but we're very different. She craves attention from men, and she'll almost always give them what they want, confusing shallow affection for real feelings. Sure, she's dating Trey's friend J.D., but it wouldn't surprise me to see her go after Trey, too.

Winning a guy makes her feel above us all. They have girlfriends, but they *want* her. It makes her feel powerful.

Until she realizes they want anyone, and then she's right back where she started.

Me, on the other hand? I'm weak. I just want to get through the day as easily as possible. No matter whom I step on to do it. Something I learned not long after that picture of me sitting alone on that bench on Movie Night was taken.

Now I'm not alone anymore, but am I happier? The jury's still out on that.

Reap, reap, reap, you don't even know, all you did suffer is what you did sow.

I smile small at Misha's lyrics. He sent them to me in a letter once to see what I thought, and they make a lot of sense. I asked for this, didn't I?

"I hate this road," Ten pipes up. His voice is filled with discomfort, and I blink, leaving my thoughts.

I turn my head out the window to see what he's talking about.

The headlights of Lyla's car burn a hole in the night as the light breeze makes the leaves on the trees flutter, showing the only sign of life out on this tunnel-like highway. Dark, empty, and silent.

We're on Old Pointe Road between Thunder Bay and Falcon's Well.

I turn my head over my shoulder, speaking to Ten. "People die everywhere."

"But not so young," he says, shifting uncomfortably in his seat. "Poor kid."

A few months ago, a jogger named Anastasia Grayson, who was

only a year younger than us, was found dead on the side of this very road. She had a heart attack, although I'm not sure why. Like Ten said, it's unusual for someone so young to die like that.

I'd written to Misha about it, to see if he knew her, since they lived in the same town, but it was in one of the many letters he never responded to.

Taking a right onto Badger Road, Lyla digs in her console and pulls out a tube of lip gloss. I roll down the window, taking in the crisp, cool sea air.

The Atlantic Ocean sits just over the hills, but I can already smell the salt in the air. Living several miles inland, I barely even notice it, but coming to the beach—or the Cove, the old theme park *near* the beach, where we're going—feels like another world. The wind washes over me, and I can almost feel the sand under my feet.

I wish we were still going to the beach.

"J.D.'s already here," Lyla points out, pulling into an old, nearly deserted, parking lot. Her headlights fall on a dark blue GMC Denali sitting haphazardly in no designated space. I guess the paint marking where to park wore off long ago.

Waist-high weeds sway in the breeze from where they sprout up through the cracks in the pavement, and only the moon casts enough light to reveal what lies beyond the broken-down ticket booths and entrances. Looming still and dark, towers and buildings sit in the distance, and I spot several massive structures, one in the shape of a circle—most likely a Ferris wheel.

As I turn my head in a one-eighty, I see other similar constructions scattered about, taking in the bones of old roller coasters that sit quiet and haunting.

Lyla turns off the engine and grabs her phone and keys as we all exit the car. I try to peer through the gates and around the dilapidated ticket booths to see what lies beyond in the vast amusement park, but all I can make out are dark doorways, dozens of corners, and sidewalks that go on and on. The wind that courses through the broken windows sounds like whispers.

Too many nooks and crannies. Too many hiding places.

I pull up the sleeves of my hoodie, all of a sudden not feeling so cold. Why the hell are we here?

Looking to my right, I notice a black Ford Raptor sitting under a cover of trees on the edge of the parking lot, and the windows are blacked out. Is someone inside?

A shiver runs up my spine, and I rub my arms.

Maybe one of Trey's or J.D.'s friends brought their own car tonight.

"Hoo, hoo, hoo," a voice calls out, imitating an owl. I tear my eyes away from the Raptor, and we all look up in the direction of the noise.

"Oh, my God!" Lyla bursts out, laughing. "You guys are crazy!"

I shake my head as Ten and Lyla hoot and holler, running toward the Ferris wheel just inside the gate. Scaling the grungy yellow poles about fifty feet above us, between the cars of the old ride, is Lyla's boyfriend, J.D., and his buddy, Bryce.

"Come on," Lyla says, climbing over the guard rail toward the Ferris wheel. "Let's go see."

"See what?" I ask. "Rides that don't run?"

She races off, ignoring me, and Ten laughs.

"Come on." He takes my hand and pulls me away from the ride.

I follow him as we head deeper into the park, both of us wandering down the wide lanes that were once packed with crowds of people. I look left and right, equal parts fascinated and creeped out.

Doors hang off hinges, creaking in the breeze, and moonlight glimmers off the glass lying on the ground beneath broken windows. The wind blows through the elephant and hot-air-balloon cars on the kids' rides, and everything is hollow and dark. We walk past the carousel, and I see rain puddles sitting on the platform and dirt coating the chipped paint of the horses.

I remember riding that when I was little. It's one of the only memories I have of my father before he split.

The yelling and squealing of our friends fade away as we keep walking farther into the park, our pace slowing as I take in how much still remains.

This place used to be full of laughter and screams of delight, and now it's abandoned and left to decay alone, all of the joy it once contained forgotten.

A few short years. That's all it's been since Adventure Cove closed its gates.

But regardless, deserted and neglected, it's still here. I inhale a deep breath, taking in the smell of old wood, moisture, and salt. *Deserted and neglected, I'm still here, I'm still here, I'll always be here . . .*

I laugh to myself. There's a song lyric for you, Misha.

I stroll behind Ten, thinking of all the musings I've mailed my pen pal over the years that he's turned into songs. If he ever makes it big, he owes me royalties.

"Kind of sad," Ten says, wandering past gaming booths and letting his hand graze the wooden frames. "I remember coming here. Still feels like it's alive, doesn't it?"

The night wind sweeps down the empty lanes between the booths and food stands, sending my flyaways floating around me. The air wraps around my legs and blows against my sweatshirt, plastering it to my body like a skin as chills start to spread up my neck.

All of a sudden I feel surrounded.

Like I'm inside the still funnel of a violent tornado.

Like I'm being watched.

I cross my arms over my chest as I hurry up next to Ten. "What are you doing?" I ask, trying to cover my jitters with annoyance.

He pulls at the shutter of one of the wooden gaming booths, and although it gives a little, it won't lift completely due to the padlock keeping it shut. "Getting you a teddy bear," he answers as if I should've known that.

"You really think they still have prizes in there after all these years?"

"Well, it's locked, isn't it?"

I chuckle and continue to watch as he grabs the side with both hands and heaves backward.

"J.D., stop it!" Lyla's voice rings out in the distance, and I look up to see their dark forms still climbing the Ferris wheel.

"Aha!" Someone else laughs.

Ten gives up on the yanking and starts inspecting the lock, as if he can just pull it open, when I drop my gaze and notice the grungy and shredded red-and-white plastic table skirt underneath the shutter on the bottom half of the booth.

I lightly kick my foot out, seeing the plastic give way as it flaps back and forth, indicating Ten's way in.

He stops, forgetting the shutter, and scowls at the skirt. "I knew that."

"Then go get me a teddy bear," I demand, giving him a small smile.

And he dips down on his hands and knees, mumbling as he crawls through the table skirt. "Yes, Your Highness."

"Use your phone for light!" I shout as he disappears inside.

"Duh."

I laugh at his muffled attitude. Out of everyone I call a friend at school, Ten is the closest to the real deal. Not as close as Misha, but close. I don't have to fake it much around him.

The only thing that holds me back from getting too attached to him is his friendship with Lyla. If I left the security of my fragile little circle, would he come with me?

I honestly don't know.

"No teddy bears!" he calls. "But they have inflatables!"

Like beach balls?

"Are they still inflatable?" I joke.

But he doesn't answer.

I lean in close to the shutter, training my ears. "Ten?"

I hear nothing.

The hair on my arms stands on end, and I straighten, calling again, this time louder. "Ten? Are you okay?"

But then something wraps around my waist, and I jump, sucking in a breath as a voice growls deep in my ear, "Welcome to the carnival, little girl."

My heart pounds in my ears, and I yank away, whipping around to find Trey holding a flashlight under his chin. The glow illuminates his face, emphasizing his devilish grin.

Jerk.

He smiles from ear to ear, his light brown hair and cocoa eyes shining. Dropping the flashlight, he rushes up to me, and I barely have enough time to catch a breath before he dips down, lifts me off my feet, and tosses me over his shoulder.

"Trey!" I growl, his shoulder bone digging into my stomach. "Knock it off!"

He laughs, slapping me on the ass, and I cringe, feeling his hand graze down my thigh.

"Now, dumbass!" I shout, slapping him on the back.

He continues to chuckle as he sets me back on my feet, keeping his arm around my waist.

"Mmmm, come here," he says as he backs me into the wall of the booth. "So you gotta taunt me, huh?" His knuckles brush the front of my bare thigh. "You wear that little cheerleading skirt at school, where I can't touch you, and now when I can, you wear shorts."

"What?" I play with him. "My legs look different in a skirt?"

"No, they look great either way." He leans in, the beer on his breath making me wince a little. "I just can't stick my hand up a pair of shorts."

And then he tries to, as if proving a point.

I knock his hands away. "Yeah, the thing is . . ." I say, "a *boy* whines. A man doesn't let anything get in his way. Shorts or no shorts."

His eyes fall down my body and rise again, boring into mine. "I want to take you out."

"Yeah, I know what you want."

Trey's been flirting for a while, and I know exactly what's on his mind, and it isn't dinner and a movie. If I give him an inch, he'll take a mile. I may not need a ring on my finger to have fun with someone, but I also don't want to be a notch on his belt.

So I don't give in to him. But I don't reject him, either. I know what happened to the last girl who did that.

"You want it, too," he shoots back, his wide shoulders and hard chest crowding me in. "I'm the shit, baby, and I always get what I want. It's only a matter of time."

I stare right through his ego, seeing a guy who toots his own horn, because either he's afraid others won't do it for him or he needs to remind himself how awesome he is. Trey Burrowes is a house of bricks balancing on a toothpick.

Something brushes my calf, and I look down just in time to see Ten crawling out from under the gaming booth. I move out of the way and push Trey back, noticing that Ten holds something in his hand.

"I got a sword," he says, waving the plastic inflatable in front of us.

Trey snickers. "Yeah, me, too."

And I swallow the bad taste in my mouth at his crude joke.

He turns away, growing quiet, his attention immediately drawn up to the Ferris wheel.

So easily distracted. So easily bored.

"Tell you what," I say, speaking to Trey as I stroll over and hook an arm through Ten's. "I'll let you take Ten home."

Trey jerks his head over his shoulder, looking at me like I'm crazy.

"And then you can take me home," I finish, seeing his eyebrow arch in interest.

School ends in six weeks. I can fake this a while longer. I don't want to go out with him, but I don't want to wake up tomorrow to a nasty rumor that's not true plastered all over the Internet, either. Trey Burrowes can be nice, but he can be a real asshole, too.

A smile pulls at the corner of his mouth, and he turns back around.

"All you have to do is catch me," I tell him, grabbing Ten's hand. "So count to twenty."

"Make it five," Ten jokes, backing away with me. "He doesn't know how to count to twenty."

My stomach shakes with a laugh, but I hold it back.

Trey smirks, staring at me like I'm a meal he wants and nothing is going to stop him. And then he opens his mouth, slowly stepping toward us. "One . . ."

And at that warning, Ten and I spin around and dash for the back of the park.

We both laugh as we race down paths thick with wet leaves and fallen branches, and whip around broken booths. We pass the Orbiter, Log Flume, and Tornado, which I remember used to play a lot of Def Leppard.

The Zipper still stands, dark and rusted, and we weave through the old swings, the cold chains brushing against my arms. They squeak, probably giving away our position as I charge after Ten.

"In here!" he shouts.

I suck in a breath and follow as he dives into a small building that looks like it was meant for employees. Stepping into the darkness, I pull the door closed behind me and wince at the musty air that hits my nose.

Ten takes his phone out, lighting the room with his flashlight, and I do the same. The floor is littered with debris, and I hear a drip coming from somewhere.

But we don't pause to explore. Ten heads for what looks like a stairwell, rounding the railing and taking a step down.

That's weird. The stairs lead below, underground.

"Down there?" I breathe out, peering over the steel-green bars and seeing only pitch-black darkness below. Fear creeps in, sending chills down my spine.

"Come on." Ten begins down the steps. "It's only a service tunnel. A lot of theme parks have them."

I pause for a moment, knowing full well that anything could be lurking down there. Animals, homeless people . . . dead people.

"They used to control the animatronics and stuff from down here," he calls up to me as he descends with his light. "It's a way for the staff to get around the park quickly. Come on!"

How the hell would he know all that? I didn't know theme parks had an underground.

But I can feel the threat of Trey at my back, so I let out a breath and swing around the banister, heading down after Ten.

"There are lights on down here," he says as he reaches the bottom, and I come up behind him, glancing over his shoulder to see what lies ahead.

My stomach somersaults. The long, subterranean path is built solely of concrete, a square tunnel about ten feet wide from side to side and top to bottom. There are scattered puddles, probably from rain runoff, a pipe leak, or maybe cracks in the walls letting in ocean water. They glimmer with the track lighting overhead.

A black void looms at the end of the tunnel, and I run my hands up and down my arms, suddenly cold.

"The lights are probably connected to the city," I say. "Maybe they're on all the time."

Of course, I have no idea—and why would they be on all the time? But lying to myself makes me feel better.

I hear a door slam up above, and I jump, glancing up the stairs for a split second before planting my hand on Ten's back and pushing him forward.

"Shit," I whisper. "Go, go, go!"

We race down the tunnel, my heart beating against my chest as we pass random doors and more passageways leading off to the sides of the main one we're running down. I stay straight, though, feeling an excited smile creep up despite my fear.

I can't help but think if it were Misha chasing us, he wouldn't run after me. But he wouldn't lose, either. He'd find a way to outsmart me.

I hear footfalls behind us, and I glance over my shoulder to see a light bobbing down the stairwell. Holding my breath, I grab the back of Ten's T-shirt and yank him into the room on the right. The door is missing, so we swing inside and hide behind the wall, breathing hard as we try to be still.

"Careful, babe," Ten says. "You're acting like you *don't* want to be caught."

Yeah, I don't want to be caught. I'd rather be waxed. Every day. Right before a scalding-hot salt bath.

It's not that I'm not attracted to Trey. He's good-looking and built, so why wouldn't I be?

But no. I won't be one of his girls prancing down the hall at school in my skintight skirt while he slaps me on the behind and his friends pat him on the back because I'm his newest piece-of-ass trophy.

Insert hair flip and giggle.

Not fucking likely.

Pressing my head close to the wall, I train my ears, gauging how close he is to us.

Did he turn back? Take a side tunnel?

But then I narrow my eyes, noticing a faint whine instead. As if there's a mosquito buzzing around the room.

"Do you hear that?" I whisper to Ten.

I can't make out his face, but his dark form stills as if listening. And then I see him digging in his jeans for something. A moment passes, and then his phone casts a small glow into the room, and I turn, widening my eyes at the sight of a bed, mussed white sheets, and a small table.

What the hell?

Ten moves farther into the room, getting closer to the bed. "So there *is* a caretaker on-site. Shit."

"Well, if there is"—I speak low, approaching him as I study the items on top of the sheets—"why didn't he kick us out when we got here?"

Ten holds up his phone, looking around the room, while I skim over the things on the bedside table and bed. There's a watch on an old black suede cuff lying on top of a picture of what looks like nearly an identical watch. There's also a couple of paperbacks sitting on a pillow, an iPod with headphones attached, and a notebook with a pen lying next to it. I pick up the notebook and flip it over, seeing what looks like a man's writing.

Anything goes when everyone knows
Where do you hide when their highs are your lows?
So much, so hard, so long, so tired,
Let them eat until you're ground into nothing.

Don't you worry your glossy little lips.
What they savor 'ventually loses its flavor.
I wanna lick, while you still taste like you.

My chest rises and falls in shallow breaths, and my thighs clench.

I wanna lick . . .

Damn. A cool sweat spreads down my back as a picture of lips whispering those words against my ear hits me. I've never been much into poetry, but I wouldn't mind more from this guy.

A familiar feeling falls over me, though, as I study the tails of the *y*'s and the sharp strokes of the *s*'s that look like little lightning bolts.

That's weird.

But no, the paper is cluttered with writing over more writing and scribbles and scratches. It's a mess. The rest looks nothing like Misha's letters.

"Well," I hear Ten's voice mumble at my side, "that's creepy."

"What?" I ask, tearing my eyes away from the rest of the poem and turning my head to look at him.

But he's not watching me. I follow to where his flashlight is shining, and I finally see the wall. Dropping the notebook to the bed, I peer up as Ten runs the light over the entire surface.

ALONE

It's written in large black letters, spray-painted and jagged, each letter nearly as tall as me.

"*Real* creepy," Ten repeats.

I inch backward, glancing around the room and taking it all in.

Yeah. Photos on the wall with faces scratched out, ambiguous poetry, mysterious, depressing words written on the wall . . .

Not to mention someone is sleeping in here. In this abandoned, dark tunnel.

The distant whine suddenly catches my attention again, and I follow it, leaning down closer to the bed. I pick up the headphones and hold them to my ear, hearing "Bleed It Out" playing.

Shit. I immediately drop the headphones, a breath catching in my throat.

"The iPod's on," I say, shooting up straight. "Whoever he is, he was just here. We need to go. Now."

Ten moves for the doorway, and I turn away from the bed, but then I stop.

Spinning back around, I dip down and rip the page out of the notebook. I have no idea why I want it, but I do.

If it is a guy living here, he probably won't miss it, anyway, and if he does, he won't know where it went.

"Go," I tell Ten, nudging his back.

And I fold up the page and stuff it in my back pocket.

Holding up our phones, we step out of the room and turn left. But just then someone catches me in their arms, and I yelp as I'm squeezed until I can't breathe.

"Gotch-ya!" a male voice boasts. "So how about that ride now?"

Trey.

Squirming, I pull out of his hold and twist around. Lyla, J.D., and Bryce stand behind him, laughing.

"Damn!" Ten shouts, breathing hard. He was obviously caught off guard by their sudden appearance, too.

"You might've turned off the flashlights," Lyla scolds with a smirk on her face. "We could see them as soon as we came down."

I move past them, back toward the stairs, ignoring her. If we hadn't been investigating that room, the flashlights on our phones *would've* been off.

"What are you guys doing down here anyway?" J.D. asks.

"Just go," I order, losing patience. "Let's get out of here."

Everyone moves ahead, back down the tunnel, and I glance over my shoulder, scanning the nearly pitch blackness and the doorway to the room where we just were.

Nothing.

Dark corners, shadows, dank glimmers from the fluorescent light hitting the puddles of water . . . I see nothing.

But I breathe hard, unable to shake the creepy feeling. Someone is there.

"This was not the kind of fun I was thinking of when you guys suggested the Cove," Lyla whines, sidestepping the small pools of water.

I turn back around, ignoring my fear as I rush up the steps. "Yeah, well, don't worry," I mumble just loud enough for them to hear. "The back seat of J.D.'s car isn't far away."

"Hell yeah." J.D. chuckles.

And I resist the urge for one more glance back down the dark tunnel.

I climb the stairs, still feeling eyes on me.

3

Ryen

Let's go, ladies!" Coach pounds her fist on the lockers twice as she passes by. The girls giggle and whisper around me, and I comb my fingers through my hair, sweeping it up into a messy ponytail.

"Yeah, I hear they're installing cameras," Katelyn Stephens says to a group as she sits on the bench. "They're hoping to catch him red-handed."

I roll on some deodorant and toss the container back into my gym bag before checking my lip gloss in the mirror on the locker door.

Cameras, huh? In the school?

Good to know.

I pull the top of my cheerleading uniform down over my head, covering my bra, and smooth my shirt and skirt. We're recruiting new team members, since so many of us are graduating soon, so Coach has been asking us to wear our uniforms to school some days to hopefully get more freshmen interested.

"I was wondering what their next move was going to be," another girl chimes in. "He keeps getting past them."

"And I, for one, hope he keeps it up," Lyla adds. "Did you see what he wrote this morning?"

Everyone falls silent, and I know exactly what they're looking at. I turn my head, glancing at the wall, right over the doorway to the gym teachers' offices. Flapping ever so gently from the AC blowing out of the vent is a large piece of white butcher paper taped haphazardly to the wall.

I smile to myself, my heartbeat picking up pace, and turn back to finish getting ready.

"Don't knock masturbation," Mel Long says, reciting the message we all saw lying behind the butcher paper before morning practice a while ago. "It's sex with someone I love."

And everyone starts laughing. I bet they don't even know it's a Woody Allen quote.

They discovered the graffiti this morning, here in the girls' locker room this time, and while the teachers covered it up with paper, everyone saw what was behind it.

The school has been vandalized twenty-two times in the last month, and today makes twenty-three.

At first, it was slow—one occurrence here and there—but now it's more frequent, nearly every day, and sometimes several times a day. As if "the little punk," as he or she has come to be known, has developed a taste for breaking into the school at night and leaving random messages on the walls.

"Well," I say, hooking my bag over my shoulder and slamming my locker door shut. "With the cameras going in all the hallways and covering every entrance soon, I'm sure he or she will either wise up and quit, or get caught. Their days are numbered."

"I hope he gets caught," Katelyn says, excitement in her eyes. "I want to know who it is."

"Boo." Lyla pouts. "That's no fun."

I twist around and head out of the locker room. Yeah, of course it's no fun if Punk gets caught. No one knows what to expect when they come to school in the morning, and it's gotten to the point where the first thing on everyone's agenda is to look for whatever message the vandal has left. They think the intrigue is fun, and while they're curious, Falcon's Well would be just a little bit more tedious without the mystery.

Sometimes the messages are serious.

I POLISH UP MY SHEEN, BUT YOU CAN'T SHINE SHIT.

—PUNK

And then everyone is quiet, visibly brushing off the cryptic message as if it's nothing, but you know it's in their heads all day, a thought without a leash.

And then sometimes it's comical.

FYI, YOUR MOM WOULDN'T DATE YOUR DAD IF SHE COULD MAKE THAT CHOICE AGAIN.

—PUNK

And everyone laughs.

But the next day, I heard, several parents called the school because their sons and daughters had given them the third degree to see if it was true.

The messages are never signed, and they're never directed to anyone in particular, but they've become anticipated. Who is he? What will he write next? How is he doing it without being seen?

And they all assume it's a "he" and not a "she" even though there's no proof it's one or the other.

But the mystery buzzes around school, and I'm pretty sure attendance is up just so no one misses what happens next.

Strolling up to my locker, I drop my bag to the ground, pulling in a long breath. The sudden weight on my chest makes it a struggle to inhale as I twist the dial on the lock, keying in the combination.

My head falls forward, but I snap it back up.

Shit.

Opening the door, shielding myself from all the eyes around me, I reach under my skirt, under the tight elastic of my spandex shorts, and grab my inhaler.

"Hey, can I borrow your suede skirt today?"

I jump, releasing my inhaler and pulling my hand out.

Lyla stands to my left while Katelyn and Mel hover at my right.

Picking up my backpack, I dig out my books from last night and load them into my locker. "You mean the expensive one that I sold half my closet to a consignment shop to pay for?" I ask, shoving my books onto the shelf. "Not a chance."

"I'll tell your mom about all the clothes you hide in your locker."

"And I'll tell your mom about all the times you weren't actually sleeping at my house for the night," I retort, smiling as I place my bag on the hook in my locker and look to Katelyn and Mel.

The other girls laugh, and I turn back to my locker, retrieving my Art notebook and English text for my first two classes.

"Please?" she begs. "My legs look so good in it."

I pull in a breath with everything I have, the struggle to fill my lungs growing like there's a thousand pounds sitting on my chest.

Fine. Whatever. Anything to get her out of here. I reach into my locker and pull out the skirt hanging on a plastic hook I'd stuck in the back.

I toss the smooth, tan fabric at her. "Don't have sex in it."

She smiles gleefully, fanning out the skirt to have another look at it. "Thank you."

I grab my small bag filled with drawing pencils, and my phone.

"What do you have right now?" Lyla asks, folding the skirt over her arm. "Art?"

I nod.

"I don't understand how you can't get out of that. I know you hate it."

I close my locker, hearing the bell ring and seeing everyone around us start to hustle. "It's almost the end of the year. I'll live."

"Mmmm," she replies absently, probably having not heard me. "All right, let's go." She jerks her chin to Mel and Katelyn and then looks to me as she backs away. "See you at lunch, okay? And thank you."

All three of them disappear down the hallway, lost in the throng of bodies as they head for Spanish, their first class of the day. Everyone flits about, rushing upstairs, slamming lockers, and diving into classrooms . . . and I feel the ache in my chest start to spread. My stomach burns from the strain of trying to breathe, and I make my way down the hallway, my shoulder brushing the lockers for support.

I shoot a quick smile to Brandon Hewitt, one of Trey's friends, as I pass, and soon all the doors start to close and the footsteps and chatter fade away. A tiny whistle drifts up from my lungs as my breath shakes from the inside as if little strings are flapping in my throat.

I blink hard, the world starting to spin behind my lids.

I draw in as much air as I can, knowing they don't see my white knuckles, me clenching my books, or the needles swishing around in my throat like a swizzle stick as I struggle not to cough.

I'm good at pretending.

The last door closes, and I quickly reach under my skirt and pull out the inhaler I usually keep hidden there. Holding it to my mouth, I press down and draw in a hard breath as the spray releases, giving me my medicine. The bitter chemical, which always reminds me of the Lysol I caught in my mouth when I was a kid when my mom sprayed it around the house, hits the back of my throat and drifts down my larynx. Leaning against the wall, I press down once more, drawing in more spray, and I close my eyes, already feeling the weight lifting from my chest.

Breathing in and out, I hear my pulse throb in my ears and feel my lungs expand wider and wider, the invisible hands that were squeezing them slowly releasing.

This one came quick.

Usually it happens while I'm outside or exerting myself. Whenever the air gets thick, I excuse myself to the restroom and do what I need to do. I hate when it happens all of a sudden like this. Too many people around, even in the bathrooms. Now I'm late for class.

Slipping the inhaler up under the hem of my spandex shorts again, I take in a welcome deep breath and release it, readjusting the books in my arm.

Spinning back around, I turn right and take the next hallway, climbing the stairs up to Art. It's the only class I have every day that I enjoy, but I let my friends think I hate it. Art, band, theater . . . they're all targets for ridicule, and I don't want to hear it from them.

Gingerly opening the classroom door, I step in and look around for Ms. Till, but I don't see her. She must be in the supply closet.

And I don't need another tardy, so . . .

I walk briskly across the room and head up the aisle, raising my eyes and pausing when I see Trey. He lounges at my table, in the seat next to mine.

Annoyance pricks at me. *Awesome.*

He must be skipping Chemistry—which he's already failed and has to pass in order to graduate. This is my happy hour, and he'll ruin it.

I let out a small sigh and force a half smile. "Hey."

He pulls out my chair with one hand, relaxing back in his seat and gazing at me as I sit down. Ms. Till probably won't even notice he's not one of her students.

"So I was thinking . . ." Trey begins as everyone chatters around us. "Are you doing anything May seventh?"

"Hmm . . ." I play cavalier as I lean back in my chair, fold my arms over my chest, and cross my legs. "I seem to remember something going on that night, but I forget."

He places his hand on the back of my chair, cocking his head at me. "Well, do you think you can get a dress?"

"I . . ." But then I stop, seeing someone enter the room.

A guy walks in, his tall form strolling across the classroom and up the aisle toward us. I don't breathe.

He looks familiar. Where do I know him from?

He carries nothing—no backpack, books, or even a pencil—and takes a seat at the empty table across the aisle from mine.

I glance around for Ms. Till, wondering what's going on. Whoever he is, he isn't in this class, but he just walked in as if he's always been here.

Is he new?

I steal a glance to my left, studying him. He relaxes in his chair, one hand resting on the table, his eyes focused ahead of him. Black stains coat the outside of his hand, from his wrist to the top of his pinky, like mine gets when I'm drawing and resting my hand on the paper, grinding it into the ink.

"Hello?" I hear Trey prompt.

I tear my eyes away, clearing my throat. "Um, yeah, I'm sure I can manage it."

He wants me to buy a dress. Prom is May seventh, and no one else has asked me because rumor has it Trey was asking me. He took his time, and I was starting to get worried. I want to go to prom, even if it is with him.

I let my eyes drift to the new guy again, looking at him out of the corner of my eye. Dirt smudges his dark blue jeans, as well as his fingers and elbow, but his slate-gray T-shirt is clean, and his shoes look in decent shape. His eyes are nearly hidden beneath thick lashes, and his short dark brown hair hangs just lightly over his forehead. There's a silver ring on the side of his bottom lip, catching the light. I fold my lips between my teeth as I stare at it, imagining what it feels like to have a piercing there.

"And maybe your hair done?" Trey goes on at my right. "But leave it down, because I like it down."

I turn back, pulling my eyes away from the boy's mouth, and right myself as I refocus my attention.

Prom. We were talking about prom.

"No problem," I answer.

"Good." He smiles and leans back. "Because I know this great taco place—"

He bursts into laughter, the guy next to him joining in on the joke, and I warm with a moment's embarrassment. Oh, you thought he was asking you to prom? Stupid girl.

But I don't pout at his attempt to make me feel like an idiot. My armor deflects, and I advance. "Well, have fun. I'll be at prom with Manny. Ain't that right, Manny?" I call out, kicking the leg of the boy's chair in front of me a few times, drawing the emo kid's attention.

Manny Cortez jerks but keeps facing forward, trying to ignore us.

Trey and his friend keep laughing, but it's focused on the weak kid now, and I can't help but feel a sliver of satisfaction.

The other feelings are there, too. The guilt, the disgust at myself, the pity for Manny and how I used him just now . . .

But I amused Trey, and now Manny and any shame I feel are far below where I sit. I look down at it. I know it's there. But it's like seeing ants from an airplane. I'm in the clouds, too high for what's on the ground to be of much concern.

"Yeah, Manny. You going to prom with my girl?" Trey jokes, kicking his chair like I did. "Huh, huh?" And then he turns to me. "Nah, I don't even think he likes girls."

I force a half smile, shaking my head at him and hoping he'll shut up now. Manny served a purpose. I don't want to torture him.

Manny is ninety pounds, at most, with hair so black it's almost blue, and a face so pale and smooth that, with the right clothes, he could easily pass for a girl. Eyeliner, black nail polish, skinny jeans, cracked and dirty Converse sneakers . . . Check to all.

He and I have gone to school together since kindergarten, and I still have the heart-shaped eraser he gave me with a Valentine's card in second grade. I was the only one who got one from him. No one knows about that, and not even Misha knows why I keep it.

I raise my eyes, seeing him quietly sitting there. The muscles under his black T-shirt are tense, and his head is bowed; he's probably hoping we won't say anything else. Probably hoping if he stays still and quiet, he'll become invisible again. I know that feeling.

But something to my left pulls at me, and I glance at the new kid, who's still focused ahead, but his brow is hard and tense now as if he's angry.

"No, seriously," Trey continues, and I reluctantly turn back as he addresses me again. "Prom. I'll pick you up at six. Limo, dinner, we'll put in an appearance at the dance . . . You're mine all night."

I nod, barely listening.

"Okay, let's go ahead and get started," Ms. Till announces, coming out of the closet and setting a caddy of art supplies on her table.

She pulls down her screen, turns off the lights, and I glance to my left again, seeing the new kid just sitting there, scowling ahead. Does he have an admittance slip? A class schedule? Is he even going to introduce himself to the teacher? I'm starting to wonder if he's even real, and I'm half-tempted to reach out and poke him. Am I the only one who noticed him walk in the room?

Ms. Till begins going through some examples of straight-line drawing while I notice Trey tear a piece of paper from my notebook.

"Manny?" he whispers, balling up a piece of the paper and

tossing the pea-size wad at Manny's head. "Hey, Manny? The emo look is over, man. Or does your boyfriend like it?"

Trey and his friend chuckle quietly, but Manny is a statue.

Trey balls up another paper, and now my guilt—heavier than before—creeps in.

"Hey, man." Trey flings the paper ball at Manny. It hits his hair before falling to the floor. "I like your eyeliner. How 'bout letting my girl here borrow it?"

A movement to my left catches my eye, and I see the new kid's hand—resting on the table—curl into a fist.

Trey tosses another paper, harder this time. "Can you even find your dick anymore, faggot?"

I wince. *Jesus.*

But then, in a flash of movement, the new kid reaches over the table and grabs the back of Manny's chair, and I watch, stunned, as he pulls the chair with Manny in it back to his table and places himself between emo kid and us. Then he quickly reaches over, grabs Manny's sketchbook and box of pencils, and dumps them on his workspace, in front of his new table partner.

My heart races, but I lock my jaw, trying to appear less shaken than I am. *Oh, my God.*

Students turn their heads to check out the action as the new guy slams back down into his seat, doesn't say a word or cast a look at anyone, and resumes frowning. Manny's breathing is hard, his body tight and rigid at what just happened, and Trey and his friend are suddenly quiet, their eyes locked on the new guy.

"Fags stick together, I guess," Trey says under his breath.

I shoot a glance at New Guy out of the corner of my eye, knowing he must've heard that. But he's as still as ice. Only now the muscles in his arm bulge, and his jaw flexes.

He's mad, and he let us know it. No one ever does that. I never get called out.

Trey doesn't say anything more, and the rest of the class

eventually turns back around while the teacher gets started. I try to concentrate on her instructions, but I can't. I feel him next to me, and I want to look. Who the hell is he?

And then it hits me. The warehouse. *Holy shit.*

I blink, looking at him again. It's the guy from the scavenger hunt. I still have our pictures in my phone.

Does he remember me?

That's so weird. I'd never actually posted our pictures to the page we were supposed to post on. After I left him and his friend, I was so preoccupied the rest of the night, unable to stop myself from looking around for him again, that I never finished my hunt.

But I never found him. After I walked away from him, he seemed to disappear.

Ms. Till finishes her brief instructions, and I spend the rest of the hour stealing glances and messing around on pointless little drawings. I'd been working on a project for a week, but I ignore it today because I don't want Trey to see it.

And even though this is the class I enjoy most, it's also the one where I feel the least secure. Art isn't my calling, but I enjoy doing things with my hands and being creative, so it was either this or Auto Shop. And I wasn't spending five months in a room with twenty guys trying to look up my cheerleading skirt.

So instead I'm here, drawing a picture for Misha. Designing his first album cover as a surprise graduation gift. Not that he has to use it—I wouldn't expect him to—but I think he'll get a kick out of it. Something to motivate him.

Of course I don't want Trey to see it and ask about it. He'll just make a joke out of something I love.

No one knows about Misha Lare. Not even Lyla. He's mine and too hard to put into words. I don't even want to try.

Not to mention, if I don't tell anyone, he won't be as real. And it won't hurt so much when I eventually have to lose him.

Which I will, if I haven't already. All good things come to an end.

"It's him," Ten whispers in my ear before sitting down at the lunch table with Lyla, Mel, and me. "That's the guy vandalizing the school."

He twists his head, jerking his chin behind us, and I look up from my math homework and turn around, following his eyes.

The new kid sits at a round table by himself, legs spread out underneath and crossed at the ankles, his arms folded over his chest. Black wires drape his chest, leading to the earbuds sitting in his ears, and the same hard expression from this morning is focused on the tabletop in front of him.

I hold back a smile. So he is real. Ten sees him, too.

And then my gaze drops to his right arm, seeing the tattoos scaling the length. A flutter hits my stomach.

I didn't notice those this morning.

I can't make out what the pictures are, but I can tell there is script mixed in. Glancing around the room, I notice others looking at him as well. Curious sideways glances, closed whispers . . .

Turning back around, I put my pencil to the paper again, finishing the assignment I got this morning so I won't have to do it tonight. "You think he's sneaking into the school? What makes you say that?"

"Well, look at him. Jail's in his future."

"Yeah, that's proof," I mumble sarcastically, still writing.

Honestly, he doesn't look that bad. A little dirty, a little angry, but that doesn't imply he's a criminal.

I glance behind me again, taking in his face for a moment . . . the muscles of his jaw, the strong, dark eyes, the slant of his nose and eyebrows like he's in a constant state of displeasure . . . He looks more like the type who would punch you for saying hello, not spray-paint song lyrics on school walls.

His stare suddenly rises, and he looks up. I follow his gaze.

Trey is walking this way, saying something to Principal Burrowes as he passes by, and New Guy watches them.

"Is he new?" Lyla asks across from me, and I see her taking in the new guy. "He's not bad-looking at all. What's his name?"

"Masen Laurent," Ten answers.

I can't help it. I say the name in my head, letting it roll across my mind. So that's the name he was trying to keep his friend from telling me at the warehouse?

"He was in my physics class this morning," Ten explains.

"He was in my first period, too," I add, turning the textbook page and jotting down the next problem. "He didn't speak."

"What do you know about him?" Lyla asks.

I shrug, not looking up. "Nothing. Don't care."

Trey and J.D. sit down, one on each side of Lyla, and begin digging into their sandwiches.

"Hey, babe." Trey presses a fry to my closed mouth. I grab it and fling it over my shoulder, hearing him and J.D. laugh, while I continue my homework.

"I don't think he's said anything to anyone," Ten says. "Mr. Kline asked him a question in Physics, and he just sat there."

"Who?" J.D. asks.

"Masen Laurent." Ten gestures to the new kid behind us. "He just started today."

"I wonder how he's getting in at night," Lyla says in a low voice.

I drop my pencil to the table and raise my eyes, looking at her pointedly. "Don't say 'he' like you know it's him doing the vandalism. We don't know that. And besides, he just started today. The vandalism has been going on for over a month."

I don't want him taking the fall for something I know he's not doing.

"Fine," she snaps, rolling her eyes and picking at her shaker salad. "I wonder how 'the guy' is getting in at night, then."

"Well, I have an idea," Ten offers. "I don't think he leaves the school, actually. The one doing the vandalism, I mean. I think he stays in the school overnight."

J.D. bites into his hamburger again. "Why would he do that?"

"Because how else would you get around the alarms?" Ten argues. "Think about it. The school's open late—swim lessons at the pool, the GED class, the teams using the weight room, tutoring . . . He can leave after school, eat and do whatever, and make it back before the doors are locked around nine. And then he's got all night. Maybe he even lives here. The attacks are happening nearly every day now, after all."

I finish my final equation, my pencil digging slowly into the paper. It's a good point. How else would someone get around the alarms, unless they hide out and wait for the doors to be locked?

Or unless they have keys and the alarm code.

"There are no homeless kids at this school," I point out. "I think we would know."

It's not a huge high school, after all.

"Well, like you said," Lyla shoots back, "*he* just arrived, so we don't know anything about him yet." I see her look over my head, and I know exactly whom she's watching. "He could've been here for the last month before starting school and no one would've known it."

"So peg the dirty new kid with no friends?" I retort. "What possible reason would he have for vandalizing the school? Oh, wait. I forgot. I don't care."

And I lean over my assignment, filling out the header, continuing, "Masen Laurent is not living in the school. He's not vandalizing the walls, the lockers, or anything else. He's new, you're scheming, and I'm bored with this conversation."

"We can get it out of him," Trey chimes in. "I can sneak into my stepmom's office and check his file. See where he lives."

"Hell yeah," J.D. agrees.

The sinister tone to their voices unnerves me. Trey gets away with everything, especially since the principal is his stepmother.

I close my book and notebook, piling them on top of each other. "And how would that be any fun for me?"

Trey smiles. "What did you have in mind? Name it."

I rest my forearms on the table and turn my head over my shoulder, watching Masen Laurent. His stoic expression is confusing. As if everyone around him doesn't exist.

They bustle about, passing by him, their voices carrying across his table, laughter to his left and a dropped tray to his right, but a bubble surrounds him. Life carries on outside of it, but nothing breaches it.

But I feel, even though he responds to nothing going on around him, he's aware of it. He's aware of everything, and a chill runs down my arms.

Turning back to Trey, I take a deep breath, shaking it off. "Do you trust me?"

"No, but I'll give you a long leash."

J.D. laughs, and I rise from the table, pushing back my chair.

"Where are you going?" Lyla asks.

I spin around and walk for Masen, answering over my shoulder, "I want to hear him talk."

I head over to his table, a small round four-seater on the outside of the room, and rest my ass on the edge, gripping the table with my hands at my sides.

The boy's eyes catch my thighs and slowly rise up my body, resting on my face.

I can hear the beat of drums and guitar pounding out of his earbuds, but he just sits there, the indents between his eyebrows growing deeper.

Reaching over, I gently tug out his earbuds and cast a look over my shoulder at my friends, all of them watching us.

"They think you're homeless," I tell him, turning back and seeing his eyes drift from them up to me. "But you're not eating, and you don't speak. I think you're a ghost."

I give him a mischievous smile and drop the earbuds, placing my hand over his heart. His warmth immediately courses through my hand, making my stomach flip a little. "Nope, scratch that," I add, pushing forward. "I feel a heartbeat. And it's getting faster."

Masen just watches me, as if waiting for something. Maybe he wants me to disappear, but he hasn't pushed me away yet.

I take my hand off his chest and lean back again. "I remember you, you know? You were at the scavenger hunt in February. At the warehouse in Thunder Bay."

He still doesn't answer, and I'm starting to wonder if I have it wrong. The guy that night was of few words, but he, at least, ended up being friendly. How do you toy with someone who won't engage?

"Do you like to go to the drive-in, Masen?" I ask. "That's your name, right?" I look down and fiddle with his pen, trying to act coy. "The weather's getting nice enough for it. Maybe you'd like to come with my girlfriends and me sometime. Wanna give me your number?"

His chest caves with every exhale, and I feel my skin start to hum as he just holds my eyes. His deep green pools glow with a fire I can't place. Anger? Fear? Desire? What the hell is he thinking, and why won't he speak? I force the lump down my throat, feeling like I'm waiting for the jack to pop out of the box.

"You don't like people?" I press, leaning in and whispering. "Or you don't like girls?"

"Miss Trevarrow?" a stern female voice I recognize as Principal Burrowes' calls. "Off the table."

I turn my head to acknowledge her, but then, all of a sudden, hands grab my waist and pull me forward.

I gasp, shocked, as I land in Masen's lap, straddling him.

"I like girls," he whispers in my ear, and my heart is pounding so hard it hurts.

Then the tip of his tongue glides up my neck, and I'm frozen, breathing a mile a minute as heat races through my blood.

Fuck.

"But you?" His deep voice and hot breath fall over the skin of my neck. "You kind of taste like shit."

What?

And then he stands up, and I tumble off his lap, landing on the floor. I shoot my hands out, catching myself.

What the hell?

Laughter echoes around me, and I dart my head around, seeing a few people at nearby tables chuckling as they stare at me.

Walls close in around me, and I burn with embarrassment.

I don't have to turn around to know Lyla is probably smiling, as well.

Son of a bitch.

And then I watch as Masen Laurent grabs his notebook and pen, drapes his earbuds around his neck, and walks around me, leaving the cafeteria without another word.

Asshole. What the hell is his problem?

I stand up, brushing off my skirt, and head back to my table.

That wasn't the first time anyone's laughed at my expense, but it will be the last.

4

Ryen

I'm going to Banana Republic." Ten rushes up and hooks an arm around my neck. "Want to come?"

I shake my head, taking a left down the hall. "I need to get home. It's my turn to make dinner tonight."

The school is empty, and we just finished practice, but while everyone else is showering and getting ready for wherever they're rushing off to, I'm still in my shorts, sports bra, and tank top. I just want to get out of here. This day threw me off track, and I need to regroup.

That new kid, Masen, is a real piece of work, and I had to turn off my phone to ignore the Instagram notifications after lunch. Thank goodness no one had time to snap a picture of him dumping me on my ass in the cafeteria, but that didn't stop Lyla from posting a meme online, joking about it and tagging me.

Of course, she was "only teasing."

Whatever. I need to get home anyway.

I was able to get precalc done at lunch, but I still have some questions from Novel Study and Government to do tonight.

"Whoa. Is that your locker?" I hear Ten say.

I look down the hallway and spot a pile of belongings spilling out onto the floor. About right where my locker is located.

Ten releases me, and we both jog up to the mess, seeing my locker door hanging open and part of it bent, as if it's been pried open with a crowbar or something.

What the hell?

I kneel down, my lungs emptying as I sift through my clothes, iPod, and a mountain of papers lying astray from the folders they were neatly organized in previously.

"What the hell happened?" Ten bursts out. "Is anything missing?"

I swing the locker door open wide and survey the remaining contents. The little pink shelves and overhead lamp I installed are still in there, as well as my umbrella and fleece jacket I keep at school just in case. I survey the items on the floor and see that all of my books are accounted for as well as the Louboutins and the shirts I hide from my mom.

"I don't think so," I say breathlessly, still confused.

Why break into my locker and not take anything?

I look around nervously, noticing no one else's locker has been vandalized that I can tell.

"I wonder what that means," Ten says.

"What?" I look up, following his gaze.

He holds my locker door closed, showing me the word written in black Sharpie on the front.

EMPTY

I stare at it, confused. *What?*

My lungs feel heavy, and I search my brain, trying to figure out what the hell is going on.

Empty? And why just my locker?

I gather up all of my belongings and pack them in my duffel, completely creeped out that someone was doing this while I was at practice. The office is closed now, but I'm definitely reporting this in the morning.

Slipping on my black fleece jacket, I head out to the parking lot with Ten and climb into my car as he hops into his. I immediately lock my doors.

I'll have to get a new locker tomorrow, too. I can't carry all this shit with me every day. Even if there's only a little over a month left of school.

Goddammit. Who would root around in my stuff? Not everyone likes me—in fact, Ten is the only person who probably doesn't have a motive to piss me off—but no one in particular sticks out. And what if it happens again?

I quickly drive home and pull into my driveway, parking in the garage and seeing no other cars home yet. My sister is probably still in class, and my mother's car is parked at the airport, waiting for her when she gets back tomorrow morning.

I stare down at my phone screen, sending a quick reply to her text that she sent earlier.

I'll be home late tomorrow. Cheer . . . swim . . . , I type.

K. Dinner will be waiting, she replies. Don't forget to pack extra food tomorrow.

Yeah, yeah. I stuff my phone in my duffel. A couple nights a week, I stay late at school for cheer practice and then to teach swim lessons for a couple of hours afterward. I have a small break in between to eat something, since I won't be home for dinner, and to get some homework done.

Closing the garage door, I gather my bags and enter the kitchen through the door off the carport, grabbing a water bottle out of the fridge before dashing up the stairs.

I'll feel better after a shower.

With what happened to my locker and the episode in the cafeteria today, it's been a long time since I've had that feeling. People don't laugh at me, and guys like him don't put me in my place. I'm not going to let him in my head like I let them in all those years ago. I'm stronger now.

I swing my bedroom door open and walk in, my bags falling from my hands.

What the fuck?!

"What the hell are you doing?" I shout.

Masen, the new guy, sits in my desk chair, leaning back with his hands locked behind his head. I hear music and glance over at my iPod dock, seeing that he's playing Garbage's "Stupid Girl."

He smirks and stares at me, relaxing as if he hasn't broken into my house and planted his ass somewhere it doesn't belong.

"Hello?" I bark. "What are you doing in my room, asshole?"

Exhaling a slow breath, he jerks his chin at me. "I went to what I assume is your sister's room first. That seems more you. Hot-pink princess bullshit with the zebra-print bedding."

I quickly close my door, not wanting my sister to get home and see him in here. "How did you get in?"

But he ignores me and keeps going. "However, I don't think it was your name in purple neon lights above the bed." He starts laughing, probably at my sister's stupid narcissistic decorating, and stands up. "Ryen, right?" he asks, looking around my room. "I must say, this is not at all what I expected."

I'm a lot of what you're not expecting, dickhead. "Get out."

"Make me."

I fist my hands. "How did you get in?"

"Through the front door." He steps toward me. "So where is it?"

I pinch my eyebrows together, confused. "Where's what?"

"My shit." His teeth are bared, his smile gone.

His shit? What's he talking about?

"Get out!" I yell. "I have no idea what the hell you're talking about."

"You seem nervous."

"You think?!" I retort. "I don't like strange guys in my house, and I really don't like anyone in my room."

"Don't care," he replies, looking bored. "You took something of mine. Two things of mine, actually, and I want them back."

"No, I didn't. Now, get out!"

He reaches behind himself and pulls something out of the back of his jeans, holding it up. My face falls, and a knot tightens in my stomach.

Shit. My notebook.

A large white leather-bound diary of rants and pity parties I've thrown for myself over the past three years, and something I don't want anyone to see. Ever. Every bad thought or feeling I've ever had about myself, my family, and my friends that I couldn't voice out loud is in that book.

How did he find it?

"Under the mattress isn't exactly a novel idea, you know?" he says. "And yes, I read that part. And the other one. And the other one."

My heart pounds in my ears, and a scream creeps its way up my throat.

I lunge for him.

I grab hold of the book, but he shoves me back, and I stumble onto the bed, his body coming down on mine.

I grunt and cry out, trying to get the book.

He reaches for something, and then my scissors from my desk are pointing at my face. I freeze, staring at the tip.

"Don't worry," he taunts in a dark voice. "I won't make sure this falls into your mom's hands. I'm going to rip out every fucking page and plaster them all over school, so listen loud and clear, you stupid cunt. I'm done talking to you, and I'm done looking at you. I want the locket, and I want the piece of paper you took at the Cove."

"The Cove?" I gasp under the weight of his body. "Wha—"

What the hell is he talking about?

And then I pause as it hits me. The Cove. Last night. The piece of paper.

I want a lick while you still taste like you.

And then today . . . *You taste like shit.*

I stare at him, dumbfounded. "Oh, my God."

That was his room?

I was right. There was someone there in the tunnel. He saw us.

And then I widen my eyes. He was the one who broke into my locker! That's why nothing was missing. He didn't find what he was looking for.

He snaps the scissors, and I wince as he brings the scissors back up, a few of my light brown hairs floating in the air.

"Stop!" I yell. "I don't . . . I . . ."

His dark green eyes narrow on me, threatening and cutting right through me.

I growl, grappling for my pillow and reaching inside, pulling out a folded, worn piece of paper.

I shove it at his chest.

He takes the paper. "Now the necklace."

"I didn't take a necklace!" I shout. "Just the paper."

He snaps the scissors at my hair again, and I scream. "Dammit! I told you! I didn't take it! It—"

Ten. Ten was with me. He took it.

Shit.

"What?" Masen growls, probably seeing the realization on my face.

I breathe hard, flexing my jaw. "My friend was with me. I'll get it. All right? I'll get it. Now, get off me!"

He pauses, staring down at me. But eventually he pushes off the bed and tosses the scissors onto the desk, sliding the poem into his back pocket.

I shoot up, grabbing at my ponytail and finding the small bit of hair that was snipped. Only about half an inch from a few strands.

I scowl at him. "Prick."

"Tomorrow," he orders, ignoring my insult. "The parking lot after school." And then he holds up my notebook. "I'm keeping this as insurance."

"No. I don't trust you."

"What do ya know, Rocks?" He smiles. "Something we have in common. I don't trust you, either." He curls the notebook, squeezing it in his fist. "Now, don't waste any more of my time. Tomorrow."

I grind my teeth, watching him walk toward the door. He stops in the doorway and turns around, taking a last look around my room.

"You know . . . I really do like your room," he muses. "Maybe if you were more like this at school, people wouldn't talk behind your back so much."

He walks out, slamming the door behind him, and my face falls.

I stare at the word written on the back of my door, in large, chalk letters that I didn't write.

FRAUD

The next morning, I make my way to Ten's locker, but only after stopping by the school office and reporting my own vandalized and getting a new one assigned. Students crowd the halls, and I hold my books in my arm and turn inward, trying to avoid any attention.

"Do you have it?" I ask without saying hello first.

He glances up from his locker and sighs, looking a little embarrassed. I'd texted him last night, demanding he bring the locket today.

Reaching into the pocket of his knee-length shorts, he pulls out a long chain with a circular silver locket hanging off it.

I take it, instantly feeling a little relief at having what that asshole wants. Now I can get my notebook back.

"Why would you take this?" I snap. Did he think it would go well with his J.Crew T-shirts?

But Ten just shrugs. "It looked like an antique. I thought maybe it might be worth something."

I slip the necklace into my pocket. "Klepto."

"How did you know I took it anyway?"

Because the hot new guy, who also happens to be squatting in an abandoned theme park, broke into my bedroom last night, cut my hair, and threatened to expose my hideous inner musings about all of my friends if I didn't get it back.

Yeah, no.

"I'll see you at lunch," I say, ignoring his question and turning around to head to Art.

Digging the necklace back out of my pocket as I walk, I flip it over, studying the aged silver and intricate detail around the large moonstone set in the middle. Ten is right. It looks like an antique. There are several scratches, and the metal feels thicker, more solid, than your typical Target jewelry.

What does the necklace mean to Masen Laurent, though? I open the locket, slowly climbing the stairwell, the people jogging and laughing around me a distant echo.

But as soon as I pop it open, I dig in my eyebrows, seeing, not pictures as I expected, but a tiny folded-up piece of paper.

Taking it out, I unwrap it and turn it over, reading the words.

Close your eyes. There's nothing to see out here.

I slow to a stop, staring at the note and saying the words to myself again.

It sounds familiar, like I've heard them before. Or said them or something . . .

The second bell rings, our one-minute warning, and I fold the paper back up, stuffing it into the locket and closing it.

Everyone around me hustles up and down the stairs, and I jog to my class, slipping the necklace back into my jean shorts.

Who does the locket belong to? A family member? A girlfriend? Maybe he stole it. He's living at the Cove, after all, and judging by the state of his hands and jeans, it doesn't look like a parent is watching over him. He probably doesn't have any money, and if he can break into my house without leaving a scratch, then I'm sure he's done it before.

I'm tempted to seek him out now and get my notebook back, but it's probably in his locker or his car, and I don't trust him to be able to do a quick exchange without others spotting me talking to the weirdo who dumped me on my ass yesterday. I don't want to be seen with him again.

And luckily, I don't see him in Art today. Perhaps he got out of the class.

Or—my heart sinks a little—maybe he's not at school today. Agitation boils under my skin. If I have to go back to that junkyard again and search him out, I'll be pissed. I'm getting that book back.

After Art, I head to English IV, carrying my text, notebook, and copy of *Lolita*. But as soon as I step into the room, I spot him sitting in the row to the left of mine, one desk back.

Relief and a touch of annoyance both hit me. He wasn't in this class yesterday. Is he going to be in any more of my classes?

But he doesn't seem to see me. Just like yesterday in Art, the guy simply sits there, staring ahead with a slight scowl on his face as if this is all such an inconvenience to him.

I take my seat, noticing his jeans are actually clean today.

Mr. Foster fires up his projector, the screen of his laptop appearing on the big whiteboard in front of the class, and he begins making the rounds, handing back our latest essays. The final bell rings, and the class lowers their voices, quietly chattering as the teacher walks up and down the aisles.

"So I'm going to go out on a limb," Foster says, stopping at my desk and holding my paper as he peers down at me. "Did you actually read the book, or did you read reviews?"

I hear a snort behind me—from J.D., no doubt—and I smile.

"You asked for an analysis of the story, so I watched the movie," I explain, plucking my *Anna Karenina* paper out of his hand. "Spoiler alert, there was a lot of sex in it."

Laughter breaks out, and I feel a rush hit my veins, pumping me up after my minor humiliation yesterday.

Mr. Foster and I constantly go head-to-head, and while Art may be the class I enjoy the most, Foster is my favorite teacher. He encourages us to use our voice and is one of the only adults to talk to his students like adults.

"I asked for an analysis of the *novel*, Ryen."

"And I tried," I tell him. "I honestly did. But it was depressing and in a pointless way. What was I supposed to learn? Women, don't cheat on your husbands in nineteenth-century Russia, or you'll be cast out of society and forced to throw yourself in front of a train?" I sit up in my seat. "Got it. And the next time I'm in nineteenth-century Russia, I'm going to remember it."

I hear J.D. chuckle again behind me, and more giggles break out in the room.

But Foster lowers his voice, looking me deep in the eyes. "You're better than this," he whispers.

I stare at him for a moment, seeing the plea in his eyes. Seeing how highly he thinks of my intellect and how angry he is that I don't make better use of it.

He backs away, moving on to the next student but still speaking to me. "Read *Jane Eyre*, and redo it," he demands.

I should quietly accept my punishment and be grateful he's giving me another chance instead of accepting the C that's written on my *Anna Karenina* paper right now. But I can't resist smarting off some more.

"Can I at least read something written in the past hundred years?" I ask. "Something where a middle-aged man isn't conning an eighteen-year-old girl into committing bigamy?"

He turns his head, a stern expression on his face. "I think you've dominated the class's attention long enough, Ms. Trevarrow."

"In fact," I go on, "I'm seeing a trend this semester. *Anna Karenina*, *Lolita*, *Girl with a Pearl Earring*, *Jane Eyre* . . . all stories featuring older men and younger women. Something you want to tell us, Mr. Foster?" I wink twice, teasing the older man.

The class's laughter is louder this time, and I can see Foster's chest rise with a huge, exasperated breath.

"I'd like the report tomorrow," he says. "Do you understand?"

"Absolutely," I answer and then drop my voice to a mumble. "There are tons of *Jane Eyre* movies."

The students around me snicker under their breath, because of course I can't read a whole novel and write a report on it with cheer and swim tonight. I end my taunting, satisfied that I won that argument. In their eyes, anyway.

The air is cool and fresh as it fills my lungs.

"What about *Twilight*?" someone calls out.

I pause at the deep voice behind me. Mr. Foster stands in front of his desk and looks up, focusing over my head.

"*Twilight*?" he asks.

"Yeah, Rocks?" Masen prompts me. "Did you like *Twilight*?"

My heart starts beating harder. What is he doing?

But I turn my head to the side, fixing him with a bored expression. "Sure. When I was twelve. You?"

The corner of his mouth lifts, and I'm once again drawn to the piercing on his lip. "I'll bet you loved it," he says, the entire class listening. "I'll bet it was what got you interested in reading. And I'll even bet you were at the movies opening night. Did you have an Edward T-shirt, too?"

A few chuckles go off around me, and the little high I felt a moment ago is sucked away at the sight of his gloating eyes. How could he have known that?

I picked up a *Twilight* paperback when I was younger, because Robert Pattinson was on the cover, and hey, I was twelve, so . . .

But immediately after reading it, I asked my mom to go buy me all the books, and I spent the next two weeks reading them with every free moment I got.

I arch an eyebrow, looking at the teacher. "While it's fascinating that it's finally speaking and all, I'm, again, wondering what the point is."

"The point is . . ." Masen answers, "wasn't Edward like a hundred years older than Bella?"

Eighty-six.

"See," he keeps going, "you're judging stories about older men and younger women as some sick, superficial perversion on the males' part, when actually it was quite common during those times for men to wait until they had finished their education and established a career before being ready to support a wife."

He pauses and then continues. "A wife, which was almost always younger, because she needed to bear many children. As society dictated. And yet, your precious Edward Cullen was over a hundred years old, still in high school, living with his parents, and trying to get in the pants of a minor in the twenty-first century."

The whole class erupts in laughter, and my stomach sinks.

I catch sight of Masen out of the corner of my eye, leaning his desk forward, closer to mine, and whispering, "But he was hot, so I guess that's all that's important, right?"

I keep staring ahead, the knots in my stomach pulling tighter and tighter. Sure, Edward was decades older than Bella. But the fact that he was good-looking had nothing to do with her loving him anyway.

Masen continues his attack. "Now, if he looked like most hundred-year-old men looked," he calls out, and I see him stand up, "it wouldn't have been romantic, would it? There would be no Bella and Edward." He walks up to the front of the class and rounds the teacher's desk, gesturing to the laptop. "May I?"

The teacher nods, looking wary but allowing it.

Masen leans down, and I refuse to look as he types something into the search engine. But when more laughter breaks out, louder this time, I can't help myself.

I glance up at the screen and instantly feel anger curl my fingers into a fist.

A huge image of an old man, withered with wrinkles, missing teeth, and bald but with wiry silver hairs sprouting from the top of his nose, smiles back at us, and I glare at Masen, who grins back.

"Old geezer Edward is a happy guy," he gloats, "because he's about to get naked with Bel-la."

"Aw, yeah!" J.D. hollers, and everyone loses control. Students double over laughing, and their amusement surrounds me like a wall closing in. Everything is getting smaller, and I start to feel the space in my lungs shrink as I pull harder to take in air.

I clench my teeth together. *Motherfucker.*

Masen crosses his arms over his chest, looking at me like a meal he can't wait to eat again. "Shake your pom-poms, Rocks," he says. "You just reminded all of us that love is truly *only* skin-deep."

I walk as quickly as I can, a cool sweat spreading down my neck and back as I dive into the girls' locker room. The weight on my chest gets heavier, and I pass girls undressing for PE as I slip into one of the shower stalls, draw the curtain closed, and turn on the water.

I step to the left so I don't get hit with the spray. The white noise of the water shields me from listening ears, and I grab my inhaler from my pocket, taking two quick pumps and leaning back against the shower wall, closing my eyes.

Four years. I haven't had a fucking attack triggered by panic in four years. It's always exercise-induced. My lungs start to open up, and I slowly breathe in and out, forcing myself to calm down.

What the hell is wrong with me? The guy's not a threat. I can handle this. So he was challenging me. So what? Am I going to flip out every time that happens? Sooner or later I'll leave safe Falcon's Well, and I'll no longer be queen bee. I'm acting like a baby.

But for a moment, everything went dark. Slowly the world in my vision got smaller and smaller, like I was in a tunnel going backward. The light ahead of me—Masen, Mr. Foster, the other students—became tiny as the darkness ate up the room, and I felt completely alone.

Just like before.

"All right, everyone!" Ms. Wilkens, my fourth-grade teacher, calls as we line up at the door inside the classroom. "If you're staying in for recess, there's no talking. You're working." Then she looks up to us. "The rest of you . . . walk, please."

The line leader pushes through the door and everyone bolts, running outside to the playground. Some students dash for the tetherballs, others for the bars, and some stroll around the blacktop, figuring out what they want to do.

Everyone passes me by, and I slow to a walk, fidgeting and watching them as they find their groups and begin playing. The sun is hot, and I slowly step into the chaos, looking around and not sure where to go or who to talk to.

This happens every day.

Girls run up to other girls, smiling and talking. Boys play with other boys, tossing balls back and forth and climbing the equipment. Some of my classmates sit on the grass and play with little things they snuck into school, and everyone has found each other, pairing off.

But no one's looking for me.

I shuffle my feet, feeling my stomach twist into knots. I hate recess. I should've just stayed in the classroom and colored or written in my journal or something.

I want them to know I'm here, though. I want them to see me. I don't like being forgotten.

I look over at Shannon Bell and a few other girls from class, their hair and clothes always so cool and pretty. Why can't I ever look like that? I run my hands down my knee-length skirt and polo shirt, looking like such a good girl. My mom always pulls my hair back in a ponytail, but I want to curl it like them.

I lick my lips, swallow the big lump in my throat, and walk over to them.

"Hi," I say, feeling like I can't breathe.

They stop talking and look at me, not smiling. I gesture to Shannon's hand. "I like your nail polish."

Actually, I don't. Yellow grosses me out, but my mom said complimenting people is a good way to make friends, so . . .

Shannon lets out a little scoff, looking embarrassed that her friends see me talking to her. She shoots a look to them.

I feel an invisible hand pushing me away from them. They want me gone, don't they?

But I force a smile and try harder. "Hey," I tell another girl, seeing her Mary Janes. "We have the same shoes." And I look down at mine, showing her.

She laughs, rolling her eyes. "Ew."

"You guys," another girl chides her friends, but they don't stop laughing.

"What's that?" Shannon points to the bulge in the pocket of my skirt.

My heart sinks a little. No one else in my class has an inhaler, and now it makes me even more different. "It's just my inhaler," I reply, speaking low. "I have allergies and asthma and stuff. It's no big deal."

I keep my eyes down because I don't want to see the looks they give each other. I twist my lips to the side, feeling tears creep up. Why can't I be cool?

"So do you think Cory Schultz is cute?" Shannon speaks up.

I blink, my guard going up. "No," I answer quickly.

Cory Schultz is in our class, and he's really cute, but I don't want anyone to know I think that.

"Well, I think he's cute," she says. "We all do. You got a problem with him?"

I look up, shaking my head. "No. I just . . . Yeah, I guess he's kind of cute."

A girl behind Shannon breaks into laughter, and Shannon suddenly walks away, toward the basketball court.

My heart starts racing. She walks up to Cory and whispers something in his ear, and he turns to look at me, scrunching up his face in disgust.

No.

Everyone starts laughing, and I turn and run away, hearing behind me, "Ryen likes Cory. Ryen likes Cory."

I start crying, tears streaming down my face and shaking with sobs. I run behind the wall of the building and hide myself as I break down.

"What's wrong with you now?" my sister, who's in fifth grade, asks as she charges over to my side. She must've seen me running away.

"Nothing," I cry. "Just go."

She growls under her breath, sounding mad at me. "Just find some friends, so I can play with mine, and Mom stops making me play with you. Can't you do that?"

I cry harder as she storms away. She's embarrassed by me. I don't know what's wrong with me.

I dry my tears and walk to my classroom. I'm sure my face is all red, but I can just hide behind my folders and put my head down on my desk.

I quietly step into the classroom, seeing a few students sitting at their desks who wanted to get work on their projects done, while Ms. Wilkens sits at her computer with her back to me. I slide into my desk and take out two folders, standing them up to make a fence around me. I put my head down and hide.

"Wanna help me?" a voice says.

I look to my right and see Delilah working on a piece of butcher paper on the floor. She holds out a marker, her fingernails dirty and her blond bangs hanging in her eyes. She always stays in for recess. Unlike me, she stopped trying to fit in a long time ago.

I take the marker, coming down to the floor with her.

"Thanks," I say, looking at her hand-drawn Eiffel Tower that's almost as tall as me.

She smiles, and we begin working, coloring it in as the weight starts to lift from my chest.

She's always nice. Why do I care so much what the other girls think? Why do I want to be friends with them?

I try to be nice, but it's never good enough.

But they're mean and everyone loves them.

Why is that?

I bend over in the shower stall, resting my hands on my knees and pushing the memory away. That's not me anymore. *I'm fine. I've got this.* He pushed, they laughed, and I choked. I got complacent. I just have to push back next time. I'm good at that.

Or just ignore him. This was no big deal anyway. None of these people will be a big deal in a couple months.

Damn *Twilight*. How could he possibly have guessed that? I breathe in and out, my muscles finally relaxing. Masen Laurent is consistently a step ahead.

I slip the inhaler back into my pocket, shut off the water, and exit the stall, leaving the locker room. I'm late for Math, but I push forward and act like the episode in English never happened.

No one's talking about it. No one's texting about it. Masen Laurent is still far off anyone's radar, and no one believes I'm the superficial brat he's making me out to be.

Absolutely no one.

———

The rest of the school day passes mercilessly slow as I brave lunch and every single class, feeling like another shoe is going to drop at any second. But as soon as the final bell rings, I drop off my books at my locker and grab my duffel for cheer and swim, hurrying out of the school and to the side parking lot.

"Ryen?" I hear Lyla yell behind me.

But I just keep going. "I'll be back!" I call over my shoulder.

She knows we have practice and is probably wondering why I'm leaving the school.

Making my way through the parking lot, seeing students piling into cars and hearing engines fire up, I scan the crowd for the new guy. I finally see him, stepping up to a black truck and not carrying a single thing. No books, no folders, nothing.

As I walk toward him, I notice a couple of guys greeting him while my friend Katelyn approaches him, coyly grazing her hand along the side of his truck and acting all shy and shit.

My hopes are dashed. He's definitely on people's radar.

I hesitate, watching her hug her books and talk, giggling at something she said, while he stares down at her, calm and cool, looking no friendlier than he did with me.

Why does that please me?

I guess it's a relief to know that maybe I'm not special. He's rude to everyone, except the guys who came up to him just a moment ago.

Or maybe I wouldn't have liked seeing him smile at her and not at me or . . .

I take in a deep breath, growing impatient. I don't want her to see me talking to him, but I need that notebook.

I walk over to them, tipping my chin up and nodding once at Katelyn. "I'll see you at practice."

She pauses, looking taken aback. I hold the strap of my

duffel hanging on my shoulder and stare at her, waiting for her to leave.

She eventually gives a little eye roll and walks off, leaving us alone.

No doubt to tattle to Lyla.

I dig in the pocket of my bag, pulling out the locket and handing it to him.

He takes the necklace, almost gently, and stares at it for a moment before stuffing it into his pocket. He raises his eyes to me, and something gives. For a split second I see something different. Like he's . . . disappointed or something.

"Now give me the book," I demand.

"Sorry," he says, holding my eye. "I'm afraid I don't have it."

"Don't piss me off," I growl in a hushed tone. "I got you what you wanted."

"What I want . . ." He laughs quietly to himself as if there's something I don't understand

He opens the driver's-side door and climbs into his truck. But before he can close the door, I reach out and grab it.

"We had a deal."

He nods. "We did. But right now I'd love nothing better than to piss you off." And he yanks the door out of my hand, slamming it shut.

Starting it up, he steps on the gas, and I run my hand through my hair, despair curling its way through me. But I hesitate only a moment before I drop my bag and race up to him, jumping up on the cab step.

"You asshole," I bite out, and he slams on the brakes and glares at me.

I'm probably attracting attention, but I'm not taking any more of his shit.

"Get off the truck."

I shake my head. "I don't know who you are or where you come from," I snarl, "but I don't get pushed around. In case you haven't heard."

He jerks his chin, indicating something behind me as he smiles. "I guess we'll see."

I turn and see Lyla and Katelyn sitting on the ledge at the top of the steps, watching us. Great. How am I going to explain this?

"Watch out. You're being judged," Masen taunts. "Don't choke."

I step down from the cab, and he puts the truck in gear again. But before he can take off, I call out, "You're living in an abandoned theme park."

He stops the car again and lifts his chin. I stroll up to his window, feeling a bit of my power return as I give him a small smile.

"I'd only be doing the compassionate thing," I tell him, "letting a responsible adult know about your homeless situation."

He stills at my threat, and I offer a sympathetic sigh. "Social services would come in, find out where you come from and if anyone's looking for you . . ." I go on, putting my finger on my chin in mock contemplation. "I wonder if Masen Laurent has a criminal record. Maybe that's why you're hiding out? You definitely want to stay invisible. I'd bet money on that."

His scowl is hot, and I can see his jaw flex. Yeah, he might be eighteen and perfectly able to squat wherever he likes, but that doesn't mean he's up for any attention, either. Maybe his parents are looking for him. Maybe a foster family.

Maybe the police.

Not many kids transfer schools six weeks before the end of their senior year, after all. He's running from something.

He shifts the gears again and finally speaks. "I'll bring it tonight."

"You'll bring it now."

He turns to look at me. "If you have me picked up, you'll never get it back," he points out. "I got shit to do. I'll see you tonight."

5

Misha

Dear Ryen,

I hold the pen over the paper, frozen, the millions of things I want to say to her every day lost once I sit down to write. What did she always tell me? *Just start.* Don't worry about what I'm going to say. Just start, and everything will open up.

I couldn't write lyrics before Ryen. And now, since that night three months ago, I can't write anything.

I stare out into the empty warehouse, black soot from past bonfires coating the walls and the warm breeze whipping through the broken windows and hitting my back.

A chain hanging somewhere in the vast space above me blows in the gust and bangs against a rafter while a shiver creeps up my spine.

It feels different here. At night this place is packed, but during the day it's quiet and empty. My favorite place to come when I need just that.

I stare down at her name, trying to remember how easy it was to always open up to her.

I hate this, I tell her. *Everything fucking hurts. They weren't supposed to bury her. I shouldn't have let them. She saw a movie when* she was a kid, about a woman buried alive, and it scared the shit out of her. She didn't want to go underground, but my father said we needed a place to visit her as if her wishes weren't the most important thing.

I close my eyes, wetness coating the rims of my lids. Anger churns inside me, and it flows down my arms as I carve the words into the paper.

> I can't write you. And when I can, I can't send the goddamn letters. I want to hurt you. I don't know why. Probably because you're the only person I have left to hurt. Every letter you send that I don't answer is the only thing that makes me feel good anymore. You want the truth? That's it. It feels good to play with you like this. It gives me pleasure, knowing you're thinking about me but wondering if I'm thinking about you.
>
> I'm not. I never do.

I keep writing, letting every ugly thing spill out, because she loves me, she wants me to be happy, and she wants me to smile and do mundane shit like talk about *Star Wars* and music and what I'm doing for college. Who the hell is she to assume there aren't more important things than her going on in the world?

> All your letters, over all the years, immediately went into the garbage after I read them. Didn't you see how pathetic you looked? Sending five letters for every one of mine? I'll bet you deluded yourself, too. Did you fantasize I kept them? Maybe with a little red bow tied neatly around the stack as I jerk off to them, because I love your pretty words so much?
>
> No. Because after I eventually fucked you, I'd get bored. That's all it was about.

I draw in air through my nose, locking my jaw together as I press the pen into the paper. Guilt creeps in.

Ryen.

The liar. The poser. The superficial bitch who's no different from all the others.

But then I drop my eyes, remembering . . .

Ryen.

The kid who slipped five bucks in a letter in fifth grade when I told her my dad took away my allowance.

The girl who makes me smile when she argues about how sausage overpowers the taste of pizza and sent me a Veggie Lovers Pie for my birthday to prove me wrong. She didn't. Meat Lovers is way better.

The girl who gets all my movie references, knows when something's wrong, tells me everything I need to hear, and stops the world from spinning around me.

Ryen. The beautiful, perfect girl who's so different from all the others.

I run my hand over my forehead and through my hair, my throat tightening into a knot and my eyes burning.

Fuck. I put the pen to the paper and scrawl what my goddamn heart can only whisper.

I miss you every day, I write. *You're my favorite place.*

And then I drop the pen and tear the paper out of my notebook. I dig a matchbook out of my jeans, the one I use for lighting my lamp in my room at the Cove, and strike a match, watching as the tip glows orange and yellow. I bring it up to the letter, setting the corner on fire. Quickly the edges burn black as the flame spreads across the paper, eating every single word as the blue lines slowly disappear.

I let out a sigh, pulling my lip ring in between my teeth. The girl I saw yesterday in the classroom—she disappointed me. My

Ryen, the one I thought I knew, would never treat someone the way she treated that kid, Cortez. The way she just stood by and let that cocksucker mess with him. I waited for her. I sat there and waited for her to stand her ass up and speak up for him, to say something, to do anything, but . . .

Nothing.

Everything makes sense now. The cheerleader she talked about in her letters and everything she hated—she was talking about herself.

I drop the small fire in my hand to the cement floor and stand up, grinding my shoe into the dust, stamping it out.

I look at my watch and see it's after seven. I'd stopped by my house after school, before my dad got home, to check my mail and pick up some things, and then I grabbed some food and came here. I remember Ryen saying in her letters that she teaches swim lessons Tuesday through Thursday nights at the school's pool. That's where I'll probably find her now.

I should've just given her the book back. She'd found Annie's locket, and I don't want to start any shit with her, especially when she's not the reason I'm here and I'm skipping town as soon as I get what I came for.

And she and I will never have to cross paths again.

But, I have to admit, fucking with her in class today was the first time I've smiled in a while. It's hard to resist.

I walk out of the warehouse to my truck and climb in the cab, slamming the door.

But then I see the passenger-side door swing open, and I jerk, startled.

Dane hops in the truck and shoots me an easy smile as he sits back, looking at ease. "Netflix and chill?"

I scoff and turn my keys in the ignition. "Get out."

The engine rumbles to life with a smooth purr that I've worked hard to maintain. My cousin left me this truck when he was "indisposed" for three years, but now that he's around, he hasn't come to claim it, so I guess it's mine. I was grateful when he passed the keys to me all those years ago. I hadn't wanted to ask my dad for a car when the time came.

"So I had this date last night," Dane goes on, ignoring my order. "Do you remember that girl from Sigma Kappa Whatever? She was at the gig last night, and everything was going great, both of us eye-fucking for like four frickin' hours . . ." He pauses and turns to me, his voice turning urgent. "She takes me home, dude, and I'm sitting in the living room while she's in the bathroom, and I'm so ready, because she's so hot, right? And who walks in?"

"Dane." I close my eyes, willing him to shut the fuck up.

"Her mom, dude!" he bursts out. "Her mom in her light pink nightie with legs for days. And let me tell you, man . . . Stacy's mom has got it going on."

I can't help myself. I break out in a laugh at the song reference and pinch the bridge of my nose, tired but a fraction more relaxed, even if I'd never admit it to him.

Such an idiot.

Dane is twenty-one, but he never quite figured himself out after high school. He still lives in his parents' house, loves to make music, but he's in no hurry to be someone by a certain age. I wish I could let things go as easily as he does.

I let out a calm breath and look over at him, guilty that he's still a good friend and I've been a shitty one lately. "I'm sorry about the band."

After Annie died I couldn't see anything beyond that. I started skipping school, I left the band, I stopped trying to have a relationship with my dad . . .

He was destroyed, losing Annie, and I went through the motions for a couple months, sticking around, but we couldn't mourn together, and I couldn't stay to watch. He was sad. I was angry. Losing her only broke whatever small link we had to each other.

And my piece-of-shit mother never even showed up to the funeral. Every day I think about it, I get more livid.

But Dane just shrugs. "We're killing time until you're ready to come back," he tells me. "You know we're not shit without you."

"Yeah, well . . . I haven't written in months. It's gone, so don't wait for me."

After I left the band, the guys all stepped in and carried on with three people. They still perform here and there, and the summer tour is still on. I know Dane is hoping I'll be back on track by then, but I have zero interest. When I lost Annie, I lost Ryen, too, and now nothing is speaking to me. I don't know if I'll ever have anything to write or anything more to say.

"What's this?"

I cast a glance over at Dane, who holds Ryen's white notebook, fanning the pages as he looks inside.

"Are you writing, after all?" he asks but then stops on a page. "Nope. This is a girl's writing." He continues to read and then lets out a little laugh. "A very bad girl's writing. Who is she?"

I snatch the notebook away from him and drop it to the seat. "My muse."

"Does she want it back?"

I smile to myself. "More than anything."

And he grabs his seat belt, fastening it. "Well, then, let's go."

Walking into the school, I hear the distant hum of a vacuum cleaner, probably coming from the library, since that's the only room that I've noticed in the school with carpeting.

I cast a look left. A janitor must be in there. I'm not sure how many there are, but there has to be more than one with a school this size.

My school, Thunder Bay Prep, is a bit smaller but, in many ways, a lot nicer. Falcon's Well has almost no security—I glance up at the cameras that are being installed but are not yet active—and the athletics here suck.

The hallways are dark, classroom doors are closed, and since we noticed the parking lot was nearly empty on the way in, that means the lacrosse, cheer, and track practices must be done for the night.

Maybe a few teachers are lurking on the second and third levels, but other than the janitors, only Ryen is left, teaching down in the pool.

I walk up to the front office doors, glancing around me to make sure we're alone, and hand the notebook to Dane. "Hold this."

"What are we doing?" He pulls up the hood on his black sweatshirt, nervously looking up at one of the dead cameras.

I slip out a tension wrench from my jeans pocket and immediately dig back in, feeling for the paper clip I swiped off a page in Ryen's notebook. I unwind the clip and straighten it, bending the end just slightly.

Dane watches as I insert the wrench, applying pressure and feeling which way has more give, before sticking the paper clip into the lock and working the pins, pressing all five of them up until they click. I add pressure to the wrench and then . . .

Click.

The lock turns, and the door opens.

"Where'd you learn that?" he whispers, sounding surprised.

"YouTube. Stop talking."

We both dive into the dark office, quickly scanning the area to make sure it's empty. The desks behind the counter sit vacant, and I shoot my eyes left, seeing MRS. BURROWES written on a door. I walk over and jiggle the handle, finding it locked as well. Inserting the wrench, I work quickly and feel relief when the handle finally gives way, the door opening wide.

I stare into the office, amazed that this actually worked. I've never picked a lock before, until I Googled how this afternoon and practiced on some rusty old doors at the Cove.

"The principal's office." Dane inches in, filling the doorway with me. "I spent a lot of time in one of these. I think they gave me my diploma just to get rid of me."

His voice is thick with humor, and I stuff the tools back in my pocket. "Shhh."

Stepping inside, I immediately go for the cabinets and begin opening drawers, looking for anything even close to resembling what I'm searching for.

I sift through student files, budgets, receipts, teacher records, disciplinary records . . .

"What are you looking for?"

I open drawer after drawer, dragging my fingers over the files as I quickly scan. It has to be here. Annie told me once she mailed the stuff here.

"Dude, we should get out of here," Dane urges, sounding nervous.

And then I see it. A thick brown pocket folder labeled *Private* with a rubber band wrapped around it.

I grab it, quickly opening it and peeking inside. It's filled with pink envelopes and a small photo album, and an ache shudders through my chest as I force down the lump in my throat.

Annie.

I close the folder and wrap the rubber band around it again, shutting the drawers and walking out of the office. There are people still in the building, and I don't want to get caught.

Dane follows in my wake as I turn around and push the button, locking and closing the door behind us.

Unfortunately, the double doors in front are locked with keys, so I can't cover my tracks on those. Hopefully the office staff will just think they forgot to lock them on their way out this afternoon.

Dane looks down at the folder in my hand. "What does this have to do with the notebook?" He holds up Ryen's diary.

"Nothing." I walk down the hallway toward the locker rooms at the back of the school, taking the book out of his hand. "Not a damn thing."

Ryen isn't why I'm in Falcon's Well, but I knew I would run into her here. Something I feared.

She doesn't deserve my attention. Annie's all that matters. But after months of not giving a shit about anything—my family, friends, or music—having Ryen close is kind of distracting. In an almost pleasant way.

It doesn't matter, though. I have the file, and as soon as I have what else I came here to collect, I'm gone. I earned enough credits to graduate in January, and I'm not going back home. I'm taking my fake name and my fake ID, and I'm going to try to forget.

Forget that I was taking selfies with Ryen that night, ignoring my instincts and responsibilities, while my sister was dying alone on a dark, cold road.

We walk into the locker room, knowing that the pool is accessible from it. Passing by the offices and through the locker bay, I see something out of the corner of my eye and catch a glimpse of two bodies in the shower.

I enter the hallway and slow to a stop. Did I just see . . . ?

I jerk my chin at Dane and point ahead. "There's a pool through there. Give me a sec."

He nods lazily and heads out of the locker room. I turn around and, keeping my body close to the wall, I peer carefully around the corner again.

Amusement pulls at the corners of my mouth. Well, it looks like not everyone in cheer and lacrosse has gone home for the night, after all.

Trey Burrowes, the guy who thinks Ryen is his, stands in the shower, holding her best friend—Lyla, is it?—up against the bathroom wall, both of them naked, wet, and fucking as the shower sprays around them.

Classic.

Lyla's dark hair is up in a wet ponytail, and her arms and legs are wrapped around him, holding on tight while he grips her ass and goes at her, both of them breathing hard and moaning quietly.

This is the guy Ryen wants to take her to prom? She chooses her dates about as well as she chooses her friends. I wonder how long they've been screwing behind her back.

But hopefully, if he's fucking this girl, then he might not be getting it from Ryen.

An ounce of pleasure hits me.

I turn around and walk down the hallway again, pushing through the locker room door and seeing the impressive ten-lane indoor pool.

Parents sit on the bleachers, observing and taking pictures, while Dane leans against the wall. I walk over and stand next to him, following his gaze.

Ryen stands in the pool with four students—all kids, probably younger than ten—and moves her arms in big circles as she dips her face in the water.

The students count. "One-two-three-breathe!" they scream, and Ryen twists her head to the side, taking a breath before dipping it back in. She circles her arms again, pretending to push herself through the water, doing three strokes as they count. "One-two-three-breathe!"

She lifts her head up and stands up straight as she pushes her hair back off her forehead. "Okay, now your turn!"

All the kids begin mimicking her as she counts.

And I just watch her. She lets out a big smile, clearly proud as they all fall into sync, completing their strokes and breathing when they should, and I have to fight not to laugh when one of the boys splashes her accidentally. She feigns a growl and splashes him back.

"All right, again!" she shouts. "One-two—" And then she stops, her eyes falling on me.

They narrow, and I hold her gaze, recognizing the temper flaring as her smile falls.

"Again!" she bites out at the kids, her eyes dropping to my hand with the notebook.

"That water looks cold," Dane comments, a quiet laugh following, and I know what he's referring to.

I let my eyes fall to her breasts, seeing the hard points of her nipples straining against her long-sleeved black rash guard. A pretty impressive feat, considering the wet material is clinging to her skin, and I can see that she's also wearing a bikini top under the shirt, adding extra padding.

Which I'm grateful for. I look up at the bleachers, seeing a few dads gazing down, and while they're probably looking at their kids, I don't like that they *might* be looking at her. She doesn't need to give them a show.

I drop my eyes back to her, watching her smile at the kids.

"Great job, everyone!" She walks down the line, giving them high fives before standing in front of the last one, asking, "Washing machine or cannonball?"

"Washing machine!" the little girl with freckles squeals.

Ryen picks her up, cradles her in her arms, and twirls in the pool, whipping left and then whipping right as the kid squeezes her eyes shut and laughs.

"Shoo, shoo, shoo, shoo," Ryen says, mimicking a washing machine sound.

I shift and draw in a breath, realizing I'd forgotten to breathe for a moment.

"Me, me!" The next kid waves his hand in the air and shouts, "Cannonball!"

Ryen picks him up. This kid she vaults into the air, and he flies a couple feet above the water and then plunges below the surface, making a big splash.

I tear my eyes away, reminding myself that I don't care. I stand with Dane and wait for her to finish all the kids, and as soon as she dismisses them to their parents, I walk over to the bench where she's drying herself off.

"And here I thought you ate children," I muse, handing her the notebook.

She throws her towel down and takes the book, immediately opening it and scanning the inside. "Well, I do like to play with my food a bit before I eat it."

She fans the diary, probably looking to see if anything is missing.

"I didn't tear out any pages," I assure her.

"How do I know you didn't make copies?"

"Because I *don't* play with my food before I eat it."

Dane clears his throat at my side, speaking low. "I'm going to go wait in the parking lot. Take your time."

He follows the parents and their kids out of the gym through the side door. Ryen stuffs the diary in her bag and picks up the towel, continuing to dry off her legs. Her black bikini bottom, unlike her rash guard, is not as conservative as I would like. Her toned legs look tight and smooth, and the droplets of water on her thighs have my heart skipping a beat.

She realizes I'm still here and scowls. "Well?" she snaps. "You can leave now."

I slide my hands into my pockets. "And why would I do that, Rocks? When it's so warm in your presence."

"Why do you keep calling me Rocks?"

I ignore the question, keeping my eyes locked on hers. But then I notice her shiver, and without thinking, I glance down, seeing that her nipples are harder than ever. She's obviously cold, and visions of her in a hot shower invade my head. Naked, steam, heat . . .

Wait . . .

Shower. I glance behind me at the men's locker room door. Her friend and that fuckwad could still be in there. What if she hears something? Or sees them come out together?

I turn back to her. So what? She should find out what goddamn sleazes those people are whose opinions she cares so much about. She should find out exactly what a bad investment that was. She has this coming.

But, for some reason, I don't want her to confront that. Not unprepared. If she sees her prom date and best friend together, no one will take her side when the fallout happens.

Probably no one will be surprised by Lyla's behavior, and Trey will be the man.

Ryen will just be the stupid girl who was duped.

And I'm not sure why I care.

"Come on," I say, "it's dark. I'll walk you out."

"Piss off."

She pulls on some shorts, tying the little string, and then slaps on a baseball cap, not even sparing me a glance.

"There's someone breaking into the school at night," I point out, my voice turning angry. "You shouldn't be here alone."

She laughs, leaning down to zip up her bag. "Yeah, maybe it's you, and you just want me out of here so you can get going on writing stupid crap on the walls."

I hesitate.

Okay, yeah, I've broken into the school a couple of times. She's right about that. But I'm not the one breaking in and vandalizing the place. That is definitely not me.

I didn't risk coming here to get caught doing stupid shit.

She straightens and turns to fix me with a look. "You called me a cunt and cut my hair. You think I'd actually trust you to protect me? Don't blink too hard, Shit-for-Brains. You might lose your last few brain cells."

I widen my eyes, and every muscle in my body squeezes so tight it burns. What the fuck did she just say?

Before I know what I'm doing, I sweep her up into my arms and carry her to the side of the pool.

"Cannonball or washing machine?"

Her eyes widen. "Wha—?"

"Cannonball it is!" I shout out. And I throw her into the pool, hearing her scream as her entire body hits the water and she completely submerges.

I storm out of the gym without looking back. Hope the swim teacher knows how to swim.

I dig my keys out of my pocket and head for my truck. *Shit-for-Brains? Blink too hard?*

She's got a nasty mouth on her and an answer for everything. Does she ever shut up?

I climb into the truck, slamming the door. "Dammit!" I growl. "What a fucking—!" But I stop myself, breathing hard. I'm so damn angry I almost wish we had a gig tonight. Or a practice. I want to take what I'm feeling out on something.

I hear a snort next to me, and I suddenly remember Dane is with me.

"I told you," he says. "She looked kind of cold. I'll bet she feels good when she warms up, though."

"I couldn't care less."

I stick the key in the ignition, yank the shifter to drive, and lay on the gas.

"Yeah, it looks like it," Dane comments dryly.

6

Ryen

Dear Ryen,

What do you think of this line to replace the ending of the chorus for Titan? You know, that song I sent you last time?

"Don't hold your breath, 'cause you weren't first! Someone had to build the stairs that you climb."

I was at the warehouse last night, and it just popped in my head. I think it fits the song a lot better, and with the beat, I think I'll like the way it's going to come out. Thoughts?

And yeah. Before you give me shit, I was at a party last night, sitting by myself and writing music. So what? I think it helps my street cred, to be honest. You know . . . the quiet loner? The mysterious, hot rebel? Something like that? Maybe?

Whatever. Fuck it. You know I don't like people.

Anyway, you asked me my favorite place in your last letter. The warehouse is one of them. During the day, when no one is there, you can hear the pigeons flapping through the rafters, and you can take in all the graffiti without everyone around. Some of it's pretty incredible.

But I guess my absolute favorite place, other than you, of course, is my house. I know, I know. My dad is there, so why would I want to be? But actually . . . After my dad and sister have gone to sleep at night, when everything is dark, I crawl out my window and up to the roof. There's a little hidden valley between the ridges where I sit back against the chimney, sometimes for hours, dicking around on my phone, taking in the view, or sometimes I write you. I love it up there. I can see the tops of the trees, blowing in the night wind, the glow of the streetlamps and stars, the sound of leaves rustling . . . I guess it makes me feel like anything is possible.

The world isn't always what's right in front of you, you know? It's below, it's above, it's out there somewhere. Every burn of every light inside every house I see when I look down from the rooftop has a story. Sometimes we just need to change our perspective.

And when I look down at everything, I remember that there's more out there than just what's going on in my house—the bullshit with my dad, school, my future. I look at all those full houses, and I remember, I'm just one of many. It's not to say we're not special or important, but it's comforting, I guess. You don't feel so alone.

Misha

I hold his letter in my hand, the last one he sent me in February before he stopped writing, and stare at the handwriting probably only I can read. The rough strokes and abrupt marks crossing the *t*'s and dotting the *i*'s, and the way he never puts the appropriate amount of space between words, so his sentences end up looking like one big, long hashtag.

Amusement creeps up. I've never had a problem reading his writing, though. I grew up with it, after all.

So many times I've read this letter. Looking for clues—any clues—to figure out why he stopped writing after this. There's no hint that this was a goodbye, no indication that he was going to be any busier than usual or that he'd gotten bored or tired of me . . .

The emptiness is getting bigger and wider and deeper, and I sit on my bed, "Happy Song" playing from my iPod, and study his words, which always put the perfect light on anything.

I'm not ready to start my day.

Why don't I want to get up or even muster the energy to worry about what I'm going to wear?

He's the only thing I look forward to. The only reason I rush home from school, so I can see if there's mail for me.

I look up and stare at the words I wrote on my chalk wall last night.

Alone

Empty

Fraud

Masen's words are in my head now. Not Misha's.

"Ryen!" my mom calls and knocks on my bedroom door. "Are you up?"

My shoulders fall a bit, and I force myself to answer. "Yeah."

I'm not entirely lying. I am awake and sitting up in bed, cross-legged and reading.

But as I hear her steps retreat back down the hallway and the stairs, I glance at the clock and see that I've procrastinated long enough. Folding the letter back up, I slip it into the white envelope and stick it in my bedside drawer. The rest of Misha's letters are under my bed, every single one close in case I need them.

Standing up, I make my bed and pack my school bag before walking to my closet and snatching out a pair of white shorts and a black top. I may have already worn that outfit this week. I'm not sure. I suddenly don't care.

Once dressed, I head for the bathroom to do my hair and makeup since I already showered after swim lessons last night.

I can't believe that asshole threw me in the pool. It was my turn to stand up to him, and I was doing a damn good job, but just like a guy, when he can't win with wit, he uses brawn.

Slow clap for Masen.

He may have had the last word, but he'd had to step up his game to do it. I feel an ounce of pride and smile as I enter the bathroom.

I straighten my hair, getting rid of my bedhead, and begin applying my makeup, getting rid of the dark circles I have from staying up too late doing homework last night. I also add some blush to make me look healthy and happy.

Someone walks in and tosses something in front of me. I look down and see my black envelope addressed to Misha. I pick it up.

It's the letter I wrote him a few days ago. I can tell, because it has the stamps with the planets on them I just bought at the post office last week.

I look over at my sister, seeing her hair up in a messy bun and that she's wearing a summer dress with my black flats she didn't ask if she could borrow.

I frown. "Why do you have my letter?"

"I took it out of the mailbox when I left for class the other day."

"Why?"

"Because he hasn't written you in months," she snips. "You need to let it go."

Anger boils under my skin as I watch her twist toward the mirror and mess with her bun. "Tell me again how that's any of your business," I snap, and I don't care if our mom hears.

"Ryen, it's pathetic," she says, looking at me like I'm a child. "You look like you're chasing him. When he gets his shit together, he can find you."

I throw down the letter and grab my lipstick, facing the mirror again. "He's not my boyfriend who needs to check in, and I don't have to explain myself to you. Don't touch my mail again."

"Fine." She turns and walks for the door but stops and turns her head to look at me. "Oh, and Mom's waiting for you at the kitchen table. She saw your essay score online."

She walks out, and I close my eyes, entertaining the idea of taking a cue from Masen for a wonderful split second.

Cannonball or washing machine, Carson? Maybe a haircut?

I walk out of my house and past my Jeep, holding the strap of my school bag over my shoulder as I carry my letter to Misha back to the mailbox. I stick it inside and raise the flag so the mail carrier knows to pick it up.

But then my eyes fall to the trash cans next to the mailbox, and I pause.

You look like you're chasing him. It's pathetic.

Pathetic.

I swallow the bitter lump in my throat.

Maybe she's right. Maybe I'm not a priority anymore. Maybe he got a girlfriend and she made him stop writing me. Maybe he got bored. His letters have been slowing down over the past couple of years, after all. I didn't mind, because I also got busier in school, but still . . .

Misha *never* wrote me as much as I wrote him. I'd never really thought about that until now.

I snatch the letter out of the mailbox, crumple it up in my fists, and toss it on top of the pile in the garbage can. Screw him.

I charge back toward my Jeep, my heart starting to race as the fresh dew on the grass wets my feet through my sandals.

But then I stop, feeling a wave of loss wash over me. *No.* It's not pathetic. Misha wouldn't want me to stop writing him. He made me promise. *I need you, you know that, right?* he said. *Tell me we'll always have this. Tell me you won't stop.* That was in one of his rare letters where I got a glimpse of everything he keeps hidden. He seemed afraid and vulnerable, and so I promised him. Why would I ever stop? I never want to lose him.

Misha.

I swing around and jog back to the garbage can, digging the crumpled envelope out and straightening it again. I flatten it as much as I can and stick it back in the mailbox, shutting the lid.

Without giving myself time to dwell on it, I hop in my car and drive to school. It's almost May, and even though it's a bit chilly, I brave it in my shorts and thin blouse, knowing the afternoon will be warmer. With ten minutes to spare, I park in the lot, seeing crowds of students milling about as I walk up the sidewalk to the front entrance.

Music plays from phones, people text, and I feel an arm snake around me, a familiar scent hitting my nose. Ten wears Jean Paul Gaultier cologne every day, and I love it. It makes my stomach somersault.

"What's this?" he asks, lifting up my right hand.

I look down, seeing blue paint on my index finger and a little under my nail.

Shit.

I pull my hand away, my heart picking up pace. "It's nothing. My mom is painting the bathroom, and I helped," I tell him.

Curling my fingers into a fist, I hide my finger under the strap of my bag. I guess I need to wash in the shower a lot better at night.

"Look." He gestures to my right.

I turn my head, seeing people circle around the lawn, and we both drift over to the edge of the sidewalk, reading the huge message, in big silver letters, spray-painted on the grass.

LYLA GOT LOST. GOT HER SALAD TOSSED

IN THE MEN'S LOCKER ROOM LAST NIGHT.

SOMEONE WAS IN AWE. FUCKING HER RAW.

BUT WHO COULD IT BE? IT WASN'T J.D.

"Oh, shit," Ten whispers, surprise heavy in his voice.

I stare at the words on the lawn, my mouth going dry with a sudden urge to laugh.

Uh, okay. Who the hell . . . ?

Students crowd around, gasping and laughing, some taking pictures, while Ten and I back away.

"That's the first time he ever got personal by naming names," Ten says.

"Who?"

"Punk," he answers as if I should know. "Now we know it's someone who goes to school here. Someone who knows us."

I groan inwardly. *Yeah, but "Punk" always signs their messages. This is getting out of hand.*

I hear a noise and look up to see one of the janitors rolling a pressure washer outside and trying to maneuver it down the stairs.

"Let's go," I tell Ten.

We walk into school and pass groups of students surrounding more messages on the walls, these ones signed.

YOU KISSED MY HAIR WHILE STICKING ME IN THE HEART.

BUT YOUR HOUSE WILL BREAK BEFORE I FALL APART.

—PUNK

I see a couple of girls take out pens and add more under the lines, dissing old boyfriends and writing things like, *Yeah, Jake.*

I hold back my laugh.

"This is killing me," Ten exclaims as we make our way to our lockers. "I want to know who Punk is, and I want in."

I snort. Leave it to Ten. Of course Lyla is our friend, but Ten knows as well as I do that what's written on the lawn isn't a lie, and I'm sure he's excited to see the showdown with J.D.

"I've got to hunt that bitch down and find out who she was in the locker room with," Ten says as he stops in front of his locker.

I keep walking, calling over my shoulder, "See you at lunch."

I'm sure no one will discover whom Lyla was messing around with last night. She probably won't even admit it's true.

Coming up in front of my new locker, I key in the combination and open it, glancing to my left and noticing another janitor scrubbing away another message on the wall. He's erased the first few words already, but I know what it says.

YOU LOVED ME, WE WERE BESTIES, I LENT YOU MY EYE SHADOW.

BUT SOMEDAY ALL YOU'LL BE IS SOMEONE I USED TO KNOW.

−PUNK

And underneath is a collage of ripped-out yearbook pictures from last year, showing sports teams and groups of students smiling at rallies and games, hugging and laughing with each other.

I hang up my bag in my locker and take out the travel-size nail polish remover from the shelf. Glancing around to make sure no one is looking, I walk over and hold it in front of Mr. Thompson, the janitor.

"Nail polish remover will take off anything," I suggest, seeing his face sweaty and red from the exertion of scrubbing so hard.

He pinches his eyebrows together, probably taken aback by my being nice for once. Not that I've ever talked to him, but I may have missed the trash can a few times when tossing away my Starbucks cups. But he accepts the bottle, nodding in thanks.

Luckily nothing used to write on the walls is permanent, but it's still a hassle for the cleaning staff. Not that I care, but . . .

I turn to go back to my locker, but my eyes instantly lock with Masen's, and I pause. He's leaning against the lockers across the hall, watching me with his arms crossed over his chest and a curious expression in his eyes.

Has he been there the whole time?

I force myself to ignore him and start grabbing my books out of my locker for my first class.

"There you are."

I turn and see Lyla, looking a little worse for wear. There's sweat on her brow, and her cheeks are flushed. I hear her phone buzzing. "What happened to your other locker?" she asks.

I raise my eyebrows at her. Is she really going to act like there's not a big, flaming slap to her face on the school's front lawn right now?

Oooookay.

"Someone broke into it," I answer, turning back to my locker. "Was it you? After my black Bebe top?"

She tosses me a dirty look. "Like it would fit. I'm softballs and you're baseballs, babe."

I hold back my eye roll as I stuff what I need in my bag, making sure I have my water bottle. I cast a quick glance behind me and see that Masen is gone.

Lyla's phone keeps buzzing, and I don't know if it's Instagram notifications or J.D. burning her up, but I really don't care.

Some girls pass by, covering their mouths with their hands, and Lyla shoots them a scowl. "Bite me, bitches," she growls. And they look away, carrying their smirks with them as they walk down the hall.

Manny Cortez comes up behind her and tries to open his locker, but she turns around, facing both of us. "Well, well, well, maybe it was Manny who broke into your locker. Did you need some lipstick to go with that eyeliner?"

I see his expression harden as he keeps his back to her and doesn't respond.

"Nah," I step in, shutting my locker. "Two different color palettes. I'm a Mountain Sunset. He's a Smokey Night."

Lyla laughs but then she stops when we hear a yell.

"Heads up!"

We both dart our eyes upward and see a football flying down, coming straight for us. We scurry back, but there's no need. The ball slams into the left side of Manny's head, and he's knocked to his right, his hand immediately shooting to cover his ear as he winces in pain.

"Oh, shit." Trey runs up to us, laughing. "Sorry, dude. I honestly didn't mean it. This time," he adds.

I watch as Manny breathes hard, his black eyebrows wrinkled up in pain. He brings his hand away from his ear, and I see blood. My eyes go wide, and I suck in a breath.

Oh, my God. Is that coming from his ear or out of it? Before I can find out, though, Manny slams his locker door shut and charges off, disappearing into the bathroom as the bell sounds.

"Nice going, asshole," I scold.

"Hey, it was an accident."

I see him cast a look at Lyla, and then I see J.D. pop up behind him as all of the students hurry to class.

"Get in class," J.D. tells Lyla, his jaw flexing.

"Excuse me?"

"You heard me. I'll finish talking to you later."

She stands there, looking angry, but I don't stick around to watch the outcome.

Walking past them, I head to Art, but I don't see Masen in his seat. And by the time the bell rings, he's still not there.

I just saw him in the hall. How does he get to just come and go as he likes and skip classes?

Luckily, though, Trey isn't crashing class, either, so I make it through the entire period getting work on Misha's cover done and being left entirely alone.

Even Manny is missing, probably having gone to the nurse to get his ear checked. I hope he's okay. That had to hurt.

After class ends, I make my way to English, weaving through students as I slip into the classroom. Masen is sitting in his seat, and I pause, taken aback.

Jesus. What does he do? Put in appearances whenever he feels like it?

No books again, no visible pencil, and looks like he just showed up because he has nothing better to do. Isn't he worried about graduating?

"All right, take your questionnaires and go set the rest of your things down," Mr. Foster instructs as we file into the room and he passes out papers. "And don't forget to take a pencil. Once I call your names, you can pair up, take your things to the library, and begin working."

Oh, that's right. It's Research Day.

Once in a while, Foster sends us to the library to let us work on our skills. He pairs us up, hands us a worksheet of information to find, and then we're on our own for the whole period. It's a reason to get out of class. I never complain.

"Lane, Rodney, and Cooper," Foster calls from his roster.

Three students stand up, take their materials, and leave the room.

"Jess, Carmen, and Riley."

He keeps going, one group after another, as the room slowly

empties, and my nerves start to turn anxious when I realize there's only a handful of people left, including Masen and me.

Please not him.

But Foster calls the next group. "Ryen, J.D., and Trey."

I let out a breath of relief.

"Hell, yeah," J.D. boasts, and I see him swipe a high five at Trey next to him. I start to stand up, taking what I need.

"And last two . . ." Foster announces. "Lyla and Masen."

I falter for only a moment and then swing my bag over my shoulder, hurrying out of the classroom.

Lyla and Masen. *Great.* She won't be able to control herself.

I step out of the classroom, hardening my expression. Why do I even care? I don't like him. I don't give a damn if she flirts with him, which she'll definitely do, so let her have at it. Fine.

She's J.D.'s problem anyway.

And it doesn't matter. Someone else already has my heart, and Masen Laurent isn't him. He'll never be Misha.

"My parents are out of town in a couple weeks." Trey jogs up to me and places his hand on my waist as we walk. "I'm having a party, and I want you there."

"Yeah, the pool's heated," J.D. adds behind us.

I look back, seeing Lyla and Masen following us, Masen's eyes on me.

"Yeah, I know," I tell J.D. "I've been in it. Remember?"

"Great," Trey chimes back in. "So bring a swimsuit. Or don't. Either way."

Heat blankets my back, and I suddenly feel surrounded. I cast a quick glance back again, and I see Masen looking away as Lyla chats about something, but then he must sense me looking, because he meets my eyes again.

Trey follows my gaze, noticing my attention is not on him. Before I even realize my mistake, he whips around and grabs Masen by the collar, throwing him into the lockers.

"Hey," he says in an overly friendly voice. "I don't think we've met. I'm Trey Burrowes. You're Masen Laurent."

J.D., Lyla, and I stand and watch as Masen remains still, simply staring at Trey.

"Now that that's over," Trey goes on, closing in and getting in his face. "Let's get a few things straight."

"What the hell are you doing?" I inch closer.

"Yeah, Trey, come on," J.D. speaks up. "He's a good guy."

But Trey just holds up his hands. "Relax. We're just having a talk. I promise."

I look down and see Masen's fingers curl into fists, but he doesn't move as Trey and he stand eye to eye.

"Now, you've been having a little fun with my girl in class, and I also hear you were hassling her in the parking lot yesterday," Trey states. "Whatever bullshit you've got going on stops now. Leave her alone."

Masen's gaze flickers to me, and a weight hits me in the chest. His eyes look sharp and angry at first, but that seems to change to disappointment along with something else. Sadness, maybe?

What's going on in his head? Why is he looking at me like that?

"Don't look at her," Trey growls, getting in Masen's face. "What's the matter? You can't speak?"

"What's going on?"

We all turn to see Principal Burrowes standing in the middle of the hallway, her black suit and burgundy blouse crisp and ironed.

Trey stands up straight and backs off Masen. "Nothing, Gillian," he mocks his stepmom and then looks back to Masen. "We're cool. Right?"

Masen's eyes are on the floor, and he doesn't speak.

"Where are you supposed to be?" Burrowes asks Trey.

But I answer instead. "Foster is sending us to the library to research."

"Then, move."

I nod, and we all quickly start walking down the hall.

"You, too," I hear her say behind us, probably to Masen.

Why didn't he do anything? Not that Trey's a small guy he could easily take, but I get the impression Masen has been in fights before. He's volatile and impulsive, so why did he hold back?

We jog up the stairs and enter the library. All of the other students are already here, whispering, moving about, and gathering the materials they need. Some are on the computers, and some are in the stacks. Our library consists of two floors and a nice view into the main level from the balcony up above. I dump my bag on a table toward the back and see Lyla and Masen take seats two tables up.

J.D. and Trey plop down in the seats at our table, and Trey puts his feet up.

Yeah, not happening. "You guys go to the computers and look up 'annotated bibliographies,'" I tell them. "Print off some examples, and I'll go find some from secondary sources."

I'm not doing this worksheet on my own.

Trey heaves a sigh, and J.D. laughs to himself, both of them getting back up off their asses.

I twist around and head back to the nonfiction section.

The shelves loom high, and I skirt around a rolling ladder and turn left, diving farther into the back of the library, away from the tables of students and their hushed whispers.

I reach out and graze my hand along the spines of the books as I pass. My mom's going to wonder why I haven't even started *Fahrenheit 451*. Not that I'll get into trouble, but she'll wonder what's been distracting me.

"You know, that kid," I hear someone say, and I jerk my head to look behind me.

Masen approaches, and my heartbeat picks up pace.

"The one writing on the walls at night?" he continues. "We have something in common. I like to write on things, too." He stops in front of me and takes my hand. "But you know that, right?"

My skin warms where he touches it, and I try to jerk my hand free, but he holds on tight.

He likes to write on things, too? What? And then I remember the wall at the Cove, my chalk wall in my room, my locker that first day . . .

I jerk my hand harder, yanking it free. "What? Did you find Trey a bit too big and scary, so you're going to take your fight to me instead now?"

He gives me a casual grin and snatches my hand again, pulling out a Sharpie from his pocket with his other hand.

"Let go."

He sticks the marker in his mouth, bites off the cap, and flips the pen around, shoving it back inside the cap. "But I thought you wanted my phone number. For the drive-in, remember?"

He looks down at me with an innocent expression on his face, and I don't know what he's doing, but I have to admit I'm kind of afraid to put up a fight this time. Throwing me into a pool when no one's around isn't that embarrassing, but I highly doubt he's going to give a shit that we're not alone right now if he deems it necessary to put me in my place again. I don't want his fucking number.

He takes my left index finger and starts writing on the inside of it, while I grind my teeth and glare at him.

"You know, I remember so much of what was in that diary," he muses as he writes. "I can say whatever I want. I don't need proof. Not with them." He jerks his chin, indicating all the students sitting over in the table area that we can't see.

I pull away again, but he tightens his hold.

"Don't worry." He smiles down at my finger as he sketches. The velvety tip tickles my skin. "I have no interest in tormenting you.

Not like that anyway. I just have one question." And then he stops drawing and looks up, peering at me. "Who's Delilah?"

I freeze and stare at him, forgetting that he's holding my hand as the hair on my neck stands up.

"What?"

"You had her name doodled all over your notebook," he tells me. "Who is she? Secret girlfriend? Secret shame?" He drops his eyes and continues writing. "A regret?"

"You read my notebook. You should already know."

"I didn't read anything," he retorts.

I glare at him. He didn't read it? But . . .

"I flipped the pages and saw her name on the inside cover," he explains. "You think I give a shit about what goes on in your mind? I've got better things to do."

Then why are you asking if you don't care?

I yank my hand away, growling under my breath. "You're an asshole."

I keep my voice low, even though I don't see anyone around.

But before I can walk away, he places his hands on the bookshelves, locking me in. "You know I could've taken him and his friend in one breath just now. What was I waiting for?"

He stares into my eyes, searching for something.

"Maybe the same thing that Cortez kid waits for when your boyfriend's pushing him around," he says in a low voice, his lips inches from mine. "Maybe for someone in their perky little ponytail"—he flips my hair—"and come-fuck-me short-shorts to grow a dick and stand up to the asshole."

I knock his arm away, my stomach tight with anger. But he locks me in again, bearing down.

"Was that what Delilah was waiting for, too?" he presses. "Did she wait for you? And you never showed?"

He grabs my hand and turns my finger, showing me what he wrote.

I look down at the thick black letters written on the inside of my finger.

SHAME

"Don't worry," he says. "I won't say anything. Your secrets are yours. You have to live with them."

And then he lifts my finger to his lips, making the *shh* sign.

I pull my hand away and slam my hands into his chest, pushing him off.

"The next time he lays a hand on me, I'll end him," he warns, curling his lips in a smirk. "And then I'll take his prom date."

7

Misha

I was getting a little lonely," Lyla purrs, resting back in her seat with her arms folded over her chest and her legs crossed. "You were gone so long."

Lonely? I doubt she even knows the meaning of the word. Not that I have any opinion of a chick who messes around on her boyfriend—unless the boyfriend is me or one of my friends—but I don't like her for other reasons. She's like Ryen on crack.

At least my Ryen is still in there somewhere. I see it in how she's uncomfortable when that Cortez kid is bullied. I saw it this morning when she gave the janitor nail polish remover to help take off the graffiti.

And I see it all over her room. The collages, the poetry, the lyrics I've sent her for review, the quotes and colors everywhere . . . That's the Ryen I know.

But in ten years she could be Lyla. Self-serving, false, and screwing anything to forget how much she hates herself.

And everything I've always found incredible about her will be gone.

I pull out my chair and sit down, knowing damn well I have no intention of doing this assignment. Misha Lare is as good as done with high school, so I'm not here for that.

"Here." She sits up, pushing some books toward me. "I dug up some primary resources, so we can start on this questionnaire."

But before I can tell this chick she's on her own, I'm shoved forward from behind, a body slamming down on my back and an arm pressing into my neck.

"What the hell?" I shoot out my arms to keep my head from hitting the table, and then I feel breaths in my ear.

"Ryen!" I hear someone exclaim. I think it's Lyla.

"Don't move," Ryen whispers in my ear, and I feel a sharp point digging into the back of my neck. "I'd hate for this pen to slip."

I shake with a shocked laugh. She didn't like being served back in the stacks, and now she's lost her mind. Excellent.

I do exactly what she asks, even though my heart is racing and my groin is throbbing with heat.

I feel the pen glide over my skin in long, slow strokes, and I'm actually amused. I know people are watching. Everyone is suddenly silent, even Lyla.

The pen digs deep, and I wince as I feel a sting. She finishes and stands up, taking her weight off me and throwing down the pen. I feel her leave, and I sit up straight. Everyone is looking at me, and I see Ryen brush past my table with her bag on her shoulder, storming out of the library.

"Are you okay?" Lyla asks.

"Yeah." I nod and glance behind me, seeing J.D. smiling and shaking his head, while Trey leans forward on the table and glares at me.

She did that in front of him. Good girl.

I turn back to my partner. "What did she write?"

Lyla rises from her seat and takes a look. I hear a snort. "Um, are you sure you want to know?"

Great.

I nod.

"Um . . ." she starts, reading in slow syllables. "Needle Dick Douchebag Asshole."

I break into laughter. Awesome. Stuck-up Ryen Trevarrow is learning how to play in the mud, and I feel a little excitement course through my veins.

"Do you want me to go get you some wet paper towels?" Lyla puts a hand on her hip, hovering.

But I just wave her off. "Fuck it. Just leave it."

What do I care?

"Masen Laurent?" someone calls.

I sit there for a moment before I blink and look up, remembering that's my name. The librarian is holding the receiver of the phone at the circulation desk and looking around.

"Yeah?"

She follows my voice and meets my eyes, hanging up the phone. "The principal would like to see you. Take your things just in case."

But I don't move. The principal? Heat floods my veins, and I feel weighted to my seat.

Why the hell does she want to see me? Does she know?

My breathing quickens, and I stand up, grabbing nothing because I brought nothing, and make my way toward the doors. I ignore the curious glances and snorts, probably because, as I pass them, they can see the shit Ryen wrote on my neck.

I should just leave. Walk out the front doors right now. But as I come up on her office, I find myself opening the doors, my resolve hardening. I haven't gotten everything I came here for yet. I'm not running away, so let's see what she has to say.

If she knows, she knows. Or if she found out my records are fake, supplied by one of my cousin's shady connections, Masen Laurent is a name I made up, and I live in a dilapidated basement and sneak into the school to shower at night, then I'll deal with it.

Either way, I'm not leaving. Not yet.

Stepping inside the front office, I nod at one of the receptionists. "Masen Laurent," I tell her.

"You can go in." She gestures to my left, but I already know where to go.

Walking up to the door, I knock twice, feeling my hands shake just slightly as I push it open.

"Hi, Masen," the principal greets, looking up from her desk and smiling.

She stacks a large pile of folders, clearing a space on her desk, and stands up, holding out her hand for me to shake.

I lock my jaw tight and straighten my back. Her eyes are warm, and I suddenly don't want to be here.

I force myself forward, slowly raising my hand and taking hers but letting go nearly immediately.

I shift my eyes to the side.

She's silent for a moment, and I can tell she's watching me. "Please sit down," she says finally.

I take the seat in front of her desk and keep my gaze averted, making eye contact only briefly.

"Don't worry," she tells me, humor lacing her voice. "You're not in trouble. I just like to try to meet everyone when they register, but you slipped in under my radar."

Okay. That's good news, I guess.

"So how are you liking Falcon's Well so far?"

I unclench my jaw, replying flatly, "Fine."

"And your classes?" she presses. "Are you finding the transition easy?"

Her eyes won't leave me, and I shift in my seat, nodding as I stare at the picture frames she has on her desk. I remember seeing them the other night. Pictures of her family.

"Well," she keeps going, starting to sound uncomfortable. "There's so little time left in the school year, but judging from your records and your grades, you should have no trouble passing your finals." She flips through transcripts and forms, from my fake file, no doubt. "Are you looking at colleges?"

I shake my head.

"Well, we have a great college-career center here. The counselor can help you make some decisions about where you're going after high school and see about getting applications in."

I nod, and we both just sit there, the silence growing more awkward. She clearly wants to be attentive but is probably figuring out whether or not I'm worth the effort when I'll be out of her school in six weeks. Sooner, actually, but she doesn't know that.

She inhales a deep breath and softens her voice. "Trey Burrowes is my stepson," she points out. "He can be a handful, but . . . he's my handful. Let me know if you have any more problems, okay?"

He's my handful. I squeeze my fists, finally raising my eyes to hers. *Don't worry, lady. I know exactly how to handle my problems. Your son will stay out of my way, or I'll make him stay out of my way.*

She smiles, and I stand up, not waiting to be dismissed. I walk out of her office, feeling my stomach uncurl and taking in quick, shallow breaths when the adrenaline finally hits me, coursing down my arms and legs. Once outside the office doors, standing in the empty hallway, I stop and smile to myself.

She didn't find me out. Not only can I leave whenever I want, but I can stay as long as I like.

No one knows.

8

Misha

"Y ou're just smearing it," an amused voice says behind me.

I turn my head to see Ryen standing with her back to her open locker, smirking. I take my hand away from the back of my neck, throwing the wet paper towel in the trash next to the water fountain. While I thought I wouldn't care about having "Needle Dick Douchebag Asshole" written on my neck for everyone to see, I was wrong. I feel like an idiot.

She turns and reaches into her locker, pulling out a long piece of fabric. "Wanna borrow a scarf?"

She laughs, and I arch an eyebrow, unamused. Glancing into her locker, I see the bottle she loaned the janitor this morning back on the shelf, and I walk over. "Nail polish remover. Now."

But she simply folds her arms over her chest and positions herself in front of her locker, not budging.

"Don't play with me." I hold out my hand. "We've been keeping our shit PG. I can go R if you want."

She twists up her lips and lets out a small sigh. "Fine. I can pick my battles, I guess."

She twists around and takes out the bottle, flinging it toward me. I catch it and twist off the cap, quickly pulling the scarf out of her hands, too.

"Hey!"

But it's too late. I dump some of the acetone onto the soft beige fabric and use it to rub the pen off on the back of my neck.

"Bastard!" she cries out. "That's cashmere!"

I pull the scarf away from my neck, seeing the black ink now on her scarf and off my neck. At least most of it, I think.

"Yeah." I toss the scarf back at her and cap the bottle. "It works great. Thanks."

She twists up her face in anguish and holds up the scarf with both hands, inspecting the damage.

I set the bottle back on her shelf and walk off before we have time to get into it again. I hear her let out a little growl behind me and slam her locker shut as I make my way for the front of the school.

I need to stop challenging her, despite the amusement I feel. Engaging her is just too easy. Why, when I walk into this building, is she the first thought that comes to my mind and not the real reason I'm here?

If she hadn't happened upon my spot at the Cove and stolen my shit that night, I might never have crossed her path here. Maybe we would've been in some of the same classes, while I lurked quietly around, waiting to take care of business, but I never intended to . . .

No. That's not right. I knew better. I kind of knew this would happen, and I knew I was walking into a temptation. I knew Ryen would be here, I knew I would see her and hear her, and I knew my attention would be drawn to her, because despite everything else on my mind, I wouldn't be able to contain my curiosity.

And then when I found out she was popular, not an outcast, and a cardboard cutout, not at all original, I became angry. She led me to believe those things, and my muse was a lie.

Until yesterday in the parking lot when I bit and she bit back.

That's my Ryen.

And I want to see more.

I take out my keys and glance around me, checking the windows of the main house. I didn't see my dad's car in the driveway, but it could be in the garage, too. Since he deals in antiques and art, owning a few shops along the coast, his schedule is flexible. He can be gone all day or home at any time.

I unlock the guesthouse door and step inside, closing it behind me. It's not even noon, so it's still light out, but I blacked out most of the windows when I moved in here after Annie's death. I take out my small flashlight and switch it on. I don't want to turn on the big light in case my dad sees.

Most of my clothes and belongings are still here, and since Dane wants to grill me every time I mooch off his washer and dryer, I decided to come back here and pick up some more stuff to avoid his third degree this time.

I left school after the scarf thing with Ryen, leaving my truck in the parking lot and taking the ferry to Thunder Bay. I didn't want my dad or anyone else we know to spot my car.

He doesn't know where I am, and I'd like to keep it that way. It isn't like he's called, either.

Digging a duffel bag out of the closet, I empty drawers and stuff the clothes in the bag, bringing a folded T-shirt to my nose. The scent brings needles to my throat.

Annie's fabric softener. She was good about doing the laundry, since my dad was busy and I always did it wrong. I complained about the flowery scents she used for my clothes, but now I close my eyes, feeling only home. I made sure to keep using it after she was gone. Nothing would change. We would never change anything she did.

Annie. I blink, feeling my eyes water. I finish gathering the clothes I need and pack an extra pair of shoes as well as the pictures of Annie and me that I have taped to the wall above my desk.

I pass by my guitar, resting on the stand, and a pile of our band's posters that never got used. Three months ago I had three things I loved. My music, my sister, and . . .

Everything empties from my lungs, and I turn away from the guitar, unable to look at the fucking thing. It doesn't matter what I had. Annie's gone now. My words are gone, and Ryen's . . . I don't know what she is.

And that's when it occurs to me. I got a letter from her last week. She's probably sent me another one by now, since she writes like I breathe air. Not that I ever minded, though. They were the best things to come home to.

I leave the guesthouse, carrying the duffel bag and locking up behind me. I notice that everything seems darker, and I look up and see thunderclouds hovering low. *Shit.* Did I leave the windows down in my truck? I better get back to school. Falcon's Well might not get hit with the rain, but it's possible.

I hurry to the back door of the main house and unlock it, dashing inside. The kitchen is dark, so my dad must be out. Heading over to the counter, I find the pile of mail, all of it mine, and immediately scan for a smoky black envelope with a skull seal.

But I don't find one. There's nothing there but college brochures and credit card applications. Has she stopped writing me, then?

Relax, dude. You came home last week and checked, and there was a letter there. It's only been six days.

But I'm curious to see if she writes about Masen. What will she say about him?

Ryen rarely ever mentions another guy in her letters. After the one she told me about when she was sixteen—the one she lowered her standards for—she seems to have kept guys at a distance. In fact, it's almost like she's lost interest, because she told me that foreplay is overrated in a letter once.

I told her I might consider that a challenge. After all, seven years of writing letters is epic foreplay, and she's addicted.

Six days. My last letter from her was six days ago. Her last letter from me was over three months ago. I made her promise never to stop writing me, and she never has. She remains constant, even despite the lack of faith she must have by now that I'll ever write her again.

My shoulders slump a little, thinking about how she's always been there for me. Her bullshit pisses me off, but to Misha, she's been a friend. And a very good one.

Annie would be disappointed in me if I treated badly the only person left who loved everything about me.

Goddammit. Fuck.

I let out a hard sigh and walk into the hallway, rounding the banister and jogging up the stairs. Approaching my sister's room, I slowly twist the doorknob and enter, her smell and the remnants of her carpet freshener suddenly wafting over me.

My heart aches, seeing everything the way she left it. Tidy and ready for her to come home from her jog that night. A bed she would never sleep in again, makeup she would never touch again, assignments that lay unfinished on her desk . . .

An ache lodges in my throat, and I feel like I want to scream. *Annie, what were you thinking?* But then I'm angry with myself, too. And my dad. How did we not see it? Why didn't we take care of her better?

I walk slowly over to her dresser and open drawers carefully and quietly, as if she'll come bursting in at any moment, scolding me for being in her room. When I open the top drawer of her chest I see her scarves, folded neatly and stacked in two piles. I smell her perfume, and my chest shakes with a sob that I force back down as

I sift through, finding one that feels like Ryen's. It's not beige, but it's cashmere. I feel a moment's guilt, but my sister would rather Ryen have it than let it sit in her empty room, forgotten.

I pull out the light blue scarf and close the drawer, sticking it in my duffel bag.

"Hello?" I hear a muffled call from the hallway.

I jerk my head toward the doorway, recognizing the voice.

My father. "Shit."

I look around, knowing there's no other way out of here. I slip behind the privacy screen my sister put up as decoration by the wall and lock my teeth together to calm my breathing.

I see a shadow block out the hallway light streaming through the doorway and falling on the carpet.

"Misha?" my father asks hesitantly. "Are you here?"

He knows I'm here. He has to. I left Annie's door open when I came in, and it's always closed.

But I don't move. I can't talk to him.

I peer through the holes in the screen, trying to see him, but I can't. He's not in my line of sight.

He doesn't say anything more, but I watch as his shadow falls farther into the room, my pulse pounding in my ears.

He enters my sight as he sits at the end of the bed, wearing his usual shirt, tie, and sweater vest. He used to dress me like that when I was a kid. Until I turned nine and started having an opinion. That was the beginning of our fighting.

"You were always so different," he says, staring off.

I can barely breathe.

"T-shirts and jeans to family functions, guitar lessons instead of the violin or piano, always so difficult to get motivated for anything other than what you wanted to do . . . always so difficult. Period."

My eyes water, but I don't budge. He's right. In his head, I fought about everything. I made arguments where there weren't any.

In my head I just wanted him to accept me. That's why I held on to Ryen so hard for so long.

"I stopped being able to talk to you," he nearly whispers. And then he drops his eyes, correcting, "I stopped finding a way to talk to you."

He picks up my sister's blanket at the end of the bed and slowly brings it to his nose, and then his body immediately shakes as he lets out a sob.

I pull my lip ring in between my teeth and tug until I feel a sting. Everything hurts, and I hate this. I hate that Annie's room is empty. I hate that our house is dark. I hate that I don't know where I'm supposed to be—I don't belong anywhere. And I hate that I hate he's alone. He didn't comfort me after Annie's death. Why should I want to be here for him?

And why do I feel a sudden need to tell Ryen everything? For her to know what I haven't said and to tell me just the right thing, just like she does in her letters. To forget Falcon's Well and what I'm doing there.

To go back, simply because that's where she is.

I make it back to the school just as the final bell is ringing. The rain had started in Thunder Bay just as I jumped on the ferry, but it still held off here, the clouds threatening but not giving in yet.

My father left Annie's room as soon as he started crying, and once I heard the hum of Brahms coming from his office, I knew it was safe to get out of the house. He'd be in there the rest of the night, drinking scotch and working on his model World War II battlefield.

I can see the soccer team practicing on the field off to my right, and I hook the duffel bag over my head, hanging it across my chest. Digging the scarf out of my bag, I reach into Ryen's Jeep and set it on the driver's seat. I pull my Sharpie out of my pocket and look around, pulling out a small piece of paper I spot in a cup holder. I leave a note on the back of the receipt.

You'll look better in blue. (And no, I didn't steal it.)

I drop it on top of the scarf as students start flooding the parking lot and climbing into their cars. It's Friday afternoon, so I doubt Ryen has any team practices, but I keep an eye on her Jeep anyway as I head to my truck, making sure no one tries to take the scarf out of the open cab.

I toss my duffel in the bed of my truck but suddenly look up, noticing people crowding around my hood, at the front of my vehicle. They stare at something, and unease coils its way through my body. What now?

Gasps and whispers fill the air, and more people head over. I charge to the front of the truck and stop, finding a whole fucking mess.

Large circles of white paint are splattered on my hood, shooting out in all directions and spilling down the sides, as if someone took a paintball gun and used the car for target practice. Some of it is already dried, which means it was done a while ago, probably right after I left campus.

And right in the middle, on top of the hood, in big white letters, is the word "FAG" sitting bright and loud, glaring back at me.

Rage heats up every single muscle in my body. *Motherfucker.*

I raise my eyes, anger and readiness boiling under my skin as I let my gaze slowly scan the parking lot. I spot Trey Burrowes near what I assume is his car—a blue Camaro that his doting little step-mommy probably bought him. I ignore the people gathering around and narrow my eyes, seeing him stroll around all cocky, chewing on a straw and shooting Lyla a lascivious glance that his best friend probably doesn't see.

I take off. Stalking right for him, I dig in my heels, ready to slam his fucking face into the hood of *his* fucking car. I'm almost glad he's picking a fight right now. I've wanted to hit something all day.

I hear someone call, "Masen," but I don't stop to find out who. I lunge straight for him and grab his collar, throwing him around and slamming him up against his car.

He growls, taking my jaw in his hand and trying to push me off, but I twist away from him and swing my fist back, landing a punch in his stomach.

I hear screams and shouts around me, feeling a crowd close in, and I quickly grab him again, slamming him against the car.

"Fuck you, faggot," he bursts out, swinging his fist back and knocking me in the face. The metallic taste of blood seeps into my mouth from the inside of my cheek, but I still don't release my hold on him.

"Can't take a joke?" he yells.

I bring my knee up, hitting him in his stomach. He hunches over, and I raise my fist high, pounding down on the back of his head twice.

"Masen, stop!" I hear someone yell, and I think it's Ryen.

I grab him by the collar again and throw him down on the ground, sweat covering my back and my lungs begging for air. But before I can get to him and land another hit, hands grab my upper arms and haul me back. I struggle against the hold, and the guy holding me stumbles forward, trying to keep a grip on me as I glare at Trey.

"What's going on?" a woman barks.

"It took you long enough!" Trey snarls at the guy behind me, and I gather it must be J.D., his friend, holding me back.

The principal appears between us, looking at me as Trey pushes himself off the ground. "Calm down!" she orders me.

I breathe hard, dragging in air through my nose. Every muscle in my body is tight, and I keep my eyes on Trey as the arms behind me finally let go.

"What happened?" Burrowes demands, looking between us.

"I didn't do anything!" Trey shouts. "This asshole shows up and jumps on me!"

She looks to me for an answer, but I don't say anything. Everyone stands around us, their attention held captivated, a few people putting away phones now that the principal is here, and I can't help but let out a small smile, seeing a drop of blood at the corner of Trey's mouth.

"Whose car is that?" the principal questions, gesturing to my truck off to the right.

But Trey and I are locked in a stare, both of us refusing to say anything.

She seems to draw her own conclusions, though, because she looks at Trey, her voice turning stern. "You will get a bucket and the hose, and you will clean every inch of it. Both of you! That better not be permanent paint."

"But—"

"Now!" she cuts him off. "And I warned you what would happen if you pulled anything else . . ."

"It wasn't him, Mrs. Burrowes."

I blink, hearing Ryen's voice. The principal stops and turns toward her.

"Trey's just covering for me," Ryen says. I hear her voice off to the side somewhere, but I refuse to look at her.

What the hell is she doing? I might believe she'd vandalize my car, but to write "FAG" on the hood? Not a chance.

"Excuse me?" Burrowes asks her.

"Yeah," Ryen goes on. "It was a stupid prank. I'm sorry."

Voices sound off around us as everyone starts whispering, and I blink long and hard. Her prom date was about to get in trouble, and she couldn't let that happen, could she? It would just be too humiliating to show up to prom alone.

Stupid girl.

"You did that to his car?"

"It was a joke." Ryen's voice is calm and convincing. "I'll take care of it. I'll take it for a car wash and pay for it. Right now."

"Hell no," Trey chimes in.

"Just shut up," Ryen snaps at him and then lowers her voice. "I'll be right back."

I don't wait to be dismissed. I shoot Trey one last scowl and walk away, the crowd of students clearing as I head to my truck. I dig my keys out of my pocket and yank open the door, climbing in.

This isn't over.

Ryen climbs in the passenger side, dropping her bag on the floor, and I can feel her eyes on me.

I bite my tongue, too fucking angry to deal with her right now.

I start the engine and lay on the horn, barely waiting for the nosy little shits to move their fucking asses before I step on the gas. Students squeal and rush out of the way as I speed out of the parking lot, putting as much distance as possible between me and everyone there.

Everyone except Ryen.

I pull out onto the road while light sprinkles of rain hit the windshield, and I stare at the paint and shit all over my hood, my hands gripping the steering wheel. I'm going to kill him.

"Here," Ryen says. "I don't want this."

I'm glaring ahead, but I shoot a glance over, seeing her hold up Annie's blue scarf. She must've seen it in her Jeep before the fight happened.

"Just take it," I bite out. "It was a dick move, ruining yours. I owed you."

"I don't want it," she insists and tosses it at me. "Another girl's perfume is on it, so you should let your skank know she left it in your back seat."

I shake my head.

Bitch.

I take the scarf and stuff it in the center console. "Fine," I grit out.

It was on the tip of my tongue to tell her. To let her know that it was my sister's and somehow I liked the idea of Ryen having a part of her, and what a dumb idea that was, because why would I want a vile brat like her to put her hands on anything that belonged to Annie?

But I would never show her weakness. I never want her pity.

I take a left on Whitney and drive down the road, sparsely populated with a few gas stations and trees, and pull into a self-service car wash, parking in one of the empty bays.

Actually, they're all empty, since it's raining. The light sprinkle has turned heavier now, and the sky looms with dark clouds, rolling on top of each other and sending down a steady shower. The white noise actually feels good. My heart and breathing start to slow, and I roll up my window and turn off the engine but keep "Mudshovel" playing on the radio.

We sit there silently, neither of us moving.

I look to Ryen. "Well?"

"Well, what?"

I lean back, locking my hands behind my head and relaxing. "You're the one who fucked up the car."

She frowns. "You know I didn't."

"Yeah, I know," I reply, amusement lacing my voice. "And it's real touching and all, you taking the fall for your man, but you're washing it."

Her lips twist in a little snarl as I catch half an eye roll. She pushes open the door, plops down onto the ground, and slams the door shut, heading up to the display on the wall and digging in her pocket. I close my eyes, leaning my head back in my hands, and try to quiet my head.

I'm suddenly so tired.

Ever since I can remember, I've had others' voices in my head, trying to tell me what to do. I fought back, stood up for myself, and I've been proud of the decisions I've made, but that doesn't mean I haven't had doubts. My dad and why he can't love me as much as my sister. The guys at my school who thought it was cooler to play sports and bang five girls a weekend. My mother and how she left when I was two and Annie was one and maybe the reason she left was because she didn't want us.

I'm glad I never listened to others' voices in my head, but . . . I still hear them. They're still noisy, and I'm still walking against the wind.

Don't change, Ryen wrote in a letter once. *There's no one like you, and I can't love you if you stop being you. I guess I shouldn't say that, but I'm a little drunk right now—just came back from a party when I saw your letter—but what the hell? I don't care. You knew I loved you, right? You're my best friend.*

So don't ever change. This is a big-ass world, and when we leave our small towns, we're going to find our tribe. If we don't stay true to ourselves, how will they recognize us? (Both of us, because you know we're in the same tribe, right?)

And even if it's just the two of us, it will be the best.

God, I loved her. Whenever my worries or anger got the best of me, she always said just the right thing to put everything in perspective. There were times growing up when I felt aggravated or tortured by her letters, especially when she'd talk about *Twilight* or how Matt Walst was just as good a lead singer for Three Days Grace as Adam Gontier—I mean, what the fuck?—but I never felt bad after reading a letter from her.

Never.

I hear spray hit the car, and I open my eyes, finding her in front of the truck, blurry through the water she's shooting onto the windshield.

Why did she never take the advice she so readily gave me?

I keep my hands locked behind my head and watch her, moving

around the hood and fanning the hose up and down, spraying every inch. I notice some of the paint coming up and running down the truck as she tries to remove as much shit with the hose as possible.

She then releases the handle, stopping the flow, and drops the gun to the ground. Grabbing the hem of her loose black shirt, she pulls it over her head, revealing a thin white tank top with glimpses of a dark pink bra peeking out from underneath. Heat floods my groin, and I feel it start to swell. *Shit.*

She walks to the passenger-side door, opens it, and barely glances at me before she tosses her shirt inside and slams the door closed again. Taking the brush with the long handle off the wall, she shuffles her feet, like she's taking off her sandals, and heads for the front of the truck, stepping up on the bumper.

I didn't think of that. She's probably too short to be able to scrub the middle of the hood if she stands on the ground. Maybe I should help her.

But I look out the windshield, streaked with water, and see her beautiful body leaning forward over the hood, scrubbing so hard her breasts shake just enough to send me reeling. This was a bad idea.

And I can't take my eyes off her. Her tanned thighs bob against the grill as her tank top rises with the exertion, and I can see inches of toned stomach, her hair hanging around her and her chest in perfect view. My cock starts to grow hard, and I want her in here, not out there. I want her straddling my lap, close and in my hands.

She jumps down and rounds the car to my side, stepping up again, this time on the tire. Leaning into the hood, right in front of me, she scrubs the paint off, the small muscles in her arms flexing and her scowl getting deeper the harder she works. My eyes flash to her stomach again, and my hands are begging to touch her skin there.

What a double-edged sword. Am I angry she's a fake, weakassed little liar? Yes. But am I happy she's also got the body of a porn star? Hell yes. She doesn't have to talk for me to look.

All of a sudden I see her turn her head, and I meet her eyes, hers looking like she wants to kick me in the nuts. She flips me a middle finger, seeing me watching her, and I start laughing to myself.

Trey is nearly forgotten. For the moment.

She hops down and takes the brush back to the wall, and then she picks the hose up off the ground again. Spraying the truck, she washes away all of the paint, the white-tinted water spilling off the hood and onto the ground. I close my eyes again, enjoying the sound of the rain and the water covering the truck.

But something cold and wet suddenly hits my face, and I jerk, opening my eyes. Ryen stands on the passenger side, spraying the side of the truck and hitting the inch-wide slit in the window left open on the passenger-side door.

Dammit!

She fans the hose, spraying more, and I growl as water splatters all over the inside of the cab and the leather seats.

"Shit!" I yell, opening my door and jumping out. "Knock it off!"

My black T-shirt is damp, and I round the truck, glaring at her. She casually sprays the hood of the car, pretending to whistle. "What? What did I do?"

"Give me the hose." I hold out my hand.

She shrugs, feigning innocence. "I didn't know the window was down. Water can be dried. Relax."

I stalk toward her, because she's the one with the weapon. "Give me . . . the hose."

She purses her lips, clearly trying to hide a smile. "Come and get it."

I inch toward her, knowing she's going to spray me, but maybe if I'm quick I can—

All of a sudden, she swings the gun toward me and sprays, the cold water hitting my arms, hands, and making my shirt stick to my chest.

I growl, lunging for her, and she squeals, throwing the gun at me and yanking open the back door. I pick up the gun from where it dropped and swing around the door, seeing her lying on the back seat, her head arched up, breathing hard, and holding out her hands in defense as she watches me.

She licks her lips, out of breath with a hint of a smile. "Don't, please," she begs. "I'm sorry."

Her body shakes with a silent, nervous laugh, but I can't move. The sight of her there on the seat, her breasts rising and falling and her thighs slightly spread with one foot on the floor and the other leg arched up, sends my body reeling.

Jesus.

Sweat—or water, I'm not sure—glistens across her chest, and a blush covers her cheeks.

I step up and set the hose, still locked on, onto the roof. The water spills in a wide, steady stream down the front windshield.

I hold her eyes. "You got me wet," I point out. "Fair's fair."

Her breathing falters, and she stares at me, frozen. Will she run away?

I lean down, bowing my head into the cab and hovering over her body, holding myself up with my hands. Her eyes flash to the windshield; she's probably nervous we can be seen. But the water distorts the view, creating a blur.

She arches up on her hands, meeting me halfway as her hot little breaths fan across my lips. Her eyes fall to my mouth.

"What does it feel like?" she asks quietly, reaching a timid finger out and touching my lip piercing.

I groan, challenging her. "You tell me."

She locks eyes with me as if scared, but then her gaze falls again to the piercing. Opening her mouth just slightly, she darts out her tongue and flicks the ring.

I groan again, unable to keep my eyes from falling shut. The wet heat from that small spot filters across my face, down my neck, and swoops low in my stomach, making my fingers dig into the leather seats.

Her breath hits my skin again, and I open my eyes to see hers watching me intently as she goes back for more. Her tongue slowly traces a trail over the ring before she darts out and bites my lip around it, pulling the whole thing in her mouth.

My skin burns and tingles everywhere, and I nearly lose the fucking strength to hold myself up. Her eyes stay open, watching me pant and groan at everything she's doing. She sucks and bites and licks and tugs as I just hover there, not moving and not kissing back as I let her explore.

A horn honks, but I barely register it.

"Masen," she whispers, running her lips over the ring, again and again, and snaking a hand around the back of my neck.

Masen.

I reach out and splay a hand across her stomach, finally taking her in my hands. I want her to say my name, dammit. I want to hear my name from her lips right now.

"Yo, idiot!" A car horn honks again, and I blink, realizing someone is here. "Where's my girl at?"

Oh, shit.

Ryen pulls away, hearing Trey's voice, too, and stares up at me, a hint of fear in her eyes.

I glance out the window, seeing the blue blur of his Camaro sitting in front of the bay. I can't see him, though, so he can't see us through the water. If he could, I'm sure I would've felt him before I saw him.

I look down at Ryen, still feeling the desire roll off her.

"She's right here, Burrowes." My voice is low so only Ryen can hear me as I run my hand across her stomach. "And she feels really good."

Ryen bites her bottom lip and shakes her head, pleading.

"Hello! Wake up, asshole!" Trey barks again.

I stare down at Ryen. "Are you wet now?" And I climb off her and out of the truck, shooting her a smirk. "Stay down."

Slamming the door closed, I see Trey sitting in his car with his window down. The rain is still pouring and the clouds have grown darker.

I grab the hose and shut it off, hanging it up. "She bailed," I bark. "Walked home. Now, fuck off."

He laughs, shaking his head. "Don't worry, man. You can have her all you want after our baseball game against Thunder Bay next week. I like a little pussy after I win, so until then, you wait your turn."

What the fuck did he just say? I watch as he speeds off and disappears down the road, curling my fists.

I will not wait my turn.

He can't have her.

9

Ryen

I lick my lips, feeling the warm metal graze my tongue.

Misha.

But then I blink awake, my room coming into view and the fog in my head slowly clearing. Misha? I was kissing Masen in my dream. Why did I call him Misha?

Damn. I take my pillow out from under my head and cover my face with it. I'm a mess. I'd fantasized about Misha before, in one of my kinky alternate realities where he writes me dirty letters and finally sneaks into my room, and that's the first time I meet him, when he's sliding into me.

But he never has a face. I always got the impression he was tall and dark, though, but I never knew for sure. I guess after everything last night, and how this new guy is in my head now, my brain made a connection.

My fantasies finally found Misha a face.

Taking the pillow off my head, I drop it to the side, yesterday's events playing in my mind. I bring up my hand, twisting it around to see the remnants of his Sharpie on the inside of my finger. I glance at my chalk wall ahead and see where I added "Shame" to the bottom of the list.

Alone
Empty
Fraud
Shame

The words hurt, but last night I realized something. There's more I'm not seeing. The first word, "Alone," was written in his bunk at the Cove. That's not about me. It has to do with something else. These words mean something else.

And then the car and the fight . . . I'd walked out to the parking lot after school, immediately spotting Masen putting something in my Jeep. I'd charged down the steps, ready to tell him off, especially after what he did to my scarf, but when I saw what was sitting on the seat of my car I paused.

Of course it was tacky to give me another woman's scarf, but I was a little thrown off that he would feel guilty enough to want to make up for it in the first place. It was beautiful and soft and I wanted to keep it.

And then the car wash. How excited I felt when he stalked me like I was prey. How the smooth curve of the piercing felt when I slipped the tip of my tongue through the hoop. How he was so patient and not greedy or selfish, just letting me explore.

How his hand inched possessively up under my shirt, sending me reeling.

I bring my fingers up to my mouth, grazing the tip of one with my tongue. It tickles a little, but it's teasing, too. Did he like it when I did that? I wanted to feel good to him, even if I only admit it to myself.

I trail my hand across my cheek and down my neck, wishing it was his hands. Wishing I could go back to last night and not cut him off, making him take me back to school so I could get my car and run away.

But the truth is . . . I'm starting to think about him. A lot, and

I don't know why. Especially when he's constantly in my face, telling me what I'm doing wrong.

I've never been in danger of losing my heart to guys like Trey, but with Masen, I find him consuming my attention. I'm always aware of him.

And the closer I get to him, the farther away from Misha I feel. It almost feels like I'm betraying him. Not that we're romantic, but he has my heart, and I don't want to give it to anyone else. I feel like Masen threatens that.

I said I would give Misha a few days, but I need to know. Is he safe? Is he alive? Has he just moved on?

Pulling off the covers, I sit up and swing my legs over the side of the bed. I look at the clock and see that it's after nine.

It's Saturday. I have the whole day free. I could just drive by.

Not like an obsessive stalker girl who just can't take a hint. No, I can just drive by. Make sure the house hasn't burned down or isn't empty because his father committed some gruesome murder and left town, on the run, with Misha and his sister in the middle of the night.

Who knows? Maybe I'll see a young guy pulling into the driveway and entering the house, and I'll be able to tell that it's him, and then I'll know that he's alive and well. I don't have to have any more answers than that, do I?

Standing up, I throw on a pair of workout shorts, a T-shirt, and a fleece jacket. Pulling my hair up into a messy ponytail, I'm not going to worry about how I look. If I go shower and fix my hair and makeup, I'll be tempted to knock on his door. If I look like shit, then I won't leave my car.

After I brush my teeth, I jog down the stairs and swing around the banister, heading into the kitchen.

"Morning," my mom says.

I look up to see her and Carson sitting at the table, looking through a magazine together. Probably some home renovation thing, because Mom wants to expand the garage. I open the refrigerator and pull out a bottle of water. "Morning," I reply.

"The principal called last night," my sister's voice rings out.

I falter, slowly closing the fridge door and not looking at her. *Shit.* That's right.

Did she tell them about what I did to Masen's truck? Or what I told her I did?

Dammit!

But no. My mom would've reamed me last night when I got home. She wouldn't have waited until this morning.

Plus, I doubt the principal really believed me, but there was little she could do.

"She said you're going to prom with Trey," my mom says, walking over to me in her bathrobe, her hair up in a bun. She empties her coffee cup into the sink. "She wanted to know your favorite color for the corsage. Why didn't you tell us he'd asked you?"

"I forgot." I shrug, relaxing a little. "You were gone, and I've been busy."

Actually, I didn't feel it was worth mentioning. Popular girl is going to prom with popular guy. My place in the yearbook is secure.

But I care so little all of a sudden. I wonder how that happened.

She nods, her blue eyes smiling at me as she brushes a flyaway off my cheek. "You're *too* busy. You leave for college soon. I want to see you."

I kiss her on the cheek and grab an apple out of the bowl on the center island. "I'll be home later."

"Well, where are you going now?"

"To see a friend," I tell her, turning and walking for the foyer. "I'll be back."

"Ryen?" my mom protests.

"Oh, just let her go," my sister grumbles, standing up and

carrying her plate to the sink. "Ryen is so busy and important now. We should be grateful when she graces us with her presence."

I grab my wallet and keys off the entryway table, clenching my jaw. I don't remember the last time my sister said anything nice to me. Or I to her, for that matter.

"Carson," my mom warns.

"What?" my sister says. "I'm happy for her. At least it's not grade school when she had no friends and I had to take her everywhere with me so she wouldn't be alone."

I swallow the bitter taste in my mouth, not looking at her. She always knows what to say to make me feel small again. The smile I can usually force for my mother's sake is pressed down deep in my stomach, contained under a pile of bricks, and the agreeable words I can always spit out don't want to play this time. I'm tired.

I walk out the front door and hop in my Jeep before she says anything else. I don't care if it's just his town, just his house, or whatever. I need to see something that's Misha.

I drive down the quiet, pristine lanes of Thunder Bay, the wind blowing through the open cab of my Jeep as loose strands of my hair fly wildly around me. The sun flickers through the leaves in the trees above, and the sea air wafts all around, filling my lungs with its fresh scent.

Avril Lavigne's "Sk8er Boi" plays on the radio, but I don't sing along like I usually do. And I barely notice the slight wheezing coming up from my chest as I gape at the homes and lawns on both sides of me.

Holy shit. I'm way out of my league.

Two- and three-story homes with gates and acres and circular driveways bigger than my house stand before me, and the cars that pass by probably cost just as much.

Jesus, Misha.

Not that my house is shabby, of course. It's more than big enough, and my mother has done a beautiful job decorating it, but these houses are the high life. For once, I'm really glad I'm driving a Jeep so I can blend in. It's the only car on the market that doesn't give away how much or how little you're worth. There are rich and poor Jeep enthusiasts.

I continue driving, glancing at the map on my GPS and taking a right on Birch and then a left on Girard.

Two forty-eight Girard. I've known his address by heart since I was eleven. At first I thought, with us being only a half hour away from each other, of course we'd see each other eventually. When we got our licenses and had more freedom.

But by the time that day came, we had lives, friends, and obligations, and it seemed to be enough to know we *could* see each other anytime we wanted to.

If we wanted to.

I pass the houses and read the numbers written on the columns, walls, and gates at their entrances: 212, 224, 236, and then . . .

I see it. On the left with a hedge of trees and two small rock columns featuring a walk-through gate and a drive-through gate, which is currently open. It's a three-story Tudor-style house, balancing the wood and stone beautifully, and I pull to a stop on the other side of the road to stare at it for a minute.

It's quaint and picturesque but not as massive or pretentious as so many of the homes I saw on the way here.

But it does have a fountain in the front.

He grew up here. This is where my letters have been coming.

No wonder he complains so much. I laugh to myself. It's a great house, but it isn't him at all. Misha, who got suspended for fighting twice, plays the guitar, and thinks that beef jerky and Monster Energy drinks make for a healthy breakfast, lives in a house that looks like it could have a butler.

I feel my lungs growing heavy and thick, and I take out the extra inhaler I keep in a secret compartment in the console. Spring is here, and my allergies are going haywire.

I take two puffs, slowly feeling my lungs start to open up again.

I check my phone, seeing the time is nearly ten. I can't sit here all day, can I? I look up, noticing a couple of women jogging toward me on the sidewalk, and I hear a kid yelling from somewhere in the neighborhood. I tap my foot against the pedal, suddenly torn.

I said I wasn't going to get out of the car, but . . . Being this close, possibly only feet away from him, I miss him so much. I need to know what's going on.

If I go up to that door, our relationship is over as I know it. Maybe it will go on in some other way, when I find out what's wrong with him, but it won't be the same once I see his face. Things will change, and I will have broken what worked. It will be awkward, and he won't have been prepared for me just to show up like this. What if we both just sit there, twiddling our thumbs and not saying anything, because I'm the crazy stalker who hunted him down, and now he feels weird?

"Screw it," I snap, realizing I'm talking to myself, but I don't care.

I rely on him. I have a right to. We've had that commitment for seven years. If he doesn't want me to show up, then he damn well should've written back and told me it was over. I have a right to know what's going on.

Pushing open my door, I hop out of my Jeep and slam it shut. With weak legs and shallow breaths, I jog across the street, pushing my fear out of my head.

Don't think. Just go. He's driving me crazy, and I need it to end. I just need to know.

Walking up the driveway, I dart my eyes around, looking at the windows to see if anyone sees me approaching. I smooth my hair back, readjusting my ponytail as I step up to the door.

I should've dressed right. I should be wearing makeup. What if he's home and sees me and starts laughing? I'm a mess.

No, Misha knows me. He's the only one who knows the real me. He won't care what I look like.

I pull the collar of my shirt away from my body and dip my nose in, sniffing. I shower twice a day—at night because I usually get sweaty at cheer and swim and in the morning after my workouts—but I didn't have one yet today.

Smells fine, I guess. Although my sister did say once that you can't smell yourself.

I bring up my hand and rap on the door several times. Then I see a doorbell to the right. Dammit, I should've rung that.

It doesn't matter. I fold my arms over my chest, hugging myself, and shift on my feet as I bow my head and close my eyes.

Misha, Misha, Misha, where are you?

I hear the door open, and my heart skips a beat.

"Yes?" someone says.

I blink up and immediately relax a little, taking in a little more air. It's a man, much older than Misha would be, with graying dark hair and green eyes. His dad?

He's wearing a dark blue robe, tied over a full set of pajamas, and embarrassment warms my cheeks. It's a Saturday morning. Maybe he just woke up.

"Uh, hi," I finally say, unfolding and then folding my arms again. "Is, uh . . . Misha here? By any chance?"

I see his back straighten a little, as if on guard. "No, I'm sorry, he isn't," he replies quietly.

He isn't. So he lives here. This is his house. I don't know why having that confirmed fills me with dread and excitement at the same time.

And this guy must be his father.

"Do you know when he'll be back?" I ask as politely as I can. "I'm a friend of his."

His chest rises with a heavy breath and his gaze falls. I notice his cheeks look sunken, and he has bags under his eyes, as if he's sick or tired or something.

"If you're a friend, I'm sure you can call him and find out," he says.

I falter. Yeah, if I were his friend, why wouldn't I have his cell number?

Maybe he knows who Ryen is. Maybe I should tell him who I am.

"Would you like to leave a message?" he prompts, starting to inch back and preparing to close the door.

"No," I rush out. "Thank you, sir."

He nods and swings the door closed.

But I shoot my hand out, stopping him. "Sir?" He looks up, stopping. "Is he okay?" I ask. "I just . . . I haven't heard from him in a while."

His father is silent for a moment, watching me, before answering with a resolute tone. "He's fine."

And then he closes the door, and I stand on the front step, frozen and confused.

What does that mean?

I guess I should be happy, right? He's fine, isn't he?

He lives here. His father says he's not home right now, which means he's home sometimes, so he hasn't moved or died or joined the Army.

But I don't feel happy.

He's fine. He lives here. He's not home right now. Everything's normal. Nothing's changed.

So if he hasn't moved or died or joined the Army, then why the hell isn't he writing me anymore?

I spin around and charge for my Jeep, knowing what Ryen, Misha's friend, would do. She'd never give up. She'd keep writing with undying loyalty, trusting that he has a good reason.

But the Ryen who Misha doesn't know, the survivor, is taking hold right now, and she doesn't like being played with.

You know my address, asshole. Use it or don't.

I'm not holding my breath anymore.

C an you believe Masen Laurent?" Lyla sneers, standing next to my locker as Ten texts on his phone beside her. She stares over her shoulder at Masen and a group of guys on the other side of the hallway. "He probably got kicked out of his last school for fighting, and Trey's getting tons of shit on TikTok for that fight." She narrows her eyes on Masen. "Definitely hot, but what an asshole. He should be arrested."

Trey's getting shit for that fight? I keep my smirk to myself. *You mean for getting his ass kicked.*

I glance over at Masen, who's surrounded by four other guys, all of them laughing and joking around as if they've been best friends forever. Masen smiles at one of them and shakes his head, sucking a straw between his lips as he takes a drink from a 7-Eleven cup.

I feel my cheeks warm. Those lips. I couldn't get enough of them Friday night, and he didn't even kiss me.

What if Lyla and Ten found out right now that he had me in the back seat of his car and I didn't want to stop?

He seems to sense me watching him, because he turns his head toward me, both of us locking gazes across the crowded hall. His green eyes pin me to my spot, something hot flashing in them, and I suddenly can't move a step. I spin back around, throwing my books in my locker.

"Yeah, well," I reply, forcing my voice flat and bored. "He seems to be finding his crowd."

"Yeah, the bottom of the barrel," Lyla jokes, looking at the guys Masen is standing with. "All those guys will be in jail in a year."

They seem like the type. Masen has been here less than a week and already has a crowd of friends, all of whom seem to fit his style. A few piercings here, some tattoos there, and probably all of them well-versed in the bail process.

"So I heard you ditched him at the car wash." Ten tosses his gum into the gray trash can against the wall between my locker and a classroom door. "You're so bad."

"Yeah, well." I pull out my phone so I can take it to lunch. "My time is precious. He better get used to manual labor, anyway."

Lyla and Ten snort, all of us shooting amused glances over at the delinquents.

Friday Masen didn't have any friends, and now . . . I'll bet anything they came to him, too. Not the other way around.

Now everyone knows him.

"He keeps looking at you," Ten says.

I pretend disinterest as I cast a quick glance over to Masen.

My pulse starts to race.

He stands, leaning his back against the locker, and his eyes are on me. Challenging, amused, hot . . . like he hasn't forgotten where we left off at all.

"He can look all he wants," I say, slamming my locker door and meeting his eyes as I speak to my friends. "He's never gonna get it."

The corner of Masen's mouth lifts in a smile across the hall, like he knows I'm talking shit about him.

"But if he does," Ten chimes in, "make sure I'm the first to know, okay? I want details."

"I'm going to prom with Trey." I hood my eyes at Ten. "Masen Laurent can admire from afar and enjoy the view."

Both of my friends laugh, but just then, something hits the garbage can and a stream of clear liquid shoots out and right for us. Soda splashes onto the floor; I gasp as it hits my legs and causes Lyla and Ten to jump back as sticky fluid hits their ankles and shoes.

"Asshole!" Lyla screams across the hallway.

Masen pushes off the lockers, still holding his straw as he chews on it, smirking. His friends follow, all of them chuckling.

He must've thrown his soda from over there, into the garbage can.

Prick.

"Sorry, Rocks." Masen pulls the straw out of his mouth, a cocky look in his eyes as he stares at me. "Didn't mean to make you dirty."

His words are filled with innuendo, and his friends laugh louder around him. I flex my jaw, dying to slap that smile off his face as he and his new friends walk away, down the hall, and toward the lunchroom.

He never fails to make an impression, does he?

"Jerk," Lyla grits out. "I'm going to the bathroom to clean up."

She brushes past me and Ten follows her, shaking his head with an amused smile. "We'll meet you in the lunchroom," he says as he passes.

I turn and reopen my locker, taking out the cashmere scarf Masen ruined. It's already dirty, so what does it matter? I dry off my legs and ankles and throw it back in the locker, making a mental note to take it home tonight and get it cleaned.

The bell rings, and I head to the cafeteria, actually feeling hungry enough to leave my books in my locker today and eat something.

But when I pass the physics lab, I see something dark come at me on my left, and I barely have time to realize it's Masen before he shoves me through the door. I stumble into the empty classroom, sucking in a breath as he shuts the door and advances on me, backing me up into the wall.

My heart pounds in my chest, and butterflies flutter in my stomach. But I stamp it down. I look at him with my hands on my hips and my chin up, forcing myself to appear calm.

He stares down at me, not saying anything as his chest touches mine. The room is dark, except for the dim light coming through the windows, and muffled sounds of laughter and talking drift through the wall from the lunchroom.

He's close.

Everything heats up under my skin, and his breath falls across my lips.

"This cheerleading outfit is fucking lame," he says.

I cock my head. "Funny, 'cause you couldn't seem to take your eyes off me in it a minute ago."

His eyes drop to my lips, and he leans in, both of our breaths turning shallow, and I can almost taste him.

I lick my lips.

And he loses it.

He reaches down, grabs the backs of my thighs, and hauls me up, and I wrap my arms and legs around him, letting out a small whimper. *Yes.*

I part my lips, running them over the lip ring and savoring the feel as he groans and digs his fingers into my thighs. I tighten my legs around him, needing to feel him.

"Bitch," he whispers.

"Loser."

And when I dart out the tip of my tongue to lick the little piece of metal again, he's done being patient.

Masen Laurent slams his lips down on mine, moving hard over my mouth and brushing his tongue with mine, the heat and taste sending my mind reeling. I stop breathing. I don't care. I just go in for more and more.

He bites my bottom lip, moving his hands to my ass and squeezing, and I let out a little cry, the feel of him driving me mad. I don't want people to hear us, but right now I don't care about anything.

My eyes close as his lips and teeth move over my neck, sending shivers down my spine. Heat gathers low in my belly as I tighten my thighs around him.

I want to be closer.

He presses his groin into me, and I come back down, taking his lips and dipping my tongue in, teasing him like that every time I come in for a kiss.

"Keep doing that," he gasps.

I hear laughter outside and jump, twisting my head toward the door.

But he doesn't let my head leave the game. He reaches over and twists the lock and then carries me over to a chair at a lab table and sits down, keeping me straddling him.

Grabbing my hips, he brings me chest to chest. "Did you think about me this weekend?" He bites my lip and lets go. "Hmm?"

The feel of his teeth sends my stomach flipping, but I bite out anyway, "You wish."

I press my body into him and sink my lips into his as he pulls my hips in again.

"You were talking shit to your dumb friends, weren't you?" he pants, his kisses and nibbles quick and teasing. "I never wanted to teach someone a lesson as badly as I wanted to teach you one just now." He pulls me again, my clit grinding against the bulge in his jeans. "I should've walked over, flipped up your skirt, and started going down on you right there, so they all know what you really like."

I start rolling my hips, slow and taunting, but when he darts out and tries to catch my lips again, I pull away, teasing him. "You don't know what I like."

"I don't think I'm going to disappoint."

His threat lingers between us, and I look down, seeing the tip of a tattoo coming out of his shirt from his shoulder and drifting up just about an inch onto his neck. I can't tell what it is, but I lean down and kiss it, trailing my lips slowly up his neck, to his ear.

"Sorry to eat and run," I whisper, "but my friends are waiting for me."

I don't want to leave, but I have to.

I move to get up, but he yanks me back down. "That's not how this works, princess."

His eyes challenge me, and I feel his fingers squeeze around my thighs.

My heart beats faster. "Someone could come in," I warn.

"And what? Find out I'm your dirty little secret?"

"Mas—" But he leans up and snatches my lips, cutting me off. He kisses me deep, and all of a sudden I just want to wrap my arms around him again.

"Don't call me that when we're like this," he whispers against my lips.

Don't call him Masen? "Why?" I ask.

"Just don't." He shrugs me off and stands up, forcing me to climb off his lap. "Now do me a favor and go in the lunchroom and sit in Trey's lap, would you? I wanna look while your fucking prom date has no clue that I just had that ass grinding my cock a minute ago."

He gives me a cruel smile, and I inhale a deep breath, raising my chin and trying to look unfazed.

But my heart pounds like a jackhammer. What an asshole.

Before I can reply with a witty, sarcastic, or utterly childish remark, he walks past me and out the door while the sound of the students in the lunchroom floods in.

An ache digs into the back of my throat, but I refuse to cry. Turning, I look out the window and see my reflection in the glass. I blink away the tears and check my face to make sure my mascara and lips aren't smeared. Checking that my hair is smooth and perfect again.

Making sure the girl who got out a few minutes ago is tucked back inside, down deep.

I take a deep breath and walk out the door, joining my friends in the cafeteria.

10

Misha

Sitting in an empty Ferris wheel car, I tip my head back and close my eyes, letting the night wind blow across my face.

The ocean waves in the distance curl and crash ashore, filling the darkness with a steady presence at my back as a car above me creaks in the wind, the rest having been rusted silent a long time ago.

The camping lamp I've been using in the room sits under my propped-up legs, and I hold a pen in my hand and a notepad on my lap.

Fifty-seven times I didn't call
Fifty-seven letters I didn't send,
Fifty-seven stitches to breathe again, and then I fucking pretend.

I open my eyes and jot down the last two lines, barely able to see what I'm writing in the near darkness. Doesn't matter, I guess. I can write it tonight and read it tomorrow.

I've been writing this song for two years, ever since Ryen started talking about "the cheerleader" in some of her letters. I got stuck halfway through, because I wasn't sure where the story was going, just that I needed to tell it. I had Ryen's impression through her words, but I couldn't get further than that.

But leaving school two days ago, after finally having her in my arms in the lab, I needed to write. I was feeling things.

She knows how to work me. How to drive me insane, acting like I'm dirt under her shoe in public but like she can't get enough of me in private. Her tongue and mouth, the little obsession she has with my lip ring, the way she ground into me, and if it weren't for a couple layers of clothes, I would've been inside her . . .

Yeah, that prissy little act drops like a bad habit, and she can get so hot, I want to take off everything *except* that lame-ass skirt and see how every inch of her feels.

If her whole stuck-up crew knew how their little princess melts for me . . .

But I look up, staring out at the theme park and realizing.

No. Not for *me*.

For Masen.

Damn, I can't keep this up. I have to leave, or I have to tell her. She'll never forgive me for betraying her like this. For being right under her nose and damn near seducing her.

"I'm ashamed I didn't guess you were here a long time ago!" a voice calls out, and I jerk, looking down at the ground.

Dane stands below with a flashlight in his hand.

I watch him start climbing the beams up to where I sit about five cars off the ground, and let out a sigh. I'm working. For the first time in months, I'm writing. Just my luck.

"You and your cousin loved this place as kids," he yells up. "I should've known you'd be hiding here."

He crawls up, past the empty cars, and heaves himself over the beam where my car sits. The wheel creaks with the extra weight, but it doesn't budge. Years of rain and moist sea air have taken care of that.

He takes a seat, and I notice he's wearing our band's black T-shirt. Our name, Cipher Core, with some artwork Dane designed, is on the left side of the chest. I have a few at home. Even Annie has some, which she used to sleep in.

I see Dane's eyes fall to my notepad, and then he raises them to me, the wheels in his head probably turning.

"You got something there for me?" he prods, meaning lyrics.

I laugh to myself, tossing him the book. What the hell? Let him tell me it sucks, so I can give up, and we can go to Sticks and get drunk instead.

He barely looks at the pad, though. He eyes me hesitantly, as if he's searching for words.

"Your dad isn't looking too good, man," he says, keeping his tone even. "The stores are closed, and no one sees him anymore. He misses you."

"He misses Annie."

"He still went to work after Annie," he points out. "It was when you left that he retreated."

I prop my arm up on the back of the seat and rub my forehead. He's not going to the shops? To open up or anything?

Dane's right. My father was in pain after Annie's death, but he didn't abandon his responsibilities. Other than me, of course. No, he gave me all the space I told him I wanted.

But he still took care of the house, ran the shops, did the paperwork, and went on his morning runs.

He hasn't called me, though.

If he's hurting—if he needs me—would he tell me?

I stopped being able to talk to you. I stopped looking for a way to talk to you.

Guilt chips away at some of my anger. Annie loved him. She wouldn't want him alone.

I look over at Dane and see him holding up the flashlight and reading the lyrics I wrote. His eyes move intently but slowly over the paper, and I can tell he's reading every word.

He looks up and meets my eyes, nodding. "We're ready to get back to work. You coming home?"

I don't know. There were reasons I left, but now I worry that I have reasons to stay. And they're not the reasons I came for. That's the problem.

I should never have gotten this close to Ryen. It's complicated now. Either leave and keep my friend or stay and lose her forever.

"I still need to get one more thing," I tell him. "And then I'll be home."

C oming up on the house, I slow to a stop and check the clock on my dash. It's after midnight, and the street is silent, all of the houses dark.

Except one.

I gaze out at the two-story brick home, a single light coming from the den and a figure moving inside. All the cars are in the driveway, Trey's Camaro sitting in the middle.

What I need is in that house.

Something of mine—something of my family's—and I'm getting it back. Fuckface has a baseball game Saturday night, and the whole family will be there. I can do it then, and then I can get out of here.

The shadow passes in front of the large den window again, and I follow it with my eyes, the warm light from inside so inviting, making my chest ache. How nice to think your children are safe under your roof, warm and sleeping peacefully, surrounded with love in their perfect world.

That's about to change.

I put the truck in gear and speed off, heading around the corner toward the school. Ryen's house is on the way, and I want to see her all of a sudden.

I've wanted to talk to her for the past two days, but yeah . . . I'd just dig myself into a bigger hole, because that's all I know how to do, it seems. I want to crawl in through her window and just touch her and talk to her and see if she can make me see the end of this. Make me figure out how to rewind and start over, before I abandoned her all those months ago when I should've clung to her and let her know how much I need her.

But if I could go back—to before I met her in person—would I really want to?

No. I wouldn't trade those minutes in the lab for anything. Or the ones in the back of my truck.

Eventually we all have to weigh what we want more: wanting back what we had or wanting what could be. To stay or to risk everything to move forward.

I pass her house. She has a temper, and I'm tired tonight.

Besides, I need a shower before I try to crawl into bed with her.

Parking on the other side of the street, in front of the school, I grab my duffel with a change of clean clothes and jog across the road, keeping an eye out for passersby. Not that it's not dead as doornails at this hour, but you never know.

I run across the school parking lot, not seeing any cars, but I look around just in case. I heard they were going to start hiring security to do sweeps every so often, trying to catch the little vandal who's decorating the walls, but I don't see any security vehicles. And they're still in the process of getting the cameras working, so for now, it's safe.

Jumping the fence to the practice field, I hike up onto some old football equipment and lift up the loose screen leading into the men's locker room. Raising the window, I hop up and plant my ass on the sill and swing my legs over. I throw my duffel on the floor and jump down, turning around to close the window again.

I've only risked this a few times in the past couple of weeks, but I'm tired of mooching off Dane for his shower, too. Plus, I could take all night here if I wanted. Even the couches in the library are more comfortable than the Cove.

I grab a towel and strip, stepping into a stall and turning on the water. The hot spray spreads chills down my body, and I damn near groan at the pleasure. This is definitely a perk of not living at the Cove. I miss my shower at home with my dry-erase marker I used to write on the wall and all the time alone I want.

I wash my hair and body, savoring the soothing temperature of the water probably longer than I should. As soon as I'm done, I dry off and dress in a clean pair of jeans and a black thermal, packing my dirty clothes back in my bag.

But suddenly I hear a beeping and then quick stutters of white noise. I freeze, training my ears.

"Yeah," a male voice says. "I'll sweep down here and meet you upstairs."

"Shit!" I whisper. I stuff the rest of my clothes in the bag and jump behind a row of lockers just as the door opens.

Fuck. Okay, my car's not in the school parking lot, I closed the window on the way in, I picked up all my shit, and . . . My eyes fall on the steam from my shower still floating around the ceiling.

Son of a bitch.

I peer around the corner, seeing the security guard flash his light into the shower. My fucking heart pounds in my chest, and I shoot a glance to the window, knowing there's no way I'm getting out that way. Darting my eyes to him once again, I see him check out the steam hovering high and then immediately shoot his light around, looking for me. He knows someone's here.

I bolt. Twisting on my heel, I dart down the row of lockers and swing open the door, a huge creak filling the quiet.

"Hey!" he shouts. And then I hear him getting on his radio, alerting the other one.

I bypass the nearest stairwell and race for the next one, skipping steps as I charge up to the main level, carrying my bag. I enter the hallway and glance in both directions, taking off left and jogging down the next hallway, keeping my eyes and ears peeled.

I pass exits chained shut, and I keep running, searching for a way out.

But then I pass the cafeteria and see something written on the windows looking in. I slow down, glancing around me to make sure the guards aren't coming.

I read the message.

I SEE YOU, LIKE PICTURES IN A FRAME,

BUT I CAN'T TOUCH, AND I CAN'T BE THE SAME.

—PUNK

I smile to myself. Looks like the little punk struck again.

The message is spray-painted in dark blue in two lines across all four of the large windows. Is he getting in the same way I have been? And even better, how is he getting out through the chains and without setting off the alarms?

I look around, trying to figure out which window I should try to slip out of, but then I hear another door swing open, and I take off. I run down the hallway from one door to another, twisting knobs to check for open classrooms.

The physics lab Ryen and I were in two days ago opens, and I dart inside just as I see the glow of a flashlight bobbing up and down the floor from the other hallway.

Closing the door gently, I scan the room, seeing the supply closet. Heading over, I open it and dart inside.

I hear a small gasp.

From right behind me.

Every hair on my arms stands on end, and I turn around, my mouth suddenly dry.

I'm not alone in here.

Reaching up, I grab the chain for the light, but a soft hand takes mine and pulls it down.

"No," a female voice whispers. "They'll see the light."

Ryen?

I blink, trying to get my eyes to adjust to the darkness, but she pulls me back, leading me around the partition of shelves to the other side, by the window. Moonlight streams through, and I see she's wearing some black shorts and her rash guard. She must've been teaching lessons tonight. Her hair hangs loose and kinky from air drying, and she clutches the loop of a black backpack in her hand.

"What are you doing here?" I ask her.

She stands close, her breathing shaky and nervous. "Nothing."

"Ryen—"

"Shh!" She grabs my wrists and pulls me down, both of us squatting low as I notice the muffled sound of talking coming from the lab.

"No, I heard a door shut," one of the guards says.

"This was the only door open," another says. "You check it out. I'm going to search the cafeteria."

I hear her shallow breathing as both of us look to the crack under the door, seeing the glow of a flashlight. *Shit.*

I look back to Ryen and suddenly drop my eyes, stopping. There's something on her hands.

I shoot my eyes back up to her and then back down, taking one of her hands and turning it over.

Blue paint.

Or blue . . . spray paint.

I survey the smudges all over her fingers and palm as realization starts to hit.

Holy shit.

I look up again, locking eyes with her. Well, well, well . . .

"You just got a whole lot more interesting."

Fear flashes in her eyes, and she pulls her hand away, her breaths sounding like she's about to cry.

I smirk, and she shoots a glance to the door and then back to me. "Please don't say anything," she begs in a whisper.

Why would I say anything? This is hilarious. Ryen Trevarrow, Queen Good Girl, sneaks into the school at night, breaking more than one law, to anonymously leave messages and air dirty secrets for the student body right under their noses.

Excellent.

I hear the guard's radio beep and more muffled chatter, and I listen, hearing him talk, his voice moving away from the door.

I take my bag and inch toward the door, listening again.

His voice is farther away now, and I crack the door just a sliver and peek out. If we stay here, we'll get caught. This isn't the first time I've run from cops, and you don't choose a hiding place without an out.

"What are you doing?" Ryen asks.

I look out, seeing the beam of his flashlight outside the classroom door as he talks on the radio. I glance across the lab, behind the teacher's desk, and see the door to another classroom, connected to the lab. Grabbing her hand in mine, I pull her quickly across the room, hearing her suck in a breath as we tread softly and hurry into the next room.

Pulling her through the doorway, I whip around a tall set of file cabinets and back her into the dark corner, squatting down and hiding.

We hear him enter the other room again, a door creaks open and then shuts, and a grumbled "little shit" before he talks to the other guy on the radio again.

I stare at Ryen.

She's Punk.

Oh, my God. She's been sneaking around right under everyone's noses, carrying on this secret life at night. And then watching everyone's reactions in the morning as they scurry about, trying to find out which of their own it is. Never suspecting her.

Why would they? I guess. She's never given the impression she's any deeper than a teaspoon. The perfect cover.

How long has she been doing this?

"Stop looking at me," she whispers, her tone finally finding its fight again.

"I'm going to head downstairs," I hear the guy on the radio say.

"I'll finish checking here and meet you down there," replies the other one.

I keep still, our bodies close as I look down at her. "Why do you do this?"

She shoots her eyes up, her parted lips inches from mine. "You can't tell anyone. No one will understand."

"Who cares?" I shoot back. "Your friends are losers."

"So are yours."

"At least I don't have to fake anything around them," I grit out. But then I realize that's not true. The guys I've been hanging out with don't even know my real name, do they?

I push forward. "Why are you two different people, Ryen?"

"What do you care? You don't know me."

"Hey, who's there?" one of the guards shouts.

Shit! I grab Ryen's hand and we bolt for the classroom door.

"Hey!" he yells.

Ryen cries out as she struggles to keep up, and we rush into the hallway, turning left.

"Stop!" I hear him say, and I see the glow of his flashlight shining on us.

His radio crackles, and I hear him talking, but we're already around the corner. Passing one of the exits, I notice it doesn't have a chain, and I push it open, hearing the alarm go off. But we don't leave. I pull Ryen in the other direction and bolt up the stairs.

"Masen," she gasps, breathing hard.

We could've just run, I guess, but my truck is on the other side of the school, and I don't know where her Jeep is. We might not make it without being recognized. Hopefully, with the alarm going off, they'll think we bolted, though.

I pull her into the library and let the door close softly before rushing up the stairs, hearing her struggle behind me. We hurry to the back, hidden behind stacks and rows of books, near the couches and chairs. The library is dark, only the faint moonlight coming in from the windows high above. Our steps are soft, thanks to the carpeting, and I drag her behind a shelf, far, far above and away from the doors in the front.

We're secluded.

The alarm still goes off, but it's faint.

She collapses into me. "Masen . . ."

She breathes fast and hard, only able to take in shallow breaths, and I wrap my arms around her, feeling her go limp.

What the fuck?

Worry floods through me, and I cup her face as she fights for air. Her lids are hooded and she looks like she's in pain.

"My bag," she breathes out.

What? And then I widen my eyes, remembering. Oh, fuck. She has asthma. That's right.

I shoot down to her backpack on the floor and dig in the front pocket, pulling out a red inhaler.

I stand back up, wrapping her in my arms and holding her up. "Here."

She leans into me, her head resting on my chest as she takes a puff and waits a moment before inhaling another one.

Her chest rises and falls fast, and I lower one arm, wrapping it around her waist as I hold her to me.

Her weak body sinks into me as her breathing starts to slow down and she's taking in deeper breaths.

Dammit. She tried to tell me as we raced through the school, and I didn't listen to her.

What would I have done if she'd dropped her bag somewhere and I couldn't find her medicine?

I hug her close, feeling, for the first time, how small she is in my arms. Ryen is always so large around me. Never backing down, her confidence always appearing larger than life.

I hold her head to my chest with the other hand and bury my nose in her hair.

"You're okay," I say gently. "I got you."

"My heart won't stop pounding," she says, her fragile voice starting to come around.

"I know." I smile. "I can feel it."

The beat of her heart is hitting my chest, and I can feel her body slowly get stable as her breathing calms.

What am I going to do with this girl? Just when I think I have her figured out, she pulls at me a little more.

Just when I think I can't stand her, and I can leave, never looking back, I turn right around and want to make sure nothing hurts her.

Her arms, hugged close to her body as I hold her, start to drop as she pulls away from me.

She raises her eyes, looking a little embarrassed and not saying anything as she kneels down, grabbing her backpack.

Standing up, she purses her lips and looks around.

The alarm stops, and I have no idea what's happening out there—if they think we left out the door or what—but she's not leaving yet.

"You don't tell anyone about tonight, and I won't tell anyone you were here, either," she says. "Got it?"

She turns to leave, but I grab her hand. "I think people would enjoy this version of you."

"My friends would hate me."

"They already hate you. Everyone does."

For a split second, I see a frown cross her face, but it quickly disappears. She faces me, a light brown eyebrow arched in defiance.

"Why fake it?" I charge. "Why compete with people and play the games?"

She takes a step, trying to leave, but I pull her back. "Don't walk away from me."

"This is none of your business!" she whisper-yells, yanking her hand free and scowling at me. "You don't know me."

"Does anyone?"

She looks away, her eyes suddenly glistening. After a moment, she speaks, her voice low. "I don't want to be alone," she admits. "They may hate me, but they respect me. I can't be invisible or laughed at or . . ." She trails off and then continues. "I don't know why. I just never had the courage to stand apart. I always wanted to fit in."

"Everyone wants to be accepted, Ryen." Does she think no one's ever had those same feelings? "Why do you write on the walls?"

She stands there, staring off and looking like she's struggling to find words.

"Misha . . ." she says, trailing off again.

I tense, my heart picking up pace.

But then she shakes her head, letting the thought go. "It doesn't matter. I just had ways to vent before, a way to be heard, and now I don't. I just started doing it a couple of months ago."

A couple of months ago. Shortly after I stopped writing her.

I blink long and hard.

The fake friends, the hovering parent, the worry and stress of wanting to fit in just like most any other person out there . . . I was her bouncing board.

I was so caught up in my own loss and anger, I never stopped to think how suddenly abandoning her after seven years would hurt her. Not that I'm responsible for her actions, but I am responsible for mine. She relied on me.

"Why are you here?" she asks, turning it around on me.

I look at the duffel bag in my hand, unashamed I needed a shower, but then that answer would lead to more questions. Why am I living at the Cove? Where are my parents?

"Mmmm," she gloats, a fake smile on her pretty face. "So others have to own up to you, but not the other way around, huh?" She backs away toward the stairs. "My mom is only a phone call away. I'll get taken straight home with a slap on the wrist. Hope you enjoy your long, hard night in a cold cell," she taunts and then calls over her shoulder. "Oh, Mr. Security Guard? Help!"

She spins around, and I reach out and grab her, pulling her back into me. "Shut up!" I growl, clamping a hand over her mouth.

But she immediately slams her elbow into my stomach, trying to get away, and I stumble backward, pulling her with me. She loses her footing, falls into me, and we both tumble to the floor.

I grunt, my back hitting the ground and my arms still around her struggling body. She lies on top of me, her back against my chest.

She squirms, trying to get away, the friction of her ass pressing into my groin. I tense, heat blanketing me.

Fuck.

She pulls my hand away, gritting under her breath. "Let me go."

"Stop moving, then."

"You don't get to judge me," she goes on, turning her face to me, her breath falling on my cheek. "Or jerk me around or make demands. I'm none of your business."

Her body struggles in my arm, and her ass rubs against me again, making me groan.

But then I hear something.

I take her jaw, forcing her still as I whisper against her ear. "Shhh."

She suddenly stills, and we both stop breathing as the guards enter the library.

I catch a flash of light through the stacks and hear keys jingle. They're talking, but I can't hear what they're saying.

Ryen casts a worried look up to me, and I stare back, holding her gaze.

"What are you going to do?" I whisper low, for only us to hear as I search her eyes. "You gonna turn me in?"

She lies there, breathing in and out but not making a move. My arm around her waist tightens, and I can't stop myself from moving my thumb over the skin of her jaw.

Her eyes—those blue eyes—have a dozen different emotions going on in them when she looks at me. She can say the nastiest things, but if I see fear or sadness in her eyes, I'm done for.

Her rash guard has ridden up in the struggle, and a few inches of skin are exposed. I slowly slide my fingers over her stomach, watching as her eyelids flutter closed.

"Yeah, I told you, man," one of the guards calls out. "They bolted out the door. Let's search the grounds."

I graze my lips across her cheek, her neck arching up more and more until her lips are millimeters away from mine. I can taste her fucking breath.

"Pull up your shirt."

She opens her eyes and shakes her head, looking scared.

I lean in, whispering against her mouth. "Come on. I think you like danger."

My finger is sitting over the pulse in her neck, and I can feel it speed up as I grab her bottom lip between my teeth and drag it out gently.

Her ass slowly grinds into me and I keep my moan silent as I see the flashlights retreat and finally leave the library.

As soon as I see the two sets of boots disappear and the doors close behind them, I slide my hand down the front of her shorts and cover her mouth with mine, letting out the groan I've been holding back.

Her pussy is soft and smooth, and I shudder at the heat as I dip my fingers inside of her, feeling how tight she is.

"You're not my business, huh?" I challenge. "You're so wet around my fingers. That is my business." I slide in a second one.

"Oh, my God," she whimpers. "Masen, no."

"Why not?" I hold her jaw, trailing kisses across her cheek as I pump my fingers inside her. "You think your friends will hate you when they find out you're a slut who loves getting finger-fucked on a floor."

I slide my fingers all the way in and back out a few times in long, full strokes, before bringing them up and rubbing her clit.

She moans, arching her back, and my cock strains against my jeans, begging to grow.

"Yes." She licks my lip ring, rubbing her ass into my dick. "I'm afraid they'll find out I like it."

Yes. I kiss her fast, moving over her mouth hard and strong, because I feel like eating, and she's the only food I want.

"Your secret's safe with me," I tell her. "I've waited too long for this."

"Huh?"

But I dive back inside her, ignoring her and kissing her neck and jaw and pulling her earlobe in between my teeth. I taste any bit of skin I can reach, never slowing my fingers down. Of course she doesn't understand my comment, and I won't explain. She has no idea that she's been in my head and body for years instead of just days.

My fingers keep going, deep and steady, coming out to swirl around her clit every so often and feeling her shiver against me. She spreads her legs wider, and I bring my fingers out, covering her whole damn pussy with my hand, because I just want to savor the feel of her. All of her in my hands.

"Masen." Her pant is wanton and filled with lust.

Masen. I want her to say my name. Not someone else's.

"I can feel how hard I'm making you," she whispers up at me, kissing my jaw. "What the hell's happening?"

I don't know, but I can't stop it any more than you can.

"Pull up your shirt," I demand again.

But she shakes her head.

"Now," I growl, leaning into her cheek. "I want to look at you."

Her whisper tickles my jaw. "But you won't just look. You'll touch."

Hell, yes, I will. "You got a problem with that?" I ask. "Because your pussy is kind of in my hand already."

She kisses me light and soft, biting and teasing. "But if I take off my top," she teases, "you're going to want me to take off my bottoms, too."

I groan, my cock swelling painfully. The thought of her naked has the room starting to tip on its side.

Please.

She covers my hand on her pussy with her hand and presses it into herself, grinding against it. "And then your hands won't be enough, and you'll want to fuck." She moans, her body grinding against mine. "And my prom date won't like that."

I squeeze her waist, baring my teeth. God, she knows how to fuck with me.

"He doesn't have to know," I tell her, "as long as you do what you're told."

I bring my hand slowly up to her neck, and an excited smile flashes across her face as she reaches down and lifts up her rash guard. I briefly let go as she pulls it over her head, revealing a peach-colored bikini top underneath. Her breasts rise well off her chest, the curves of her smooth olive skin looking like hills in front of me, and her hard nipples poke through the fabric. My mouth is so dry. I want to taste her everywhere.

"Good girl," I whisper. "Now take off the other top."

She sucks in a quick breath, and she looks up, holding my eyes as she timidly reaches behind her neck and pulls the string in one long, fluid motion.

The straps fall loose at her sides, and I come up, slowly peeling off one triangle of fabric, exposing her pretty flesh.

Christ. More than a solid handful.

She pulls away the other triangle, and I stare in awe at her. So stunning. And not even her body so much as the way she plays me, saying just the right thing to drive me insane and make me angry, turned on, possessive . . .

She suddenly brings up her arms, covering herself.

"Did I tell you to do that?"

She slowly lowers her arms, exposing her skin for me again.

"How long do you want to look at them?" she asks shyly.

I slip my hand back into her bottoms and slide my two fingers deep inside her again.

"Until you come," I answer, pumping her and watching her tits bounce as her body sways back and forth.

She squeezes her eyes shut, moaning.

"You like it?" I taunt.

"Yeah."

"Tell me."

"I like it!" she cries out.

Her nipple stands up like a point, and I can't take my eyes off her as I fuck her and kiss her lips.

"Come on, Rocks. Buy my silence," I growl as she rolls her ass against me, dry-fucking my dick as I finger her. "Spread those legs and come on my fingers, and I won't tell everyone you're the little shit writing on the walls."

She rests her head on my shoulder and reaches back with one hand, holding the back of my neck as she fucks my hand. Something builds low in my stomach, and the friction of her rubbing against my cock sends need rolling through me as we go harder and harder. Her tits are bouncing rough and fast, and I watch them, imagining my dick inside of her, fucking her.

"Don't tell anyone. Please?" she begs, thrusting against me.

The blood rushes to my cock, and I feel cum drip out of my tip. *Fuck, I need to be inside of her.*

"Just a little more, baby," I urge. "How good are you willing to give it to me to keep me quiet? Huh?"

"Ah," she whimpers. "Yeah, whatever you want."

"Whatever I want?"

She nods frantically, crying out. "Yes!" She moves faster and faster, chasing her orgasm, and then finally throws her head back and stills, moaning and shivering as she comes. "Oh, God!"

I push my fingers deep inside her, rubbing her spot and feeling her body's little convulsions as the orgasm works through her.

She breathes hard and fast, her body tense, and my cock is hard and ready to go, aching in my jeans. I wouldn't want to screw her for the first time in a library, but I didn't expect to get myself this worked up, either.

Her orgasm ebbs away, and she calms, her chest rising and falling slower and slower. I look down at her body and her beautiful face, a wave of shit I don't know what to do with washing over me.

Guilt, because she still doesn't know who I am, and I've just dug myself in deeper.

Longing, because I miss her. I miss talking to her as me.

Lust greater than I've ever known, because when we're like this, it's the only time she softens and changes and gives me an inch, and it's a need that's in my head just as much as my body. It keeps me on my toes.

And something else growing that I don't want to be there. Something that might make it very hard to leave her.

And impossible to forget her.

I watch her face, her body still and her eyes downcast, and a bad feeling creeps through me. She's not looking at me.

After a few moments, she sits up and crawls off me, standing up and grabbing her clothes. I hesitate only a moment before I sit up, as well, watching her warily. She dresses and pushes her hair behind her ear, looking anywhere but at me.

The moment is gone.

But I stare at her anyway, not letting her off the hook.

She picks up her backpack and finally looks at me. "You started it," she snips, her guard back up, "so if you're expecting a blow job, then—"

"Then I know where to get one," I reply, cutting her off. "You're not my first rodeo."

A chill settles under my skin, and now I'm pissed. Her jaw flexes, and she arches an eyebrow.

How quickly she can go from hot to cold.

She puts on her backpack and twists around, heading down the stairs. I stand up and walk over to the railing, watching her leave the library.

Fine. She wants her jock prom date in order to live some lie for everyone else's approval? I can understand that.

But it doesn't mean she's going to own every round we play.

Trey's game is on Saturday, so I have a few days to kill until then. If she wants to play, I can play.

11

Ryen

I haven't spoken to Masen in almost two days. Not since Wednesday night in the library, and now it's Friday afternoon, and he wasn't in our first class today again. How does he just come and go like it's no big deal? Has he even turned in any work? I've never seen him with books, and I'm tempted to go to the Cove and check on him. Is he even still there?

I don't know why I care. He's constantly getting in my face, I know next to nothing about him, and he's dangerous for me. I'm not looking to break the mold when the year's almost over. I've come this far, and I don't want any drama. He *should* stay away.

But I find myself looking for him. In class. In the cafeteria. In the parking lot. Even when I go home, this small hope lights up that he'll ambush me in my room just like that first day last week.

I want to be alone with him again. Those few stolen moments—the car, the lab, the library—they're like my letters from Misha. Something to look forward to.

I didn't leave any graffiti last night after swim lessons, partly because I almost got caught the night before with him and it was a good idea to back off for a few days, but also because I suddenly didn't want to.

Masen was the release now.

And I hated that.

When Misha disappeared and I didn't know if he was getting my words, I started leaving them at school for people to read. It's stupid and childish, but one day a couple of months ago, when things got to be too much, I was afraid I'd start screaming. So that night, before locking up the pool, I made a snap decision and took out my Sharpie. I wrote on a locker—a special message for just that person.

It was a fluke. It wouldn't happen again.

But the next morning when I saw him read it over and over before finally writing it down and taping it to the inside of his locker, before the janitor could clean it off, it became something I wanted to do again. The messages became more frequent, bigger and louder, but never personal. Never with students' names.

Not until last week with Lyla's business aired on the front lawn. That wasn't me, and it was all the more reason for me to stop. Others were following my lead now, and I didn't want it to get any more out of hand. They'd hired security, so it was only a matter of time before they got the cameras working and someone got caught.

Especially when I'd been using washable spray paint and only using markers on things, like metal, that could be cleaned, and not damaged, with nail polish remover. But the lawn had to be cut, since whoever did it had used permanent spray paint and the pressure washer didn't work. How long before it got really destructive?

Well, it won't fall on me. I didn't write anything last night, and I'm not going to sneak in tonight, either. We're all going to the drive-in, and my mom will be holding me to my curfew.

But what would happen if Masen wasn't around anymore? What if I decide it's too risky to keep sneaking into the school at night? Will I act out some other way?

No. Weak people have vices. I don't need Misha, Masen, or anything else to make it through the day.

But as I walk out to the parking lot at the end of school, I can't help but look for him again. His tall form, his dark brown hair, his green eyes that always find me and send an electric current through my body . . .

I was mean the other night. Again.

On the floor, in the library, after the dirty talk and the name-calling and the touching and kissing . . . he'd turned gentle and held me. After he made me come, and I could feel his eyes eating me up, he didn't push me farther than that. He didn't try to take off the rest of my clothes or climb on top of me and rush me into something I might not be ready for. He just lay there, holding me.

And I pushed him off and ran away.

I'm attracted to Masen, excited by him and intrigued by him, but he isn't forever. I don't want to go to the prom with Trey, but I want to go, and Masen hasn't asked me. I don't even know if he's going to be here in a week.

I'm not risking Trey and my friends for someone who's never given the impression he actually wants me.

No matter how much I'm starting to like him.

Lyla and Ten are already at my Jeep, waiting, since we were going to go get food after school today. She stands on the rear driver's-side tire, holding on to the roll bar and yelling to someone farther away in the parking lot, while Ten sits in the back.

I toss my bag in beside him.

"Where have you been?" I hear a voice ask.

I turn around and see Trey standing in front of me. I would usually consider his navy blue T-shirt and white baseball cap attractive on him, but now I just see bare arms, devoid of tattoos, and boring blue eyes with boring pierceless lips.

I want my delinquent.

Lyla hops down from the tire and stands next to me, too nosy for her own good.

"I've called, I've texted, and I don't like being ignored," he warns.

I look around me, lifting up my arms to see if I have anything on my clothes. "Oh, I'm sorry. I must have lost my dog tags," I tell him. "You know the ones that say I'm your property and I report to you."

I can hear Ten's quiet laugh off to the side. Trey's eyes narrow to slits.

"You know," he starts, "a little reciprocation from you wouldn't be out of line. Especially when the whole school sees you and Laurent fucking around with each other."

I stare at him, keeping my expression emotionless. Yeah, I'm sure the school has drawn several conclusions about Masen and me, given our arguments and the fact that they think I vandalized his truck. But Trey and I aren't dating, and I don't for one second think he's not out there having a little fun of his own. I have no obligation to him, except to look nice for prom pictures.

A prom I agreed to go to when Masen wasn't a factor.

"You can't possibly be insecure," I say, trying to work him. "You're Trey Burrowes, and Masen Laurent will be walking your dogs someday."

He stares at me for a moment and then he lets out a snort, visibly relaxing. Lyla laughs to herself, and I let out a breath.

"Did you get your dress?" he asks.

But Lyla nudges me, answering him, "We're going shopping this weekend."

"Good." He comes in and takes my hips, pressing himself to me.

I don't want him to kiss me, so I quickly turn my head, but his lips brush my forehead anyway.

I look up and see Masen.

He has his back to me, talking to J.D., but his head is turned, watching me over his shoulder. His eyes flash to Trey and then to me again, narrowing. My breathing hitches. Did he just get here? Or has he been around and I just missed him?

"I'll see you at the drive-in tonight." Trey's thumb grazes my stomach, and then he gives me one last look before he leaves.

I feel crowded. Trey is demanding, Lyla's in my business, and Masen is . . . everywhere. I feel his presence in the parking lot now, off to the right, like the sun burning on that side of my body.

"What's the matter with you?" Lyla scolds. "If you don't start being nicer, he'll find someone who will."

I shoot my eyes over to her, feeling them burn. "Nice, like you?" I ask. "Doesn't look like being nice did you any good." And I gesture over to J.D., who's laughing with Masen.

Her boyfriend has barely spoken to her in days, probably because he knows what was written on the lawn last Friday was true—we all do—no matter how much Lyla denies it.

But then I do a double take, it finally registering that J.D. is talking to Masen. When did they start being buddies?

"I can handle my boyfriend," she says.

"And I can handle Trey. Thanks."

I turn around and open the door, climbing into the Jeep. Lyla rounds the front of the car and slides into the passenger side, our little tiff still thick in the air. I wish she'd just go home. Every day is heavier and heavier with things I want to say to her, because I know she hates me. I want to call her on it, but I don't know why. I can barely stand her, either, and there's just as much bullshit to call me out on. Masen's been doing it since he got here. Lyla and I are both hypocrites.

"Y'all, look at Katelyn," Ten says, leaning up and gesturing out the front windshield.

I put my key into the ignition and stop, looking up. Katelyn is talking to Masen again.

J.D. is gone, and she's standing close to him, smiling and typing something into a phone. She then hands it to him, and he slips it in his pocket, looking down at her with all of his attention.

What?

My heart pounds in my chest, and I curl my fingers around the steering wheel, wanting to take her by the hair and pull her ass away from him. Really? Why is he looking at her like that? Why did he let her have his phone?

"Oh, God," Lyla groans. "What is she doing?"

"She really is as dumb as a box of rocks." Ten chuckles. "Five years from now, she'll have four different baby daddies. Just watch."

My pulse rings in my ears as they laugh, but I blink, dropping my eyes.

Rocks.

Dumb. As. A. Box. Of. Rocks.

I raise my eyes, glaring at Masen Laurent. *Motherfucker!* That's what he's been calling me?

I turn my head away so they can't see me seething. *Asshole.*

Katelyn strolls away from him, looking all pleased with herself as she heads toward us.

"Did you just give him your phone number?" Lyla asks her, kneeling on the seat, one hand on a roll bar, another on the windshield.

Katelyn bites her bottom lip, trying to look coy as she holds my door and leans back playfully. "Well, I thought he might want it after last night."

"Last night?" Ten presses.

"Yeah, I ran into him in the parking lot after cheer yesterday," she admits, blushing as she drops her voice. "We were up late."

She's insinuating a lot more in those words, like she has a secret. My stomach fills with knots.

"What's he like?" Lyla asks in a hushed voice, suddenly interested.

"Like an animal." Katelyn grins. "I'm surprised I don't have any bite marks."

"Mmmm." I hear Lyla's soft coo.

Jesus Christ.

Katelyn walks away, smiling, and I do my best to act like I'm not sitting here shattering right now. I want to believe she's lying. He wouldn't go for her. He's not after a quick thrill, is he? He wanted me in the library. *Me.* He wouldn't forget that. Not so soon.

But . . . he did say he knows where to go to get what he wants.

Like an animal. The biting, the roughness, the way his eyes and hands and mouth take what they want . . . She described him perfectly.

I swallow the lump in my throat. I feel nauseous.

"Well, I guess there's something to be said for the bad ones," Lyla muses, watching Masen climb into his truck. "And that piercing? I'll bet it feels good. Everywhere."

Ten squeezes my shoulder from behind, and I snap back into focus, uncurling my fingers from the wheel. My knuckles are as white as snow.

"Let's go eat and raid my mom's liquor before the drive-in," he tells me. "Lyla's driving tonight, so I'm getting wasted."

Yeah, I don't think I can eat.

But watching Masen take off out of the parking lot, probably going to do who-knows-who, I might just take a drink.

Friday nights at the drive-in are just an excuse for every teenager with a car in Falcon's Well to hang out in one place. Especially since it just opened back up a few weeks ago in time for spring. The weather's nice, there's a concession stand with food, car stereos blast music, and I doubt even a quarter of the people here are watching the movie tonight.

One of those stupid nouveau slasher flicks with lots of gritty pain and an ambiguous ending, I'm sure.

After dinner, I'd gone home and changed into some jean shorts and a tank top before Lyla and Ten swung by to pick me up.

Trey arrived with J.D. just as we got here, all of us parking up in the front row. They started making the rounds, going off to talk to different people and hang out, while I headed for the concession stand. My mom doesn't let us drink our calories, so the movies is one of the only chances I get to have a Coke.

I walk inside the concession area and move down the line, grabbing a cup and filling it with ice.

"You dropped this the other night," a smooth voice says.

I jerk my head up to see Masen, standing right at my side. Butterflies take off in my stomach.

I look down to see him holding out my inhaler and then quickly glance around, making sure no one is watching. I snatch it out of his hand and slip it into my pocket. *Shit.* I must've left it on the library floor after we . . .

I turn back to the soda machine, not saying anything as I fill my drink up and secure the lid.

"How've you been?" he asks.

But I refuse to engage. I take my drink and move down the line, grabbing a straw and flexing my jaw in anger. Images of Katelyn, half naked with her legs wrapped around him as he lies on top of her on the back seat of his car, flood my mind. I tap the straw on the counter, trying to unsheathe it from its wrapper, but it snaps and breaks instead.

I toss it in the trash can and grab another. How could he look down at her and want her over me? How could he kiss her? Does it even matter who it is? I thought he was different.

"You heard, didn't you?" he says, following me as I pick out candy. "I'm glad. I wanted you to hear."

I bend down and pick up a bag of Sour Patch Kids. "No one cares what you do, loser."

He takes a step closer. "You have a boyfriend," he points out, shrugging. "Katelyn's got a hell of a body, she's good in bed . . ."

My fingers curl around my paper cup, the lid pops off, and Coke overflows, spilling all over my hand.

Dammit.

He snorts, and I scurry, grabbing napkins and cleaning myself up.

Good in bed? The thought of him enjoying her—touching her—makes me want to shove a rubber dick up his nose.

Asshole.

And I do not have a boyfriend. I have a prom date.

He leans in, his voice full of self-satisfaction. "You're jealous."

I fix the lid back on the drink, throw the soiled napkins away, and turn to him, my eyes burning. "Rocks?" I bark, changing the subject completely to avoid the one we're on. "Dumb as a box of rocks? Are you kidding me?"

He breaks into a laugh. "It took you long enough."

"Don't you ever call me that again!" And then I dart my eyes to the side, seeing a couple of girls from school cast us curious glances. I lower my voice. "And I'm not jealous. I just don't appreciate you filling me in on all your sleazy bullshit."

He takes a step closer, putting us chest to chest with both hands on the counter at my sides, caging me in. "And I don't like him touching you." He scowls down at me.

He must be referring to the parking lot today when he saw Trey kiss my forehead.

I reach over and grab a popcorn box, tipping it over and shaking it to show that it's empty. "Here you go." I shove it at his chest. "All the fucks I give."

And I push through his arm, taking my drink with me.

"Hey. Everything okay?" someone asks.

I look up, seeing Ten as I approach the register. I pause, seeing his gaze flash between Masen and me as he holds his silver water bottle, which I know is filled with rum and Coke.

Ignoring his question, I glance back at Masen. He tosses the popcorn box to the counter and walks toward me, holding my eyes as he glares down. I feel the heat coming off his body, but I stand tall, daring him to even try to pick another fight. He's a jerk whose only kick in life is to make mine miserable.

He doesn't say anything, though, and keeps walking out the doors.

After he's gone, Ten exhales a long sigh and turns back to me. "In case you're still trying to figure it out," he says, "he wants you bad."

I turn away, unable to shake the desire to go pick another fight. He wants me bad? Well, he certainly doesn't look like he's suffering with need. Not at all.

I pay for my drink and candy and head out of the stand with Ten. He heads for a group of guys at a convertible, while I walk through the cars toward Lyla's BMW up front and try not to look for Masen. The sky is black now, but the screen is shedding lots of light, and I hear the crickets buzzing in the grass out in the distance. I spot Trey standing by his car, flirting with some girl.

Awesome.

I keep walking, but I stop when I pass a big black truck. *Masen's.*

I glance around, finding him over by his new friends, including J.D., talking and laughing. People loiter about, caught up in their conversations, and no one is looking at me. I stare at the truck, suddenly feeling inspired.

Holding back my smile, I set my drink and snack on the ground, next to the tire, and open the back door on the driver's side, quickly climbing in. I shut the door and immediately notice how dark it is inside. I hadn't noticed that the afternoon at the car wash. The windows must be heavily tinted.

The leather interior shines black, just like the paint on the outside, and it smells heady and rich, intoxicating, like him. I lick my lips, leaning up and opening his console between the front seats, looking for something to write with.

I sift through change, a few receipts, and some tools. I see a pen and pull it out, clicking the top to load it and scribble on my hand.

Black.

Everything in here is fucking black. Anything I write won't show up. I dig back inside the console and my fingers curl around something long with a grip on it. I pull it out, seeing that it's some kind of pocket knife.

My heart starts beating faster. He's a prick, but I'm not quite sure I want to get that destructive. Carrie Underwood's "Before He Cheats" starts playing in my head.

I pinch the groove on the dull side and unsheathe the blade, jumping when it snaps out. The curve is scary and intense, and I hold it up, studying it and wondering if I really want to leave him what's sure to be a very expensive message.

And then I think about Katelyn straddling him on this very seat, riding him, and I want to do a lot more than just cut up his truck.

But the door suddenly opens, and I jump, seeing Masen step up and come right for me, slamming his door shut.

I gasp, tossing the knife up to the front, and twist around, yanking the handle of the other door.

It opens, but he grabs it and pulls it closed again, pushing down the lock.

The truck is dark again.

His arms come around me, and I gasp as he hauls me back against him, holding me as I struggle.

"Get off me!" I yell, trying to get free.

"Were you jealous?" he growls in my ear, and I can hear the smile in his voice. "Were you mad you could be so easily replaced? Is that why you're in here, trying to do some shit to my car?"

I jerk, trying to twist out of his hold.

"Get over it," he says. "A pussy is a pussy, after all, and if I don't get it from you, I can get someone else with a lot less hassle."

Dickhead. Of course I'm no one to him. I'm not even surprised.

I struggle loose, but he pulls me tight again, taunting, "If it doesn't bother you, then you shouldn't want to run away."

I breathe hard, a cool sweat breaking out on my neck. I stop struggling and calm my breathing, forcing my tone even. "Let me go now."

His arms relax around me, and I slide away from him, reaching for the handle.

But he reaches out and grips the door, holding it closed. "I didn't think about you at all when I was in bed with her last night," he tells me. "She was hot, she turned me on, she liked my hands on her, and I liked how she felt . . ." His breath falls across my hair, his words cruel and unforgiving. "She wasn't average or boring or stuck-up. *She* excited me."

My bottom lip shakes and tears fill my eyes. But I tense every muscle in my body, trying not to let him see. *Stuck-up. Average. Boring.*

"Tell me you're jealous," he demands.

"If it doesn't bother me, why would I be jealous?"

He leans closer, and I can feel his body at my back and his lips next to my ear. "Tell me you're trying not to think about how much I loved fucking her. Tell me something true, and I'll let you leave."

Something true? Tell him what? What does he want to hear? That this hurts? That I loved kissing him the last time we were in here and every time after that? That I don't want anyone touching him? Screw him. I'm not saying any of that shit.

"You can't, can you?" His voice is quiet and almost sad. "You can't talk to me."

And then I watch through blurry eyes as he leans up and exhales on the window in front of me, fogging it up to draw a word with his finger.

FEAR

I shake my head.

Alone, Empty, Fraud, Shame, Fear . . . What is he doing? What does that mean? A tear spills over, and I growl out a breath, wiping the word off the window.

"You're a prick. Just stay away from me."

I go to open the door, but he grabs my hand.

"I didn't sleep with her."

I freeze, turning my head just an inch. What?

"I lied," he tells me. "I asked her out for food yesterday to make you jealous, and today, when she insinuated shit that didn't happen, I let her. But I didn't touch her."

The heat of his breath hits my neck, and I can tell his head is bent to my hair.

"I don't want to hurt you," he whispers, his voice thick with emotion. "I don't want anyone else. I only think about you." He pauses, his voice shaky. "I think about you all the time, Ryen."

Me.

"I'm sorry," he continues. "I had to push you. I wanted to know."

I turn my head, glaring at him through my tears. "You didn't touch her?"

He shakes his head.

I swing my hand to hit him, but he grabs it and pulls me into his lap, taking my face in his hands. "I had every right to," he bites out, "especially since you're still letting Fuckface drool all over you while making me hard as a rock for a damn week."

I bite my bottom lip, trying not to cry. I never cry in front of them.

"*You* turn me on." He cups my face, brushing my hair away from my eyes and a tear off my cheek. "God, you turn me on. You're driving me crazy. I want you to need my hands on you. Do you?"

I hold his eyes, seeing the pleading in his. Seeing, for the first time, the need. He's desperate to hear me say it.

And I know right then and there I want to be the only girl he ever looks at like that.

"You're not boring," he says softly. "You're not average, and you're not stuck-up. You piss me off, but *you* excite me."

His face is shrouded in shadow, but I can feel him everywhere. He puts his forehead to mine, his whisper thick and heavy, spinning like a cyclone inside me. "They don't get you and me. I know that's what you're afraid of. You're perfect. I'm never in line. You're beautiful, and I'm bad, right?"

His breath hits my lips, and I reach up and touch his hand on my face, sliding my cold fingers between his warm ones.

"They'll never matter to us, Ryen. No one knows how this feels."

Tears ache behind my eyes, and I breathe hard, giving in to it. I slide my thigh over his lap and straddle him. I fist his T-shirt, our lips inches from each other. "If you touched her," I cry softly, "it's not going to be pretty."

He nods. "I know. I'll keep the knife in here for you."

I laugh and kiss him, his hands falling to my hips as I press my body closer. I hold the back of his neck as I deepen the kiss, the heat of his mouth sinking to the end of every limb in my body.

But I pull away, turning my head toward the front windshield. Shit. People walk about, and I can see a couple guys in the car ahead of us, as well as a couple next to us.

Masen buries his lips in my neck, kissing and biting. "The windows are blacked out," he mumbles against my skin. "So tinted it's illegal."

I turn back to him and dive into his mouth again, hearing their music and laughter only feet away, all around us, and not giving a shit. I catch a glimpse of someone passing by the truck, and I let out a moan.

He moves from my mouth to my neck again, getting greedy, and I close my eyes, holding on to him.

Coming up, he cups my face again, wiping away the tears with his thumbs. "Tell me something true."

I lick my lips, hungry and wanting his mouth back, but his eyes are holding mine. He's not letting me off the hook.

I lean in and put my forehead to his again. "I don't like cheese on my sandwiches," I admit, chewing on my lip. "*Bridge to Tera-bithia* is my favorite book." My fifth-grade teacher read it to us, and it always stuck with me. "I make jalapeño bagels sometimes, be-cause my mom told me once that they're my dad's favorite." I glance up at him to see his eyes still open and on me. "He left when I was four, and I haven't seen him since. I don't make them when she's around, though."

I press my teeth down on my lip harder, but his thumb nudges my lip back out, probably seeing how nervous I am.

"I don't get along with my sister," I admit, "and I don't feel close to my mom anymore. I know a lot of it is my fault. My armor got too thick, and I stopped letting people in." I pause and add, "Most people."

New tears spring up, and a small sob escapes. He kisses me and pulls back just enough to rub my mouth with his. "I can't get enough of you."

I smile a little.

"And sometimes," I keep going, snatching his lips in another kiss. "Sometimes I want to vomit on Lyla when I see her."

He suddenly snorts, breaking into laughter. A wide smile spreads across his face as his whole body shakes. I kiss him again, our lips melting together.

"And last Friday night," I whisper, nibbling on his bottom lip as I grind on him, "after the car wash . . ."

"Yeah?" He lowers his hands to my hips, grunting as I rub harder.

"I thought about you," I whisper in his ear. "I thought about you when I was in bed that night."

I feel his fingers dig into my hips, and he growls low as he kisses me again and again, breathing hard.

His lips move down my neck, and I barely notice the strap of my shirt being slipped down my arm as the heat of his mouth covers my shoulder.

He grabs the back of my neck, holding me in place as he runs his nose and mouth back up my neck, inhaling me. "Do you feel me?" he whispers, pressing my hip down hard into him. I whimper as I rub against his thickness between my legs.

"Yeah." But then I notice something is loose and air is caressing my skin where it didn't before. My bra. He's unhooked my bra at the back.

The straps fall down my arms, and the side where my shirt fell off exposes my now bare breast. I quickly bring up my arms, covering myself. "Masen, no."

But he comes in, kissing me, and grabs my ass, pressing me to him. "I can't stop."

"But people will see."

He looks up into my eyes, nibbling my lips. "No one sees you, baby. Just me. And I want to kiss you."

"You are kissing me."

He gnaws my lip, his whisper thick and hot. "I want to kiss you in other places."

Oh, Jesus.

My chest caves and heat swirls in my belly, making my clit throb and my body crave him so badly. I've never been this turned on.

He stares at me as he gently pulls my arms away, and he slides the other strap of my shirt off my shoulder, my loose tank top and bra falling to my waist.

"Masen," I say nervously, trying to bring up my arms again.

I twist my head and look around me, seeing two guys standing right next to the front of the truck. But Masen takes my hands, guiding them away and shaking his head with a slight grin on his face.

Fear races through me, making my heart pound, but I'm excited, too.

"God, look at you," he breathes out, his eyes feasting as they fall down my chest and stomach. "You have a hell of a body."

Chills spread down my arms, and I feel my nipples tighten and harden under his gaze.

"Take me somewhere," I say, leaning into him, "and I'll let you kiss me anywhere you want."

"Sounds enticing," he says. "Maybe next time."

Grabbing my waist, he brings me in close, forcing me up higher on my knees so that my breast is level with his mouth.

"Masen," I gasp as he grabs my left nipple between his teeth, sending shocks through my system and right down between my thighs. "Oh, my God, we can't."

But he sucks the whole damn thing into his mouth, and I grip his shoulders, my eyes fluttering closed, not giving a damn that half our class is right outside.

"Yes," I whimper, losing my breath and wrapping one arm around his neck, holding him closer.

His tongue, hot and wet, comes out and swirls around the pebbled flesh of my nipple, teasing me, and his fingers dig into my skin as he goes back for more, nibbling the whole breast.

I hear laughter outside, and I try to turn my head, but Masen leans into me, forcing me to arch back as he switches to the other breast, kissing and dragging the nipple out by his teeth.

I moan, closing my eyes and letting my head fall back. "Masen, we're going to get caught."

But my plea is pathetic, and he knows it. He sucks hard, stretching my skin, and I want to grind on his dick so badly, but it's difficult from this position.

His mouth and teeth explore, tugging and sucking until I'm sure I'm red, and I lean back up, letting his mouth trail to my neck and back to my mouth.

I roll my hips, rubbing on him as he kisses and nibbles down my jaw. I want to feel every inch of him through his jeans. I'm so wet.

He suddenly pulls away from me, and I look to see him pulling his shirt over his head. I briefly see the rest of the tattoos trailing up his arm and over his shoulder, as well as the few across his chest and stomach.

He pulls me to him again, pressing his chest against mine. "I want to feel your skin on mine."

He palms my breast with one hand while slipping the other down the back of my shorts and squeezing my ass.

I gaze into his green eyes, both of us breathing hard, but I see him pause, as if he's suddenly not sure about something.

And all of a sudden, I'm not worried about getting caught. I'm worried about him stopping.

Don't stop.

My eyes burn with tears, and I'm so tired. So tired of holding back everything I feel and want to say. So tired of being someone I'm not and making mistakes that I didn't have any fun making.

I want to feel this. I want to get lost with him for as long as I can.

"Masen?" I put my hand to his face and lean my head into his, speaking low. "Can I tell you something true?"

He nods.

I slip my hand between us and press my hand into his cock. "I want to get fucked."

His eyes widen, and I bite his bottom lip.

Yeah, he wasn't expecting that.

He expels a breath, sounding shocked, but he doesn't need to be asked twice. Wrapping an arm around my waist, he flips me onto my back on the seat, and I let out a small gasp, not sure if I'm excited or nervous. He stands up as much as he can, and hovers over me, gazing down at my body. I bite my lip, trying not to smile as much as I want to.

Reaching up, I hold his eyes as I unfasten his belt, but when I go to unbutton his jeans, he stops me.

"I said I needed to kiss you everywhere," he reminds me, eyeing my shorts. "Take 'em off."

I cast a nervous glance out the window above me, seeing someone walk by. The slickness between my legs gets wetter, and I can't help the rush of heat under my skin.

God, this is so bad.

Swallowing the lump in my throat, I unbutton my shorts and slide them over my ass and down my legs. Masen gazes down at my lacy red thong and slowly slides a finger up my thigh, under the hem of the panties, and pulls them aside, baring my pussy.

I groan at the feel of his eyes on me. *Please touch me.*

"Do you keep it bare like that all the time?" he asks, still staring at me.

"Do you want me to?"

He smiles and meets my eyes.

I run my hand up his chest and wrap it around the back of his neck. It's weird. Sometimes I feel like I know him. Like, really know him. We engage so easily, and even when we're angry, it still feels like it's familiar. And then it hits me that I really don't know anything about him.

"Where do you come from, Masen?" I ask. "Where are your parents? What are you hiding from?"

He stares at me, his expression turning wary. Then he reaches out and runs his fingers gently down my face, forcing my lids closed. "Close your eyes. There's nothing to see out here."

What?

But then I feel his tongue gliding up my slit, and I gasp, my entire body tensing. "Oh, God."

He licks me up and down slowly, dragging his tongue up my

pussy and over my clit, and then latches onto my nub, sucking it hard into his mouth.

I arch my neck up, breathing hard as I watch him. He groans, swirling his tongue around me and then tugging my clit out between his lips and going back for more—licking, sucking, and nibbling.

The pulse between my legs throbs, and I feel warmth at my entrance as I get wetter and more ready for him.

He pushes up one of my knees, opening me up, and starts going at me harder and faster, more greedily. His tongue licks, his teeth grab and tease, and then he covers me with his mouth, sucking and working my clit until I cry out.

"Please," I moan. "Ah . . ."

He reaches up and clamps a hand over my mouth, still eating me, and I shoot my eyes up, seeing Trey right above me.

I stop breathing for a second, my eyes widening. He stands right outside the rear passenger-side door, calling to someone.

Oh, shit.

"Damn, Trey," Masen says, smirking up at me and flicking out his tongue to lick me. "Your girl's pussy is so tight."

I pull away from his hand on my mouth. "Shut up!" I whisper.

He licks and sucks me again. "Thanks for letting me borrow her, man."

And then he dives in, finally sliding his tongue inside me and penetrating.

I suck in a breath, whimpering, and he covers my mouth again as he moves his tongue inside and works my clit with his other hand.

I roll my hips, trying to meet him—trying to get deeper—as my breasts sway back and forth with the small movements. I grab the back of his neck, holding him to me, feeling the tingling where his tongue touches build and build until every muscle in my body contracts so tightly it burns.

"Yes!" I cry out behind his hand.

My orgasm explodes, spreading up through my stomach and down my thighs, and I throw my head back, staring in horror at Trey and some guy standing right there above me. I slam both of my hands over Masen's on my mouth, moaning into them and hoping no one can hear me through the doors.

My chest rises and falls, the incredible feeling wracking through my body, up to my head and down to my feet.

Masen lowers his hand, palming my breast before letting go. He rises up and leans over me, putting a hand on the door behind me to hold himself up as he unbuttons his jeans. My heart picks up pace again.

His hard eyes stare down at me, filled with lust. "Take off the thong, or I'm ripping it off."

I glance up nervously, afraid of getting caught. What if the truck rocks?

He reaches into the pocket on the back of the front seat and pulls out a condom, tearing it open with his teeth. He has condoms back here?

I narrow my eyes, glaring up at him.

He meets my stare and just laughs. "Don't worry. You're the only girl I've had back here."

Then why do you keep condoms in the back seat of your truck? Just in case?

He reaches into his jeans and pulls out his cock, hard and ready, and I lose my breath, watching as he rolls the condom on.

I put my hands on his chest, not sure if it's because I want to touch him or because I'm scared. I've only done this once, and it was two years ago. It was a mistake.

But it feels like the first time again, and I'm nervous.

He stops, looking at me. "Take it off," he whispers. There's pleading in his eyes.

I lick my lips, breathing hard and my pulse racing.

I reach down slowly, a nervous shake to my body as I slide my panties off and let them drop to the floor. I want him. There's no harm in letting him feel me for just a little bit, right? I'll make him stop and take me somewhere else soon.

"Just for a minute, okay?" I plead, reaching back up and caressing his chest. "And then we have to stop."

A smile curls a corner of his mouth as he lifts my knee, his thick cock pressing between my legs.

"Just for a minute," he promises. "And then I'll stop."

Thrusting his hips slow and steady, he reaches down and works his cock inside me. I groan, feeling myself stretch as he sinks into me, going deeper and deeper and burying himself to the hilt.

"Oh, fuck," he gasps, his face twisted in pain as he stills. "Ryen . . ."

He breathes hard, lowering his body, my nipples brushing his chest. I shudder, savoring the feeling of his tip rubbing my spot, and without thinking, I bend my knees up more and spread my legs wider.

Just for a minute.

He kisses me, and I barely have time to adjust to him before he pulls out and thrusts back in, stretching me so good.

"Oh, God." The sounds of the movie play in the distance, and I hear the muffled voices of people not far off.

But all I see is him. His lips hovering over mine, his breath warming my skin, his fucking that's getting harder and faster as he thrusts between my thighs.

I look up, seeing his hand still gripping the door, the muscles in his arms bulging and tight.

"Look at me," he whispers.

I drop my eyes back down as I lick his piercing and hear him growl under his breath.

The truck creaks with our movement, and I whimper, digging my fingers into his hips as he moves in and out of me. "The truck will rock," I say, worried. "We have to stop."

But he just groans, fucking me harder. My breasts bounce back and forth, and I gasp at the pleasure of him filling me. I pull him deeper with every thrust, rolling my hips to fuck him back.

"Masen," I beg, licking and biting his neck and feeling myself coming again. "It feels so good."

He slides a hand under my ass and nestles in deeper, grunting as he fucks me rougher. I hear a noise underneath us, from the truck, and I cast a worried glance around. "Go slow!" I plead. "The truck . . ."

But he growls and comes down, kissing and biting my lips. I slide my hands down, gripping his ass and keeping him close, and he thrusts his dick inside me again and again.

"Yes, yes," I moan over and over, feeling another orgasm crest as I taunt him with quick little kisses.

"Masen, is the minute over yet?"

"Almost, baby." I hear the humor in his voice.

His cock nudges me deep inside, and I cry out, breaking loose and coming as my pussy clenches around him, holding him too tight.

"Oh, fuck," he groans, putting a hand over my mouth and thrusting inside of me faster.

He pushes in one more time and stops, his body shuddering under my hands, heavy breaths and groans fanning my ear.

I run a hand up his back, feeling his sweat as I close my eyes. My head is in a fog, and the inside of the truck is spinning.

The orgasm seeps down every limb, and I feel tired and happy and sad. I don't want it to be over.

But holy shit. We shouldn't have done that here.

He relaxes on top of me, his hand still holding the door and his head bent to my shoulder. I stay there, still and quiet.

I don't even want to look outside to see if anyone noticed. Like I really thought we could stop once we started?

He raises his head finally and looks down at me. I smile small, wishing we were parked in the forest somewhere. Somewhere we could stay all night and do that some more.

His eyebrows pinch together, and he looks like he's searching for words. "Ryen, I . . ."

"What?"

But he remains silent.

I touch his face, but he just shakes his head and looks away. "Nothing. It's fine."

Fine? A chill brushes across my skin.

What's fine?

12

Ryen

I sit in the front seat, pulling my hair over my shoulder and smoothing it down. After we finished, he climbed in the front and drove us out of the drive-in, while I stayed hidden in the back, getting dressed.

I chew on the corner of my mouth, worry setting in. The truck was definitely moving.

Anyone could've seen me climbing in before that, and everyone knows it's his truck. Not to mention, he's being quiet now, driving and not even looking at me.

Typical guy. Say all the things you need to get into her pants, but all those strong feelings and hot whispers fade when you get what you want, don't they?

Whatever.

I fasten my seat belt. The drive-in is behind us and the road ahead dark and empty. "I left my purse in Lyla's car," I say more to myself. "I'll have to make up something for why I left and how I got home."

"Well, good thing lying's not hard for you."

I shoot him a nasty look. But then I see him give me a joking smile, and I immediately relax a little.

Maybe I don't need to lie at all. Just tell her I let Masen Laurent take me home. What could happen?

I catch sight of the screen on the radio, seeing the name of the song playing from the iPod, and break out in a smile, turning it up.

Masen glances over at me, probably wondering why I look happy. "What?"

I gesture to the radio, where Eminem's "Without Me" is playing. "I have a friend. He hates my taste in music," I tell him. "I sent him this song once. It led to a lifelong argument that still hasn't been settled."

"He?"

I lean back in my seat. "In elementary school, our teachers set us up as pen pals," I explain. "When the school year ended, though, we just kept writing, and we haven't stopped. He lives in Thunder Bay, but we've never met."

Masen stares at the road ahead, his chest rising and falling steadily. He's not jealous, is he? Misha and I aren't like that.

"Do you tell him everything?" he asks, still not looking at me.

I narrow my eyes on him. Maybe he suspects Misha is important to me.

Or maybe he wonders if my pen pal is more important than him.

The truth is, Misha is irreplaceable. But even with him, I don't say everything.

I turn my head to look at the window. "I tell him more than I tell anyone else."

"Do you lie to him?"

"Yes," I reply honestly. "He gets the version of me I want to be."

For some reason, I feel no shame in admitting that to Masen. With my mom, my sister, my teachers, and my friends, I feel like I'm judged. Like there's something I need to live up to.

Even with Misha, I feel guilt for never putting my money where my mouth is and hoping he never finds out how awful I can be sometimes. I want him to think the best of me.

But with Masen, I almost feel like nothing I could do could make him want me less. Like my imperfections entertain him, my issues complement his issues, and two negatives make a positive, and all that.

"Are you going to write to him and tell him about tonight?"

I turn to him, a slight smile on my face. "Probably. Would you care?"

He shakes his head, watching the road.

"You wouldn't be jealous?"

"You'll need your friends," he replies.

I arch a brow. What the hell does that mean?

He pulls into my driveway and follows the circle around to the front door and stops. I unfasten my seat belt and glance at his right hand sitting on his lap. Not even a half hour ago that hand was on my ass.

No one knows how this feels.

I close my eyes, feeling lonely now. Why is he being so distant? I'm not dumb enough to think we're a couple now—I never have unrealistic expectations when it comes to people—but this is awkward. His vibe sucks, like tonight was a mistake or something, and it hurts a little.

Not that I'd ever admit that to him.

"Well . . ." I sigh, opening the door. "I guess I'll see you."

I climb out and slam the door behind me, walking toward my house. I hear another door slam shut, and I turn around to see Masen jogging toward me.

I stop.

He touches my face, coming in close and looking down at me.

"What's his name?"

"Who?"

He hovers close, his lips an inch from mine. "Your pen pal."

His breath lingers on my lips, and I open my mouth just a little in anticipation for him. God, he smells good.

"Misha," I whisper.

He kisses me, his lips sinking into mine as I close my eyes.

"What was that?" he teases, nibbling my lips. "I couldn't hear you."

"Misha," I gasp before diving into him and brushing his tongue with mine. I press my body into his, feeling the bulge in his jeans rubbing me.

He finally pulls away, breathless and turned on again, just like at the drive-in.

"Thank you." He kisses me one last time on the lips and turns around, heading back to his truck.

What the hell?

I watch, confused again, as he starts the engine and drives away, his taillights glowing in the darkness as he pulls out onto the street.

I know him very little, but after every encounter, I feel like I know him less.

I didn't see Masen all weekend. Saturday came and went. My friends and I spent all day on the football field, orientating the incoming freshman cheerleaders for the next school year, and Sunday I was locked in my room, playing music, doing homework, and writing Misha.

Three letters.

Two of them were just full of boring, stupid crap, and the third—the one about Masen—I crumpled up and threw away. I'm not sure why. I don't even know why I wrote it in the first place.

Walking down the hallway at school Monday morning, I stop at my locker and start to key in the combination, but I see black writing on the front, and I stop.

Anything to not need you,
Anything to not fall for you,
Anything to look at a girl who's not you,
But baby, there's nothing but you.

I smile. *Masen.*

At least I hope he's the culprit. My cheeks warm, hating how happy that just made me. Why does it feel so good to know he was thinking about me this weekend when he snuck in to write it?

I try to force away the grin, but it pulls at me still as I open my locker and stuff in my bag, taking out what I need for the morning.

I walk to Art and enter the room, immediately shooting my eyes over to his seat, relieved to see him sitting there. I don't know why, but I'm afraid any moment could be the last I see him.

He talks to Manny seated next to him, and as usual, he either doesn't notice me or acts like he doesn't.

I walk up to my table and turn to set my materials down, but someone bumps into me, and I lurch forward.

"Sorry," a deep voice says, and something is shoved into my hand.

I straighten and turn my head, seeing Masen brush past me and head to the front of the room, smirking back at me as he tosses his gum into the trash can.

I curl my fingers around the small piece of paper and sit down, acting like nothing happened. He returns and takes his seat again, resuming his conversation with Manny.

I hold the paper in my lap and look down, unfolding it and reading it.

I can't wait to kiss you.

Tingles spread underneath my skin, and I stuff the paper into my pocket, trying to appear like romantic crap like that doesn't do it for me. Nope. Not at all.

And I totally didn't replay the drive-in in my head a thousand times this weekend, remembering how awesome his kisses really are.

But then I look up and see Trey walking into the classroom.

My stomach sinks. I was looking forward to having Masen close, but Trey's the rain on the parade again. I should just cut him loose.

"I think you really like Art," I say as he pulls out the chair next to me. "People will start talking."

"They'll forgive me when they find out I only sit here to look down your shirt." He rests a hand on my chair behind me and lets his eyes fall to my loose T-shirt. He can't see down the top, but a sliver of my belly is showing at the bottom, right above my tight jeans. "You're a nice view."

"Yeah, okay—"

But I stop, hearing a scratching sound. I turn my head, seeing Masen rotate a protractor in one hand, the sharp needle digging into the wooden table and slowly slicing a circle as he grinds it. I dart my eyes up to his face, seeing that he's focused ahead, but when I look back down, I notice the black finish of the table is now marred, revealing the tan wood underneath.

I feel a smile pull at my lips. He's not happy.

Good. If he wants me to find a new prom date, then he can man up and ask me.

"Well then," I continue, pushing the envelope and looking to Trey but talking loud enough for Masen to hear. "You should see my prom dress. You're going to love it."

"Can't wait." He grins back.

I open my sketchbook and continue working on my project while Ms. Till starts drifting around the room to check on students and how they're coming along.

"Hey, Manny," I hear Trey call in a whisper. "You won't have your guard dog in PE today."

I hood my eyes, agitated. Manny remains still, shrinking almost entirely from view on Masen's other side.

"You see, Laurent?" Trey calls over my head to Masen. "You can't watch him all the time."

I continue hearing the scratching of the protractor and look up, scanning the room. Till needs to get Trey out of here. Masen attacking him won't go unpunished if it happens again.

"When you sucker punch someone, that shit doesn't go unchecked," Trey threatens, "so don't turn your back, either. I won't be alone next time."

"Jesus, I'm bored," I mumble at Trey. "Go to Chemistry, would you?"

He arches a brow.

"I'll see you at lunch," I say, pushing him to take the hint. "I have to work now."

He snorts like he's wondering what possible "work" I could have to do in Art. He finally rolls his eyes and gives me a peck on the cheek, getting up and walking out of the classroom.

I reach down, pretending to get something out of my bag as I whisper to Masen. "Tell me you're jealous."

I say the same words to him that he said to me at the drive-in. I don't want to go to prom with Trey. I don't want to even talk to Trey.

But Masen has given me nothing, and I'm not putting my life on hold in the meantime.

"Tell me I'm yours," I say.

He lets the protractor fall to the table and looks down, keeping silent.

My jaw aches, and I feel tears sting the backs of my eyes. "I feel like you're going to disappear any minute. Like you're not really real."

"I'll tell you everything," he whispers back. "I promise. Just not yet."

I wipe away the wet at the corner of my eye and clear my throat. I like Masen. A lot. But he has no roots here, and once the year ends, nothing is keeping him here. I'm nervous.

A low growl catches my attention, and I turn my head, realizing it's coming from Masen's stomach. He shifts in his seat, looking a little embarrassed.

"Have you eaten today?"

"I'm fine," he says. "I just didn't feel like gas station food again."

I watch him, the realization of his situation hitting me. Does he just go to the Cove after he leaves here? Is he alone all the time? How much money could he possibly have to eat and get gas and do laundry?

Sadness creeps in. No one's taking care of him.

He must sense me watching him, because he jerks his chin at my drawing, changing the subject.

"What is that?"

I swallow, gazing down at my third try at the charcoal sketch, which looks more like a Rorschach inkblot.

I suck.

"It's an album cover," I tell him. "That friend I told you about? Misha? He writes music. I was making him a surprise for graduation."

His eyes narrow on it, and his breathing turns fast and shallow. "What?"

He turns away, blinking rapidly. "Nothing."

I let out a sigh and turn back to my work. *Nothing, nothing, nothing.* I might lie a lot, but at least I say something.

I reach into my bag and pull out a granola bar, tossing it in front of him before I excuse myself to go to the bathroom.

It's only eight o'clock in the morning, and I think I've already had enough boys for one day.

———

Squeezing out the packet into the cup, I replace the plastic lid and shake the salad inside. The Caesar dressing mixes and coats the contents, and I grab a plastic fork and a bottle of water, moving down the cafeteria line to the cashier.

"You're eating?" Lyla steps up next to me and reaches over, taking a cup of fruit.

"Yeah." I hand my lunch card to the cashier, and she swipes it. "Spring fever. Might as well eat. I can't concentrate on schoolwork today."

Or at least not at school. My mind is on Masen all the time. Is he here? Is he close? Is he going to push me into a classroom, touch me, and kiss the daylights out of me?

Please. God. Yes?

"You know, I should tell you," Lyla says, giving the cashier some money. "You leaving the drive-in with Masen Friday night was pretty shitty."

I stop and turn my eyes on her, my heart catching in my throat. I don't really care if she knows I left with him, but does she know what we were doing in his truck at the drive-in?

She smiles sarcastically. "Him pulling out of the drive-in right in the middle of a movie, and you nowhere to be found? It wasn't hard to figure out, and I'm willing to bet Trey's figured it out, too."

I exhale, relaxing a little. Okay, she doesn't know much else, then.

"You know what?" I say. "You actually shouldn't tell me anything. You didn't see me leave with him, you have no clue what's going on between us, if anything, and *you've* given more guys a ride than a bus. When you're perfect, then we'll talk. Got it?"

Her eyes flare, shooting me a nasty look as she opens her mouth to speak again.

But I cut her off. "You're done," I tell her. "I'm hungry. Let's eat."

I turn around, but I see Trey and J.D. approach and stop.

Son of a . . .

"You wanna have some fun?" Trey comes in, placing his hands on my hips.

What? I breathe out a laugh, a little exasperated. I can't keep up with the intrigues right now.

But I blink, trying to focus myself again and find my quick wit. "Sure." I give in. "I was wondering when you'd start getting interesting."

J.D. laughs, and Trey cocks an eyebrow, half-amused and half looking like he wants to teach me how to keep my mouth shut.

"Laurent can't seem to take his eyes off you," he says.

He turns his head over his shoulder, and I follow his gaze, finding Masen sitting at a table full of the worst delinquents in school. He leans back, his long legs stretched out and his hands locked behind his head, laughing with the guy he's talking to.

"So?" I look back at Trey.

"So I think he wants you," he answers. "I want you to use that for me."

And then he leans in, holding the other side of my face and whispering into my ear. "Get him to come to my house next week for the party."

I pinch my eyebrows together, vaguely remembering him mentioning his parents being out of town soon. And he wants me to bring Masen. *So you can do what? Beat him up after I've lured him into the trap like in that eighties movie?*

Yeah, no.

Trey pulls away, and I force my tone even. "That doesn't sound like any fun to me."

Trey hoods his eyes, clearly getting aggravated with my lack of cooperation. He turns to Lyla, giving her a sexy smile. "Lyla, baby," he says, and I see J.D. tense. "You got some balls, don't you?"

Lyla grins back coyly, and I shake my head.

If I don't do what he wants, Lyla will. I catch J.D.'s sneer shoot between Trey and Lyla, and then to me before he looks away.

I heave a sigh. "Masen's not stupid, Trey. He'll see right through her."

I shove my salad at Lyla and brush past the boys, walking toward Masen's table.

Stepping up, I stop next to him. All of his buddies cease their conversation and look at me, but Masen doesn't spare me a glance.

"Hey." I put my hand on my hip, knowing he's aware of me.

A smile curls Masen's lips, and his friends' eager glances dart between him and me.

"Princess," he says. "What can I do for you?"

Oh, please. I slide in between him and the table, hopping up and planting my hands behind me, leaning back a little, well-aware my shirt is riding up as his eyes flash to my stomach.

A few snorts sound off from his friends, and I taunt him with my eyes.

"Your prom date's watching," he says.

"He sent me," I reply. "He seems to think you'll let me bring you to one of his parties."

I hear a few mumbles around the table, while Masen simply looks amused. We both know what Trey has in store, and I can feel my own friends watching us.

"You don't want your friends thinking you're a chicken, do you?" I play.

Masen's smile widens, and he glances to his side, probably seeing if Trey is paying attention.

Not that either of us probably cares. I kind of like this game. No one would believe we're actually into each other. I can play them as long as we're not playing each other.

He looks up at me and slides his hands under my knees, pulling me off the table and slowly lowering me into his lap, straddling him. Quiet laughter sounds off around the table and a need is suddenly building between my legs.

Leaning into him, chest to chest, I whisper in his ear. "I don't want you to go," I admit. "He won't be alone."

"Why do you care?" He speaks low, keeping his tone flat. "You're still taking Machismo-Dick to prom, aren't you?"

"Has anyone else asked me?"

"Would you say yes?"

I brush his ear with my nose, feeling his soft skin there. "Ask and find out."

"Trevarrow!"

I jerk, hearing my name called. I don't have to turn around to know it's the principal. Great. I move to get off his lap, but he presses his hands down on my thighs, keeping me there.

"Masen," I urge. He's going to get me in trouble. In public.

"Get off his lap," Principal Burrowes orders me. "Now."

I put my hands on Masen's shoulders, moving to get up, but he grips my hips again, keeping me down.

"She gets off my dick when I tell her to get off," he tells the principal.

My mouth falls open, and I widen my eyes. *What the fuck?*

Burrowes' expression turns furious, and I hear various laughs and snorts around the table behind me.

"I beg your pardon?" she exclaims.

But Masen just leans into my ear. "I'll see you later."

And then he stands, carefully letting me slide off his lap and onto my feet.

He doesn't spare anyone a second glance and walks out of the lunchroom with Burrowes' heels clacking after him.

Somehow, though, I doubt she's going to be able to stop him.

13

Misha

I'm going to hell. I'm pretty sure she's going to drag me there herself.

Ryen has a nasty temper, and it's the one thing about her I didn't know but was happy to find out.

It excites me.

I tilt the flowerpot and pluck out the key that's hidden underneath. Unlocking her front door, I replace the key and enter the house as the grandfather clock chimes to indicate it's five a.m. Hopefully, everyone is still asleep.

I'll tell her tomorrow. I'll take her to my father's house—my house—and show her . . .

No, I should write her a letter. Something where I can get my words out right.

No.

Fuck! She won't accept it. She won't be able to get past it. She'll hate me and cut me off, and my life will be empty without her. I have to tell her, or I have to leave.

And the possibility that I'll do just that, punk out and cut and run, is the only reason I don't claim her. The only reason I don't knock Trey's fucking hands off her and put a dent in his stomach.

I can't rob her of prom and friends when I know I won't be here to pick up the pieces. Either I'll be gone or she'll make me go.

How do you tell your friend—your *best* friend—that you've been right here, under her nose, playing with her like a puppet? That she had no idea the guy who was fucking her Friday night was the boy she grew up with?

It all just got so out of hand.

And then I blew off the one thing I came here to do on Saturday night, because all of a sudden, I wasn't in a hurry to leave anymore. Not after what had happened at the drive-in.

I close the door, gently releasing the knob to keep from alerting anyone who might be awake that someone's breaking into their house.

Looking around the downstairs, I don't see or hear anyone, so I jog upstairs, careful to keep my steps light and quick. Veering to the right, I twist the knob to Ryen's bedroom and open the door.

But I hear a gasp and look up to see her scrambling on the bed, pulling the sheet over her chest as she sits up.

I narrow my eyes, shocked she's awake already, as I close and lock the door. I was just planning on lying down next to her, savoring the feel of her for a little while.

Our days might be numbered.

"What are you doing?" she whisper-yells. "How'd you get in here?"

"Same way I got in last time," I reply, walking toward the bed. "There's a spare key under the flowerpot outside."

She rolls her eyes, probably at her mom's stupidity.

I let my eyes fall down her body, noticing her bare leg arched up, but as I drift my gaze back up again, I see the curve of her hip, completely bare, and the side of her torso, visible in her half shirt.

What the hell?

Reaching down, I lift the sheet up, seeing that she's completely bottomless. No sleep shorts, no underwear . . .

She snatches the sheet back, covering herself, a rosy blush crossing her cheeks.

"Why are you naked?" I straighten, suspicion crawling over my skin.

I don't wait for an answer. I walk to the closet and throw open the doors, wondering who the fuck she has in here. She was obviously awake and scared when I opened the door.

"There's no one here," she says. "I'm alone."

I look around the room, noticing there aren't any other hiding places. Except . . .

I kneel down and throw up her bed skirt, peering underneath the bed.

Nothing.

Why the fuck is she naked then?

I stand up, cocking an eyebrow at her as she shifts nervously.

And then it occurs to me.

Taking the sheet in my hand, I yank it off her, her little whimper falling on my deaf ears as I lock eyes on a small black bullet vibrator.

My pulse speeds up, and I feel my cock instantly swell.

She places her hands behind her, holding herself up with her knees arched up, and chews on her lip, turning her embarrassed eyes away.

I can't resist an amused smile. I lean down and hook the cord with a finger, picking it up, the black egg dangling in the air. "Thinking about me, were you?"

A little snarl mars her fresh morning face. "You wish, loser."

My chest rumbles with a laugh. Dropping the sex toy, I slide my hand between her legs, all the doubt and fear of a minute ago falling away as I slip the tip of my finger into her wet heat.

"Did you come yet?"

She tosses me another scowl, still looking away.

Leaning into her ear, I whisper, "Do you have any idea how perfect you are?"

Her breathing hitches, and she finally turns her face to me. I run my hand up her pussy, over her smooth, toned stomach, and just under her half shirt, grazing the underside of her breast.

"Show me what you do with it," I beg.

Her eyes flash up to me, worry and nervousness written all over her face.

I glide my fingers over her hard nipples. "I'll love everything you do. I promise."

She shakes her head.

I grip her breast harder, a little whimper catching in her throat.

"Do it now," I growl, demanding.

Her head falls back, and she squirms a little, clearly turned on, and I moan in her ear, my dick fucking solid.

I hear the clank of the vibrator and remote, and stand up, backing away, so I can watch her. I expect her to lie back, stick the ball between her thighs, and start rubbing it on herself, but she doesn't do that.

Instead, she slowly turns over onto her stomach and slides the egg between her and the sheet, all the way down to her pussy.

I sit down in the chair next to her bedside table, not blinking even once. I don't want to miss a second.

Bending a knee to spread herself open, she positions the ball right where she needs it, and I let my eyes fall down her body. The sexy little white T-shirt that ends halfway down her back, her perfect ass, her sexy, tanned legs, and when the buzzing begins . . .

I groan, my cock straining against my jeans.

She turns her head to me, her body supported up on her elbows, and I see her hips start grinding into the bed, her pussy rubbing against the hard little vibrating ball underneath her. I can barely breathe, I'm so fucking mesmerized.

Her ass moves, rolling in little circles as she pleasures herself, and I hear her breathing get heavier. Looking up, I meet her eyes, one nearly hidden behind her hair.

Her stare is hard, as if her imagination has taken hold and it's me she's fucking instead of the toy.

"You fuck that little ball a lot?" I ask, my voice husky.

She nods slowly.

"I like watching that ass move, babe."

"I can tell." Her amused eyes fall to my groin; she probably notices how hard I am.

She arches her neck back, running a hand up her thigh and over her ass, moaning and grunting faster as she starts to hump harder. *Oh, fuck.* The sexy movement of her hips, the way her ass thrusts in and out, is the hottest damn thing I've ever seen.

Her heated eyes fall on me again, luring me in. "I've fucked a lot in this bed. Just never with someone else."

Well, it's time to pop that cherry.

"Oh," she moans, her face twisted in pleasure. She grinds her pussy harder, digging into the bed and trying to rub her clit to orgasm.

I lean forward, my elbows on my knees, hypnotized.

"I'm so wet," she whimpers. "I can feel it dripping over my clit."

I fist my fingers.

"I like it when you watch me," she whispers. "It makes me want to suck your cock."

My eyes go wide, and I stand up, walking over to her. Cupping her chin, I lean down, forcing her head back and her eyes up to me. "You're a hot little brat," I growl over her lips. "But only for me, you got that?"

I grab her breast, squeezing it roughly and making her moan. This is mine.

She darts her tongue out, flicking my lip ring. "I can feel you down my throat already."

I groan under my breath, the blood rushing to my cock. That's it.

I reach underneath her, pull out the vibrator and fling it onto the floor.

"Wha—" she protests, but I kneel on the bed behind her, grab her hips and pull her up onto her hands and knees, smacking her ass.

She yelps but follows it with a moan, inching her knees wider apart and arching her back, welcoming me. I pull my shirt off and over my head, tossing it to the floor. Reaching into my pocket, I take out a condom and unfasten my jeans, pulling out my cock and sheathing it.

Is she on the pill? God, what I wouldn't give to feel her bare right now.

I roll the rubber on and guide my dick into her, thrusting once and hard, burying myself deep inside her.

"Ohhhh," she groans.

I close my eyes, her tight heat wrapping around me and filtering through my whole damn body.

Gripping her hips, I thrust in and out, pulling her heart-shaped ass into me hard and fast. "Damn, you feel good."

She holds herself up on her hands, her long hair spilling down her back and bouncing as I fuck her. Running one hand up her spine, I feel her body move and back up into my cock, eager to meet me halfway every time I enter her.

I slide my hand up her neck and thread my fingers through her hair, fisting it. Pulling her back, I turn her head and kiss her, her tongue teasing me as she pulls away and comes back for more.

I thrust harder, and the headboard starts hitting the wall.

"You have to go slow." She tilts her head back, closing her eyes in pleasure. "My mom and sister will hear."

"Fuck that," I growl in her ear. "I'm not holding back again."

Last Friday night was agonizing, and while I enjoyed it, it was torture trying to contain myself so the truck wouldn't rock and no one would hear her moaning.

I pound into her, the sound of skin hitting skin filling the room as I grunt and tense every goddamn muscle in my body. I know I'm hitting her deep, because her moans are getting faster and higher.

"I'm going to do something a little illegal tonight," I tell her, tugging at her earlobe with my teeth. "You game?"

"What is it?" she breathes out.

"It's a surprise. Don't you trust me?"

She scoffs. "Why would I trust you? The only thing I know about you is that you've got a nice body and you get me off good."

I can't help the stupid, fucking pleasure that swarms my chest. I don't want to be just a fuck to her, but I'm glad I please her in that area. She owns my head and my body. When she finds out who I am, will she remember how perfect we are?

"You know more than that," I whisper. "I won't let anything happen to you. You're my tribe, Ryen."

She pauses and looks me in the eyes. "What did you say?"

Every part of my body tenses.

Fuck. *Tribe*. She wrote that in a letter.

Why did I say that?

I deflect as quickly as I can. I lean forward and come down on her, pushing her down to the mattress and thrusting deeper and harder.

"I said I won't put you in danger." I reach around and cup her face, turning her head and kissing her. "Come with me while everyone is at the game tonight."

She whimpers, her eyes falling closed, and I can feel her tightening around my cock.

"Come on and make some trouble with me," I say.

"And get an insight into who the hell you are?" she shoots back, her breathing turning shallow and hard.

"Maybe."

She nods, her eyebrows pinching together and looking like she's about to come. "Okay."

I push into her, fucking her relentlessly, as electric shocks course through my stomach and stream all the way down to my dick.

"Yeah, yeah," she pants, arching up her ass to meet my thrusts.

I cover her mouth with mine, our moans drowning out as we both come, her pussy squeezing like a vise grip around me. I thrust a few more times, wishing I could spill inside of her as pleasure washes over my whole body, and I eventually still.

Damn, she's perfect.

I gnaw at her mouth in short, gentle nibbles. I love her lips, and the light sweat I can taste on her skin.

A door closing sounds from out in the hall, and I gather her family is starting to wake up. My eyelids are suddenly heavy, and I breathe hard, trying to come down.

I better get out of here.

Looking down, I see her face resting on the bed, her eyes closed, looking very content. I slip my hand between her and the bed and squeeze her breast, placing one last kiss on her cheek. "Thanks, Pom-Poms. I'll see you at school."

She makes a little growl in her throat, but her eyes remain closed, and I laugh to myself as I clean up and get dressed.

14

Ryen

"Do you think anyone will guess we got this shit from the bakery?" Lyla asks, holding up a stack of wrapped cookies.

I take the clear plastic bag from her, tied with a red bow, and set it back down on the long plastic table. "It's not shit. *Because* it's from the bakery."

School ended four hours ago, but the parking lot is packed full of cars as we stand behind our table, greeting people before they enter the ballpark. The sun has already set, and the field lighting overhead shines down, brightening the area as the last of the crowd filters through the gates.

Lyla and I were picked by the coach to work the bake sale tonight, and as a requirement, we have to wear our cheer uniforms. Fundraising is one of our many duties, and since we're not busy rallying the crowd during the baseball game that's about to start, we're trying to earn some money for the team and acclimate some of the new girls coming in next year.

Technically we were supposed to bake the goods we're selling—with the help of the team moms—but we'd dropped the ball, not planning ahead. It's spring, school's almost over, and I'm already swamped as it is. So we raided Lieber's Bakery during school today and got dismissed from final period to package everything in our own bags with ribbons of the school's colors.

"Come on, freshmen!" Lyla claps her hands. "Smile. It's your new thing. I promise."

I laugh to myself. I don't envy them at all. The will to plaster a smile I don't feel on my face has very nearly left the building.

I push the packages of cookies and brownies up to replace what has already been sold. Looking up, I see Masen standing near his truck with a group of guys from school. My stomach somersaults.

He's watching me with an amused look on his face. I'd told him about the bake sale during Art today, so we agreed to meet afterward to do whatever it is he's got planned, God help me.

After he sneaked into my room this morning, catching me with my vibrator, and damn near woke up the whole house—because he needed to get laid—the rest of the day passed relatively calmly. Everything else was easy-peasy compared to that.

I resist the urge to pull out the huge-ass black bow on top of my head that we're required to wear as part of the uniform. I can feel the laugh he's holding back all the way from here.

I see him and his friends approach.

"Jesus, it's like the Disney Channel puked all over this table," he jokes, scanning the array of polka-dotted plastic bags and the flowery tablecloth.

I put my hands on my hips.

"Nice bow." He jerks his chin, eyeing the top of my head. "If I pull it, does it have a string that makes you talk and move?"

A snort breaks into a laugh, and I shoot a glare over to Ten, standing behind Lyla. He hunches over just a little, his body shaking.

He glances up at me, sees my stare, and tries to hold it back. "I'm sorry, okay? It was funny."

I arch an eyebrow and turn my eyes back to Masen. He cocks his head, looking delighted with himself.

I grab the collar of his black hoodie and pull his face close, leaning into his ear and covering my whisper with my hand. "You left bruises all over my tits this morning," I tell him, "and if you're not nice, I won't let you kiss them better later."

He sucks in a breath.

"Now buy some cookies," I order, pushing him away.

A smile pulls at his mouth, but I raise my chin, watching him pull out his wallet.

He hands Lyla a hundred-dollar bill, and I blink, trying not to look like I'm taken off guard. Okay. I guess he's okay on money, after all.

Where'd he get that much cash? An unnerving feeling settles in my gut.

"How much will this buy me?" he asks her but keeps his eyes on me.

She takes the bill and stares at it for a moment. But then she takes a package of ten cookies and shoves it at him. "Here."

A laugh catches in my throat. That stack of sweets costs five bucks, but I don't care that she's hustling him. He deserves it.

He gives the package a look, clearly knowing he's being swindled, but he keeps quiet and tosses it to a friend behind him. Slipping his wallet back into his pocket, he holds my eyes briefly before walking away, his crew following.

"Nice." Lyla waves the hundred in front of me. "What did you say to him?"

"I forget."

I don't fear Lyla's judgment about Masen, and part of me wants people to see him touch me, but for some reason, Masen still feels like a fling, and I don't want to try to explain it to others. I'm still trying to figure him out myself.

And part of me likes the sneaking around. I love having this one thing that makes me happy that I don't have to share with anyone else.

Kind of like Misha.

Misha. Why do I feel like I'm betraying him? He abandoned me.

After the national anthem and the first pitch, Lyla, Ten, and I call it a night, sending the other girls home and then packing up. Lyla grabs the rest of the snacks, saying we'll just give them to the baseball team when they're done, and Ten heads into the game, probably to find J.D. and the rest of our friends.

I hook my bag over my shoulder, grab my water bottle, and walk for the parking lot instead of the ball field.

"Where are you going?" Lyla asks, turning with the box of cookies in her arms.

I gesture to my bag. "Taking this to my car."

I walk away, not waiting for a response, and head straight for my Jeep, seeing that Masen's black Raptor is parked on the other side of the aisle.

His eyes are on me as he leans against his door and two of his pals stand in front of him, their heads turned and watching me, too.

Tossing my bag into the back, I reach up and unclip my bow and pull out the rubber band that held the top half of my hair back. I comb the strands with my fingers and fluff it up, letting it hang loose down my back. Turning around, I lean back on my Jeep and hang my elbows over the edge of the car, looking straight at him.

"I don't know, man," Finn Damaris muses, smirking. "She looks like she wants something. What do you think?"

"Yeah." The one with the Mohawk, whose name I don't know, nods and bites his bottom lip, letting his eyes fall down my body. "She definitely wants something."

Masen watches behind them, amusement in his eyes.

"She's so clean," Finn comments, turning to his friend. "I'll bet she likes to get dirty, though."

Mohawk laughs. "Oh, yeah."

I roll my eyes, waiting. I'm sure they're loving this. The stuck-up girl playing with one of their own . . .

"You guys take off," Masen says. "I got this."

I walk over, fall gently into his chest as his friends disappear, snickering.

"So where are we going?" I hover over his lips.

He inhales a deep breath and plants a quick peck on my cheek, standing up straight. "Come on. Get in."

I cross my arms over my chest to keep from fidgeting. "I should've changed my clothes."

Masen peers over, driving past my neighborhood and deeper into the countryside. "Why?"

"Because if we're seen doing whatever it is we're doing," I explain, "I won't be hard to identify in a Falcon's Well cheer uniform."

He smiles to himself and looks back at the road. "You won't be seen."

I take in a deep breath and reach over and turn up the radio, trying to drown out the worry in my head as Breaking Benjamin's "So Cold" plays.

I try to act like a badass, but honestly, I'm nervous as hell.

I should've told him no this morning. I'd stopped writing on the walls, and doing anything more illegal would be risking too much. I have acceptance letters to NYU, Cornell, and Dartmouth. Like I'm going to jeopardize that simply because I'm infatuated with him and will use any excuse to be close to him.

Actually it was hard to refuse him anything while he was inside me. I would've told him I'd tattoo his name on my neck if he wanted.

He'd probably love that. I glance over at him, laughing inside at the idea. His brown hair, wispy and sticking up a little, is pushed forward, and I stare at his mouth, remembering the warmth of the smooth metal ring grazing the dozens of places he's kissed on my body.

I suddenly want to know everything. What he was like as a kid. What his favorite kinds of music are. Where he goes when he wants some peace and quiet, and whom does he go to when he needs to talk.

Whom does he love? Who's there for him? Who knows him best?

Who knows him better than me? I can't help the jealousy I feel at that thought. He has an entire life and history with people who aren't me.

I chew on the corner of my mouth, feeling so many things I know I shouldn't say.

But I want to.

"I like you," I tell him, looking down, my voice quiet.

I see him turn his head toward me, not saying anything.

"You said some nice things last Friday night," I go on, "and I wanted you to know—in case you don't already—that I actually kind of like you." I raise my eyes, seeing him watch me with something I can't read going on in his eyes. "I know I can be . . . me. I don't get sappy, and I don't give up what's going on in my head a lot. It's hard for me." I pause, feeling a little more resolute. I want him to know. "But yeah, I like you."

I know it's not much, but it's a lot for me, and I hope he knows that. Admitting I like him makes me vulnerable, and that's not usually a card I ever give up. Not anymore.

Because, to be honest, I don't just like him. It's more than that. I think about him.

I miss him when he's not around.

It'll hurt if he has to leave as suddenly as he appeared.

He's quiet, and the heat of embarrassment blankets my skin. Awesome. Good going, Ryen. Maybe all he liked about you was that you weren't clingy, and now you're acting like you're in love with him.

"When are we going to be there?" I ask, my tone curt as I try to change the subject.

I watch as he slowly pulls over to the side of the road and parks next to a wall of trees.

"We're here now," he answers.

I peer around the hedge, taking a better look, and then dart my eyes around, taking in the quiet, spacious neighborhood.

"This is Trey's house," I point out, my guard definitely up now.

He nods, taking off his seat belt. "There's something of mine in there. A family heirloom." He gestures to Trey's house on the right. "And I need it back."

"What are you talking about? Why would Trey have something of yours?"

He shakes his head. "Not Trey."

"What?"

He takes my phone out of my hand and punches some buttons on the screen as I try to figure out what the hell's going on. There's something of his in there? Something he wants back? Trey and his entire family are at the baseball game, so no one's home.

Are we breaking in?

"Masen, I'm not breaking into his house."

"You don't have to." He hands my phone back to me. "I programmed in my number. I think it's about time you had it anyway. Call me if anyone comes home or you see anything weird."

What?

I stare at him, appalled, but he just climbs out of the truck and jogs for the house.

Excuse me?

I push open the door, jump out, and slam it behind me, chasing after him. "I can't believe you!" I whisper-yell, catching up to him in the middle of Trey's lawn. "You won't tell me anything, and now you're breaking and entering, and you're involving me? I could get into trouble, and yes, I don't mean to seem like a hypocrite, being Punk and all, but I don't want to do this."

He stops, and I clutch my phone in my hand, kind of wanting to throw it at him. Where the hell does he get off? He has friends. Why not ask them?

"Why would you ask me to do this?" I demand.

"Because it's important."

He glares at me, but I don't think he's angry.

He lets out a breath, and his expression softens as he approaches me. "Because I need what's in there, and because . . . you're the one I trust. You're the one I want here."

"Gee, thanks."

"I'm serious, Ryen. Trust me, would you?"

"I trust people who don't deliberately put me in danger," I shoot back. "I thought we were doing something at the Cove or climbing a water tower or something. Not breaking into the principal's house."

"You break into the principal's school," he points out.

I twist up my lips, folding my arms over my chest. *Jerk.*

He regards me for a moment and then drops his eyes. Taking my hand, he places his keys in my palm. "You're right. Go ahead and take the truck to your house. I'll meet you there," he tells me, relenting. "It's only a mile away. I can walk it."

What? No—

But he turns around and walks for Trey's house, not giving me a chance to protest. I don't want to get in trouble, but I don't want him getting in trouble, either.

Something of his is in the house. So we're not taking anything that doesn't belong to him, then. Okay.

I let out a sigh and run after him.

Just go. Don't think.

I wonder how many people who got prison sentences said the same thing when they committed their crimes.

I see him head for the front door, digging something out of his pocket, but I eye the doggy door on the garage and then look around me. Anyone could drive by or a neighbor could possibly spot Masen at the door, trying to get in.

"The doggy door is a better idea," I tell him, knowing Trey's parents probably took the husky with them to the game.

He jerks his head, eyeing the rectangular hole in the door. "I can't fit through there."

Of course not. Their dog is big but not that big.

I shake my head, hesitating for a moment. But then I heave a sigh and move toward the door.

I can try to convince myself that I know this house, having been here before, and I can get him through it and try to find what he needs a lot faster than he can. But the truth is, I want to know what he's looking for and why. So far he's been like a ghost, and I'm curious.

Crouching down, I push my hand through the doggy door, listening for feet to come running or a bark. But all I hear is leaves rustling in the wind.

Masen comes up behind me, and I stick my head through, seeing only the inside of the pitch-black garage. Sliding my arm in, I turn on my side, maneuver my shoulders through the tight space, and put my hands down on the cold cement floor, wiggling my body through the small hole.

I inhale the musty air and make out the little green dot of light by the kitchen door, guessing that must be the garage door opener.

Stepping cautiously in the dark, I hold out my hands and move toward the door, trying to avoid the pool table, couch, and other furnishings I know are in the converted man cave.

"Don't turn on any lights," Masen calls.

"Duh." My foot hits the step, and I reach out my hand, pressing the button for the opener. The motor starts turning, and the garage door begins to lift up. Masen bends down and slides in under the door, and I press the button, lowering it again.

I twist the handle to the kitchen door and open it, immediately seeing moonlight streaming through a large kitchen window. Masen comes in behind me, closing the door, and I inhale, smelling Trey. It's funny how people smell like their houses. Or vice versa.

Combinations of leather and wood furniture, Febreze, laundry soap, the different colognes and perfumes your parents and siblings use, the food your family cooks . . . all coming together to create a single, solitary scent in your house.

Except Masen. He smells like the leather from his truck with a hint of soap. That's it.

"Let's go."

He leads me through the house, looking around as if figuring out where to go, which I could tell him if I knew what he was looking for. But rounding the stairs, he jogs up, and I follow.

"Are you going to Trey's room?" I ask.

"If so, I'll find it," he bites out. "I don't need to know that you know where it is."

I smile to myself. "I don't. I was just asking."

He opens a door, and I peer into the darkness, seeing pink walls and toy hot-air balloons hanging from the ceiling.

It must be Emma's room. Trey's half sister. I know Principal Burrowes married Trey's dad when Trey was about four. Even though he calls her Gillian and doesn't treat her like a mom, she practically raised him and then gave birth to a daughter several years younger than Trey.

I look at Masen, wondering why he's not closing the door. What he needs can't possibly be in here. Emma is only like six. She didn't steal anything from him.

But he just stands there, letting his eyes drift around the room. His chest moves with his shallow breaths.

"Masen?" I prompt.

But he doesn't answer.

I touch his arm. "Masen?" I say louder. "What are we looking for? I want to get out of here."

He blinks, turning away, almost like he's angry. "All right, come on."

He leaves the room, and I shut the door again, catching a flash of movement. The shadows of the leaves outside the hall window dance over the carpet, and my heart skips a beat.

Walking to the next door, Masen strolls in and stops for just a moment, looking around. Heading for the armoire, he pulls open a drawer and takes out a small flashlight from his pocket. He clicks on the small light and starts inspecting the jewelry case.

"You can't be serious?" I bark in a whisper, stepping up to him. "Did the principal steal your favorite string of pearls?"

"It's a long story, babe." He pulls open drawer after drawer, quickly scanning the contents and shuffling items around, searching for what? I don't know.

"And I'm fascinated," I retort. "But if you steal anything, I'll make you bleed."

"Hold this." He shoves the flashlight at me. "I won't take anything that's not already mine."

"What's yours? What are we looking for?"

"A watch."

A watch? "Why would the Burroweses have your watch?" I ask, confused.

"Later," he says. "Now, hold up the light."

I purse my lips, growing impatient. But I hold up the light and shine it on the drawers he's sifting through. I follow him when he moves to the dresser, dipping his hands in sweaters and shirts, feeling around.

"So do you want to take a shower tonight?" He glances up at me.

I frown. He's flirting? Really?

He chuckles. "I don't really need one, but I'd love to wipe that little scowl off your face, and I'll bet you'll feel good wet."

I shake my head, trying to look unamused at his shitty choice of timing for dirty talk.

Although a hot shower with him, kissing and touching him, sounds really good.

"Just hurry up," I whisper, wiggling my legs underneath me, getting anxious.

He searches the rest of the room—some small boxes in the closet and the bedside drawers—while I hold the light, waiting for him to give up so we can just get out of here. But he pauses briefly, standing at the foot of the bed, thinking.

And then, before I have a chance to push him again to get us out of here, he whips around and heads out of the room and across the hall.

Trey's room. *Finally.* I expected him to search there first. I don't know why Trey would have anything of his, but he'd be a hell of a lot more likely to steal something from Masen than the parents.

Glancing around the principal's bedroom, I make sure everything is put back in place—closets and drawers closed—and shut the bedroom door, hustling across the hall and following him into Trey's room.

I brave a glance around. I should feel guilty that I'm sneaking around the room of the guy I'm going to prom with, but I let my gaze fall on his queen-size bed, a navy-blue comforter with gray sheets, and I feel a shiver crawl up my arms instead.

There's no way I ever want to lie in there with him.

I watch Masen open the bedside drawer and pick up a box of condoms, flashing it to me over his shoulder.

"What do you think?" he teases. "Is he stocking up for prom?"

Oh, whatever. "You know, you keep bringing up prom," I point out, stepping up behind him and whispering in his ear. "If you're that worried about what might happen with those condoms, maybe you should do something about it."

I feel his body shake with a quiet laugh as he tosses the box back into the drawer.

"Ask me," I whisper, running my lip over his lobe. "Ask me, and I'll say yes."

He leans into my mouth, looking at me. "Maybe tomorrow."

I push away, displeased. "Douchebag."

He chuckles behind me. I flash the light around the room as Masen makes his way over to the dresser and opens the left drawer, mussing the socks as he digs.

But I notice something in the dark and pinch my eyebrows together, coming over and reaching in, touching his hand.

"This drawer should be deeper," I tell him, my fingers hitting a plank of wood. I'd noticed his hand and wrist in the drawer when the depth should've eaten up half his forearm.

We both feel around, and Masen narrows his eyes, finding something and pulling on it.

He lifts up the piece of wood, the clothes fall back, and I see another compartment underneath.

Masen reaches in and pulls out what looks like a stack of cards. He turns them over and looks at them, but then he drops his hand back into the drawer, stuffing the cards back into the compartment.

"What?" I prod, reaching in and trying to grab the stack away from him.

"It's nothing." He tries to replace the board. "It's not what I'm looking for."

But I force my way in and rip the stack out of his hand.

Shooting him a joking little scowl, I turn the cards over and look at them.

My chest caves. *Oh, my God.*

They're not cards. They're pictures. Four-by-sixes by the looks of it, and I stare at each image, shuffling the cards one after another, my stomach churning.

Lindsey Beck, a senior who graduated last year.

Fara Corelli, a senior in my class this year.

Abigail Dunst, another senior.

Sylvie Lanquist, a junior.

Georgia York. J.D.'s older sister. He probably doesn't have any idea about that.

Girl after girl, naked and in a variety of different poses. Some of them are selfies, some of them taken by someone else, and in one of them, Trey has a girl straddling him. His face holds a sleazy smile.

Disgusted, I curl my fingers around the pictures.

Brandy Matthews is naked and on her hands and knees, the camera catching the side of her face as Trey, I would assume, kneels behind her and takes the picture.

My heart races, and I feel like it's going to jump out of my chest, I shuffle the next card and see Sylvie, her mouth open and . . .

I drop my hands, looking away. *Gross.*

My God. What's wrong with him? Who takes pictures of that many women—girls—committing sexual acts? Did they know he was doing it to all of them? And Sylvie's the sweetest kid. How long did he sweet-talk her to get what he wanted?

"I'm sorry, babe."

I scoff, tossing the pics on the dresser. "You think I don't know what he's about?"

"Well, you are still going to prom with him."

I shoot a look over to him, aggravated he keeps bringing that up.

No. I'm not going to prom with Trey. Not anymore. If he treats girls he's able to get naked like that, how will he treat someone he can't get into bed?

But I won't tell Masen that. He'll just gloat.

I look down and see another picture in his hand and inch forward. "What is that?"

He hoods his eyes, shaking his head like I need to leave it alone. I dart out and snatch the picture, holding it up in front of me.

Lyla is naked and wet, her hair soaked and sticking to her cheeks and neck, and she's posing against what looks like a shower wall, her arms over her head and her breasts on display. Her eyes taunt the camera—or whoever's behind it.

Trey. If he's not the one with the camera, he still has the picture of her.

But I'm not fooling myself. They fucked. And recently, too. Lyla's wearing the bronze wrist cuff she bought when we shopped three Saturdays ago.

I don't care about him, and I don't really like her, so why do I feel my eyes burning and my throat aching with a scream?

I'm not jealous he got from her what he wasn't getting from me, and I'm not jealous they got off on each other. But why did they feel they could do it behind my back?

I feel a warm hand touch my face. "You know what she's about just as much as him," Masen says. "This doesn't surprise you."

I shake my head, blinking through the thick tears I can't stop from welling up. "No," I barely whisper, staring at the photo.

No, I'm not surprised. I just feel like shit for some reason. The whole time I thought I was winning. I thought I was on top. But behind my back, the people I thought I could handle were handling me. They think I'm stupid, after all. Someone they find easy to humiliate.

Just like before.

I knew Trey wasn't holding out for me, so I didn't care. But I did think I had Lyla figured out. I thought I had her respect.

What fun she must have had, standing next to me and knowing that she's getting a piece of someone she thinks I might want.

Fat tears spill over, and I feel a weight on my shoulders. It's not Trey. It's not Lyla. It's me. I don't know who I'm supposed to be.

"You know, I turned into this," I tell him, my voice cracking and an ache settling behind my eyes, "because I was a kid and I thought there was something more. I traded friends I didn't think were good enough for friends who really aren't good enough."

I blink long and hard, my wet lashes falling against my cheeks. "Even Misha gave up on me."

Masen cups my face gently. "I'm sure Misha has a reason," he says sadly. "Because there's nothing wrong with you."

"There's so much wrong with me." A sob shakes my chest, and I cry harder. "I don't have any friends, Masen."

I don't. Not really. I can understand people at school. I got what I deserved. I chose shallow, I acted shallow, and I got nothing that would last.

I don't know if Ten will stick with me, and now Misha is gone, too. I don't know what I did, but it had to be something, because when you find that everyone hates you, it's not them. It's you.

"You have a friend," Masen tells me, his tone hard and sure. "The rest of those fucking losers are deadweight. Do you hear me?" He runs his thumbs over my cheeks, wiping away the tears. "You're beautiful and smart, and you have this fire in you that I'm addicted to."

Warmth fills my chest, and I raise my eyes to his.

He leans in, forehead to forehead. "You're an incredible pain in the ass, but God, I love y—" He stops, and my breath catches in my throat.

"It," he finishes. "I love it. I can't get enough. I think about you all the time."

I sniffle, taking some deep breaths and wiping my tears. My heart skipped a beat there. It almost sounded like he was going to say something else.

"Let's just get out of here, okay?" I pull away, replacing the board in the drawer and closing it. I know he hasn't found what he needs, but I have to get out of here. I need a shower after those pictures, or I want to do something with Masen and forget coming here.

Gathering up the pictures, I head out of the room and take a left to head down the stairs. But Masen grabs my arm, stopping me.

"What are you going to do with those pictures?"

"Burn them," I answer. "He probably printed them, because he didn't want his parents finding them in his phone, so he won't have copies. I wouldn't put it past him to be showing these to his friends."

But Masen shakes his head. Taking them out of my hand, he makes a U-turn and opens the parents' bedroom door.

"What are you doing?" I whisper-yell.

But then I see him throw out his hand, sending the pictures flying all over the room, falling to the floor and even the bed.

"Oh, my God." I choke out a laugh and cover my mouth.

"Let the parents sort him out," Masen says, taking my hand and closing the door behind us.

I laugh quietly, but I still laugh. I can't stop. The Burroweses will definitely know someone was in their house tonight, but judging from the photos, they'll probably just assume it's a disgruntled girl pissed at Trey.

We leave the house, going out the same way we came in, and hurriedly hop into his truck, looking around to make sure there's no one around.

The street is dark and quiet, and Masen starts the engine, getting us out of there.

"I'm sorry you didn't get what you wanted."

He gives me a weak smile. "I got what I want."

Flutters hit my stomach, and I bring up my hand, running my fingertips over the top of his hand that's resting on the console.

After a couple minutes, he pulls up in front of my house and puts the truck in park, leaving the engine running.

I sit up and lean over to him, not wanting to say good night.

Never wanting him to leave, actually.

"There's a tree house in the backyard," I look up at him teasingly. "You game?"

He smiles. "I would love to. But I have something to do right now," he tells me, whispering in my ear.

I feel disappointment, but I brave it and plaster on a flat expression like I always do.

"Do me a favor, though?" he asks, kissing my cheek slow and soft. "Make sure the key's under the pot. And don't touch yourself tonight. Save it for the morning when I can watch."

My body warms with excitement, and I smile. If it weren't so dark in the truck, I'm sure he'd be able to see me blush.

"Be early," I beg. "I might not be able to wait."

He kisses me, and I linger for a moment before pulling away. Climbing out of the truck, I look back at him once and then unlock my door, entering the house.

As soon as the door's closed, I hear him pull away.

How easy it is to get lost with him. A few minutes ago I was crying, and now none of that seems to matter. I want friends, of course. I want to know Ten will stay by my side, and I want Misha back, but . . .

Masen just makes everything seem smaller. Like I have a new perspective. He's becoming a part of my heart, and I feel good when he's around.

Almost like none of my fears matter as long he's there.

Tomorrow he said he would tell me everything, but honestly, part of me isn't sure I want to know anymore. Of course, the more I know about him, the more I'll feel like he's real and the more I'll be a part of his life instead of him just being a part of mine, but I like him. A lot.

I walk up the steps and down the hall, entering my room. Switching on the lamp, I kick off my shoes and collapse onto the bed, hanging my head off the end and staring upside down at all my chalk-wall scribbles.

My eyes feel heavy with exhaustion, but I'm not tired.

Misha's words and my words mix together, running into each other along the wall, and I can't even remember whose are whose anymore. His thoughts and lyrics, my dreams and musings, his anger, and my confusion about everything in my life . . . Misha is everywhere, and I miss him. For a long time, he was my savior.

But Masen makes me feel courage, too.

I don't need him to fill the void Misha left, but I like how he pushes me and expects more. He's a reminder of what I want to feel every day, whether it's with him or on my own. He's taught me that who I am when I'm with him feels too good to sacrifice for the approval of everyone else. The way I dress, the guys I talk to, the games I play . . . it's all plastic, and when I'm with him, I'm gold.

My eyes fall on the list of words I drew over the past couple of weeks.

Alone

Empty

Fraud

Shame

Fear

And below it, I added the line he spoke to me in the back of the truck at the drive-in.

Close your eyes, there's nothing to see out here.

I loved that line. As if everything we needed to know, we couldn't see. It was all inside of us.

I blink at the list, reading them over and over in my head.

Alone, Empty, Fraud, Shame, Fear,

Close your eyes, there's nothing to see out here.

Hmm. I read them again in my head and once more out loud.

It rhymes. Like a song.

Alone, Empty, Fraud, Shame, Fear,

Close your eyes, there's nothing to see out here.

I flip over and study the words again. It's kind of weird how they fit together like that.

Of course, he'd given the words separately, and he never indicated a connection between them, but I knew there was some kind of meaning other than what he was telling me. The first word was at the Cove, not meant for me, after all. I'd had a feeling the words were coming from somewhere specific.

Hopping off my bed, I pull out my desk chair and have a seat, waking up my laptop. Typing the words into the search engine, I hit *Enter* and wait.

Pictures and YouTube videos immediately load onto the screen, and I sit back, scanning the hits to see if it's from a song, and if so, which one. One of the YouTube videos is titled "Pearls," and I click on it.

The video is grainy and dark, but I can see the stage and lights of the small venue, and I hear a crowd shouting and calling out.

And then I peer closer at the guys onstage, not blinking and my heart picking up pace. A band with their drums and guitars, and . . .

Masen?

I breathe harder and faster. *What?*

Everyone is positioned, one guy sitting behind his drums, two others flanking Masen with guitars, and Masen looking casual with a hand in his pocket and no instrument. My blood runs hot, and my chest aches. What the fuck is this?

The song starts, hard and loud, the drummer pounding in steady beats and the crowd jumping up and down as Masen bobs his head. I dart my eyes down, underneath the video, and see the band name.

Cipher Core. He has a band?

The scavenger hunt. *Oh, my God.* I'd thought he was just a guest that night. Some random guy hanging around, but he wasn't. That was his band's event.

My hand shakes as I move the cursor and click on the "Show More" section. The lyrics are written there, and I see Masen close his eyes and hold the microphone on its stand as his smooth, deep voice starts singing the words I'm reading.

A picture is worth a thousand words,
But my thousand words slice deeper.
What doesn't kill us makes us stronger,
Fuck that. I've become a hide and seeker.

Treat others how you want to be treated,
But what if tonight I want to be burned?
You told us it's better to be safe than sorry,
And little sister listened, but I was the one who learned.

Reap, reap, reap, you don't even know,
All you did suffer is what you did sow!
Necessitate, medicate, eradicate, resuscitate.
Swallow your pearls, but for me it was too late.
Alone, Empty, Fraud, Shame, Fear,
Close your eyes. There's nothing to see out here.

Do better, be more, too many, too much,
I'm about to fucking choke, I can't force it down.
So string up the little wisdoms and wrap them 'round my neck,
I'll strangle myself with your pearls of wisdom and die a wreck.

The lyrics ring a bell. I repeat them in my head. *Reap, reap, reap, you don't even know . . .*

Misha and I put those lyrics together. The entire fucking song is Misha's. I remember it, and something terrible and hard curls through me as I stop breathing and read the short bio at the bottom.

**Cipher Core is an American rock band
based out of Thunder Bay.**

A band in Thunder Bay. *No . . .* I swallow, acid bile rising in my throat.

MEMBERS:
Dane Lewis—guitars and backing vocals
Lotus Maynard—bass
Malcolm Weinburg—drums
Misha Lare—lead vocals, guitars

"Oh, my God." I crumble, sinking out of my chair and to the floor, sobbing and shaking my head. "Oh, my God," I cry.

I run my fingers through my hair, holding my head and my chest growing heavy. I suck in short, shallow breaths. I can't breathe.

Masen is Misha. "What the fuck?!" I yell.

The whole time. All this time I've been missing him, worried about him, wondering where the fuck he is and why he hasn't written, and he's been right in front of me the whole time!

I scream, slamming my hands down on the floor and curling my fingers into the carpet.

I can't believe it. He wouldn't do this to me. He wouldn't make a fool out of me and play with me like that.

Shooting up, I wipe my nose with the back of my hand and glare at him on the screen. He finishes the final note, long and languorous, into the microphone, and from the distance in the crowd, I can see him dip his head as if still lost in the song after it's over. People cheer, the last chords of the guitar ringing out, and I hear a couple girls call out for him.

Calling for Misha.

Everything is shaking, and the room is spinning as my mind races.

Masen. Mysterious, quiet Masen who no one knows anything about and who came out of nowhere. The guy who knew I loved *Twilight*, where I lived, and exactly what to get out of my backpack when I had my asthma attack without me telling him.

Oh, my God, how did I not know? I close my eyes, angry tears streaming down my face.

Misha, my best friend who got me into bed and fucked me with a lie.

You have a friend, he'd said earlier.

"No," I whisper to myself, rage building as I slam my laptop closed and leave the room to get my sister's car keys.

I have no friends.

15

Misha

Everything is dark, not a single light shining through any of the windows. My dad has to be home, though. It's pretty late.

I slip my key into the lock, always nervous that I'll find it doesn't work. Of course, my father wouldn't have any reason to keep me out—he never told me to leave, after all—but I'm not really sure he wants me here, either.

Stepping inside, I close the door behind me and stick my keys back into my pocket. A pungent odor hits my nostrils, and I wince, gazing around.

Trepidation creeps in. The house is a mess. My dad was always a neat freak, and with my sister and me helping with chores, we kept a nice house.

But I look around, seeing mail and newspapers on the floor, some laundry on the stairs, and I smell something that's a mixture of old food and dirty clothes.

Walking past the sitting room, I notice a light coming from the living room and peer in, seeing the TV playing. The sound is low, and my father is lying on the recliner in his pajamas and robe. A table full of coffee cups, napkins, and a barely eaten plate of food stands next to his chair.

I walk over and gaze down at his sleeping form, guilt weighing on me. Dane was right. My dad is an active guy. Even after Annie, he still took care of things around here. But I can see the sallow tint to his cheeks and how rumpled his clothes are, like he's worn them for more than a day.

My eyes start to burn, and I suddenly want Ryen.

I need her. I'm scared, and I don't know what to do right now.

I couldn't get back what I needed from Falcon's Well, but I'm not sure I care anymore.

But I don't want to leave yet, either. I want Ryen, but I also feel like if I walked out now and left my father for good, Annie would truly be gone. Any semblance of the life we had before would be a memory.

I lower myself to the ottoman, watching him. His head is turned to the side, and I spy a pill bottle on the table.

I don't have to look to know it's Xanax. My dad's kept it around for years, something to take the edge off when raising two kids by himself got stressful. Honestly, though, I think he started taking it because my mother left. He'd loved her, and she skipped out. No notes, no calls, no contact. She left her kids and never looked back.

I dealt with it, my father buried himself in his kids, work, and hobbies to not think about it, and Annie waited. She always seemed to think our mom would come back and want to see us eventually. She'd be ready for her.

I still feel my sister in this house. As if she's going to walk in the door, sweaty and out of breath from exercising, and barking orders, reminding me that it was my night to cook dinner and telling Dad to throw the clothes in the dryer.

"I miss her, Dad." I speak low and quiet, despair overtaking me. "She called me that night."

I look up at him, wishing he was awake but also glad that he isn't. He knew she'd called me, probably only a minute before she collapsed on the road, but he wouldn't hear any more. He'd fly into a rage because he knew this was my fault.

"I didn't answer, because I was busy," I continue. "I assumed it was something little. You know how she always got on my case for not washing my dishes or stealing her chips?" I smile to myself at the memories. "I thought it was something unimportant, and I'd just call her back in a minute, but I made a mistake."

I let out a breath and close my eyes. If I'd answered . . . I might've gotten to her in time. I might've gotten an ambulance to her before it was too late.

"When I called back she wasn't answering," I say, more to myself, reliving the night in my head as tears build. "I still wake up, frightened out my mind, and for a moment I think that it was all a nightmare. I grab my phone, scared that I missed a call from her."

I bury my head in my hands.

In the weeks that followed Annie's death, my father and I either fought or ignored each other. He blamed me for not being there when she needed me. She'd called me, after all, not him.

And I blamed him, too. If he'd just stopped pushing her and convinced her that our mother was never coming back, she might not have been destroying her body to try to be the perfect student, the perfect athlete, the perfect kid . . . And then her poor body might not have given out on her on that dark, empty road.

If he hadn't popped Xanax when it was convenient, then maybe Annie would never have gotten the idea to put herself on amphetamines to give herself the boost to do more than she should handle and be perfect.

Annie was going to be great. She fought for what she wanted in life. So much wasted talent.

"Sometimes I wish it was me instead, too." I look up, seeing him still asleep.

He'd said that to me one night when we'd gotten in each other's face, and I'd been hurt, despite how I acted like I wasn't. I knew he didn't mean it, but I do know he'd be happier still having the one child of his he had a good relationship with.

With me, what does he have?

But I can't let him go. Annie is in him, she's in this house, and we're her family. We have to stay that way.

"We're never going to have a relationship like you and she had, but I'm here."

I stand up and quietly start clearing off the cluttered table, heading to the kitchen to do the dishes.

Hey," Dane calls, and I look up, seeing him walk back out of the gate at the Cove and head toward me.

"I've been texting you," he says.

"Yeah, I saw." I slam the truck door and reach into the bed of the truck, taking out some boxes.

After cleaning the kitchen at home, I'd opened some windows to air the house out while I threw in a load of laundry, sorted through the mail, took out the garbage, and cleaned up my bedroom. Which is pretty impressive, because I never do that.

I'd covered my dad with a blanket, and hopefully, when I bring groceries home tomorrow, he will be okay with me being back.

I guess I'll find out.

"I've been going over this song you gave me with the guys. We were up until three last night," he tells me. "I think we really got something."

I nod, not really that invested in that right now. My head is in a million other places. I still have no idea how I'm going to fess up to Ryen.

God, she's going to kill me.

Dane walks with me as I head through the parking lot for the gate entrance. "What are you doing?" he asks. "Are you moving back?"

"I'll be home soon," I say. "I just have some stuff to clear up here first."

"Do you need help?"

I jerk my head over my shoulder. "Go grab more boxes if you want."

He runs back and collects the rest of the boxes I took from my garage at home, and we walk through the old park.

I didn't bring much with me when I decided to hide out here, so it won't take long to pack my stuff, but I'm not in a hurry.

I don't really want to leave, but I can't stay here as Masen Laurent anymore—a name I picked out of thin air a month ago when I asked my cousin to help me get my fake driver's license and forge some school records. I just kept my same initials.

Once people—two people, in particular—find out I'm Misha Lare, the jig is up.

And I can't lie to her anymore. Things were never supposed to get this far.

I don't have any friends. Hearing her words and seeing her eyes tonight, that moment when she broke, I hated myself. What is she going to think tomorrow when she finds out her best friend stabbed her in the back and looked her in the eye doing it?

Dane and I climb down the field house stairs, and I head over to the opposite wall, throwing some switches. Lights spark to life, illuminating the long hallways as we make our way straight to the room I've been using.

"I don't know how you slept down here," he mumbles. "It's like a horror movie."

I give a weak laugh. It's definitely creepy, but . . . "I wasn't really thinking a lot back then."

I figured because it's close to Falcon's Well, I probably wouldn't be discovered—or so I thought—and I have good memories of coming to this place with Annie when I was a kid.

I swing into the room, Dane following, and I walk the short distance to the bed table and switch on the light.

"Whoa," Dane says.

"What?" I look up and follow his gaze, but I quickly notice what he's referring to, and I stop breathing for a moment.

Wha—

"What the hell have you been doing in here?"

I turn in a circle, seeing the flood of papers scattered over nearly every inch of the room. Posters are ripped off the walls, my clothes are strewn about, and a table with some candles is tipped over, all of my personals lying on the floor.

I suddenly feel the pulse in my neck throb like the vein is trying to punch through the skin.

"I didn't do this."

I lean down and grab a fistful of the papers off the floor, seeing my name at the bottom of every letter, a couple of them a year or two old, and one from grade school. I can tell, because I signed my name *Mish* during an asinine spell to sound less girly.

These were all letters that were sent to Ryen. She's had them. How did—

Something tightens around my stomach, and I wince, knowing there's no other way these letters got here.

"What's that say?"

I sway, off-balance, but I look up, following where he points. On the wall, written with a can of black spray paint, are huge letters glaring down at us.

YOU TRICK ME? WATCH YOUR BACK, WAIT, AND SEE.

"Oh, shit." I can barely fucking move. It's a lyric from one of my old songs Ryen helped me write.

I dive down to the shelf on my bedside table, seeing that the few items that were stashed in there are pulled out. I grab the pocket folder where I kept some of her letters—my favorite ones that I reread—but as soon as I pick it up, I already feel the weightlessness of it.

"No, no, no, no . . ." I flip open the top and look inside.

"What is it?"

"Fuck!" I growl. Every single one of them gone. I fling the folder away from me. "Shit!"

"What? Who?"

Jesus Christ. I shoot up and run my hands up and down my face. She knows who I am, she found her letters, and she took them back.

I spin around and run out the door.

"Misha!" Dane yells.

But I don't stop. I race for the stairs, run up to the main floor, and dash outside, speeding through the park.

She'll listen to me. She'll understand. All this wasn't meant to happen.

I dig in my jeans for my keys and climb in my truck, charging out of the park and onto the highway.

The letters. Goddammit! Knowing Ryen's temper, they're probably shredded at the bottom of a garbage disposal right now. *Fuck!*

I grip the steering wheel, rubbing my eyes with my other hand. The road is blurry, and I try to calm my breathing.

Those letters are everything. They're her and me, kids just trying to figure themselves out and going through all our growing pains. They're where I first started to fall for her and need her. They're my fucking songs and a part of me.

Our history is in those letters. Every beautiful thing she ever said to me to tilt my world on its side.

My stomach rolls. If they're gone, so help me God . . .

And if Ryen won't hear me out, I don't know what I'll do.

After ten minutes, I'm finally parking on the street in front of her house. I kill the car and jump out, running up to her front door.

The house is dark and quiet, which is expected at one in the morning. But when I lift the flowerpot, the key is missing. I curl my fists.

I round the house, checking windows to see if they lift, but then I spot a ladder propped up on the side of the house and stop. Gazing up, I see no light coming through Ryen's window.

Fuck it. If she's not there I'll wait.

I start climbing.

Making my way up the ladder, I step onto the roof and walk over to her window. The room is pitch black, but I hear music, "True Friends" by Bring Me the Horizon, playing, and I don't hesitate. Lifting the window, I swing a leg in and bow down, sliding in.

And I immediately feel her.

Standing upright again, I hear an intake of breath and turn, spotting her dark form sitting with her knees bent up in the corner of the room.

She shoots off the ground and charges for me. "Get out."

I take in her red and wet eyes, her rumpled sleep shorts and tank top with teardrops soaking through the pink fabric, and her hair hanging in a mess around her. She looks like she's been crying for hours.

But still, that temper of hers is there.

I step toward her. "Where are the letters?"

"Get fucked!" she bursts out. "I burned the letters!"

I whip around and slam my hand into the wall.

"Stop!" she whispers. "My mom will hear you!"

"I don't give a shit," I say, turning around and getting in her face. "You belong to me more than you ever did to them."

She shakes her head, eyes filling with tears again. "How could you do this? I was supposed to trust you, and this whole time, you were right here, watching me. You ruined everything!"

"I didn't come to Falcon's Well for you," I shout back, bearing down on her. "But believe me, I'm not sorry. What a waste of time you were all these years. Now I know."

She chokes on a sob. "Get out."

But I can't leave.

I never thought I'd make Ryen Trevarrow cry, but both times I have, it's been in the past two weeks.

We kept writing because we needed each other, because we made the other one's life better. But even after knowing her for years, it took no time for me to break what we had.

We were perfect for each other.

Until we met.

I realize now as I'm staring into her angry eyes that hold a pain she's trying to shield from me that there is so much more to her than what was in her letters. And so much in her letters that she let me see and no one else. I want it all.

"You're so selfish," she cries softly. "You take and take and take, and you didn't even think of me, did you? I was never real to you."

The despair in her eyes comes through, and hatred winds its way under my skin. I hate that she's looking at me like I'm one of them.

Walking toward her, I force her back against the wall and pull my shirt over my head, clutching it in my hand.

She stares at me, confused. "What the hell are you doing?"

"Look." I hold her eyes, willing her to look at my body. We were too consumed at the drive-in, and in bed this morning I was behind her, so she hasn't gotten a good look.

I light up my phone and hold it up, illuminating my skin.

Her eyes drop, looking hesitant, but slowly she starts letting her gaze drift over me. And I know exactly what she's seeing.

Her eyes fall over the cassette tape high on my torso, musical notes stringing out of it, and the label on the tape reading THE HAND THAT RULES THE WORLD. It was a play on words from a poem Ryen quoted in a letter once when she was encouraging me to start a band.

Her gaze trails down to the small black birds taking flight on the side of my stomach and over my hip. Words float along with the art, reading, *And flights of angels sing thee to thy rest*. It's from *Hamlet*, Ryen's favorite Shakespeare play. I got the tattoo after Annie died.

She takes my phone and slowly circles me, shining the light and taking in my chest and back, the Pearls of Wisdom down my arm—another letter about our parents—the decaying heart on my shoulder, stitched up down the middle and reconnecting the words "You're My Tribe"—inspired by her words, which even led to a song I wrote. And then there're the countless other little quotes and designs, the scenes of things we talked about, dreamed of, and laughed over.

I wasn't covered, and I didn't have full sleeves going on, but it was a lot to take in. And almost all of it, she was the root of.

She comes around my front again, her breath shaking and her eyes glistening with tears.

"You were the only thing that was real to me," I tell her.

She looks at me like she has no idea how to process all this. I mean, really. What did I expect? Even tomorrow, when I meant to tell her everything, how was I planning on doing that? Was there any way for her to find this out in a way she was going to understand?

"Misha?" she whispers, and all of a sudden she's scanning me up and down, looking at me like she's finally seeing me.

I take the phone from her and slip it in my pocket. Moving in, I bring my hands up to hold her face, but she flinches.

I immediately drop them. "You have to listen."

"Ryen?" someone calls, knocking on the door.

It's a woman. Probably her mother.

"Get rid of her," I whisper.

Ryen blinks up at me, wiping her eyes. "Ye . . . yes?" she stammers, calling out. "I'm in bed."

"Okay," her mom says. "I thought I heard the TV or something. It's late. You need sleep."

"Okay, good night."

I pull the shirt back on and lower my voice, hearing her mother's door close.

"I never intended to let it get this far," I explain. "I had business here, and I wanted . . ." I trail off, searching for the right words, because I'm scared. "Part of me couldn't resist being this close to you. I think part of me needed you. I never thought we would speak again after the scavenger hunt. I didn't want to ruin what we had, but then I came here and . . ."

She runs her hands up and down her face, starting to cry again, and I can tell I'm losing her.

"But then you steal my shit," I keep going, "and I see you harassing Cortez. And then you try to fuck with me in the lunchroom, and one thing leads to another, and we were constantly in each other's faces. It was like . . . It was like, even if we'd never been pen pals, we still would've found each other, you know?"

"Why didn't you tell me?" she cries. "At any time you could've said, 'Hey, I'm Misha!'" She shakes her head, glaring at me. "I kissed you. I went to bed with you! The whole time you knew me, and I had no idea. You humiliated me! You've been right here in front of me this whole time. Do you have any idea how fucking creepy that is?"

"I had no reason to tell you!" I growl in a near whisper. "I didn't even know if I liked you anymore that first day! And I definitely had no reason to trust you. You were a snotty little brat, and you know it. Why did *you* lie to me?" I scowl. "Why did I think, for seven years, that you were strong and fucking nice? Someone who has balls and stands up for herself?"

Her shoulders shake, and little gasps escape as she struggles to breathe. I quickly look around, angry and guilty at the same time. Seeing an inhaler on her desk, I grab it and hand it to her, but she knocks it out of my hand.

"I lied about the people in my life and the parts of me I fake for others," she explains. "Everything else was true. The movies and the music, my ideas and my dreams, everything else was true. The rest wasn't important."

"I trusted you, too," I point out. "I believed in you."

"I'm everything I said I was."

"You can *say* whatever you want," I retort. "Doesn't make it true."

Her head falls, and she inhales shaky breaths through her nose, clearly trying to calm herself and get her body under control. The inhaler lies on the floor. I wish she'd just take the fucking thing. She's making me nervous.

"I was the real me when I wrote you those letters," she says quietly. "I was everything I wanted to be."

And I can understand that. There are definitely some minor things I haven't told her, because I wanted to be free with her, like I can't be at home. But she has to know that, even though what I did was crazy and things got way out of hand, it hurt me, too, to be tricked. To find that the person you care about and hold on a pedestal is shallow and mean to the rest of the world.

"And when you would write me," I ask her, "telling me to stand up to my dad, believe in myself, stay true with no regrets . . . Why would you tell me those things when you didn't follow them yourself?"

She looks away, but I don't back off. I stare at her, holding her hostage. *Why preach to me all the things you didn't have the courage to do yourself?*

"Hmm?" I prod, dipping my head down to meet her eyes.

"Because . . ." she whispers, avoiding my eyes. "Because you want good things for the people you"—she breathes fast, barely whispering—"love."

I suck in a sharp breath. God, what is she doing to me?

I'd give anything—anything—to have her in my arms right now.

I reach for her, cupping her face, my mouth less than an inch from hers. "Ryen, please . . ."

The tears and quiet sobs start again, and I try to comfort her, but she pushes me away. "Oh, God, get out," she cries, holding up her hands to keep me away. "I can't look at you right now. I can't wrap my head around this. I feel sick."

"Ryen, please," I beg, feeling the ache in my chest spread. "I love you—"

"Oh, God!" she cuts me off. "Get out!"

I wince, my eyes burning with tears. I feel like my heart is ripping apart.

I watch as she buries her head in her hands and stands there, breaking in two.

There's no way I can go back and change this. While she may have been vile to others, she was always a good friend to me, and I can't say the same. She aggravated me and pissed me off, but I broke this. I'm responsible.

I bend down and pick up the inhaler, putting it on the desk in case she needs it.

And then I climb back out through the window and head back to the Cove. I'm not going home.

I'm not going anywhere until she's mine.

16

Ryen

"Where were you this morning?" Ten asks, a hint of worry in his voice. "Lyla said you skipped practice."

I walk down the hall at school with him beside me, having left myself barely enough time to hit my locker and race upstairs to Art before first period starts. He walks at my side.

"I was tired." I pull my baseball cap down a little farther to shield my red eyes.

"You slept in?" His tone is confused. "Coach is going to make you run laps for that."

I'm sure he's right. But I can't bring myself to care right now.

While I showered, blew out my hair, and put on makeup this morning, my brain kept drifting back to Misha, and I started tearing up again. I couldn't keep mascara on, so I gave up and grabbed a hat.

My eyes burn, and my lids just want to close forever. I blink hard at the shot of pain digging into my skull between my eyes and clutch the strap of my bag tighter, hoping against hope that he isn't here today. If I can't think about him without crying, I certainly can't look at him.

Veering toward my locker on the right, I spot a group of students ahead, some pausing to read something on the wall and some taking pictures of it. I look up, immediately recognizing the Eminem lyric.

Needles prick my throat, and I look away. He can go screw himself. He doesn't like that rapper, and even though I do, quoting his songs isn't going to get him on my good side.

"Well, well, well," Ten muses. "I thought he got caught or something. He's been slacking on the messages."

I walk up to my locker and start dialing in the combination. Ten follows, fiddling on his phone.

"'Love the Way You Lie' by Eminem," he says. "Hey, he's speaking your language now."

I force a little smile for Ten's sake. He's the only one in my life who's easy, and I don't want him to know anything is wrong. Our friendship is uncomplicated.

And in all honesty, he's been good to me. I may not be sure where his loyalties truly lie, but he's here now. I'm grateful for that.

I empty my bag, stuffing in the books I took home over the weekend and pulling out what I need for the morning. I haven't seen or talked to Misha since our fight, and I'm still in shock. I'm angry, but I'm sad, too. I would've thought that the reality of Masen being Misha would've set in by now and crystallized into hatred.

But it hasn't. I'm hurt.

"Are you okay?" Ten asks, hovering close, his eyes on my face. "You look like you were up all night, *not* sleeping in."

"I'm fine."

I finish getting my things and close my locker, Ten and I walking farther down the hall. But then I glance up and notice more writing on the wall.

EVERYTHING WAS REAL.

I suck in a small breath, feeling my chest shake with a sob. It's in large strokes of black paint, surrounded by messy paint streaks of blue—my favorite color—and purple. I stop and stare at it, my shoulders feeling heavy.

He broke into the school this weekend and did this.

"What's wrong with you?" Ten whispers, this time sounding more concerned. "Tell me the truth."

I wipe away a tear before it has a chance to fall. "Nothing," I say, forcing my voice to stay even. "My sister's just harassing me about mixing whites and colors in the wash again, so, you know . . ."

He scoffs, but I can tell he doesn't buy that excuse.

I make a quick right into the stairwell. "I'll see you at lunch, okay?"

"Ryen?"

But I keep going, jogging up the stairs and pausing briefly when I see yet another message written on the wall, reading it as I pass by.

I DIDN'T MEAN TO LIE, BUT I MEANT EVERY KISS.

Damn him. I break into a run.

I shouldn't have come to school today. I hoped he'd gone back to Thunder Bay, but he must've painted those messages last night. There are too many people in the school over the weekend and too much of a chance the staff or janitors would've gotten all of it taken down by this morning if he'd done it earlier than that.

No. He was still in Falcon's Well last night.

I want him gone. I can't help my heart and what it wants despite the pain, but I can help what I do with those feelings. Everything I told him—about Misha and how he didn't like my music and the stuff at the drive-in and all the things he wanted to know that were true—he already knew all of that shit from my letters. What a kick, to sit there and humor me to get my clothes off.

I approach the door and arch up on my tiptoes, peering in the window. He's sitting at his seat, one earbud in his ear while he twirls a pen in his fingers and stares at a notebook.

I slump back down.

Great. You would think he could back off, at least for a while. It's not like he needs to be at school anymore anyway. Misha had written me last fall and told me that he had enough credits to graduate early, so if he didn't come here for me, then why the hell is he playing student when he doesn't need to?

Why is he really here?

I whip open the door and make my way down the aisle, trying not to look at him but already feeling his eyes on me.

He's all I'm aware of, and the memory of the physics lab suddenly hits me, the feel of my legs wrapped around his body and his piercing between my lips.

He can't be here. I can't do this. Tears spring to my eyes.

But then someone standing in the aisle suddenly turns toward me, and something wet and orange slams into me, covering my hands and T-shirt.

"Ugh!" I growl, inspecting my hands and clothes.

Manny Cortez scurries backward, taking his freshly painted clay bowl with him. "I'm sorry!" he exclaims, looking scared.

"You're gonna be," I threaten, pointing behind him. "The kiln's that way, moron. Do you need a map?"

He winces, his eyes dropping as others around him laugh. My stomach rolls, and I grind my teeth together to hold back the sob as I push past him and charge toward my seat in the back.

He walks away, diving into the supply room.

Dropping my bag, I sit in my seat and pull out my sketch pad and pencils. Misha's presence is heavy next to me.

"Yeah, I know," I bite out, not looking at him. "I'm a vile bitch, right?"

"No," he says quietly, staring ahead. "Just weak and stupid. And

I'd tear you apart in front of this whole school if I wasn't so sure you already feel like a pile of shit inside."

I crack, my chin trembling.

"All right, let's get started!" Ms. Till says.

But my stomach is shaking with sobs I can't let out. He's right. This is who I am.

And we both know it.

"Ryen, are you ready to talk about your project and where you are on it?" Till asks.

But I just pick at my thumbnail as my hands rest on the desk in front of me. Everything on the table is turning blurry.

I lashed out at Manny because he's an easy target. Because he's weaker than me. Because he's the *only* thing weaker than me. Everyone else sees through me, and Misha is disgusted by me. He hates me.

"Ryen?"

Who I am and how no one likes me isn't Misha's fault. I did this. I'm stupid, weak, and a waste.

I feel tears welling, and I choke on a sob. Reaching down, I grab my bag and hook it over my shoulder as I walk through the class, avoiding stares and hushed whispers as I leave the room.

"Ryen?"

But as soon as I hit the hallway, I let the tears loose and run to the bathroom.

Where have you been?" Lyla charges as she walks up to my side in the lunch line. "You weren't at practice this morning, and Ten said he saw you before first period, but then no one's seen you since then. And rumor has it you broke down crying in Art?"

Her tone sounds disgusted, and I don't spare her a look as I grab a salad shaker and a packet of dressing. I'm not hungry, and my limbs are tired and heavy, but I can't hide out in the library any-more. I feel like I'm losing everything, and I need to stand the fuck up and get over it.

"Trey got in major trouble this weekend," she says as if it's my fault.

Well, I guess it is, although she can't know that.

"All of us, including the whole team," she continues, "went to his house after the game Friday night. His stepmom went upstairs, came back down, and kicked everyone out."

Her voice grates on my ears.

But she keeps pushing. "Which you might've known if you were ever around anymore."

"I don't care," I grit out, turning to her, unable to control my-self. "You got that? And I'm sick of you thinking that I should. Now, leave me alone."

She rears back, giving me a WTF look, and then narrows her eyes, looking angry. "You want to be left alone?" she asks. "I can do that. We can *all* do that, because we're sick of your shit." Her eyes fall down my body, surveying me like I'm a piece of crap. "Always disappearing, treating Trey like crap . . . and don't think it's es-caped anyone's attention all the little looks you and Masen Laurent are giving each other. If you want to play with that piece of trash, do it quietly, because I'm not going to act like I like it."

I squeeze the plastic shaker in my hand and take a step, advanc-ing on her. *Bitch.*

But then a guy steps between us, Misha's friend with the Mo-hawk, and grabs a grape out of a fruit bowl. He pops it in his mouth, looking at Lyla. "Hey, baby. Wanna fuck?"

She grimaces, and I nearly snort. What the hell?

Her mouth falls open as she stares at Mohawk guy, but then she spins around—probably having lost her train of thought—and storms back to wherever she came from.

Mohawk guy turns to me, winks, and then leaves.

What was that about?

I run a hand over my eyes, adjusting my baseball cap, and feel a sudden need to crawl in a hot shower and sit there for a year.

Turning back to the lunch line, I see Misha on my other side and jump, my heart skipping a beat.

"I need to talk to you," he says.

I move around him and continue down the line. "I don't want you here, Masen." And then I stop, correcting myself. "Misha. Just go home. Go back to Thunder Bay."

"I can't." He comes up behind me, placing his hands on the counter, blocking me in. "I have no life there if you're not in it. You're part of everything good I've ever done, Ryen. Please."

People come up in the line and veer around us, continuing down to the cashier. I want to push away from him, but I can feel eyes on us already, and I don't want to make a scene. Maybe I'm being paranoid, but I know better. Lyla is taking note of everything I do.

"You're in the music." His low voice falls across my ear. "You've made me strong. I won't do anything with my life if you're not there. I'm sorry. I never meant for any of this—"

"You broke my heart," I cut him off, turning around and looking up into his eyes. "I look at you, and I don't see Misha." Sadness burns my eyes, and I don't care if he can see. "All the years, all the letters, it's getting further from my memory now. Like Friday night clouded everything."

His stare narrows.

"You tainted it all," I tell him. "All the history. And soon, I'll barely remember you or how we used to be friends."

I leave my food and push his arm away, walking over to where Ten sits.

I don't know if everything I said to Misha right then was true, but my head is in a constant fog. My feelings are clouded, and maybe I just need a long nap, a long swim, or a long drive to clear my head.

All I do know is that I can't look at him. Hell, I don't even think I can look at myself right now.

I sit down at the table and snatch one of Ten's fries, nibbling just so I can do something.

"What about your parents?" J.D. asks Trey, obviously in the middle of a conversation.

"It's better to ask forgiveness than permission, right?"

"What are you guys talking about?" I ask.

Trey looks at me, and I can feel the chill in his body language. "I'm having a party, remember?" His tone is clipped. "My parents are out of town for the night, but they didn't say I couldn't have people over. I don't suppose you'll still be able to make it."

He says it as if he already knows the answer, and I hear Lyla and Katelyn snicker.

A party. I look over my shoulder, seeing Misha plop down in a seat with all of his friends, and I don't miss the glare he shoots my way.

"Will there be drinks?" I ask, turning back to my table.

"Of course. Lots of drinks." Trey smirks.

"Well, then. Maybe that's just what I'm looking for."

He smiles, and Ten slaps the bill of my cap, joking around. "Hells, yeah."

Ten and I tread over the Burroweses' lawn, past the driveway and the street, which are already packed. Visions of the last time I was here make my heart pick up pace, and I feel a little weird walking into the house.

Why did Misha need to search this place the other night? Why is he in Falcon's Well? I was so consumed with the revelation this weekend and dealing with my bullshit meltdowns that I didn't actually think about why he's here. I was too busy feeling betrayed.

What had he said? Something about coming here for something and then we were in each other's faces constantly, and things just got out of hand, one thing led to another, blah, blah, blah . . .

Yeah. Ten and I took his things at the Cove, and I was the one to go up and harass him in the lunchroom that first day, but he was still here in the first place. Knowing I was here, too. And hiding in plain sight. The second I kissed him in the truck at the car wash, he should've come clean.

"Shit, look at all the people here." Ten laughs as we walk in.

The floor is flooded with our classmates, crowded into the living room and trailing up the stairs, and I look beyond, out onto the patio, and see the pool and deck packed, as well. People are dancing and drinking, and music blares from speakers set up around the room.

Lots of distraction.

I wear my bikini under my jean shorts and shirt, even though I'm not really planning on getting in the pool. But Ten said he might, and I'm not leaving his side, so . . .

I'm trying not to think about Trey being a piece-of-shit pervert or about Lyla and how she would be thrilled to see me fall off my pedestal tonight. If I stay with Ten, maybe I'll have a drink, dance and laugh, and get sedated long enough to forget the last few weeks for just five damn minutes. I need this. I need to do something to feel normal again.

"I doubt he's going to make it to prom, girl," Ten tells me. "If his parents haven't taken it away already, they will after this."

"I'm not worried." I don't even know if I'm going anymore, and I'm definitely not going with Trey.

We trail outside and hook ourselves up with a couple of beers from the keg, but when Ten lifts a bottle of tequila, I push it back down.

"Nope." I shake my head.

"Why?"

"I'm driving," I remind him. "You go for it. I'll stick with a beer."

He shrugs and pours a dram into the little plastic cup. I wince, smelling the pungent odor. I've done tequila before, but that isn't chilled. How can he do that?

He licks the salt off his hand, tips the shot back, and gives a little grimace before sticking a lemon wedge in his mouth.

I laugh. I've known him long enough to know he usually likes his liquor mixed with Coke or juice or something.

"Come on!" He pulls me along. "Let's dance."

I smile, taking my beer and feeling a little better already as he leads me over to where the music is. "Dirty Little Secret" plays, and the warmth hitting my stomach from the beer filters through my limbs, as I sip my drink and join everyone else, getting lost in the noise and excitement.

Over the next hour, we do nothing but dance. He replaces my empty cup with a water bottle and another beer, and I double check to make sure he's the one who poured it. The slight buzz I had from the first one has smoothed away the edges, but I think it's more the music and the energy of everyone around us that's intoxicating.

We jump up and down, laughing and dancing, and Ten leans into my ear. "You feel better now?"

I nod, shouting over the music, "Yes! A lot more relaxed, actually."

"Yeah, they say alcohol isn't the answer, but it's nice to be able to turn off your brain for a little while."

I finish my drink and toss my cup away, grabbing a bottle of water to drink for the rest of the night as Ten joins me at the bar.

"Another one?" I chirp, pouring him a shot.

He smiles, shooting it back without the salt and lemon this time.

I lean into him, smelling his heady cologne. It feels kind of good to be there for him for a change.

I keep everyone—my friends, my sister, my mom—at a distance, because I started to believe that no one could really like me for me. That's why I had to change. And any attention my family or Ten gave me was simply them pretending.

That's why I loved Misha so much. It wasn't distant. It was close and real, and it felt good.

But good things are still around me, despite what I've done to keep them at arm's length. They've been around me the whole time.

Ten pulls away and picks up the bottle again, grabbing the shaker and turning around to look at me. He studies me up and down, twisting his lips to the side.

"What?" I ask.

He jerks his chin at me, a smile playing on his lips. "Spread your legs."

Huh?

"Come on," he teases, shaking the salt. "I want to see what you taste like."

I snort, widening my eyes. "Absolutely not."

"Pleeeease?"

"No!" I burst out, nearly laughing at his sad face.

No way in hell! I am *not* doing that.

Not a chance.

17

Misha

Malcolm beats through the fill, the kick drum vibrating under my feet, and Dane eases in, playing the transition while I keep time on the guitar, backed up by Lotus.

Belting out the lyrics, I feel a high hit me as I close my eyes.

Bookmark it, says the cheerleader
I promise we'll come back to this spot.
I have shit to do first. You won't wait a lot.

I can't make her stay,
And I can't watch her go.
I'll keep her hellfire heart,
And bookmark it 'fore it goes cold.

Malcolm is razor, keeping the energy up, and sweat glides down my back as I savor the rush of playing again. Sticks, a favorite Thunder Bay hangout, has been closed for renovations for over a month, but the owners are still great about letting us use the space when we need to practice without an audience.

Dane's guitar whines as he cuts off the note and stops playing. "All right, stop, stop, stop!" he interrupts. "I think we should break it up at the point, add a riff." He points to Malcolm at the drums. "You back me up with something creative, before we dive back in with vocals."

"Keep it high-energy," I say.

But he just sneers at me, like *duh*. "Yeah, I know what you like."

"All right, count it off," Lotus calls out, but I hold up my hand, pulling the guitar strap over my head.

"I need a drink."

I step off the stage and walk to one of the tables, taking a swig out of the water bottle.

A girl stands behind the bar—one of the owner's daughters, I think—her chin resting on her hand as she looks at me. She's about my age. Maybe a year younger.

She looks like Annie. Blond hair, pert nose, slender shoulders . . . Annie never listened to me play, though. She wasn't unsupportive. She was just too busy to take an interest. Of course, I could say the same thing about myself and her hobbies. The only reason I attended as many girls' volleyball games as I did was because she asked me to be there. She needed people to be proud of her, and I knew why.

The girl smiles at me, and I smile back and then quickly look away.

There was a time when she might've been my type. Cute, soft, sweet. But just the memory of Ryen's nervous breath across my lips before she kissed me that first time in the truck has my body stirring. She's a complicated, temperamental little mess, but she gets me going.

I pick up my phone and check to see if I have any messages. I'm hoping for anything. A rant. Insults. A bitchy text, telling me to fuck off.

But nothing. I know I should leave her alone and give her space. There are just so many things yet to say, so much she doesn't know, and I need to tell her before she pushes me away for good.

Maybe she'll meet me. Tomorrow at my house, and I can tell

her everything. I don't want to ambush her, but maybe she'll give me a chance if I open myself up and lay everything on the line.

Clicking my Instagram app, I type in her name and go to her profile, deciding I'll just send her a message and leave the ball in her court. I have to try. If she doesn't go for it, then I'll wait for as long as I need to.

But when her profile pops up, I see a video she's tagged in, and I hesitate. Without giving myself time to think, I click on it, noticing it was posted only a few minutes ago.

Ryen is standing by a pool, surrounded by people drinking and dancing, with one of her thighs turned out as some guy kneels between her legs.

What the fuck?

I watch as he dives in, licking a long stroke up the inside of her thigh, as she breaks into laughter and everyone cheers.

The asshole has his back to the camera, tips back a shot as the crowd eggs him on, and Ryen laughs, sticking a lemon wedge in her mouth and inviting him in to suck it from her.

The music is blaring, and Ryen wraps her arms around him, their mouths touching before she breaks away and starts shaking her body to the music.

"Son of a bitch." I squeeze the phone in my hand, scrolling the comments to see the party is at Trey's house. She's at his house?

And people are sharing this video of some guy licking her, too.

"What's up?" Dane asks.

I grab my keys off the table and stuff the cell in my pocket. How the fuck is she at a party at that asshole's house, and who the hell is she screwing off with?

"Let's go," I bark at the guys.

"Where?"

"I'll explain in the truck."

I head through the pool hall, hearing them put their instruments down and run after me. Once outside, I hop in the cab.

Dane climbs in the passenger side, and Lotus and Malcolm jump in the bed behind us.

Firing up the engine, I speed away from Sticks and hop onto the highway. I lay on the gas, determined to make the thirty-mile drive in ten minutes. Is she actually drinking at his house? She has to know how stupid that is.

She wants to party? Fine. She wants some space? Okay. But going anywhere near that asshole or being entertainment for some horny little shit who wants to touch her is pushing me too far. Ryen doesn't do fucking body shots. She's trying to piss me off, and it's working.

And I think of Annie and what she did to herself, because she wasn't thinking straight, either.

By the time we make it to Trey Burrowes' house, I'm more worked up than I've ever been, but I know if I go in there half-cocked, she'll just fight back, and I'll walk out of there without her.

We climb out of the truck, and I can feel the vibrations of the music out to the street. "Bad Girlfriend" plays, and I glance around, seeing the houses all a good distance away from each other, but some of them have to be able to hear this noise. I'm tempted to call the cops myself, if they haven't been called already, just to break it up and send Ryen home. But no. I'll let her choose.

As we walk into the house, a group of girls runs past us to the stairs, laughing and falling into the wall as they stumble up the steps.

"Nice." Lotus laughs, making like he's going to follow them.

But I grab his black ponytail and pull him back. We're not here for that.

"Hey, man." J.D. comes up, shaking my hand. "I'm glad you're here. You going to set off some fireworks?"

I laugh to myself, knowing he knows I would rather swallow needles than be in this house. "I wasn't planning on it. Have you seen Ryen?"

He shakes his head. "Not in the last fifteen minutes." And then he narrows his eyes on me. "You going to tell me what's going on between you two?"

"No."

He snorts. "Okay." And then he moves around me toward the family room. "I'll be close. If you need me."

I nod and look back at the party, scanning the crowd as we step down into the living room.

"Well, well, well," Trey says, stepping through the crowd and approaching me. "What the fuck do we have here?"

He's flanked by a couple of his friends, and I steel my spine, keeping my expression hard as I stare at him.

"You want trouble?" he says. "We can give you trouble."

I feel my bandmates inch in closer, and Trey's eyes flash to them as if finally realizing I'm not alone.

"Not in my parents' house, though," he clarifies, suddenly nervous.

Enough. "Where's Ryen?" I demand.

He laughs. "Have you checked in one of the rooms upstairs? Little cocktease had some liquor tonight, so she might finally be giving up that pussy. I can't wait for my turn."

I lunge out and grab him by the collar of his T-shirt, both of our crews moving in.

But I catch sight of something to my left, and I look down, seeing a cuff wrapped around Trey's wrist.

And on the cuff, secured by two straps, is an antique Jaeger-LeCoultre timepiece.

My heart pounds in my ears. "Where the hell did you get that watch?"

His eyebrows dig in, and I shake him, feeling a thick swell of bile rise in my throat. He didn't get it from her. She wouldn't have given it to him. *No.*

"Misha!" someone calls. But I ignore them.

All I see is Trey.

"Misha?" someone murmurs. "Who's Misha?"

The music is still going, but I stare at him, feeling more people start to crowd around us.

I push him away, releasing him as I tighten my fists. She gave it to *him*?

"Leave," Ryen orders, appearing at my side.

I jerk my eyes to her and stare down, hovering. "Don't talk and don't move," I bite out, taking in her tits, plain as day in her bikini top and off-the-shoulder shirt that hangs on her like a shredded piece of fucking Kleenex. "You're all over Instagram, shaking your ass and doing body shots. I'm not happy."

Her eyes go wide, shock and anger flaring. "Excuse me?" she yells as a couple of girls giggle.

But I turn back around, advancing on Trey. "Where the fuck did you get that watch?"

"What's your problem?" he snarls. "Go fuck yourself!"

I rear back and punch him across the face, knocking him to the ground. The whole place erupts as his friends and my friends go for each other and partygoers scream and jump out of the way. I dive down and dig my keys out of my pocket, unsheathing the knife on my key chain and leaning over Trey. Everyone above me goes crazy, and I grab Trey's wrist as he winces from the pain in his face.

"Get off me!" He tries to yank his arm away from me.

But I slide the dull knife between the watch strap and his wrist and pull hard, slicing it off his arm.

"Misha!" I hear Ryen call, and I stand up as everyone stumbles around me.

"Everyone stop now!" a deep male voice bellows from behind. "Turn off the music!"

I look behind me, seeing two cops in black uniforms enter the house, one of them holding his hands around his mouth and shouting.

Shit. I guess someone did report the noise. The whole crowd scurries, running out the sliding glass doors or into the kitchen, where there's probably a back door.

I shove the watch and key chain at Dane. "Take my truck. Get the guys and go!"

He grabs the stuff from me and alerts Lotus and Malcolm as the two cops busy themselves, trying to stop kids from leaving. My friends dive out the back and disappear, while I stand still, looking over and seeing Ryen, surprised she's still here.

Her cheeks are flushed, but her eyes are steady on me. She doesn't look drunk.

Why did I let Trey bait me like that? Ryen wouldn't do something as reckless as get wasted and follow someone upstairs. I was just looking for a reason to hit him.

And then I look at the guy standing behind her and notice that it's Ten. It takes a moment, but I finally make the connection. Blond hair, blue shirt . . . He's the guy from the video.

Dammit. So I charged over here to beat up a guy who's probably more attracted to me than to Ryen. Great.

"Hey!" Trey shouts, standing up. "He stole my watch!"

I stay rooted in place, but I take out my phone and shoot a text to Dane that I'll probably be arrested. He'll know what to do.

The music cuts off, and a cop comes around, standing between Trey and me.

"What are you doing here, son?" he asks me.

"Just partying."

"He has my watch," Trey grits out.

But I just shrug. "Search me. I don't have anything."

Trey comes in close, invading my space and glaring at me, but the cop pushes him back. "You're in enough trouble," he tells him. "Stand back."

But Trey is a wall. He doesn't come closer, but he stays rooted.

"He wasn't invited, he started a fight, and he stole my watch," he says again.

My lips lift in a small smile.

The cop looks to me. "What's your name?"

"I don't know."

"Where do you live?"

"I forget," I answer, still staring at Trey.

I hear the cop breathing hard, turning angry. I don't want to be difficult, but Dickwad can't know who I am. I don't want Misha Lare on the radar in this town. Not yet.

"Put your hands behind your back," he orders.

I do as I'm told, and he moves around to put handcuffs on me.

"Wait, no!" Ryen argues.

But I look at her, softening my expression. "It's fine. Don't say anything."

Don't tell them who I am.

"All right, I'm taking this one in," the officer tells the other cop, who's busy on his walkie-talkie. "Clear this out and call Mr. and Mrs. Burrowes."

The other officer nods and gets back on his radio.

The cop leads me out of the house, and I look at Ryen. There's a million things I want to say.

I'm done here. I'm going home.

I'll be anything you want, even gone if that's what you need.

I love you.

But I just shoot my eyes up to Ten and tell him, "Make sure she gets home safe."

An hour later I'm sitting in the police station, no longer handcuffed. I lean back in one of the chairs against the wall, my legs stretched out and crossed at the ankle, and my arms folded over my chest. A female cop is talking on the phone behind the counter, and I tap my finger under my arm, playing the tune we were working on at Sticks tonight in my head.

At least I got the watch back. I got both of what I came here for, so I should be happy.

Unfortunately, though, those things that seemed so important three weeks ago seem kind of trivial now.

"Why did he have your watch?" I hear someone ask.

I jerk, startled, and look up. Ryen leans on the corner next to my chair, probably having just come down the hallway from the entrance.

"That was the watch you were looking for, right?" she presses.

"How did you get here?" I sit up. "You didn't drive, did you?"

"I'm sober," she answers. "Now answer the question. What are you doing? What's going on?"

I face forward again, leaning back in my chair.

I know I need to stop dodging, and I have no reason not to tell her, but where do I start? I want her to understand, but I also want to know if we can make it back to where we were in our letters and to where we were when I was Masen. I want to get there without her pity.

"You want me to trust you," she points out, "but you're still keeping things from me."

I turn to her, opening my mouth to speak, but just then, three guys come down the hallway and enter the station, stopping when they see me.

I move to stand up, but my cousin pushes me back down.

"I'm sorry, man," I rush out, hating that he had to come all the way down here.

But Will just smiles at me. "Getting arrested is a Thunder Bay boy's rite of passage," he jokes, beaming with pride.

I roll my eyes. Will's two friends, Michael Crist and Kai Mori, stand behind him, looking amused.

I guess they would know. A few years ago, they reigned over my hometown when they were high school basketball heroes, and they haven't left the limelight since. Simply exchanging notoriety for infamy.

Will crosses his arms over his chest, giving me a condescending look. "You should've been able to get out of this yourself, you know?" he chastises. "Watch and learn."

He turns around, all three of them heading to the counter, no doubt with their best smiles on their faces.

Ryen shifts to my left, but we both remain quiet.

"Hi, I'm William Grayson III," Will says to the female cop. "Officer Webber, is it?" She darts her eyes between him and the other two, looking on guard.

"My grandfather is Senator Grayson," he tells her, "and I really hope he's your favorite person on the planet. He's always supported police officers."

I laugh to myself at his smooth voice, which is probably working on her. Kai leans on the counter, quiet but with a small smile on his face, while Michael, the lead point guard for the Meridian City Storm basketball team, stands tall and intimidating.

He reaches out a hand. "And I'm Michael Crist."

"Oh, yes." She smiles wide. "My husband is a huge fan."

"Just your husband?" he teases.

A blush crosses her cheeks, and I want to puke.

She then shakes Will's and Kai's hands, exhaling a long breath, her demeanor suddenly happy and relaxed. "Well, what can I do for you gentlemen?"

Will leans on the counter, getting intimate. "Misha Lare Grayson is also the grandson of Senator Grayson, and our grandfather would consider it a personal favor to him if you would allow the family to deal with Misha."

I can feel Ryen tense next to me, and I wince. *Shit.* Yeah, I forgot about not having told her *that* particular detail, too.

Will goes on, turning his head toward me, and the cop follows his gaze. "He's kind of the black sheep—I'm sure you can tell," he explains to her, as her eyes skim down my tattooed arms. "We'll take him back to Thunder Bay, and he will not return to Falcon's

Well. You have our word. We'll escort the little shit home right now."

I grind my teeth together. Will's eyes twinkle with laughter.

The cop regards me. "Well, the other young man is claiming he stole a watch," she explains; "however, he doesn't have it on him, and we have no witnesses. We were going to let him go anyway, but he won't tell us where he lives or his parents' names."

Will nods, straightening back up. "Trust us. We'll take him home."

She looks around at the three of them, seeing their perfect black suits, clean fingers, and not a tattoo in sight, so of course they're upstanding gentlemen. "All right," she finally concedes. "Take him home, and keep him out of trouble."

They shake her hand and walk away from the counter, looking smug as they head over to me.

I shoot out of the chair and stand in front of Will, staring him eye to eye and trying to keep my voice low. "I'm the black sheep?" I challenge. "I'm the black sheep? Did I just spend two and a half years in prison? How could she not know who you were? Why don't you roll up your sleeves and show her your tattoos?"

Will adjusts his collar and cuffs, primping himself. "I told you, never let anyone see all your cards. Didn't I say that? I'm a wolf in sheep's clothing. They have no idea what I'm capable of until it's too late."

His friend Kai quietly laughs at his side.

"I told you not to get a tattoo on your neck," Will scolds. "Didn't I say that? Did you see how we worked her? You should've been able to get yourself out of that if you had any sense."

"It's not on my neck," I argue back. "It's just like"—I gesture to my neck—"up a little and . . ."

"Hi." I hear a calm, deep voice and look over to see Kai staring at Ryen.

Michael follows suit and moves close to her. "So this is the one who was at a party, without you, doing body shots, huh?"

She scowls, and I retort, "Dane needs to shut his mouth."

But Michael just smirks down at Ryen. "If that was my girl, her ass would be red for a week."

"Yeah, I don't physically threaten my girl, okay?"

"And look where she was."

Will pushes Michael back. "Don't listen to him," he soothes Ryen. "He doesn't lay a hand on his girl. She has swords."

Kai laughs quietly off to the side, but Ryen's face is twisted in disgust. She looks to me. "Who are these pigs?"

I walk for the front door, knowing everyone will follow. "Will's my cousin. These are his friends. I called him so I wouldn't have to call my dad."

"And how's my baby?" Will calls from behind, referring to his truck. He lent it to me when he got arrested a few years ago. I had it the whole time he was on the inside, but since he's been out, he hasn't come looking for it, so I hoped he forgot about it.

"I hope you don't want it back," I tell him. "I have some good memories in that truck."

I shoot a look over to Ryen, seeing a blush cross her cheeks.

"Yeah, me, too," Will answers. "I guess I can let you hang on to it for a little while longer."

Ryen stares ahead, her jaw flexing. "I'm out of here."

She pushes through the doors, but I call after her. "No. I need to talk to you!"

But she powers toward her Jeep, which is parked on the side of a building at the left of the parking lot. I run after her, forgetting Will and his friends.

"Stop!" I take her arms and pull her to a halt next to the passenger side of her car. "What do you want me to say, huh? That I fucked up? I know I did. I'm sorry."

I'm sick of her defiance and how she won't give me an inch. *Just say you miss me.*

I take her face in my hands. "Look at me."

But she pushes my hands down. "I hate you. Let me go."

"Why?" I lash out. "So you can go back to that party? Back to your prom date? You gonna fuck him, too?"

"Maybe!" she yells. "Maybe I'll sink as low as you, and we'll have something more in common. Maybe I won't hate you so much."

I bare my teeth, staring at her. "You don't hate me. You love me, and I love you."

She slaps me so hard my head whips to the side and the burn spreads across my skin. "Don't say that," she growls low. "I want Masen. He doesn't love me. He's just good to me." Her tone taunts, turning breathy and sultry. "Really good."

I don't miss her meaning. I was a fuck and nothing more. She liked me when I was just that. When I wasn't Misha.

"Yeah?" I turn my eyes back on her, playing along. "Is that what you want?" I come in, grabbing the backs of her thighs and lifting her up. "Your dirty little secret who will fuck you in the back of a truck, hiding you so your stuck-up, shallow friends don't know how good I give it to you?"

Her breathing hitches, and she only hesitates a moment before her hands come up and grip my shoulders. I dive down, kissing her neck and reveling when she bends it back, opening for me.

But then I see something out of the corner of my eye and look up, realizing the guys are still here.

Michael and Kai are in the front seat of an SUV, Michael leaning far forward from the driver's side to watch out of Kai's window, while Will is paused at his open back door, looking amused.

"Seriously?" I snap.

Michael and Kai quickly turn away, and Will clears his throat.

"All right, we're out." He climbs into the car. "Stay out of trouble, and wrap it up. Hell hath no fury like Grandpa Grayson dealing with a teen pregnancy."

Ryen's nails dig into my skin, and I close my eyes, coming up and slamming my mouth down on hers as I hear the SUV speed away.

I kiss her lips, inhaling her and getting so fucking lost in my need for her. Her tongue brushes mine, and her teeth bite and nibble me, driving me so insane I can't think.

"Ryen," I gasp, pressing my cock into her as I squeeze her ass too hard. I need to be closer.

"We shouldn't do this," she pants as I pull down her shirt and touch her everywhere not covered by her bikini top.

"Don't act like you're going to tell me no." I pull open the passenger-side door. "I know you like *this* side of me."

She looks around, probably nervous we'll be seen, but the parking lot is dead. I pull my shirt over my head, dropping it on the ground next to hers, and start unbuttoning her shorts, going in for another kiss to quiet any protest she might dream up.

Her shorts fall to the ground, and she whimpers in my mouth.

"Get on my lap," I tell her, taking the seat and pulling her in.

She climbs on, and I shut the door, leaving our clothes outside. She reaches behind her and pulls the strings of her bikini, the whole top falling away, and I grab it and toss it before doing the same to her bottoms, pulling the strings that secure it at the sides.

"Oh, Jesus," I groan, kissing her again as I take her ass in one hand and dive between her legs with the other. She's so smooth and wet.

She reaches between us and unfastens my belt, and I do the best I can, getting my jeans down and my cock free while trying not to break the kiss.

"Give it to me," she moans. "I want it."

"I know."

Pulling out a condom from my jeans, I rip it open and roll it on, holding my cock steady as I pull her up. I slip it down her length and position myself under her. She groans, already rolling her hips in sexy little movements.

Finding her hot entrance, I thrust my hips up and put the tip in, and she does the rest. Lowering herself, she spreads her legs as far as the seat will allow, and I pull her into me, burying myself deep.

"Hell yes," I breathe out.

Her hips roll shallow and fast, in little figure-eight movements, and she stays close, her tits rubbing against my chest. I can taste her mouth, even though our lips aren't touching.

"Say my name," I whisper. "Who's fucking you right now?"

She keeps stride, her beautiful ass swaying in and out and the car filling with wet heat. "I'm fucking you," she corrects. "And I really don't care whose dick it is."

"That's bullshit."

"It could be anyone in this Jeep," she says, biting my bottom lip. "Maybe someone from that party even. If you hadn't shown up, I would've still been riding someone's cock tonight."

I dig my fingers into her ass. "Were you going to be bad?"

She mewls, nodding.

"Show me how bad, baby." I bring one hand up, palming her breast. "How were you going to screw some stranger later?"

She picks up the pace, leaning back, so I can get a good view of her gorgeous body working me. Her tits sway with the motion, and I close my eyes, letting my head fall back as I rub her clit with my thumb.

"You would've made him come good," I tease. "Sweet little pussy like this."

Her moans get higher and faster, and I open my eyes, seeing her watching me. But then she suddenly comes in close again, wrapping her arms around my neck and covering my mouth with hers, kissing me deep and hard as she rides us both home.

I come, wrapped in her arms, legs, and mouth, and feeling her sweaty and smooth skin stuck to mine. She cries out, her pussy tightening hard around me as she comes and thrusts her hips, taking me in again and again until she's spent.

I hold her as we both come down, the heat nearly unbearable. I have no idea how long before she'll let me touch her again, so I'm going to enjoy this.

She can be a nightmare, but this still feels better than any dream.

Her breathing calms, but she stays buried in my neck, sounding as if she's asleep.

"I wish we would've met in grade school," I say quietly, smiling to myself. "We would've played well together. On the playground, I mean."

She pulls her head up, and there's pain in her eyes.

I cup her face in my hands. "I know you," I tell her. "I know you now. You wouldn't have wanted this from anyone else. Because before me, you had sex once. Two years ago."

Her eyebrows pinch together, and I can see tears glistening. *Yeah, I remember the letter, babe. You were a mess, feeling ashamed and hurt, and I wanted to kill the guy.*

"Everyone told you to do it, and you did," I whisper. "He never spoke to you again, and that's why you waited for me."

"I wasn't waiting for you."

"You waited for it to feel right," I bite back, not taking any more of her shit. "I was jealous when you confided in me about your first time. That was when I realized I was possessive of you." I stare straight into her eyes, never sure about anything this much. "I want everything about you, Ryen, and I know you want me."

Her body shakes a little, and I lean in, kissing her on the cheek. "But I love the way you lie."

18

Ryen

The next day, he's not in our first class.

I know where he lives, and it brings me back to when I first noticed he'd stopped writing all those months ago. *I can check on him if I'm really worried. He knows where to find me if he wants to see me.*

But wait . . . I'm the one who doesn't want to see him. I told him to go, so what if he did?

I know he never intended for things to get so out of hand, and I believe he's sorry, but I can't wrap my head around it. Pretending you're someone else is bad enough. Lurking right under my nose with me none the wiser is awful.

But sleeping with me? How could he do it? Was he Masen or Misha in that truck at the drive-in? Was he really ever planning on telling me?

I shouldn't have relented last night. The emotions were high, I missed him, and when he took me in his arms, I just wanted to stop fighting for five minutes. I wanted to feel good with him again and forget.

But now, the light of day is so bright I want to crawl back under the covers. Everyone heard him scold me at the party last night. Acting like I'm his property.

They may not know what's happened between us, but they know *something* happened to make him that angry with me. And they know I've been lying about it.

I force down the lump in my throat and walk up to my cubby in the locker room, next to Lyla and Katelyn as they dress for PE.

"Hey," I say, trying to force a chipper tone.

But Lyla doesn't respond. Instead she lifts her nose, sniffing the air and complaining to Katelyn next to her. "God, did the janitors clean last night? I smell skank everywhere."

Katelyn laughs, and I tense.

"Can you believe that bitch didn't even bother to show up to practice again this morning?" Katelyn tells her, loud enough for me to hear. "Doesn't matter, I guess. Her fat ass was getting too heavy to catch."

Liquid heat races through my veins, and I hear my pulse in my ears. I turn to them as they get dressed. "You wanna say something, say it to my face."

But they both ignore me as if I haven't said anything.

"So did J.D. book a limo?" Katelyn asks Lyla.

"Oh, yeah. One big enough for all of us," she replies, and they both slam their locker doors, walking past me and down the aisle. "This night is going to be epic. Especially without Ryen there to stink up the car."

Their delighted laughter grates on my ears and tears spring to my eyes, but I slam my locker closed, refusing to give in.

All through PE I stay away from them, slowly feeling their bubble getting bigger and pressing me farther away. They're them, and I'm me. Over here, separated, alone, and excluded. I'm outside the bubble.

Again.

How did I get here? What do I do?

After class, I shower and dress quickly, heading to my locker before lunch when I really just want to leave.

It's easier, isn't it? Rather than facing people I don't like and being where I no longer feel I belong?

I've been here before. The uncertainty, the self-hate, the powerlessness . . . it's all so familiar. But the last time, I took those feelings and turned them outward, making others feel what I felt. What I didn't see is that those feelings came from people doing the same thing to me. I feel and fear exactly what they want me to feel and fear.

I won't respond the same this time. I'm better than this.

I'm going to be better.

Moving down the lunch line, I take an orange juice out of the cooler and walk for the cashier, but arms suddenly lock me in on both sides, keeping me from moving. My heart jumps, thinking it's Misha, but then I turn around, seeing Trey behind me.

"You know, if you wanted dirty, I could've done dirty," he taunts, staring down at me. "Maybe it was good Laurent broke you in, though. Doesn't take long for you little bitches to turn slut once you get a taste for it."

I breathe hard. What the hell did he just say?

He laughs. "You should've seen the train we pulled on this girl last week. She had guys lined up. It was so fucking good."

I push through his arm and pay for my juice, carrying my drink and books to an empty table as far away from his as I can find. I feel eyes on me everywhere, like people are laughing. I haven't sat at a table alone in a long time.

Opening my juice carton and notebook, I dive into the math homework due tomorrow, using it as a shield to not look so pathetic.

"No one wants you in here," a female voice says, and I look up to see Lyla. "I can't even eat, looking at you."

And she picks up my carton of juice and pours it into my lap. I gasp, the ice-cold drink making me shoot out of my chair as it cascades down my bare legs. I glare at her and dart out with both hands, shoving her away.

She stumbles back, dropping the carton, but comes back in, pushing me back.

"Oh!" someone shouts. "Fight!"

The cafeteria erupts in noise, chairs scraping against the linoleum and people shifting around for a better view.

Lyla reaches for my hair, but I rear back and slap her arms away. My shirt and shorts stick to my skin, and anger rages in every muscle. She comes back for me, and I get ready to lunge, to push her back again, but then, all of a sudden, there's a wall standing in front of me.

A wall in a white T-shirt with tattoos.

Misha.

Trey comes around Lyla and inches into my and Misha's space, a challenge in his eyes. "Move out of the way," he demands.

"Make me."

Trey scoffs, knowing Misha's not kidding but clearly not ready to take him on here in front of everyone. Especially when he got his ass kicked last time.

"If you want her, you're going to have to go through me," Misha states, and I step around to his side, refusing to hide.

The OJ sticks to my legs and seeps into my shoes, and I struggle to ignore the murmurs around me. Misha's standing up for me in front of everyone, and against my will, my heart warms.

"After school," Trey says. "The drive-in."

"Nah, I'll be busy tonight," Misha replies.

Trey laughs, looking round to his friends, all of them probably assuming Misha's too scared to show up.

"So how about we just do it now?" Misha tosses out calmly and then throws a punch across Trey's face, surprising us all.

Exclamations sound off around the crowd, and Trey stumbles back, cursing. "Fuck!"

Misha dives in, but then J.D. grabs him from behind, holding him back as Principal Burrowes steps between the boys.

"Stop it!" she shouts to both of them. "Stop it right now!"

Misha fights against J.D.'s restraint, J.D. turning red just from the struggle to keep him back. "Okay, calm down, man. Calm down."

"Get this asshole away from me!" Trey gestures to Misha, screaming around his stepmom.

"You fuck with her again," Misha growls, "and I'll make what just happened seem like a dream." He pauses and then speaks to Lyla. "And you. Don't talk to her again. You just want her to feel as ugly as you are."

She arches an eyebrow, folding her arms over her chest. She knows it's true just like it was true for me, but she won't credit it with a response.

"I won't fuck with her," Trey taunts. "Looks like you've already been there and done that."

A few giggles go off around me, and Misha breaks away from J.D., glaring at Trey and looking like he's dying to make sure he never talks shit again. But instead, he twists around and takes my hand, leading us out of the cafeteria.

"Mr. Laurent!" the principal calls.

But Misha ignores her and pulls me into the men's bathroom, wetting some paper towels and wringing them out.

He pushes me back against the sink and kneels down, lifting my foot and setting it on his thigh, slowly wiping the drying orange juice off my leg.

Pain springs to the back of my eyes, and I watch him carefully and quietly taking care of me.

Wetting more paper towels, he moves to the other leg and then starts untying my soaked shoes.

"Are we still friends?" I ask, my voice cracking. "Because I need Misha, not Masen."

I was wrong last night. Everything is Misha. They're not separate.

And I need my friend.

Holding my soiled Chucks, he stands up and takes my hand, still silent as he leads me out of the bathroom.

"Where are we going?"

"Away from here."

We don't bother to look back, and I'll probably be in trouble tomorrow, but no one and nothing could drag me away from him right now. I tighten my hold on his hand, ready to follow him anywhere. At least for today.

We drive for a long time, and we don't speak. The music plays, the afternoon is overcast, and my eyelids are heavy, probably because Thursday night was the last time I slept well.

I don't know if I'm ready to forgive him, but I want him. The smell of him, the sight of him, the feel of him . . . He doesn't even have to touch me. Just being near him is soothing at the moment. Maybe I'm just vulnerable, but right now I don't want to be anywhere else.

A sprinkle of rain starts as we pull into a driveway leading up to a house that's shielded behind a wall of trees.

A flutter courses through my belly. "Your house?"

We're in Thunder Bay? I didn't think I was dazed out that long.

He pulls into the garage and turns off the engine. "Have you ever been here?"

I nod. "A couple weeks ago. You hadn't written in so long, I needed make sure you were okay—"

"You don't have to explain," he cuts me off. "I should've written. You had every right to be worried."

"Why did you stop?"

He smiles gently, opening his door and taking my shoes. "A story for a different day. But it didn't have anything to do with you," he assures me.

"Your dad said you were fine." I climb out of the truck and walk around, following him into the house.

"My dad doesn't air dirty laundry. Did you tell him who you were?"

"Would he know me?"

"Of course," he replies, entering what looks like a laundry room and tossing my shoes into the washer. "He's seen your letters coming in for years."

Yes, of course. If I'd told him, maybe I would've been invited into the house and seen a picture of Misha. And then I would've found out even sooner who he really was.

Misha comes over to me and pulls up the hem of my shirt, but I lock my arms down, looking at him.

"No one's home," he reassures me. "Let's get your clothes in the wash. You can take a shower, and I'll find you something to wear."

It only takes me a moment to consider. I don't feel like I need to leave anytime soon, and the stickiness is still all over me, despite Misha's efforts to clean me up.

I nod and pull off clothes, handing him everything, one by one. He puts my shorts, shirt, and underthings in the washer, adding soap and starting it, and then hands me a T-shirt from the dryer.

Pulling it on, I let him take my hand and lead me into the rest of the house.

We walk through a large living room, and I look around, gaping. "Oh, geez," I mumble.

"What?"

I shake my head. "Nothing."

It's hilarious, really. He hangs out with the worst of the worst at school, looks like a delinquent, and everyone—including Lyla, Trey, and even me once—assumed he was a poor foster kid or nothing but a thug.

If Lyla discovers he lives in a house bigger than hers and mine put together and has a Gauguin hanging on the wall, she'll be the first one kissing his ass.

The house is dark, but even still I can tell it's stunning. There's wood shining everywhere, fancy art and knickknacks decorating the place, and I smell the rich scent of polish. What did Misha say his dad did in his letters? He's an antiques dealer?

And if he's the child of a senator, then he has to be well-set.

"Do you like peanut butter and jelly?" he asks, taking me up the stairs. "It's the only thing I make that I don't burn."

"It's fine."

He leads me into a spacious bathroom, very dark and very male, and opens the glass door, turning on the shower for me.

"Take your time." He plants a kiss on my forehead and takes a towel off the shelf, setting it on the counter for me. "I'll go make us some sandwiches."

I stare at him as he leaves, and despite the height and muscle of a man, I'm finally seeing him as the kid I envisioned so many years ago whom I became so attached to and loved. The one I pictured as kind and gentle and caring.

After my shower, I dry off and pull the T-shirt back on, finding a brush on the counter and tugging it through my ratty hair. Thankfully, Lyla's assault missed my head, so I didn't have to wash my hair.

Walking into the hallway, I hear the soft hum of music coming from down the hall, and I step quietly, following it—but carefully, in case it's his dad.

I find Misha in his room. He's walking around, picking up a few clothes, and on the bed sit plates with PB&J sandwiches and sprigs of grapes, with juice boxes sitting next to them.

I hold in my laugh. I don't think I've had that lunch since fifth grade.

P!nk plays at low volume, and I feel my chest warm at the gesture. He knows I like her, too.

But then I gaze around his room and see four office boxes, complete with lids, stacked on top of each other up against the wall.

I walk over. "What's this?" I ask, lifting the lid.

"Oh, uh . . ."

But I widen my eyes, taken aback, and drop the lid on the floor. The box is filled with black envelopes. With silver writing.

"Oh, my God." I reach in and fan the envelopes, seeing my writing on every single one.

He kept them.

He kept them?

I don't know why, but I guess I never thought he actually saved them. Why would he? Thinking back, I can't even remember what they said. Couldn't have been too interesting if I can't recall.

The other three boxes are probably filled with letters, too.

"I can't believe I wrote you this much," I say, a little horrified. "You must've been so bored with me."

"I adored you."

I look up, seeing him stare at the floor. An ache weaves its way through my chest.

"I adore you," he corrects himself. "I've read them all at least twice. My favorites, a lot more than that."

His favorites. And then I recall. The letters I found at the Cove. When he stayed there—away from home—he took those with him. The rest stayed here.

I feel guilty now. "They're in my desk," I confess. "I lied. I didn't burn them."

He gives me a little nod. "Yeah, I hoped so. I have mine, too, that you threw all over the place at the Cove. In case you want them back."

I give him a small smile, grateful. Yes, I do want them back.

I replace the lid, kind of curious to open a few letters and relive all the embarrassing things I shared with him over the years. Kissing with tongue the first time, the music I suggested that I thought was so epic but realize now was kind of lame, and all the arguments we got into.

Remembering back, I was pretty hard on him. I mean, using an

Android phone doesn't make him an introverted burner who probably won't ever have a job or a valid driver's license at the same time. I didn't mean that.

And I'm sure he didn't mean what he said when he called me a Steve Jobs cultist who worships inferior technology because I'm too much of a bubblehead high on apps to know the difference.

On second thought, no. I like the truce we have going on today. The letters can wait.

I walk over and sit down on his bed, bringing up my legs to sit cross-legged. He kicks off his shoes and lies down sideways on the bed, supporting his head on his hand.

I take the sandwich and peel off the top crust while he pops a grape in his mouth.

I stare down at the food. I'm hungry, but I'm also tired and suddenly feel like I don't give a shit. One of us has to start talking.

He wants something true? Something he doesn't know?

"I didn't have many friends in grade school," I tell him, still keeping my eyes down. "I had one. Delilah."

He's quiet, and I know he's staring at me.

"She had this shaggy blond hair that kind of looked like a mullet, and she wore these frumpy corduroy skirts," I went on. "They looked thirty years old. She wasn't cool and she didn't dress right. She was alone a lot like me, so we played together at recess, but . . ."

I narrow my eyes, trying to harden them as the image of her comes to the forefront in my mind.

"But I got tired of not hanging out with the popular kids," I admit. "I'd see them hanging on each other, laughing and surrounded by everyone, and I felt . . . envious. Left out of something better. I felt like I was being laughed at." I lick my dry lips, still avoiding his eyes. "Like I could feel their eyes crawling over my skin. Were they disgusted by me? Why didn't they like me? I shouldn't have cared. I shouldn't have thought that kids who shunned me would be worth it, but I did."

I finally raise my eyes and find his green ones watching me, unblinking.

"And in my head," I continue, "Delilah was holding me back. I needed better friends. So one day I ran off. When recess time came, I hid around a corner so she wouldn't find me, and I watched her. Waiting for her to go off and play with someone else so I could do the same and she wouldn't look for me."

I swallow, my throat stretching painfully.

"But she didn't," I whisper, tears welling in my eyes. "She just stood against a wall, alone and looking awkward and uncomfortable. Waiting for me." My body shakes, and I start to cry. "That was the day I became this. When I started to believe that a hundred people's fickle adoration was worth more than one person's love. And for a while it felt kind of good." Tears stream down my face. "I was lost in the novelty of it. Being mean, slipping in a quick insult, making a joke of others and of my teachers . . . I felt respected. Adored. My new skin suited me."

And then more images creep in, still so vivid after all this time.

"But months later, when I'd see Delilah playing alone, being laughed at, not having anywhere to belong . . . I started to hate that skin I was so comfortable in. The skin of a fake and shallow coward."

I wipe the tears, trying to take in a deep breath. He's looking at me, but the heat of shame covers my face, and I'm worried. What does he think of me?

"And when I started writing you a year later," I go on, "I needed you so much by that point. I needed someone I could be the person I wanted to be with. I could go back. I could be the girl who was Delilah's friend again. The girl who stood up to the mean kids and didn't need a spirit animal, because she was her own."

I close my eyes, just wanting to hide. I feel the bed shift under me and then his hands cupping my face.

I shake my head, inching away. "Don't. I'm awful."

"You were in fourth grade," he says, trying to soothe me. "Kids are mean, and at that age, everyone wants to belong. You think you're the only one who feels like shit? Who's made mistakes?" He nudges my face, making me open my eyes and look into his. "We're all ugly, Ryen. The only difference is, some hide it and some wear it."

I slide the food out of the way and crawl into his lap, wrapping my arms around him and burying my face in his neck, hugging him close. He gently falls back onto the bed, lying down and taking me with him.

Why didn't we do this ages ago? Why was I so scared to meet him and change things? We were there for each other during his grandmother's funeral, lengthy summer camps with hardly any communication to each other, and even a couple of girlfriends of his whom I never told him I was really jealous of.

Why did I think that all the words and letters and the friendship would fade so easily?

His arms hold me tight as I lay my head on his chest, hearing his heartbeat and the light tapping of rain against the window. This is new for me. I've been comfortable in places, but I think this is the first time I've been anywhere I never want to leave. My eyelids fall closed, sleep pulling at me.

"I have a question," he speaks up, causing me to stir.

"Hmm?"

"When you write on the walls at school, you sign the messages as Punk. Why?"

I keep my eyes closed, but I breathe out a weak little laugh. "Do you remember the letter you wrote about your first tattoo and your dad saying you looked like a punk?"

"Yeah?"

"So it was a tribute to you," I tell him. "A shout-out to the ruffians and rule breakers."

"But why not use your own name?"

I pinch my eyebrows together. "Because I don't want to get caught." *Duh.*

"Okay . . ." he says. "So what you do is hide in the dark to share words anonymously, because you want to be heard but not mocked. Is that it?"

I open my eyes, thinking. Is that what I do?

"You want to be loved without risking consequences, so you reach out to get the attention you need while enjoying the luxury of taking no responsibility for those words."

I start to shrink into myself. I don't like what he's saying or the fact that he's saying it, but I can't deny that he's right.

I don't want to hear feedback, because if they knew it was me, their reactions would be different. But it's not exactly fair to throw things in their faces and hide under their noses, either.

"Alone, empty, fraud, shame, fear," he murmurs, holding me tighter. "Don't you get it yet? You don't have to be afraid or embarrassed. No one does you better than you. You can't be replaced. Not everyone will see that, but only you need to."

He kisses my hair, and I wrap my arm around his torso. *No one does me better than me.*

I close my eyes again, hearing what he's saying. I changed because I didn't think what I brought to the table was worthy enough. I let them make me believe that, but who made them authorities? I may no longer be adored, but I might not be so miserable, either.

And I may eat alone, but that's not such terrible company, is it?

I feel him move under me, and then a blanket covers my legs and body, locking our warmth in under the covers. I slowly drift off to sleep to the sounds of the rain and his heartbeat.

A velvety tickle glides across my skin, and I strain to lift my lids. The room is darker, the sun having set, but the soft glow of the lamp on the bedside table illuminates the bed, and I glance over at the window, seeing that it's now dark outside. The rain pounds hard, echoing through the roof, and thunder rolls outside.

Misha is bare chested and propped up on his side next to me, his head down by my ass.

Which is bare, because he's pulled up my shirt.

"What are you doing?"

"Shh, don't move," he orders, moving a pen over my skin. "You're the closest thing I have to write on."

I snicker, closing my eyes again. He'd better not be using a Sharpie. That'll take days to get off.

The peaceful noise of the rain outside lulls me back into relaxation, and I fold my arms under my head, feeling the felt tip move quickly over my skin, stopping every so often to dot an *i* or poke a period.

"I wish we could stay here forever," I muse.

"Oh, you're not moving anytime soon. Your ass is too nice to look at."

I cross my legs at the ankles, teasing, "Is that all a Thunder Bay boy can do with a girl's ass?"

A light slap hits my right cheek, and I laugh.

But then, after a pause, he stops writing. "Have you ever . . ." he asks, drifting off.

It takes me a moment to connect the dots, but then I realize what he's asking.

"Anal?" I clarify. "Well, considering I've only had sex once before you, I'm sure you know the answer to that."

I certainly wouldn't have done *that* the first time, no matter how naïve I was. And since Misha and I haven't done that, then of course the answer is no.

"So we're virgins then," he says, his tone making it sound like he's kind of enjoying that idea.

"Yeah, virgins," I grumble. "And I plan on dying one, because there's no way you're sticking *that* in *there*."

He snorts, breaking into a laugh.

Capping the pen, he moves up and over me, lifting my shirt

over my head. I arch my neck back, meeting his mouth and kissing him. His teeth nibbling my skin send an electric shock down my belly and straight between my thighs.

I guess the nap helped. He slides his hand under my chest, cupping my breast, and I'm already turned on.

"Is this okay?" he asks.

I stare at his lips, dipping in for more. *Hell, yes.*

I groan, my eyes damn near rolling into the back of my head as his mouth trails down my neck, devouring me in hot, demanding kisses. He grinds his hips into me, and I feel the hardening bulge between his legs.

"Talk to me," he whispers. "I need your words."

Talk? Now?

His hand glides down my bare back, brushing my hair and making it tickle my skin. He takes my ass, kneads it, and without thinking, I bend my knee to the side, opening myself for him.

"Before I met you," I say against his lips. "I fantasized about you."

"But you didn't know what I looked like."

"I knew you were Misha," I reply. "That was enough."

He groans, nibbling my ear and dipping his hand between my legs, his fingers sliding inside of me.

I close my eyes, the pleasure of him filling me making me wetter.

"One night it was storming, like tonight," I tell him. "The lights went out, and for the whole evening, it was dark and quiet."

His fingers come out, swirling around my clit, and I shudder. My breath is shallow, and I'm unable to stop my hips from trying to rub into the bed and his fingers.

"I reread all of your letters that night," I pant. "I love the ones about when you got your first car and how you and your friends got arrested for the kegger out on some farm. You sounded so bad, so much fun." I lean back, longing for his mouth again. "But the letter I love more than all the rest is when you told me about your ex-girlfriend after you'd broken up. I was so mad at first. You had a girlfriend, and you hadn't told me, but . . . I think that's when I first realized . . ."

"What?" he breathes out.

"That I wanted you. You were mine."

"I was," he assures me. "It didn't take me long to realize that I couldn't talk to anyone like I talk to you."

And I feel the same way. I always did. I couldn't go out with anyone without comparing them to Misha. He had every right to date, and I'm sure whoever she was—or they were, because there were probably more—they weren't bad people, but I still felt territorial. *I knew him first. No one was going to know him better than me.* I know I had no right to feel those things, which is why I never told him. Until now.

"I started fantasizing about you that rainy night. It was the first time I ever daydreamed about you."

"What did you do?" He pushes his two fingers in deep, rubbing my spot and grinding himself on me. "Did you want to be her?"

I shake my head. "I wanted you to see me. I wanted you to see me and want me so much. Not just my letters, but my body, too."

"What'd you do?" he whispers in my ear.

I moan, feeling a wave of pleasure fill my thighs and pussy, and I back up into him, wanting to be filled. "I lay in bed," I say, "and I couldn't stop thinking about you. It was so dark, and the AC wasn't running. The more I thought about it, the hotter I got . . . until . . ."

"Until what?" He pumps my pussy faster, grinding his dick harder. "What'd you do?"

"I pulled up my shirt . . ."

"Yeah?"

"And imagined you were standing in the corner of my room, hidden in the shadows, watching me finger myself."

"Don't stop."

"My skin was damp with sweat, because it was so hot," I whimper, reaching over my head and holding the back of his neck, "and I slid my hand down my panties . . ."

"Did I like what I was seeing?"

"Yeah. We were always just friends. So calm, relaxed, and cute, but I wanted you to want me. I wanted you to see me and need to be inside me."

"Did you come?" he growls low in my ear as I rock into him. "Did you come, thinking about me watching you?"

I nod, completely lost in the vision and his fingers. "I knew I'd do anything you asked me to. I'd let you have anything you wanted."

"Is that true?"

"Anything."

He removes his fingers from inside me, and I hear him unzip his pants.

"And what do you want?" he asks, his fingers gliding up my ass again.

I know what he wants. My heart is pumping wildly, and I'm shaking with need.

I lean my head back again, gasping over his mouth. "I want you everywhere."

I feel his smile curl over my lips right before he kisses me. He moves his fingers between my thighs again, rubbing and getting me wetter with need.

"Everywhere?" he whispers.

I nod. I'm his. All of me.

I want him all over me.

His breath shakes over my lips. "Don't do this because you think I want it," he pleads. "I only want what you want to give me. I need to know you trust me again."

His dark hair sits over his forehead, and his beautiful eyes tell me everything I need to hear without saying anything.

He hurt me, and I hurt him, but shit happens and love doesn't change. He makes me happier, he makes me stronger, and he knows everything and still wants me. If he can say the same, then this is it. The real thing.

It's us together.

My mom told me once, "Life is fifty wrong turns down a bumpy road. All you can hope is that you end up somewhere nice."

"I trust you," I say, sinking into his mouth. "I want you."

He swirls the wetness between my legs farther up, and I slide my hand between me and the bed, rubbing my clit as he positions himself. I'm throbbing everywhere, and my heart pounds in my chest as he pushes the tip in and stops. I gasp, feeling a tiny burn.

I contract around him, breathing hard and rubbing myself faster.

"Ryen," he breathes out. "Do you want me to stop?"

I shake my head, feeling so filled and good. I didn't expect that. "No. I want more."

"Oh, God."

He slides in slowly, all the way, and I arch my ass up, giving him a better position.

"Holy shit," he growls low. "You feel so good. I need to . . ."

I close my eyes, every nerve alive and pulsing with need. He comes down on my back, kissing me as he thrusts out and back in deeper.

"Ah," I moan into his mouth.

"Are you okay?"

"No," I whimper. "Go faster."

He smiles, holding himself up with one hand and holding my thigh where my leg and hip meet. "Are you sure?"

I nod, intense pleasure washing over me and making me grip the pillows as I arch my neck back to meet his lips.

"I trust you," I tell him.

And he bites my neck and starts fucking me harder, not holding back and neither of us being quiet.

For the rest of the night.

19

Ryen

My entire body feels like I was caught in a tornado. My arm muscles are sore, my neck hurts, I have bruises on my hips, and my ass . . .

It was fun while it was going on last night, but after waking up this morning in pain everywhere, I told him we can't do that again.

He just retorted that my body wasn't used to it, and we should do it more.

Man, our fifth-grade teachers would be proud.

I pull into a parking space at school and groan as I gingerly climb out of the Jeep. We were up half the night, and while I'm not at all tired, I'm kind of regretting not staying home and soaking in a bath today. I'm supposed to teach swim tonight, and I forgot the Advil at home.

I reach into the back of the car and pull out my duffel with my swimsuit and change of clothes. After we woke up early this morning, Misha drove me back to school to collect my Jeep, and then he went to the Cove to pack up his stuff while I went home to shower and clean up.

I'm not sure if he's going to be in school today, but then I feel hands come around my waist and I break out in a shiver as a whisper hits my ear from behind.

"Are you sore?" he teases.

I arch an eyebrow and turn around, seeing him smirk down at me. "Are you kidding?"

"It was fun, though."

I can't hold back the smile as my cheeks warm. *Yeah, it was.*

We walk into the school and head for my locker, and I notice he's sticking by my side.

"I'm fine, you know," I tell him. Yesterday—Trey, Lyla, and the lunchroom—feels like ages ago. I'm not scared.

"I know."

"Masen," someone calls.

I turn around to see Ms. Till, the art teacher, carrying a pink slip. She hands it to him, speaking sweetly. "The principal would like to see you in the office. She wanted me to give you this in first period, but I just spotted you. You may as well go now."

He takes the slip, and she pats him on the arm, walking away. Misha doesn't read it, merely crumples it in his fist and tosses it to the ground.

"What are you doing?" I ask. "If she can't get a hold of your parents about the fights, she could bring in the police. Do you want to be found out?"

"I think we know how well I stay arrested," he retorts, a cocky look on his face.

I roll my eyes. Yeah, okay, Rich Boy.

Pulling out my sketchbook, I spot the cashmere scarf still hanging in the locker, and something hits me. He gave me a new scarf that first week. With perfume on it.

"Whose scarf did you try to give me that first week?"

His eyes drop, looking somber. "Annie's."

Annie's? His sister?

And then my eyes go wide, and I turn to him, remembering what I'd said. "Oh, my God," I burst out. "Annie. I'm so sorry. I didn't mean what I said."

I cringe at myself. I called her a skank, thinking she was some random girl who'd left her clothes behind in his truck. *Shit.*

"It's okay." He gives a half smile. "I know you didn't know."

Ugh. I feel sick. I'm the worst.

"Well, you couldn't give it to me anyway," I scold. "She'd want it back."

He grows quiet, avoiding my eyes.

I'd totally forgot his sister in all the drama. She's a junior. Where was she last night? His dad must've come home during my nap, because Misha had to lock the door later on so he wouldn't walk in on us, but Annie was never mentioned.

"Mr. Laurent."

I turn my head to see Principal Burrowes coming down the hall-way. Students move around her, everyone heading to their first class.

"In my office," she orders. "Now."

He turns away from her. "No, thanks."

I stand frozen, watching. *Just go, Misha.* She's not going to let him off the hook, and it's only going to escalate.

"Now."

"I'd rather not leave my friend alone when that piece-of-shit son of yours is roaming the halls," he snarls. "Aren't there laws about sexual predators not allowed to be within a certain number of feet from a school?"

Anger mars her face. "If I have to ask again, I'm calling the police."

"Mi—Masen," I correct myself. "Just go."

Burrowes puts her hand on his back and gestures for him to move.

But he whips away from her touch, scowling. "Fuck you." He glares at her and then turns to me. "I'm leaving. I'm done here. I'll be at the Cove after school."

"What?" I exclaim.

He kisses me on the forehead and shoots Burrowes one last look before walking down the hall and back out the front door. I look around and see that other students are watching the exchange.

Burrowes meets my eyes briefly, but she doesn't go after him. Turning around, she walks back down the hallway and disappears into the throng of bodies rushing to class.

Misha's gone, and I'm a little pissed he'd rather leave school and me than deal with her. If he moves back to Thunder Bay, I'll barely see him. At least until summer break.

What the hell's going on with him?

And now that I finally slow down enough to think about it, he still hasn't answered all of my questions.

Why is he here? Why did Trey have his watch? And why is he staying at the Cove?

Everyone heads to their next class or into lunch, and I stand next to the water fountain, filling up my water bottle. I don't feel like braving the cafeteria today, even though I'm a little hungry.

I know I should go in. I should sit at a table without the armor of my phone, homework, or a book, and just be there. If I hear whispers, then so be it. Let them talk.

But I don't have it in me today for some reason. Maybe I just don't want to see them. Maybe I don't feel like getting covered in juice when I have to be here half the evening.

Maybe I'm allowing myself to just wimp out today.

The hallway slowly empties, shoes squeak across the floor, and lockers slam shut. The clatter of trays and the chatter of conversations filter out into the hall, and I hear a door open to my left. Looking up, I see Trey coming out of the bathroom. He holds a black cord with a pendant attached to it, and he walks over to the garbage can, pulling it apart and breaking it and then dumping it in the can.

That's Manny's, I think. It's one of the gothy necklaces he wears with some band's name on it or something.

Trey raises his eyes and sees me, and I twist the cap back on my water bottle and walk his way, staying far to the right to go upstairs to the library.

But he rushes over and stops me, caging me in against the wall.

I exhale a hard sigh, turning angry.

"Where's your bodyguard?" he asks, leaning his hands on the wall at my sides and blocking my escape. "Oh, that's right. I heard he bailed school. Is he coming back?"

I push at his arm, trying to slip away, but he pushes me back, and I drop my bottle.

"Get the hell away from me," I growl.

"It's your own fault," he replies. "You shouldn't be caught alone with me. You've been asking for this."

I dart my eyes to the sides, looking for an adult. But the hallway is nearly empty.

"You know what I think I'll do?" He gives me a sick smile. "One of these nights, I'll get you in the parking lot after you teach swim lessons, and I'll spread those pretty legs and fuck you right there on the ground. Would you like that, baby?"

"I'm not scared of you."

"But can you outrun me?" An amused look crosses his eyes. "Your boyfriend's gone now. Every corner you turn, every night when you go to sleep, I'll be there, and I'm going to find out exactly what I've been missing."

He pushes off the wall, and I fist my fingers, realizing they're chilled to the bone.

"You're just like every other bitch in this school. They all wanted it."

I take in deep breaths as I watch him walk down the hall to the lunchroom, trying to slow down my pulse.

I don't care what he thinks he can get away with. I'll talk to my mom tonight and take this to the principal. If she doesn't handle him, then we'll go over her head. He's not threatening me again.

I move to make my way up the steps, but I see the men's room door Trey came out of and remember the black necklace.

He must've taken it from Manny. If Manny's in there, why hasn't he come out yet?

I look around, not seeing anyone in the hall, and hurry to the bathroom door, slowly pushing it open.

"Manny?" I call out.

Why the hell am I doing this? He won't want to see me. I'm sure he's fine.

"Manny, it's Ryen," I say.

I don't hear anything, and for a moment I think the bathroom is empty, but then I hear a shuffle and step inside.

Inching past the empty stalls, I walk along the sinks to the hidden space where the hand dryers sit.

Manny is standing with his back to me, his backpack dangling from his right hand, and his head bowed.

He's shaking.

"Manny?"

He raises his head but doesn't turn around. "Get out," he demands. "Get the fuck away from me."

"Manny, what happened?"

I step to the side, trying to see his face, but then I see something, and I stop. Blood trails off his ear and down his neck.

The hole on his lobe where a black gauge used to fit is now empty, and he's bleeding, although it looks like it's stopped.

Trey. Oh, my God, did he rip it out?

I take a step toward Manny, but he flinches, moving away.

Of course. Why would *she* help? He sees me as just as dangerous as Trey.

He thinks I'll victimize him. And why not? I've done it in the past.

Grief fills my heart. How many times have I made him feel alone?

I stay rooted, not wanting to make him scared, but I want to help. "It won't always be like this."

"It's always been like this," he retorts.

I stand there, thinking back to grade school. Manny and I got along okay until fourth grade when I . . . changed. But even before that he was on the periphery of whatever was happening. He was small and lanky, never picked for sports and often got in trouble for not turning in assignments. I knew then that he had it a little stressful at home, but other kids don't understand things like that. They just judge.

"When I was little," he goes on. "I used to be able to go home and get away from it. But now we're older. We have social media, and everything they say about me during the day, I get to see online every night."

I can hear the tears in his voice, and I want to get him some napkins to clean up the blood, but I don't want him to stop talking, either.

"One of you assholes pushes my tray into my clothes and dumps food all over me, and the first thing everyone does is take out their phones. And then I have to relive it through pictures on my newsfeed every hour—even days and weeks later. Over and over again. I can't get away from it anymore. Not even when I leave school."

I never thought about it like that. When we were younger, the dynamics of friendships and fitting in were only difficult at school. When we went home, we were free, and most of us, hopefully, felt safe there. Now the only thing we leave at school is school. The pressure, the gossiping, the bad feelings, they follow us home online. There's no break from it.

"It's constant. The humiliation . . ."

"It won't always be like this," I say again, moving closer.

"My family sees it, my sisters and their friends. I embarrass them." He shakes, sobbing again. "That's why I get high."

He pulls a rag and spray can out of his backpack, and I move forward, a lump stretching my throat.

"As high as I can get as often as I can get," he says, "so I can bear the fucking pain of breathing and eating and looking at people like you."

"Manny . . ."

"When everything is painful . . ." He drops the backpack and sprays the inhalant on the rag. "You start to ask yourself, 'What's the point?' No one cares, and you start to care even less. You just want the pain to stop."

He brings it to his nose, and I lunge out, knocking the cloth out of his hand and grabbing the can.

I wrap my arm around him and pull him into me, both of us starting to cry. "It's okay. It's okay," I whisper.

I drop the stuff on the floor and hold his frail, shaking body as tears stream down my face. What the fuck? How did we get here? He wasn't like this as a kid. Neither of us was like this.

He breathes hard, and I think about all the times I didn't think of him and all the things I wasn't seeing. All the times I ignored what was happening because of the fear of being alone, empty, and ashamed of who I was.

We were kids once, and we liked ourselves. We were happy. How did that change?

I pull away and toss the stuff into the garbage, wetting some paper towels for him to clean off his neck.

Handing them to him, I lean down on the counter and try to calm the sobs in my chest.

This is crazy. How can he hurt himself like that? He has to know it gets better. The world will open up, and we won't feel so trapped. You just need to hang on.

But I look over at him, seeing tears coat his face, bags under his eyes, and him staring off. He absently wipes the blood off his neck, looking completely fucking empty and like he's done hanging on.

I wipe my tears away and try to steel my tone. "It won't always be like this." I want him to know that.

But he just looks over at me, looking like he's hanging on by a thread. "When does it get better?"

My heart aches. Yeah, when? How long does he have to wait?

There should always be hope—we change, our environment changes, and our communities change. It will get better.

But that doesn't mean we're powerless in the meantime, either. I can't change his life, but I can do this.

I pick up his backpack and stand up, handing it to him. Taking his hand, I lead him out into the hallway, seeing him toss his wet cloth in the trash on the way out.

We walk across the hall to the lunchroom, and I relax my grip on his hand just in case he wants to let go of me.

But he doesn't. We walk hand in hand to the lunch line, already hearing the deafening noise fade a little and murmurs drift around the room.

I give him a tray and take one myself.

"Why are you doing this?" he asks in a low voice. "You don't like me."

"I've always liked you." I turn my eyes on him. "And I need a friend."

My being an asshole was personal to him, but it wasn't personal to me. I never stopped liking Manny.

We move down the line, and my back is hot. Hopefully it's my paranoia, feeling all those stares. If not, I guess I've laid down the gauntlet. And without Misha here this time to protect me. Here we go.

"I always eat in the library." He looks around nervously.

I take a Jell-O cup. "The lunchroom is where we eat."

"Everyone's looking at us."

"It's because you have a better ass than me, that's why."

A laugh escapes him, but he quickly diffuses it, probably because he's not sure if he can trust me. I don't blame him.

We load up our trays with chips, mac and cheese, and brownies.

I also get a soda, because fuck it, I'm hungry, and I want to drink some calories today.

After we pay, I walk over to a round table and glance back, making sure he's following me.

His eyes dart left and right as he carries his tray and backpack, and he's probably nervous as hell. After all, I can't remember the last time I spotted him in here, and everyone is looking at us.

I keep my eyes forward and set my tray down, having a seat. He quickly slides into a chair on the other side of the table, and even though the hairs on my skin are standing on end and I'm aware of every damn person in here, I inhale a deep breath and give him a reassuring smile.

"See?" I brag, opening my Coke. "It's getting better already."

But then something smashes down in front of me, my food splatters, and I gasp, instantly stilling as mac and cheese hits my arm and hair.

What the . . . ?

"Whoa!" Howls sound off across the room, followed by laughter, and I know it's coming from my old table. People around us take notice and start laughing, a few taking out their phones to take pics.

I sit there, frozen.

I look up, seeing a fat, cheesy noodle dangling from my hair over my forehead, and I lock eyes with Manny as he reaches over and picks up the red apple that came crashing into my tray. He stares at me, looking surprised, but then his eyes shoot up to the noodle, and he snorts.

"Hey," I snap. This isn't funny!

But he's smiling anyway, shaking with laughter.

I roll my eyes, feeling my stomach tighten into a knot, but I set my drink down and pluck the noodle out of my hair. Grabbing a napkin, I start to clean off my arm, where thick cheese is sticking to my skin.

"Hey," a male voice says.

I look up, seeing J.D. pull out a seat. He grabs the apple away from Manny and flings it across the cafeteria, back to where it came from. I don't look, but I hear a crash and squeals.

"What are you doing?" I ask, watching him lean back in the seat, relaxing.

He shrugs, taking my Coke and unscrewing the cap. "Well, when your girl screws your best friend, it's time for a new girl and a new best friend, I guess."

"We like you more, anyway," someone else says.

I turn my head to see Ten taking a seat next to Manny. He looks over at the kid. "Hi."

Manny sits slumped, suddenly appearing frightened to even look at anyone. "Hi," he mumbles.

J.D. takes a sip of my soda.

"When did you know?" I ask him. I'm sure Misha wouldn't have told him.

"Slightly before I wrote the message on the lawn, outing her."

I shoot my eyebrows up, and Ten stares at him, shocked. "That was you?" I shoot out.

Holy shit. If he knew then, how did he just stand by and play dumb around them this whole time?

"I guess I was afraid to stand on my own," he explains. "Until I saw you doing it five seconds ago."

"You're not Punk," Ten gauges as more of a question than a statement.

J.D. just shakes his head. "Uh, no. It was just that one time."

I momentarily wonder if I should tell them who Punk is, but no. Wrong time, wrong place, and I'm not sure Punk is done yet. I don't want to come out of the closet until I'm ready.

I finish cleaning off and open my bag of chips, grateful that everyone in the room has seemed to resume their conversations. Thanks, no doubt, to J.D. and Ten's arrival.

I guess what I always thought is actually true. There is safety in numbers.

"So I got a limo for prom," J.D. tells me, looking around at everyone. "Group date?"

Ten nods, but Manny and I are silent. I trust Ten, but I'm not entirely sure about J.D. yet. Everything I've noticed from him the past couple of weeks tells me he's on the up and up, but now I'm paranoid. I don't want to get suckered into going to prom, and whoops . . . now I'm soaked in animal blood like in *Carrie*.

"This isn't a joke, is it?" I ask him. "You're cool?"

He looks at me thoughtfully. "If Masen's not there, they'll have to go through me to get to you." And then he glances at Manny. "You, too. And believe me. No one likes to go through me."

I can't help but smile. He's a hundred eighty pounds of future USC football player, and while he's always been pretty harmless, people know they shouldn't mess with him.

"Sounds good, then. I'd love to." I turn to Manny. "You?"

"You got a dress?" Ten pipes up, asking him.

Manny frowns, shooting him a dirty look. "Do you?"

Ten smiles, and Manny seems to relax a little.

He doesn't answer, but I'll call him later. He doesn't trust us, and I don't want to push him right now.

Everyone gets busy eating. J.D. steals food off everyone's trays, and I take out my phone and go to text Misha. I hope he doesn't mind getting asked to prom.

But then I think better of it and go to Google to find his Instagram or TikTok. I've read so much about his life, and now I'd like to see it, I think. I'm guessing the last thing he wants to talk about is prom, but I'd like to put it out there sooner rather than later for him to think about at least.

But as I type "Misha Lare Grayson" into the search engine and scroll to find what I need, I'm suddenly lost in more information than I can handle.

My stomach sinks, and my heart races.

Oh, my God.

20

Ryen

The Cove looms ahead, massive and imposing under the gray clouds. I park next to Misha's truck and climb out of my Jeep, making my way to the entrance.

Now I know why he stopped writing three months ago.

I should never have let it go as long as I did. It was completely selfish to sit there and wait for him to come around and write me back—assuming his issue was small and insignificant and that protecting the status quo of our relationship was more important.

Of course he wouldn't have stopped writing for anything trivial. He'd been committed to me for seven years. Why did I think he'd be so cavalier about dropping me all of a sudden?

And now I know why he's been hiding out here, away from his dad, too. It all makes sense.

Almost.

Walking into the park, I feel the cool breeze from the downpour yesterday brush my arms. The air is thick and weighted, and the clouds overhead threaten more of the same. I hug myself against the slight chill.

Looking around, I walk past the rides and old gaming booths, spotting the field house ahead. I enter and make my way down the dark stairwell, instantly seeing a light down the corridor.

This place freaks me out. I'd heard some people from Thunder Bay were buying the property and had plans to tear down the old theme park and turn it into a hotel with a golf course and a marina and all that, but it might've been just a rumor.

I'd be sad to see the place go, but yeah . . . I turn corners half expecting to see death clowns cackling amid the decay.

Too many horror movies, I guess.

Misha's room is lit up, and I see the lamp on the bedside table turned on as well as some candles on another table across the room. He's lying back on the bed, his feet on the floor and his ears covered with headphones as he taps his thigh with a pencil.

There are a few boxes that look filled with his belongings sitting next to the door, but other than the bed, table, and lamp, everything else is packed away.

I smile softly, unable to tear my eyes away from him. The way his foot is tapping to the beat that I hear playing out of his headphones, the way the ring in his lip makes his mouth look like something to eat, and his dark brown hair—damn near black—wispy like he was just outside in the wind.

My heart aches, my stomach somersaults, and my lungs fill with air that sends a shiver down my spine.

I love him.

Stepping over, I climb on top of him, straddling his waist and planting my hands on either side of his head. He jerks and opens his eyes, his gaze turning gentle and happy when he sees me.

He pulls off his headphones. "Are you okay?"

I know he was probably concerned about leaving me at school around Trey and Lyla without him. I nod.

I'm tempted to tell him about my day. Trey's threats, Manny in the bathroom, J.D. and Ten at lunch. But no more distractions.

"Why didn't you tell me about Annie?" I ask him.

His expression turns somber, and he slowly sits up. I move off him, sliding onto the bed and sitting at his side.

"I would've," he says, avoiding my eyes as he turns off his iPod. "I was just waiting for us to calm down."

I can understand that, but I'm not talking about when he came here as Masen. I'm talking about in his letters.

"I heard about it and saw the name online," I tell him, "but . . . why did you tell me your last name was Lare?"

When I heard about the seventeen-year-old girl who died on Old Pointe Road from a heart attack, I'd read her name was Anastasia Grayson.

Annie, I gather, is short for Anastasia, but Misha never told me his real last name?

"Lare is my middle name," he replies. "A family name. Everyone in Thunder Bay knows the Graysons, and my grandfather is important. There's always been pressure to be and act a certain way. It was so aggravating as a kid, and when I started writing you, I saw it as an opportunity to kind of be free. Not really thinking that a kid our age probably wouldn't know who Senator Grayson was anyway." He gives a weak laugh. "I legally changed it to Lare when I turned eighteen, though. It suits me a lot better."

So I guess I wasn't the only one pretending to be someone else.

"She was an honor student," he explains, "an athlete, and she was always picture-perfect. I wondered how she did it—how she found the time and energy to be everything she was—but it wasn't until too late that I realized what she was doing to her body. There were signals and we missed it. Taking money out of my wallet, the hours she kept, the decreased appetite . . ."

I'd read the details when the police finally released her name all those months ago. She was jogging, it was late, and she was alone. Her car was dead, so they guessed she was trying to run to a gas station or something.

She'd collapsed with her phone in her hand, and by the time help got to her, she was gone. It was later determined she'd been abusing drugs for quite some time.

I didn't follow the story and wasn't very invested at the time. She was just a girl I didn't know. But I heard enough to know the details, and I want to cringe, thinking back to the times I thought about it, not realizing who she was.

Misha's sister.

"It was the night we met at the scavenger hunt," I say, remembering the date in the news article.

He nods absently, still staring off. "You and I were inside talking, and she was . . ."

Dying. I look away.

"I couldn't stomach anything after that," he explains. "I stopped writing because I couldn't talk about it, but I couldn't talk about anything else, either. I couldn't carry on like before, and I couldn't face the reality of her being gone. I felt sick." He finally looks over at me. "I needed you, but I just didn't know how to talk to you anymore. Or anyone. I'd changed."

"You can talk now."

He smiles, easing me back to his lap. "Yeah. I'm not sure I could ever give you up again."

I touch my forehead to his, not knowing what I would do without him. I hate that he stopped writing. I hate that he pretended to be Masen. But I'm so glad we're here.

I just really hate that it was his sister's death that brought him here.

"I understand why you stopped writing and why you came here to get away, but . . ." I look him in the eyes. "Why did you enroll at school? If it wasn't for me, what was it for?"

He shakes his head, letting out a breath. "Nothing."

"Misha—"

"Really, it was nothing," he tells me, cutting me off. "I thought I had another reason to be here, someone who I used to know, but no. It was dumb, and I feel stupid. I shouldn't have come." And then he smiles, wrapping his arms around me. "But I'm not sorry I did."

I cock my head, aggravated. He's being cagey again.

"I love you," he says. "That's all that matters."

And he looks so calm and happy, I don't want to ruin it. I take in a deep breath and relax into him. "Can I have the scarf back?"

"Yeah."

"I love you," I say, my fingers tingling as my heartbeat picks up.

His fingers grip my waist. "It's about fucking time."

I breathe out a laugh, kissing him. He's always gotta bust my chops.

"And I think it's about time I met your mom," he states.

"Ugh, do we have to?" I trail kisses over his cheek and down his neck, more interested in something else right now.

"You think she won't like me?"

I sigh, looking back up at him. My mom is lovely, but she's strict. Seeing me in love and giddy and everything, her first concern will be making sure I don't blow off college to get married.

"Well, you are the grandson of a senator, I guess," I tell him. "Can we lead with that?"

He snorts, shaking his head at me. I guess that's a no.

"Okay, fine," I snip. "But afterward, I have a favor to ask."

"Ask me now."

"Eh," I cage. "I'll tell you in the truck. It's kind of illegal."

21

Ryen

I pick up the small duffel and hear the clank of a few cans inside. Well, I guess it's better than it was. I don't want to alert my family when I take it downstairs, so I've wrapped the cans in some clothes, hoping to drown out the sound.

Tonight is my final little foray, and Misha is helping. Only this time, I have no guilt about it. We're rebels with a reason.

Okay, a little reason, at least.

Checking myself in the mirror one last time, I grab the bag and hear the doorbell ring, smiling. He's here.

Leaving my room, I lift the hem of my dress as I step down the stairs. My mom and sister are camped out in the living room, huddled around a bowl of popcorn and scary movies tonight, but really, they're just waiting to see Misha again.

When I brought him home last week, my mom immediately liked him. A lot. Especially with our history. She knows how much Misha means to me, and to finally meet him was incredible.

My sister, I think, was just aggravated. *Oh, look. He didn't ditch me. He likes me. He loves me. And he's hot.*

But she's been on my case less the last week, and I've tried to make an effort with her. After all, my relationship with my sister is as much my fault as it is hers. She may have been a brat as a kid, hating that she always had to hold my hand so I wasn't alone, but as we grew up, I was the one who pulled away. I'm trying to watch my mouth now and not build a wall every time she enters my space. It'll take some time, but I think we'll get there.

She even did my hair for me tonight.

I reach the bottom of the stairs, seeing my mom already heading through the foyer. I set the bag down and stand back up just as she opens the door.

Misha stands there, tall and dressed in a black suit, white shirt, with a black tie. Everything fits him perfectly, and he even has his tie tightened. His hair is styled, and the only thing that looks the same is the silver lip ring. His collar even covers the bit of ink that trails up his neck.

I love how he normally looks and dresses, but there's something about him in a suit. He looks so grown up. And really hot.

And I appreciate the effort he puts forth to impress my mom. When I brought him home the first time, he grabbed a hoodie out of the truck and put it on before we entered the house, pulling down the sleeves to cover up his ink. He was worried my mom would judge him before she knew him.

But that changed when she showed him the little kanji tattoo she had on her shoulder from college. Back when kanji was the rage. He relaxed a little.

His eyes lock with mine and then fall down my dress, a sleeveless red floor-length gown with a high neck and jeweled and pearled spaghetti straps across my bare back. My sister did my makeup, too, and my mom played music and made chocolate-covered strawberries while we all had fun getting me ready. Originally the plan was to go with Lyla and the girls to the salon, but today was perfect. I'm glad I spent it with my family.

I hold up my hands, posing and teasing, "So do I look cute?"

He steps in and walks up to me, leaning in to kiss my cheek. "That's not the word I would use," he whispers.

"You both look great," my mom chimes in.

"You don't match," my sister retorts, and I look up to see her entering the foyer.

She's dressed in her skimpy sleep shorts, probably for Misha's benefit, and I fantasize about putting vinegar in her mouthwash.

Match? Like his tie and my dress?

But Misha looks at her and places his hand on his heart, feigning sincerity. "We match in here."

I snort, breaking into quiet laughter.

My sister rolls her eyes, and my mom shakes her head, smiling.

"All right, let's go," I say.

I lean down to take the bag, which my mom thinks contains a change of clothes for the parties we're not going to later.

But she shouts, "Pictures!" And I stop.

Letting out a small sigh, I step down the last stair, and he turns me around, putting my back to his chest.

"Traditional cheesy prom pose," he explains.

"Oh, well, then. If we must."

My sister folds her arms over her chest, looking discontented as she watches my mom snap shots of us. Of course I want pictures. I'm not a party pooper. But I have that first picture of us at the scavenger hunt, and I feel like Misha's just doing me a favor, coming along with the boys and me. I don't want to put him on the spot.

But surprisingly, he seems to enjoy this. Turning me around, he wraps his arms around me and looks into my eyes, my mom taking a couple of quick pics.

My heart is already thumping hard, and I stare at his mouth, feeling my body warm up. I'd really just rather be alone with him tonight.

"Ugh, get a room," Carson whines and turns around, heading back into the living room.

I continue to stare at Misha.

"Ryen, be home by two," Mom says.

"It's prom," I point out. "It's kind of an all-night thing."

"Two," she repeats, looking between us, her warning clear.

But I argue anyway. "Seven."

"Three."

"Three, and Misha can come back for breakfast in the morning," I press.

She nods easily. "Fine. But beignets. Not jalapeño bagels."

"I know."

I take the bag gingerly, careful not to make the cans bang into each other, and whisper to Misha as I head past him, "Hopefully you'll be here extra early, because I'm not going to let you leave."

He laughs quietly and opens the door, leading me out. He probably doesn't want to risk getting on my mother's bad side now that they've met, but he knows he won't be able to say no to me.

We walk down the steps, and he takes the bag from me as I spot the limo sitting at the curb. Walking over, I stop and let him open the door.

"Hey!" voices drift out.

I see J.D., Ten, and Manny all sitting inside, snacking and drinking sodas, but if I know Ten, there's alcohol going on somewhere in here.

"Hey, why didn't you guys come in?" I ask as I climb inside.

"A prom picture with four guys?" J.D. teases. "Think of what Lyla would post about that."

Yeah, right.

But then the car door closes, and I dart my eyes over to see Misha leaning down and peeking in the open window.

"What are you doing?" I ask.

"I'll see you at prom."

What?

He starts to walk away, and I stick my head out of the window. "Misha!"

He turns around, walking backward, and I notice his truck behind him. He must've driven here and the guys pulled up after. "Don't worry," he calls, "and have fun. I'll be there."

I stare after him, completely confused. He's taking the bag with him, too. He's not going to do anything without me, is he?

Dammit.

I sit back in my seat, frowning. Now I don't get to walk into prom with four men.

I feel the limo start moving, and I notice the inside is also silent. Looking up, I see Manny, Ten, and J.D. all staring at me.

And then J.D. speaks up. "Who's Misha?"

The Baxter Hotel is decked out when we arrive. White lights glow in the trees and beautiful turn-of-the-century lanterns flicker with small flames, leading us into the ballroom. The fast music vibrates out into the lobby, and I can already smell the food.

We sent the limo back, hoping Misha will have his transportation when he gets here, but as we enter the prom, I still don't see him.

The room is exquisitely decorated in black and green—our school colors—with balloons, candles, and white linen tablecloths. I look up to the stage, where the band is playing a cover.

"Do you see him?" I yell into Ten's ear.

He winces, turning away from his conversation with Manny to answer me. "I haven't looked for him."

Okay. Relax. We just got here.

But things have finally calmed down between Misha and me, and we're having fun. I just don't want something dumb to screw it up.

I came clean to the guys in the car, figuring there was no harm anymore in telling them Masen's real name. Misha said he wasn't coming back to school, and I have real friends again. I feel awkward about lying.

"Do you want something to drink?" Ten asks, indicating his breast pocket.

I wave him off.

"Wanna dance?" J.D. asks at my other side.

I gaze around again, looking for Misha.

"Yeah," I finally answer. Why not? He told me to have fun.

J.D. leads me out onto the dance floor while Ten and Manny sit down at a table. I glance back at them, seeing Manny look around nervously like the other shoe is about to drop. But then . . . Ten reaches over and grabs him by the tie, pulling him in closer so he can straighten it.

I almost laugh. Manny looks taken aback, but a look passes between them, and I'm kind of curious.

Nah. Ten would never date a goth.

J.D. and I join everyone else on the dance floor, moving to the music as others laugh and talk. The energy and atmosphere are incredible. It's dark and crowded, and it feels like what Misha talked about in one of his letters. About realizing you're one of many and not feeling so alone.

I almost feel unseen—not on display—and I kind of like it. The song ends, and I fall into J.D., breathing hard and laughing. The fog machine and heat of so many crowded around is weighing on me, and I reach into my wrist purse and pull out my inhaler. I look around, hesitant. I usually go in the bathroom.

Screw it. Taking a puff, I see J.D. do a double take, but he only looks surprised as I take another one and try to inhale.

"You okay?"

I nod, giving him a thumbs-up. "I'm fine."

I slip the inhaler back into my purse and let him come in close. He places his hands on my waist as we slow dance.

"I can't believe what I'm seeing," someone says.

I turn around and lock eyes with Lyla and Katelyn, who are glaring as everyone dances around us.

Lyla's arms are folded over her hot-pink dress. "It's almost too precious for words," she muses.

Katelyn smirks behind her, and I drop my head forward, faking a snore. "Oh, I'm sorry." I pop my head up, looking at J.D. "I fell asleep. What happened?"

He chuckles.

In all honesty, though, I deserve Lyla's animosity. I wasn't a good friend. But with her, I'm not sure anyone can be.

I notice Trey lumbering toward her from behind and watch as he falls on her, draping his arms over her. His eyes are hooded, and he can barely stand.

"Hey, how goes it?" he slurs, gesturing between J.D. and me. "You, too, huh? You skip around pretty fast, girl. I like it."

Oh, please. I turn away from him but not before I see Lyla trying to shrug him off.

"Come on," he calls behind me, "friends share, J.D. You take mine for a spin, and I'll take yours."

Trey grabs my arm, but J.D. knocks him off. "Stay away from her."

Trey comes in again, but I steel every muscle inside me. "Enough!"

But just then, a voice rings out, and I stop.

"Thanks for letting us intrude, everyone," Misha says, and I blink, realizing the music has stopped.

Tearing my eyes away from Trey, I look up onstage and see Misha standing at the microphone. He's still wearing his suit, but he has a guitar draped in front of him, and we meet each other's eyes as a small smile dances in his.

I take a step, drawn in.

"We're Cipher Core, and this is dedicated to the cheerleader," he says.

My heart leaps into my throat, and I notice his bandmates on stage, the same guys with him at Trey's party.

"Hey, it's Masen," J.D. says, mumbling. "I mean Misha."

The drums count off, the beat starts, and the guitars lead in, creating a fast and hard but soulful tune. Misha's voice drifts in slow and haunting but quickly picks up pace.

Anything goes when everyone knows
Where do you hide when their highs are your lows?
So much, so hard, so long, so tired,
Let them eat until you're ground into nothing.

Don't you worry your glossy little lips.
What they savor 'ventually loses its flavor.
I wanna lick, while you still taste like you.

Bookmark it, says the cheerleader
I promise we'll come back to this spot.
I have shit to do first. You won't wait a lot.

I can't make her stay,
And I can't watch her go.
I'll keep her hellfire heart,
And bookmark it 'fore it goes cold.

Fifty-seven times I didn't call
Fifty-seven letters I didn't send,
Fifty-seven stitches to breathe again, and then I fucking pretend.

Fifty-seven days to not need you
Fifty-seven times to give up on you
Fifty-seven steps away from you,
Fifty-seven nights of nothing but you.

His eyes are closed, and his face is so beautiful. Everything inside me is crumbling, because it's the most perfect song I've ever heard, and I want him to keep going.

When did he write that? When we were fighting? Before we met?

A chaperone walks onstage after the song ends and cocks her head disapprovingly at the band. They smile and take off their instruments, quickly getting out of there, because while they may have had permission to perform a song, they probably didn't have permission to say a few of the words that were in those lyrics.

I laugh as Dane takes a dramatic bow and the crowd cheers. I don't even know what just happened. Were people dancing? Where's Trey and Lyla? I don't know, and I don't care.

Misha hands off his guitar to one of the guys, and I inch forward through the crowd, waiting for him to come to me. He hops down off the stage as the other band takes over again and starts playing.

He comes up and wraps his arms around me under my ass and lifts me up. I laugh even though tears wet my face.

I touch his cheek, looking down at him. "I didn't want to cry."

"A lot of your words are in those lyrics," he tells me. "We do more than a few things really well together, you know?"

"Good and bad."

He stretches his neck up, brushing my lips. "And I want it all."

I kiss him, everyone else forgotten. So that was "57." He'd sent me pieces of the song in the past year, but I'd never heard the whole thing.

"I love you," he whispers. "And I'm ready to leave as soon as you are, so keep me posted."

"I'm ready."

He smiles and sets me down. "Let's go have some fun."

He takes my hand, and we walk through the crowd of dancers, running into J.D. as we pass the food tables.

"Where are you guys going?" he asks.

I glance at Misha, and he shrugs.

There's a girl whose name I don't know at J.D.'s side. I don't want to take him away from her or the after-parties, but . . .

"Can you disappear with us for an hour?"

He thinks about it and sets his plate down. "I'm in."

"Remember you said that," I warn.

He whispers something to the girl and jogs after us while Misha knocks on Ten and Manny's table. "Let's go."

We all pile into Misha's truck, and I see my duffel sitting on the passenger-side floor as I climb in.

"So where are we going?" Ten asks as Misha starts the engine and pulls out of the parking lot.

"To the school."

I pull on my seat belt and put the bag in my lap, unzipping it.

"Why?"

I shoot a look to Misha, everything in his expression telling me to go ahead.

I pull out a can of the washable spray paint. "Because . . . it's nearly the end of the year, and I have a few more things to say."

I hold up the can and look behind me, seeing Ten's eyes damn near bug out of his head.

"What?" he bursts out.

"You?" J.D. looks at me, shocked.

I meet Manny's eyes, and I can see the wheels in his head turning. Maybe he realizes it was me who wrote the message on his locker that first time:

YOU'RE NOT ALONE. IT GETS BETTER.

YOU ARE IMPORTANT, AND YOU CAN'T BE REPLACED.

HANG ON.

I fill them in on everything. How it started and how I justified it, but I also tell them what I still need to do tonight. One last time to make it count.

And since they all will have something to say about the subject, I thought they might want a hand in it. Especially since Ten already indicated he'd like a piece of the action, and J.D. has already participated once.

"So are you in?" I ask them.

"Hell, yeah," J.D. replies.

I look at Manny, who remains silent. "You don't have to."

I'm not asking any of them to get in trouble. They can wait in the truck, or we can take them back to prom right now.

But he nods, indicating the can in my hand. "I want black."

All right. I dig in the bag, doling out cans and reminding them to stick to surfaces that can be easily cleaned. Stay away from screens, posters, artwork, and uniforms or clothes in the locker rooms.

We reach the school and park on the south side, slipping through the gate and running through the lot, up to the pool room.

I hand Misha my can and pluck my key out of my handbag.

"You have a key?" J.D. asks, surprised. "I can't believe they never thought of questioning you before."

Yes, I have a key. Often I'm the last one out of the pool, and this is my job. I'm entrusted to lock up this door.

"I'm Ryen Trevarrow," I joke. "I'm a bubblehead with barely enough brain cells to breathe."

Quiet chuckles go off around the group, and I unlock the door, hurrying everyone inside.

"How do you know no one will see it tomorrow and get rid of the paint before Monday?" Misha asks.

It's Saturday night, so it's possible.

But . . .

"Roofers will be here tomorrow to fix the leaks," I explain.

"Teachers are being asked to stay out of the building for safety." I look around at all of them. "You know what to do?"

"Yep."

"Absolutely."

"Ready."

Okay, then. "Let's go."

Monday morning, Misha and I walk into school, staring ahead as the storm whirls around us.

A big part of me knows we shouldn't have done it. There are all kinds of ways to handle our problems, after all. Better ways to deal with the issues.

But what Misha said was true. Everyone is ugly, aren't we? Some wear it and some hide it.

I guess I just got tired of Trey hiding it.

And of everyone allowing him to keep it hidden.

I did a bad, bad thing.

"Oh, my God," a guy mumbles off to my side, and I look over to see him reading something I wrote Saturday night.

"Hey, did you see this?" a girl gasps, asking her friend as they gape at the opposite wall.

I look down the corridor, seeing several messages written here and there and people fluttering about, taking it all in.

YOU SHOULDN'T BE CAUGHT ALONE WITH ME. YOU'VE BEEN ASKING FOR THIS.

—TREY BURROWES

CAN YOU EVEN FIND YOUR DICK ANYMORE, FAGGOT?

—TREY BURROWES

I'M GOING TO FUCK HER AND THEN FUCK HER MOM. WATCH ME.

EVERY CORNER YOU TURN, EVERY NIGHT WHEN YOU GO TO SLEEP, I'LL BE THERE, AND I'M GOING TO FIND OUT EXACTLY WHAT I'VE BEEN MISSING.

DOESN'T TAKE LONG FOR YOU LITTLE BITCHES TO TURN SLUT ONCE YOU GET A TASTE FOR IT.

YOU SHOULD'VE SEEN THE TRAIN WE PULLED ON THIS GIRL LAST WEEK. SHE HAD GUYS LINED UP. IT WAS SO FUCKING GOOD.

HEAD DOWN, ASS UP, THAT'S THE WAY WE LIKE TO FUCK.

Trey, Trey, and more Trey.

We keep walking, passing the quotes all four of us wrote on the walls, lockers, and floors Saturday night, turning down another hall and seeing even more.

Not all of them are about Trey, though. Some of them are attributed to Lyla, Katelyn, a couple of Trey's friends, and even me.

Because of course, saying you're sorry is easy. Facing the shame is where atonement begins.

ONE OF THESE NIGHTS, I'LL GET YOU IN THE PARKING LOT, AND I'LL SPREAD THOSE PRETTY LEGS AND FUCK YOU RIGHT THERE ON THE GROUND. WOULD YOU LIKE THAT, BABY?

—TREY BURROWES

"That's disgusting," a junior girl says, wincing.

Another girl takes out a pencil and writes underneath the "They all want it" message.

No, we don't, she writes.

The hallways are a flurry of activity, and we tried to keep our posts to the two main corridors, mostly because everyone passes through these hallways when they come into school.

People are captivated, though. Some girls look angry and disgusted. Some guys are surprised.

"All students please report to the auditorium," the vice principal's voice carries over the loudspeaker. "All students please report to the auditorium."

Ten stops us in the hallway, looking nervous but amused. "Looks like we broke the bank on this one."

"Yeah." I offer him a tight smile and watch more students writing under the messages on the wall. "Look at them, though."

Speak your mind, and you give others permission to do the same.

I turn to Misha, sighing. "You should leave. You don't need to be here, and she's going to pull you in if she finds you."

Since he walked out on Burrowes over a week ago, he hasn't been back to school, but I think he was worried about how all this would go down today and wanted to be here.

He shakes his head. "I don't care."

"Well, the police just got here," Ten informs us.

"The police?" I whisper. "I didn't think what we did was that bad."

"No, it's not for the vandalism. It's for Trey. A bunch of kids—several girls—are in the office, ratting him out. I guess the posts got to them."

"You should really go, then," I tell Misha.

But just then Principal Burrowes approaches us and my heart skips a beat.

"Mr. Laurent? Come with me now."

He stares at her for a moment.

But I jump in. "Why?"

"I think he knows why."

He hesitates for a moment, and I think he's going to fight like last time, but he doesn't. He takes a step.

"No, no, no . . ." I burst out. "He didn't do anything."

"It's okay," he assures me under his breath.

But Burrowes interjects, looking at me. "I show you on the log as the last person, other than the janitor, to sign out and leave the school Friday evening," she tells me. "Now, that's not unusual, since you stay late to teach swim lessons, but then it occurred to me that you have a key. And then I remembered the company you've been suddenly keeping." She glances at Misha. "Did you take her key?"

"No!" I answer for him.

"Yes," he says.

Oh, Jesus.

"It's okay," he says again. "I'll be fine."

She leads him away, and I throw up my hands, feeling helpless. Why didn't he just walk out like last time?

He doesn't have to protect me, and he knows I won't let him take the fall.

What is he doing?

22

Misha

"Sit down."

I prefer to stand, but I'm guessing I may as well settle in. I take the seat in front of her desk.

"After the fights and your behavior the past few weeks, I've been calling the phone numbers on file," she tells me, closing her office door. "None of them work or they're wrong numbers. You want to tell me what's going on?"

I stare at her as she takes her seat behind her tidy little desk. Unbuttoning her suit jacket, she scoots in and opens a file, undoubtedly mine. It's nearly empty.

But I keep quiet.

"If you had a concern about Trey, you should've come to me," she demands. "Not break into the school and write horrible accusations on the wall."

Accusations? Were the pictures she found in her bedroom not clear enough?

"Where is he?" I ask.

She straightens. "I've sent my stepson home for the day, while we sort through this mess."

I feel like smiling, but I don't. I simply stare at her. With the amount of upset students outside her door right now, I'm guessing the mess will take quite a while to sort through.

"Where are your parents?" she asks.

"My father lives in Thunder Bay."

"And your mother?"

"Gone."

She exhales a sigh and folds her hands on her desk. She knows she's not going to get anywhere like this.

Reaching over, she picks up the phone receiver and holds it to her ear. "Give me your father's phone number."

My fingers curl, but I don't give myself away. *This is it.*

"Seven-four-two . . . five-five-five . . . three-six-four-four."

"What's his name?" She punches in the number. "His *real* name."

I hear the line start ringing, and my heart pounds painfully, but I remain stoic.

"Matthew," I answer flatly. "Matthew Lare Grayson."

She suddenly goes still and darts her eyes up to me. Her breathing speeds up, and she looks like she's seen a ghost.

Well, she remembers his name. That's something, at least.

My father's voice comes across on the line. "Hello?"

And she looks back down, and I see her swallow the lump in her throat, blinking nervously. "Matthew?"

"Gillian?"

She hangs up the phone like it's burning hot and covers her mouth with her hand. I almost want to smile. Just to add to the taunt.

She raises her eyes, locking on mine and looking like she's scared of me. "Misha?"

Yep.

And awesome. She remembers my name. Two points for Mom.

Now she knows. Me choosing to come to this school and sit in this office had nothing to do with Trey. It was about her.

"What do you want?" she asks, and it sounds like an accusation.

I laugh to myself. "What do I want?" And then I drop my eyes, whispering to myself, "What do I want?"

I raise my chin and cock my head, sitting across from her and holding her fucking accountable. "I guess I wanted a mom. I wanted a family, and I wanted you to see me play the guitar," I tell her. "I wanted to see you Christmas morning and for you to smile at me and miss me and hold my sister when she was sad or lonely or scared." I watch as she just sits there silently, her eyes glistening. "I wanted you to like us. I wanted you to tell my father that he was a good guy who deserved better than you and that he should stop waiting for you. I wanted you to tell *us* to stop waiting."

I flex my jaw, getting stronger by the moment. This isn't about me. I'm done being hurt and asking myself questions when I know the answers won't be good enough.

"I wanted to see you," I go on. "I wanted to figure you out. I wanted to understand why my sister died of a heart attack at seventeen years old, because she was taking drugs to keep her awake to study and be the perfect daughter, athlete, and student, so you would come back and be proud of her and want her!"

I study her face, seeing Annie's brown eyes staring back, pained and turning red. "I wanted to understand why you didn't come to your own child's funeral," I charge. "Your baby who was lying on a dark, wet, cold road for hours alone while your new kids"—I shove at a picture frame on her desk, making it tumble forward—"in your new house"—another picture frame—"with your new husband"— the last picture frame—"were all tucked safe and warm in their beds, but not Annie. She was dying alone, having never felt her mother's arms around her."

She hunches forward, breaking down and covering her mouth with her hands again. This can't be a surprise. She had to know this was going to happen someday.

I mean, I know she hasn't seen me since I was two, but I thought for sure she would know me. That first day, seeing her in the lunchroom, I felt like she was going to turn around. Like she'd be able to sense me or some shit.

But she didn't. Not then, not when she pulled me into her office for a "Hey, how are you?" . . . and not anytime after that.

She deserted us and moved away when Annie was just a baby. After a time, I heard she went to college and started teaching, but honestly, it barely hurt.

I could understand being young—twenty-two with two kids—and not to mention the cutthroat family she married into. But I thought she'd eventually find her way back to us.

And later, when Annie and I found out she was only one town away, married to a man who already had a son, and she'd started a family with him and still hadn't made the slightest effort to seek Annie and me out, I got angry.

Annie did everything in the hope our mother would hear about her or see her team in the paper and come for her.

"Now . . ." I say, my tone calm and even, "I don't want any of those things. I just want my sister back." I lean forward, placing my elbows on the tops of my knees. "And I want you to tell me something before I leave. Something I need to hear. I want you to tell me that you were never going to look for us."

Her teary eyes shoot up to me.

Yeah, I might've convinced myself that I came here to collect the photo album of my sister's school pictures and newspaper clippings Annie said she mailed her here that I found in her file cabinet, and my grandfather's watch, but really, part of me had a shred of hope. Part of me thought she might still be a good person and have an explanation. A way to tell me why—even in death—Annie's mom still didn't come for her.

"I want you to tell me you don't regret leaving and you haven't thought about us a single day since you left," I demand. "You were happier without us, and you don't want us."

"Misha—"

"Say it," I growl. "Let me leave here free of you. Give me that."

Maybe she missed us and didn't want to disrupt our lives. Maybe she missed us and didn't want to disrupt *her* life. Or maybe that part of her life is broken and over, and she doesn't want to go back. Maybe she doesn't care.

But I do know that *I* can't care about this anymore. I stare at her and wait for her to say what I need to hear.

"I wasn't going to look for either of you," she whispers, staring at her desk with tears streaming down her face. "I couldn't stay. I couldn't go back. I couldn't be your mother."

I slam my hand down on her desk, and she jumps. "I don't give a shit about your excuses. I won't feel sorry for you. Now, say it. Say you were happier without us, and you didn't want us."

She starts crying again, but I wait.

"I'm happier since I left," she sobs. "I never think about you and Annie, and I'm happier without you." She breaks down as if the words are painful to say.

The sadness creeps up my throat, and I feel tears threatening. But I stand up, straighten my spine, and look down at her.

"Thank you," I reply.

Turning, I walk for the door but stop, speaking to her with my back turned. "When your other daughter, Emma, turns eighteen, I will be introducing myself to her," I state. "Do yourself a favor and don't be an asshole. Prepare her before that time comes."

And I open the door, leaving the office.

I step into the empty hallway and make my way for the entrance, the distance between my mother and me growing. With every step, I feel stronger.

I won't regret leaving, I say to myself. *I won't think about you a single day from now on. I'm happier without you, and I don't need you.*

I'll never look for you again.

D id you ask her why she left?"

"No." I sit against the wall in Annie's room with Ryen resting against me between my legs.

"You're not curious about her reasoning?" she presses. "How she would justify it?"

"I used to wonder. But now I . . . I don't know." It's not that I don't care, but . . . "If someone doesn't want us, we need to stop wanting them. I used to tell myself that, and now I believe it," I tell her. "It's not so hard, facing her and walking away. If she wanted to explain, she would've. If she could've, she would've. She didn't chase after me. She knows how to find me if she wants to."

Ryen smooths her hands down Annie's blue scarf. "So that's why you were in Falcon's Well."

"Yeah. She had the watch. An heirloom gifted by my father's father for her and my dad at their wedding," I say, burying my nose in her hair. "Family tradition dictates it goes to the firstborn son. She took it when she left—maybe to spite my dad or pawn it for money if she needed—but somehow she ended up giving it to Trey."

"You must've hated her for that."

"I already hated her," I shoot back. "That hurt, though. She'd already abandoned us. How could she steal one more thing—especially something that rightfully belonged to me?"

She was selfish and spiteful, and maybe she isn't the same person now that she was then, but I'm not waiting for her like Annie did. I hug Ryen close. This, right here, is everything. I can't wait to live all the days I'm going to live with her. We're going to have a hell of a lot of fun.

Especially since I no longer have to worry about that cocksucker at school with her for the rest of the year. She got a text from Ten earlier, saying he heard that the superintendent stepped in and forbade Trey from stepping foot on school grounds until everything clears up. And since a few students are pressing charges, for the photos and various assaults, it looks like the next several months of Trey's life will be spent in court.

Ryen stands and pulls me up, both of us trailing out of the room. I'd come in here to put Annie's locket and photo album back. There had also been letters with the album in the envelope I'd taken from our mother's office, too. Annie didn't tell me she'd written her, just that she'd sent her a photo album of her pics and stuff. She made sure to leave photos of me out of it, though. She knew I wouldn't have liked that.

Maybe I shouldn't have taken the album and letters. After our mother never showed up to the funeral, though, I just didn't want her to have anything of Annie's.

But Annie gave them to her, I guess. It was her wish our mother have those things.

If she wants the envelope back, she can have it. But she has to come and ask.

I close the door quietly behind me and walk into my room, seeing Ryen sitting on the bed, reading a piece of paper.

"What's this?" she asks.

I look down at the white paper. "It's a letter."

She folds it up and sets it down. "Well, I didn't read it or anything, but it could be an offer to talk about a recording contract." She smirks. "And there's several more there." She points to the bedside table. "I didn't read those, either, but I was wondering if maybe they could be letters of interest, too. I'll bet some well-connected dudes have seen Cipher Core's YouTube videos and want to talk."

They don't want Cipher Core. They want me, and I don't want to leave my band.

I plop down on the bed and pull her back, tickling her. "The only things I want to do are things that won't take me away from you. Understand?"

She laughs, squirming and trying to stop me.

"Well, college isn't far off!" She giggles, slapping my hands away. "I'll be leaving. And I looked at your band's Instagram page. They have tour dates up for this summer."

"It's just bullshit dives and fairs and festivals." I climb on top of her, straddling her and pulling her arms up over her head.

"But that sounds amazing."

I stick my tongue out and lean down, trying to touch her nose.

"Are you five?" she squeals, flopping her body and attempting to buck me off.

I dart in, licking the tip of her nose. She winces and shakes her head rapidly so I won't get a second shot in.

I chuckle, releasing her hands. "Honestly, I don't know why Dane still has that shit up. I told him I wasn't going."

"Yes, you are."

I climb off her. "Ryen, I—"

"Stop," she says. "It's not forever. You have to go. Just follow this and see where it leads."

Right now, I couldn't want anything less. The idea of leaving her makes me really fucking unhappy.

"You and I have had a long-distance relationship for seven years," she goes on. "I think we've withstood the test of time and distance. No one has ever come close to meaning to me in person what you mean to me in your letters. And now that we've met, and I love you," she says, climbing into my lap and wrapping her legs around me. "I don't doubt this. You need to go."

"I just got you."

"And I don't want you holding back because of me."

I slide my hands up the back of her shirt, savoring her warm, smooth skin.

"We're going to have everything we want," she tells me, laying down the law. "That's the only way I want this with you. If you go, and you don't like it, come home. If you do like it, I'll be waiting when you're done."

I can feel my nerves firing, and I don't know how to deal with this. I'd rather not think about it today at all.

Would I like to drive around in an old rented bus and play some music this summer? Maybe. That was the plan up until February.

But now I have Ryen, and I can't imagine not seeing her every day. I don't see the goddamn point of wasting a minute without her in it. I won't be happier just because I have the music.

But she's right. She's going off to college, and although I can, too, it won't be the same school. I could go with her, but . . . I can't follow her. We both need our own work someday, a way to be fulfilled.

"If you don't try," she says, "you'll wonder later if you should've. Don't put that guilt on me."

I give a weak laugh. Geez, punch me in the nuts, why don't you?

"If I do this, I have a condition of my own," I tell her, looking up into her eyes. "I want you to write a letter."

She breaks out in a gigantic smile. "A letter? I'll write you more than one while you're gone."

"Not to me." I shake my head. "Delilah."

Her face instantly falls. I can tell the prospect of facing that demon unnerves her.

"She left Falcon's Well in sixth grade. I wouldn't even know where she is now."

"I'm sure she's just a Google search away." Which she knows. She's just looking for an excuse to not face it.

She turns her head away, biding time, but I nudge her chin back to me again.

"What if she doesn't even remember me?" she asks. "What if it was no big deal to her, and she thinks I'm an idiot for still dwelling on it?"

I hood my eyes. "Any more excuses or are you done?"

"Okay," she bursts out like a child. "I'll do it. You're right."

"Good." And I flip her over onto her back and pin her down again. "Now get undressed. I need to make up for lost time while I'm away."

"What?" she argues as I pull her shirt over her head. "You make up for lost time when you get back!"

"Yeah. We can do that, too."

23

Ryen

So Alexander the Great, as you know, had a very close relationship with his mother, who was exceedingly influential in his life," the professor lectures.

I tap my pencil, glancing up at the clock, willing the minute hand to move faster. It's not that I'm not interested, but I'm supposed to get a package from Misha today, and I want to get back to my dorm.

"Is the movie accurate?" a young woman down the aisle to my right asks. "Did she really like snakes as much as they portrayed?"

Movie? I smile to myself. A girl after my own heart.

Although I've learned to be more tolerant and patient. I've read all the articles and other assigned reading. In addition to seeing the film, of course.

The aging professor sits on his table down front, his legs dangling above the floor. "That is accurate. She loved snakes. Too much, some say."

I blink and finally look at him, my curiosity piqued now. Too much?

Professor Jacobson sees the blank stares around the room and laughs, giving us a bigger hint as to his meaning. "She liked snakes, and . . . snakes . . . like . . . warm . . . places . . ."

I shudder, it finally hitting me. "Ew."

The whole class breaks into laughter, all of us squirming in our seats. That can't possibly be true.

He smiles, always seeming to enjoy messing with us, and looks up at the clock. "All right, let's call it a day," he says. "Have a good weekend, everyone. I'll be in my office until six if anyone needs me."

Yes. I swipe my keyboard and iPad off the table, my heart starting to race in anticipation. Stuffing everything into my bag, I shoot out of my chair and jog down the stairs, crossing the front of the classroom and pushing through the doors.

I haven't seen Misha in months—not since Christmas—and even though he sends me letters and calls on Skype all the time, it's the packages he teases me about that I anticipate almost as much as the prospect of seeing him.

I like checking my mail and seeing anything from him.

Sometimes it's fun stuff, like mixtapes, souvenirs from his tours, or things he thinks I need, like funny cookbooks such as *Thug Kitchen*, when I complain I'm tired of eating in the dining halls.

Other times I'll walk into my dorm room and find flowers or the ceiling covered with balloons, like on my birthday.

And I write him every week, even though he's not always in the same place and won't get the letters until later. But he insists. No emails.

After all this time, we're still pen pals.

His tour last summer ended better than expected. He thought he'd finish, come home, and keep writing music, trying to get a deal, but after all the exposure last year, they were knocking at his door before the tour was even done. In the months since, he and the guys have recorded an album, and even though I listen to it every day, I can't get through a twenty-four-hour period without hearing it come from someone else's iPod, car stereo, or television, either. I'm so proud of him.

Making my way past the student union and down the sidewalk

lined with newly budded trees, I cross the street and walk into Campbell Hall, my home for the past seven months. Jetting down the steps, I dig out my keys from my bag and find my mailbox, unlocking it.

I pull out mail, but pause when I don't see another key. My mailbox is small, so anytime Misha sends packages, there's a key to a bigger box where I'll find the box he sent.

I quickly flip through the mail, seeing a card from my mom, my phone bill—which I won't look at today—and some credit card offers.

Nothing from Misha.

My heart sinks. Didn't he say something was coming today? I should FaceTime him in the middle of whatever he's doing for getting my hopes up like that, dammit. I close my mailbox and slide my mail into my bag.

As I walk back into the stairwell, something on the wall catches my attention, though, and I stop, reading it.

THEY SAY WE'RE NO GOOD AND WE'RE OKAY WITH THAT,
WE'RE THE LEADERS OF THE NOT-COMING-BACKS.

The black Sharpie is written on the wood, down the side of the doorframe, and I break out in a smile at the 5 Seconds of Summer lyric, my heart lodging in my throat.

I break into a run up the stairs and see a small sign hanging on the wall, also with a lyric.

IT'S DARK INSIDE. IT'S WHERE MY DEMONS HIDE.

Oh, my God. I suddenly can't catch my breath. He's here.

I race up to my floor.

PAINT IT BLACK AND TAKE IT BACK . . . Another message as I swing through the door leading to my floor. I walk briskly down the well-lit hall, seeing message and after message written for me, leading right to my room.

HELLO THERE, THE ANGEL FROM MY NIGHTMARE.

And I smile wider, seeing an Eminem lyric in various colors, painted on the wall.

YOU DON'T GET ANOTHER CHANCE. LIFE IS NO NINTENDO GAME.

ONE MINUTE I WANT TO SLIT YOUR THROAT, THE NEXT I WANNA SEX.

I laugh, covering my grin, because yeah.

Biting my lip, I unlock my door with shaking hands and swing it open, instantly spotting Misha. Butterflies take off in my stomach.

"You know," he starts, leaning back in my desk chair, his hands behind his head, "I might see more of you if you'd decided to attend the New York School of Design instead."

I smirk, walking in and closing my door. Damn, he looks good. Dark jeans that hang on his waist just well enough to make me jealous of a pair of pants and a gray T-shirt over his long, wide torso. I glance around to make sure my roommate isn't here.

I approach him, dropping my bag. "Have you seen Cornell's library? Rows and rows of dark hidden places to get lost in."

Of course I could've had more opportunities to see him if I went to school in the city, but he was going to be all over the place, and Cornell was what was best for me, so I dove in.

"So that's why you chose this university?" he asks, spreading his legs and taking my hips as I come in close.

I nod. It was certainly one of the reasons. Fantasizing about Misha's visits and all the little places we could get lost in.

I touch his face, seeing that he's finally changed out his black lip ring for a silver one. "I missed you."

"Missed you, too." He lifts the hem of my shirt and kisses my stomach, sending shivers right down to between my thighs.

"You look beautiful," he says. "Happy."

"You won't let that deter you, will you?" I tease, referencing how we can always manage to spice up any occasion with a little banter. "I might enjoy some trouble."

He buries his nose and mouth in my skin, his voice muffled. "No problem."

"So I hear you're famous now."

His shoulders shake with a small laugh. "In my small sliver of the world for the next fifteen minutes maybe."

I bring his face up, forcing him to meet my eyes. "Your music . . . you did incredible. I listen to it every day."

"You're prejudiced."

I shrug. "Probably."

Leaning down, I kiss him, loving how I get immediately warm all over. I hope he doesn't want to crash here tonight. I'll feel guilty turning my roommate out while we try to squeeze into my twin bed. Hotel, please.

"How long do you have?" I kiss him again and again, sitting down and straddling his lap as both of us turn breathless. "Are you going on tour anytime soon or something?"

He shakes his head, speaking between kisses. "I think . . . maybe I'm not ready for the music world quite yet. I thought I might go to college, take my time . . ."

I stop and pull away. "Is this . . . this doesn't have anything to do with me, does it?" I question him. "I don't want you to miss your opportunities."

"You're my opportunity," he states. "I've grown up with you, and like I said, you've been a part of nearly everything I've done that I love. I can make music anytime, anywhere, and the opportunities will be there when we're ready for them."

But—

"Although you may have to transfer," he cuts in before I have a chance to retort. "I'm not sure I can get into Cornell."

And then I'm swept up in the reality of what he's saying, and I break out in a smile. Misha and me. Here together. Seeing each other every day. I have to admit, I'm all for it. As much as I love the letters and the anticipation of seeing him after long absences, I want to move forward, not go back like we're still pen pals in fifth grade.

Not that I didn't love being pen pals, but that was before I was in love with him, and the prospect of it being just the two of us now sounds too good.

And we're only nineteen. If he wants to slow back down and take his time, I can't begrudge him that.

I squint at him. "A bestselling rock star and senator's grandson who will bring free publicity to the university?" I muse. "I'm sure it will work out."

If Cornell doesn't take him, then there's no way I can stay in such a lame university.

I wrap my arms around him, whispering across his lips. "Can't wait to have you around every day. No parents. No drama. No shenanigans. Just us."

But then I hear someone behind me burst through the door, and I twist my head around, seeing Dane standing in the doorway, his hands up and looking worried.

"We're going to have to rent a house," he tells Misha, out of breath. "There's no way I can fit all my guitars and amps in these rooms."

I turn around, cocking my head at Misha.

But he just snorts. "He kind of goes where I go. We'll stay out of trouble. I promise."

Mm-hmm.

24

Ryen

Five Years Later . . .

Ryen!" I hear my name being called. "Ryen, come on!"

I shake my head, amused as I step up onto the curb in front of my apartment building. Delcour's doorman is already poised with the door open for me to make my escape.

"No, Bill," I say to the reporter from the *Times* as he and a few photographers rush up to me, cutting into my space.

I try to veer around them, but they're everywhere. I push through them.

"An Oscar nomination for Best Original Song?" Bill Winthrop holds up a recorder in front of me. "You have to be pleased. He has to have something to say! Come on."

"He's in the writing cave," I say, making my way to the door. "I told you that before."

I turn around, giving him and the other guys who've been camped out here forever a bored look. "Really, you've been out here for months. Take the night off. Go get a date."

Some of the reporters and photographers laugh, and shots from their cameras go off around me.

"Yes, it's been months since anyone's seen him," Bill chides. "How do we know he's still alive?"

I cock my head and put my hands on my hips, making my now-visible pregnant belly more apparent. Obviously, Misha is well enough to do this, right?

I hear laughter break out again.

"You know Misha likes his privacy," I point out.

"Will he be at the awards?"

"Not if he can help it." And I turn, heading into the building.

"You're impossible!" I hear Bill's frustrated shout and don't even bother to hide my smile.

"I love you, too!" I call over my shoulder.

Really, that has to be the most tedious job. Waiting around to see if Misha leaves to go get coffee or pick out a new pair of shoes. It won't last forever, but my husband would rather avoid attention at all costs. I guess that just makes him more alluring and mysterious, though. I think they even created an app, *Spot Misha Lare*, like it's frickin' *Pokémon Go* or something.

I can understand the desire for him, though. He ended up joining me at Cornell for college after his summer tour, saying that his opportunities could wait. We had one life, and he refused to do anything more without me at his side. He'd wait.

I was worried he'd miss out on some big chance, but Misha knows who he is and what he wants.

And he was right. It wasn't long after college before he re-formed Cipher Core, all the original members back, and they began racking up the awards and tour dates.

It's been a hell of a ride, and it's just starting.

I walk through the lobby, spotting Rika passing by the front desk.

"Hey, how are you?" she asks, carrying a duffel bag.

I take in her leggings, knee-high black boots, and oversize sweater, and here I am, feeling like a planet. When is she going to get pregnant anyway?

Michael Crist's wife—who's from Thunder Bay, as well—and I

have become very close, and since her mom and Misha's dad are suddenly *very* close, we'll all probably be family eventually.

I can't complain. Their whole crew of friends is interesting, to say the least, but they're loyal.

I look at her apologetically, gesturing to the reporters behind me. "I'm sorry about all this."

But she just waves me off. "It's happened with Michael when he makes the playoffs, just not quite like that." She laughs. "I think he's jealous, actually. But, hey, a basketball player is a basketball player. A rock star is a rock star."

"Don't remind me."

She adjusts the bag on her shoulder and keeps walking. "Well, I'm off to the dojo and then Thunder Bay for the weekend. See you Monday, and tell my future stepbrother I said hi," she jokes.

"Will do." And I head for the elevators.

I ride up to the twenty-first floor, where there are two penthouses. There's only one floor above us, and that's the Crists'. I love the view, and I'm glad Misha likes to be in the city. We frequently spend time with his father in Thunder Bay, but the nightlife, shows, and concerts are too alluring to stay away from. We like the noise here.

Once inside, I smell steaks cooking, and my stomach instantly growls. We have a gym in the building, but I like the classes at Rika's dojo, so I braved the reporters for that today, but now I'm starving. And I need a bath.

Arms come around me from behind, holding my belly, and I lean back, feeling instantly relaxed. His intoxicating scent surrounds me, and I need contact.

"Help me get out of these clothes," I beg.

He pulls my shirt over my head and helps me out of my sports bra. I'm only six months along—our son is due in March—but I'm playing up the helpless act. The more he touches me, the happier I am. And Misha doesn't like to see me mad.

After stripping out of my shoes, socks, and workout pants, I turn around, pulling my hair out of its ponytail.

He looks incredible. I like this house arrest he's been keeping himself on. All he does is walk around the apartment all day, half-naked in only lounge pants, listening to music and leaving lyrics in random places. They're written all over the refrigerator, on napkins, on Post-its stuck to the walls—which he started doing when I freaked out about Sharpie on the fresh paint in the bedroom.

It's all a part of his creative process, he says.

Whatever. It works, I guess.

"Come on." He pulls me along. "I started you a bath."

I follow him to the bathroom, watching him strip down and get in, and then he holds out a hand, inviting me in.

I climb in and sit at the other end of the large tub, smiling gratefully when he starts massaging my leg.

"The reporters are insane," I tell him. "Everybody wants a piece of you."

"Well, this piece wants you." And he takes my foot, nudging between his legs with it.

I slowly crawl up on top of him, straddling him but not able to get chest to chest with my belly.

He takes the small silver pitcher I have next to the tub and begins pouring water over my hair. I arch my neck back, the blanket of warmth coating my scalp and back and making me moan.

He kisses my neck. "Can I tell you something?" he asks gently.

I look up, meeting his eyes and nodding.

He smooths my hair back, looking at me lovingly. "I love you very much, and when we got married it was my hope that we'd be together forever," he states, "but that mirror thing"—he points behind me to the wall design I just installed—"is pissing me off. I lose my equilibrium whenever I walk in here."

I turn around and break into a smile, looking at the array of mirrors installed on the walls, which reflect the mirrors on the opposite wall.

Turning back to him, I lift my chin, nodding. "You'll get used to it."

"You say that all the time," he whines. "I put up with the gothic fireplace in our converted barn home in Thunder Bay, the sewing machine end tables, the fact that I have to walk through a wardrobe to get into the master bathroom, but this mirror thing . . ."

He trails off, and I kiss his cheek. "It's a conversation piece."

He levels me with an unamused look.

I shake with laughter. "If you divorce me, we won't still have sex."

He twists up his lips. "Yeah, I figured."

What a baby. He knew when he married me that I liked being creative. Even if I wasn't any good at it.

I reach over and flip the knob, turning on the shower over us. It falls behind me, but it creates a pleasant buzz.

"You need to put in an appearance," I say.

I hate pushing him, and I normally don't, but sometimes I worry he doesn't live it up enough.

"Will's been calling like crazy," I point out, "and he even bugged me at work today. He says you need to 'ride the ride while you can.'"

"I am," he maintains, and then he tightens his arms around me. "I just want to make music with you, and I want people to hear it and love it, but I don't need to be bigger than this. I don't need the hype. I'm happy."

I caress his face. "Most people don't get a chance to be a god," I say. "Are you sure you're not missing out? You won't live forever, after all."

"No, but my music can."

He always has the perfect answer for everything. He's right.

He's not missing anything. Would we be happier, sacrificing the time we have together to give it to others? No.

"And you and me in the lyrics," he finishes. "That's all that's important, and I won't tolerate any distractions. I've only got one shot to do this right, and that's what I'm doing."

I bring him in, kissing him. I love him so much.

But his words remind me of our favorite rapper, and I pull back, unable to resist teasing him. "Hey, 'only one shot' just like in Eminem's 'Lose Yourself.'"

And I start singing the song, belting out the lyrics at the top of my lungs.

He pushes my head back, dousing me under the shower as I squeal in laughter.

Hey, what did I say?

RYEN AND MISHA ALTERNATE MEETING

This is an alternate reality in which Ryen learns Misha's identity before he learns hers. It takes place in the fall of their senior year, about five months before they first meet in the book.

There are no plans to make this into a book. It's just a fun extra. Enjoy!

Ryen

Dear Ryen,

Tell me what to do. I might not listen (probably won't listen), but you're the only one who trusts me to know what's best for myself. Just tell me it's okay to leave.

I don't want to go to college. I don't want to stay in Thunder Bay. My family loves me. Why do I want to get away from them so much?

Except for Annie, of course.

My grandfather thinks youth is an insignificant prelude to a real life you'll earn someday if you commit to things you don't want to do right now. If I do what he says, he'll give me the keys to the kingdom.

My dad thinks everything will kill me and never wants me to see anything outside of this town.

And my cousins and my sister all follow. They want the money and the power, and they're scared to be without it.

I just want it to mean something.

I know my mind. I like the things I want. But I'm fucking sick of no one who loves me being on my side. It's just all fear. So much goddamn fear, and I'm catching it, too. Maybe *they're right. They have experience. The formula worked for them, after all. Maybe if I hire top-shelf pussy from the city, comb my hair, and tighten my fucking tie, I won't still want to hang myself with it in ten years. Maybe then I won't know how to think on my own anymore, and I'll just be numb. You think?*

And for what? To keep the money rolling in for the next generation, so my kids can keep it rolling in for the ones after them? Why?

Would you still like me if I wore a suit?

"What are you reading?" Lyla asks.

I glance up, meeting her eyes in the rearview mirror as she speeds down the highway. I fold Misha's last letter and stuff it in my bag. They don't know about my pen pal, and they never will. I'll never share him.

"Why are we dressed like this?" I ask instead.

"Like what?"

Trees fly by in the darkness out the windows, Ten sitting in the seat next to her and flicking a cigarette butt out the crack in the window.

"Like blow-up dolls," I reply.

Ten laughs, and I prop my elbow up on the door, resting my chin in my hand.

"It's a uniform," Lyla points out, "and you wear it every week, Ryen."

"It's a uniform when we wear it to games." I stare at the tree line, smelling the ocean beyond the woods. "To a Thunder Bay campout, it's a costume. I'm not sleeping with any of them."

"Be sure and say that nice and loud when we get there," Ten teases. "They're very bored and love a challenge."

No, they don't. If it can't be bought, it can be roofied. I know how the rich kids from Thunder Bay deal with their challenges.

Except for Misha, of course. He's the only person from that town I'd show up for. I've never met him, but I know him. In fifth grade, our teachers paired up everyone in our classes to write letters to each other, and Misha and I never stopped. We didn't get along at first, but then the arguing became fun. He forced me to stand up for myself, and then I started admitting things that I couldn't tell anyone else, because it was safe. I didn't have to ever face him.

I had no idea how important he would become to me.

And I know him well enough to know I won't see him tonight, which is why I agreed to step foot on his turf. He would never waste a second of his life at some self-indulgent celebration of "look how powerful we are." It's hard to even imagine him tolerating those people at school every day.

"I'm not a challenge," I retort. "I have standards."

"Too-high standards." Lyla sighs. "You're very hard to impress."

She's judging me because I won't straddle Trey Burrowes like she thinks he deserves.

But Ten chimes in. "No," he tells me. "You're not hard to impress." He checks his hair in the mirror on his visor, meeting my eyes. "You just need your mind stimulated. That's a good thing."

Doesn't everyone need their minds stimulated?

"And you might like this more than you think," Ten continues. "Thunder Bay is different. Rich people are different."

Duh.

"They're desensitized," he explains. "Whatever they want to eat, they eat. Wherever they want to go, they can go. They don't enjoy anything, because they don't know what it's like to not have it."

Sure. It's completely understandable how they can't just get laid like everyone else, nice and simple. No, according to a story I heard, a few years back they had to find a senior girl who would volunteer herself to be tied naked to a tree, and then they had a contest to see who could masturbate her the best.

It's just like how I can no longer find anything to watch on TV, because I have access to everything with streaming. We all have to work harder to be entertained now.

But Ten keeps trying to make me understand. "Several years ago," he says, "some friends got together and realized the only things they wanted anymore were the things no one dared to ask for. A freedom people didn't talk about at the breakfast table. They don't want to fuck you, Ryen. They want you to tell them what to do to Lyla and watch you watch them do it to her."

Ew . . .

"If it comes to that," Lyla tells me over her shoulder, "they can do everything. Just an FYI."

"Same for me," Ten adds.

I shake my head, seeing the outline of the dark roller coasters of the Cove in the distance. "It's sick," I say under my breath.

"Sick or sane." Ten shrugs. "Sometimes I really don't know which one is worse."

But what happens when fucking with people's heads gets as boring as everything else? Ten has a point. When your life affords you the opportunity to overindulge, it becomes harder to enjoy things. You don't long for anything anymore. There's no craving.

I hope I never have everything I want. How did Misha stay ahead of it all? He's rich. At least his family is. I've gathered that much from his letters. Not that he ever came out and said it, but he talked about falling off a horse when he was little and a painting of his mom's he found in the attic once. Average people don't often have horses *and* paintings in their lives.

As the car curves a right, I take the flask Ten hands me over the seat and swallow a swig of his vodka. Maybe I shouldn't have come tonight. It's cold, it's in the middle of nowhere, and it's Devil's Night—when Thunder Bay is at its absolute worst. I just feared missing out.

We cruise into a vast lot, the pavement broken by weeds sprouting from the cracks, the yellow lines from parking spaces faded after years of neglect. To the right sits the abandoned theme park, Adventure Cove, the old cars of the Ferris wheel creaking and the torn vinyl of the game booth tents flapping in the wind.

We climb out, and I hug myself against the chill in the October air. Other cars are scattered throughout the lot, a few people hurrying to the right, into the woods. The direction opposite the theme park.

Lyla fixes the black bow—identical to mine—on top of her head, smoothing out her dark hair.

"How did we score an invite to this?" I ask.

She doesn't answer right away, checking her lipstick in the car window and turning to follow everyone else into the trees. "We don't have an invite."

I round my eyes, darting them to Ten. What the fuck?

"Don't worry," he rushes to tell me. "They want us here."

I look down at my uniform, which Lyla told me to wear. "The outfits . . ." Like porno candy. Jesus Christ. "Are any other Falcon's Well people here?"

"Let's go!" she shouts after us.

Like hell. I round the car, prepared to leave without them if they don't get in with me, but Lyla calls out, "I've got the keys!"

And she jiggles them over her head.

I curl my hands into fists, watching them head into the brush. Ten glances back at me with a contrite grin, only a little bit sorry for me.

The last thing I want to do is crash their party like I'm begging to be here. I don't do that.

Pulling out my phone, I pause a moment before dialing my sister. She'll make the whole drive home a bitchfest, but my mom is out of town. I can't call anyone else. It'll look pathetic.

I hold the phone to my ear. "Carson, answer the phone."

When she doesn't pick up, I end the call.

"Dammit," I spit out.

I tap out a text to her. I need a ride.

I wait a few seconds, and nothing. It's after ten, but it's the weekend. She's up. She's ignoring me. She does that thing where she reads my texts when they pop up as notifications. It doesn't tell me she's read it unless she clicks on it. I know, because I do the same thing to her.

But I'm literally in trouble right now. I glare at my phone, strangling her in my head.

"Fuck," I mouth, tucking my phone up my skirt and into my Spanx before I start following everyone into the trees.

Staying out here by myself isn't a good idea, either.

I make my way down a wide path, dry leaves rustling under my sneakers, and I inhale the scent of the burning wood as I see the glow in the distance. Trees stretch overhead into the night sky, canopying the walkway as people head down the trail in front of me.

Darting my eyes around, I spot dark shadows deep into the forest at my sides and keep my eyes up, aware of my surroundings. This place is dangerous.

The kids here are threatening. Everything that happens in Thunder Bay is reported as consensual, but it's not like wealthy people can't afford to sell whatever version they damn well like.

There are caves in Thunder Bay. Catacombs. Underground tunnels. Millions of places to—

But then I pause, slowing my steps as something catches my eye high in a tree. A dark figure looms on a branch above, and I keep stepping forward slowly, not blinking as I gaze at him.

Is that . . . ?

I drift my focus to the next tree and the next.

And then . . . the next.

There's four of them. All in different trees, two on each side of the path. They stand, either holding the trucks at their sides or a branch above their heads. Statues?

Then one moves. He cocks his head, the moonlight catching his face, and I see it's gnarled and dripping with blood. I suck in a breath.

But something about the skin is off. It's too bright. Like white face paint.

Like a mask.

I let my eyes float around to all four of them, seeing each creature, frozen except for the subtle sway as they balance in the trees. They look like they're staring at me.

Misha goes to school with these people?

"They don't bite," someone whispers, and I turn to see a guy in a black bomber jacket at my side. "They swallow you whole."

Amusement crosses his eyes, but he maintains enough of a distance.

He doesn't invade my space.

"Why are the girls always the prey in Thunder Bay?" I ask.

"All human predators were once prey." He jerks his chin at the boys in the trees. "They weren't born this way."

I arch an eyebrow. That actually sounds a little profound, but I don't have the patience to unpack it right now.

"Ryen Trevarrow," he says, holding out his hand. "Riley Costigan."

"How do you know my name?"

"I know everyone."

I stare at him. *Riley Costigan.* I've heard of him.

He invented the fleet parties off the coast. I wouldn't tell him, but I would actually love to see one of those bashes. They all get their parents' boats together in the ocean, like one giant barge. There's one to kick off the summer and one before school starts every year.

I take his hand, shaking it.

"Come on." He keeps hold of it for another second, pulling me along before letting go. I follow him into a clearing where a giant bonfire rages, and it's full of people dancing and laughing.

Two kegs sit to the left, between two trees, while camping tents of various colors glow with lights and the sporadic shadows coming from inside. Ten and Lyla flirt with a couple of guys, the taller one passing a bottle among them all, and people run around, some in costumes. Tomorrow's Halloween.

Devil's Night is the real party, though, and I'm still not sure I understand it. It's like they try to look for things to do that they'll regret.

Two people fight off to my right, and it takes only a moment to realize it's a guy and a girl. I straighten, watching her beanie fly off and her blond hair whip around. I open my mouth to . . . I don't know—say something—but then I realize she's winning. With her arms wrapped around his neck and her legs around his waist, she's stuck to his back. He crashes down onto the ground, her head jerking back, and I think she's going to lose hold as the wind gets knocked out of her, but she doesn't. He flips over, taking her with him, and no matter what he does, he can't shake her. Running out of breath, he taps out.

She breaks into a smile, releases him, and rolls away before climbing to her feet. Cheers fill the air around her as she swipes her hat off the ground and pulls it back onto her head.

He probably let her win. What does she get as a prize? A kiss from him?

"I remember that feeling," Riley Costigan says, staring at me. "Looking but not seeing."

"And what am I supposed to see?"

His blue eyes dance as he slips his hands into his jeans pockets. "It's not for anyone to tell you that, Trevarrow. But it's less a matter of what to see and more a matter of how."

I draw in a breath, looking away. I'm already bored. This isn't my first conversation with a Thunder Bayer, and they all speak like Zen masters, as if their sordid indulgence is some profound meditation.

"You look at them like you're afraid you're not invited," Costigan says. "And you're ready to turn up your nose if you're not."

I flash my eyes back to him.

I'm not looking at them like that.

"And how should I look at them?" I ask instead.

"Like you extended the invitation." He smiles, leaning in a little. "Every time, baby."

A buzz lights under my skin, and for a second I almost wonder if he's actually Misha.

He tips his chin off to my side. "Watch."

I see the young woman from the fight, her black T-shirt covered with dirt and bits of leaves, as she pulls the shirtless guy she was fighting behind her. Of course. She gets her prize, which, of course, is no real chore for him. He's going to love every second of this.

"Follow them," Riley tells me.

Do I have to?

But my curiosity gets the best of me. We follow quietly, into the dense cover of trees, past tents and to where it's emptier, and darker.

A green tent sits alone, surrounded by tall trees and boulders, and Riley and I shield ourselves behind a trunk. The last thing I want to do is watch this girl take off her clothes for him.

They reach the tent, she turns, and he smiles down at her. I'm about to roll my eyes when someone else steps into view. I watch a guy in a black hoodie grab the shirtless one by the neck and swing him around to face him. The one from the fight scowls, shoving him off, but the one in the hoodie takes hold of his throat in both hands and plants their foreheads together, the other guy not fighting him anymore. They both breathe hard, and in one quick movement, Black Hoodie shoves the other one into the tent. I watch his shadow fall inside as the other one pulls off his sweat-shirt, drops it to the ground, and climbs into the tent with him.

I stare at their shadows, and it almost looks like they're fighting again before . . . they start kissing. The one on top starts ripping at the other's belt and dives back down to his body before the light inside is extinguished, and I blink.

I drop my gaze. I didn't mean to watch.

I glance around quickly. The girl has disappeared. I'm not sure when she left.

"The one in black is her brother," Costigan tells me.

It takes a minute to put together what happened. "So, she won a prize for him with that fight?" I ask.

But instead of nodding, he studies me. "You think Shirtless was the prey?"

Well, wasn't he?

I watch the tent, the nylon moving here and there as they shift inside.

I stare at Costigan. "Are you saying the brother was? The other one fought to get his attention?"

He shrugs. "Maybe." He gazes at the tent, whispering, "Or maybe you're the prey in this entire scene."

I dig in my eyebrows. Me? I'm definitely not letting myself be coerced into . . .

But I did watch, didn't I? Not all seduction is sex.

"Or maybe you are," I say, a smile crossing my lips.

He breathes out a laugh. "Very good." He taps his temple. "Per-spective. Nothing is how it seems. Ever. Everything is about per-spective. Everything. You understand?"

And for some reason, I nod.

"Control your perspective," Zen Master tells me, "and the world is so much more beautiful."

"And what happens when fucking with people's heads gets old?"

"Oh, honey. High school is just practice." He plants a hand on the small of my back, guiding me back to the party. "It'll be so much more fun in five years. You'll see."

I remove his hand but stay at his side.

"Don't worry," he says. "You're not my type."

And he eyes the bow on top of my head. I suddenly feel it tugging at the hair right at my scalp. I move it from side to side, trying to loosen it. "It's stupid. Not my idea . . ."

"It's a costume," he says.

Exactly what I said, but I think Lyla was hoping we'd look like bait.

"Who are you going to be tonight?" he taunts. "Sexy cheerleader? Virgin cheerleader?" And then in a low voice: "Daddy's cheerleader?"

Unable to stop myself, I let out a snort. *Constantly playing a role . . .*

And I have a feeling that the kids in Thunder Bay are always in character, Devil's Night or not.

I lean in, my nose nearly touching his. "Killer cheerleader."

But to my surprise, he isn't amused.

A gleam hits his eyes like I've issued a challenge. "You sure about that?" he presses. "The last time a Falcon's Well girl tried to play in Thunder Bay, she's the one who ended up dead."

"Reverie Cross." I tighten my half ponytail, lifting my chin.

Everyone knows about her. The seventy-year-old murder and the underlying reason why our towns are enemies.

"Guess that means it's our move," I tell him.

Finally, he smiles. "You can stay."

He walks away, leaving me to go have my fun now that I have a proper invitation to hang with them.

I watch spectators cheer as two climbers race up a tree in a game of chicken to see who will go the highest. Guys in masks lurk around the periphery, and I pass by a guy blindfolded, trying to guess the name of the girl he's got in his hands.

I will give these people one thing. They don't seem to care about talk. As if rumors are trite and reputations are earned instead of dreaded. Very different from Falcon's Well.

"Misha!" a young woman squeals.

I freeze.

My heart lodges in my throat, and my skin vibrates. A girl leaps past in front of me and disappears out of the corner of my eye.

"Hey!" she chirps, and I almost can't breathe.

Misha.

He's here.

He's here?

It can't be. My pulse starts to race, and I focus on where she ran off behind me. To him. He's behind me.

Don't look.

You can't.

It might not even be him. Misha isn't a common name, but it's not uncommon, either. It could be a girl.

My Misha wouldn't be caught dead at a gathering like this.

But heat crawls up my neck, and I can't run. I want to turn around.

Don't . . .

Don't.

But I don't stop myself.

I twist around, watching the young woman jog into the trees, toward a red tent.

She wraps her arms around the guy standing next to it, tucking her head into his chest.

I stare at him, the world tilting on its side around me. I almost stumble.

It's him.

I know it's him. And barely thinking twice, I start to step closer.

He strips off his Thunder Bay Prep school tie, gives the girl a squeeze, and then pulls the back of his white button-down shirt, slipping it off over his head. My eyes instantly drop to his naked chest and arms, tattoos covering him and his dark brown hair lying in messy wisps just above his eyes. I see ink that looks like words all over his body, a cassette tape on his torso, a string of pearls, a pained-looking heart on his shoulder, and so many other little things that I can't make out unless I get closer.

My stomach swirls. Misha?

He's a foot taller than the girl, with broad shoulders and a narrow waist. He gives the young woman a playful scowl while she digs in his pocket and pulls out his wallet. Flipping it open, she plucks a few bills out and gives him a sweet smile.

A pang of jealousy hits me. She's so familiar with him.

I would be like that with him. No one knows him better.

But she tosses his wallet back at him, nearly hitting him in the face.

The looks he gives her . . .

It's his sister. Annie.

I exhale with relief, but I don't know why. He's talked about girlfriends before. Of course he would have one from time to time. I mean, look at him.

My eyes trail up his toned stomach, the muscles in his arms, his long, beautiful fingers . . . Hands that have played a guitar, opened my letters, and written me thousands upon thousands of words over the last seven years.

"I don't need company, sweetheart," he suddenly says.

I blink. Huh?

I look up, realizing he's talking to me.

I suck in a breath, realizing I'm only ten feet away from him. I'm standing right in front of him. *Shit.*

Annie looks at me, then down, counting her money like she's a little embarrassed for me.

I watch him dig in a duffel bag, pulling out a black T-shirt. I almost spin around to leave, but . . .

I can't bolt. I don't want to.

He doesn't need company? Did he seriously just say that to me?

"Misha," I say, forcing my voice to steady. "Lare?"

"Yeah?"

My heart thumps hard. It's him.

Fucking hell.

He doesn't look at me, just slides his arms into the shirt like he's used to young women fainting in his presence. I cock an eyebrow, squaring my shoulders.

"You have a . . . a band." I move in a couple of steps. "Right?"

"Everyone wants the lead singer," some guy teases, coming in and dropping a cooler on the ground.

Annie dives down to open it, but Misha grabs the collar of her jacket and hauls her back up. It must have beer inside of it.

"Of my band . . ." The new guy breaks into song, Annie joining him. "My band, my band, my band, my baaaaand . . ."

Misha flashes a little snarl, and they both laugh. I smile, too. It's a D12 song. Sung by Eminem. He hates Eminem. And they seem to know that as well as I do.

"I'm not in the mood," he says again, this time to them.

Annie hugs him again. "Sorry," she says. "You don't have to stay if you don't want to."

"Fine." He pulls on his shirt. "You ready to leave?"

She pulls away, unamused. "I'll be at the bonfire."

His friend slaps Misha on the back and follows her, but I stay, watching him don a black hoodie over the shirt.

Music and hollers go off behind me, but we're alone.

It's weird. I've never imagined him, because I never had to. He's been in my head for so much of my life. Every word he ever wrote owns a place inside me.

"Sweetheart?" I say, repeating what he called me. "That's how you talk to women?"

"Sorry." He smiles to himself. "I don't have a fountain of pre-conditioned responses like 'Go, team' and 'Victory, victory, that's our cry' to tap into."

His eyebrows have an arch most women would envy. I almost hate him for being good-looking. I don't know if I'll be able to write him now, knowing that.

"Victory, victory, that's our cry . . ." I take a step closer. "All I ever wanted was for you to be my . . ." I think. "My . . . My end."

He stops, raising his eyes to me and pinching his brow.

"You write your own lyrics?" I ask.

He doesn't say anything, but that's okay. I have his attention now.

Riley Costigan was right. Perspective is everything.

I just want to talk to him for a minute. "Can I ask you something, Misha Lare?"

He still doesn't speak.

I soften my expression. "Does my bow bother you?"

He darts his eyes up to the top of my head and then back down. A snort escapes him.

He tosses his duffel inside the tent, his demeanor softening a little. "It's, uh . . . it is kind of . . ." He rises and looks at me. "Wow."

"You don't like cheerleaders?"

He shrugs. "I don't know any."

I gaze at the piercing on his bottom lip. Did he tell me about that?

"Yeah," I whisper, having a hard time tearing my eyes away from his mouth. "I guess it would be bad to judge someone without knowing them, right?"

I take the bow, unsnapping the clasp, and pull it off my head. The rest of my hair falls around my shoulders, caressing the sides of my face. I could be any girl here.

"See?" I tell him. "It's not all lip gloss and back handsprings. I'm made from the same stuff you are."

His gaze zones in on me, and this time it's him taking a step closer. "I know someone who goes to your school. She doesn't like the cheerleaders."

Sparks light under my skin. He's talking about me.

"All of us or just one of us?" I inquire.

"Might she hate you?" he asks instead. "What's your name? I'll ask her."

Nice try.

I sigh. "I find that judgy people are usually just jealous. Is she ugly?"

His expression falls, and I see his jaw flex.

Something warm swells in my chest.

He's protective of me.

"Too ugly to get laid?" I continue, pressing my luck to see how far he'll go. "She sounds bitter. Like she's looking to place blame and hate on everyone who's getting good dick when she's not."

He closes the distance between us. "Stop talking."

"Or what?" I taunt. "No one who's getting it is *that* unhappy."

I hear the air he draws in through his nose, and I know that if I were a guy, he would've hit me already.

"She's dying of the cold," I say in a low voice, "because she won't ask anyone to keep her warm."

His eyes falter. "Dying of the cold . . ."

And I know he's getting ideas for lyrics to a song. I help him with his music a lot.

He locks his jaw again, hardening his gaze.

"I know." I nod. "It's bad to judge someone without knowing them."

Just like he fucking gave attitude because I'm in a cheerleader uniform.

"You seem like a good friend." I start to back away. "She's lucky."

He doesn't move or blink.

"It was really nice to meet you," I tell him and turn, walking away.

I feel like I'm being pulled back, but I force my feet forward. I have to be satisfied with that. In case I die, I know I met him and talked to him. That's enough.

I don't want him to know, though. He might like me when I have all the time in the world to figure out what I want to say in a letter, but I'm not ready for him to really know me. What if it's weird? What if I don't live up to his expectations?

He was exactly as he seemed in his letters. And more. I'm not, though. I can't risk losing him.

I head to the bonfire, glancing over my shoulder. He's writing on the inside of his forearm, as if he's afraid he'll forget something and doesn't want to waste time looking for a piece of paper.

Someone steps up to my side. "You shouldn't be here."

Trey Burrowes stands next to me, his hands casually resting in his pockets.

But his gaze is hard.

I shift my gaze to Lyla, seeing the gleam in hers.

She called him. She just loves to start shit, doesn't she?

And just as I was thinking I might be having fun.

"Afraid of a little competition from some Thunder Bay guys?" I ask him.

He takes the last step up to me, staring down. "I have no competition."

I can't think of a retort fast enough. Trey Burrowes scares me.

He's the one everyone wants. He's hot, popular, active in every social circle at school (the important ones anyway), and if I show him that I want him, I'll be queen.

And finally, people will want to be me. I've wanted that since forever.

"You shouldn't have come here without me," he says, swinging his eyes around the Thunder Bay party. "These people are dangerous."

So is he. I've heard the talk, which is why I haven't given in to him yet. Once he has me, he'll treat me like shit, too.

I see a dark form move out of the corner of my eye.

"Well . . ." I fix my attention back on Trey. "As you see, I'm in one piece."

So far.

Another figure moves into my line of sight; both of them circle Trey and me.

Masks. They wear masks, like the guys in the trees. One of them is yellow and another is white with blood around the eyes and mouth.

I look to my left and then right, seeing the black holes of their eyes dip down and back up as they slowly take me in.

Horsemen. I've never seen them, but I've heard of them. They don't come to Falcon's Well, and I never come here.

Some years ago, four friends started a tradition where everyone gets permission to act like an animal. Thunder Bay Prep, Misha's school, always has a group of them. They reign until they graduate, and then others throw down over who gets the crown next. Sometimes there are four, sometimes there are more. And Devil's Night is their night. This is their party.

And my cheerleading uniform from a rival school has gotten their attention.

"We know just what to do with you," the one in the yellow mask says.

They stop, eyeing me. Trey straightens.

But before he can get in their face, Yellow Mask turns to him. "Don't."

He takes off his mask, and I see it's Jarek Anders. Captain of their basketball and baseball teams. He's going to MIT, and rumor has it, he actually got in on merit.

His blond hair lies messy over his forehead, his dark brown eyes meeting mine. "We know just what to do with you."

"Your imagination doesn't stretch far enough to shock me."

His eyes dance. "Because you expect the worst from people."

I don't expect it. I'm just ready for it.

A couple more of his friends show up, one in a silver mask with blacked-out cheekbones and another in a deep green one with fangs.

"I know your type," Anders tells me. "With your intolerant morality."

He literally *just* met me.

"You're in love with the boundaries you set for everyone else and feel so much more comfortable pissing on things than opening your eyes," he says. "No, I think what shocks you the most are things that make you feel or look weak, right?"

I go still.

"And feeling things that change you," he goes on, all four of them starting to circle me. "You've never fucked someone you love, have you?"

I clench my teeth.

"In fact," Anders continues, the amusement in his tone clear. "I'll bet you a million dollars that you've never been in love. You want to take that bet?"

My skin vibrates with awareness, and I actually wish Trey would shut him up now.

"Do you know what it's like to feel physical pain in your chest when you look at someone else?" Anders asks me. "I've felt that. Have you?"

I suddenly find myself wondering about the person he's talking about. And hating that maybe Misha was right. Everyone has a story. Not everyone is forgivable, he once told me, but everyone is relatable. There's always a reason.

Nevertheless, I don't deserve to be toyed with.

"She's boring," White Mask says as they move around me.

Anders cocks his head at me. "But salvageable."

And he's going to save me himself. What a hero.

"I can shock you." He leans in, and I feel the party close in on us as everyone notices them fixated on me. "And I won't even touch you. Here's your challenge . . ."

I glance at Trey, but I don't know why. I can handle myself. I raise my chin a little.

"You are going to take your phone to the caves," Anders instructs, "and you are going to be our videographer tonight. You don't talk to anyone. Not a single person. You drift, and you record. Photos, videos, whatever you want. Just watch and absorb." He starts to don his mask again. "I'll catch up—"

"No," I reply.

He stops, looking at me.

Silver Mask sways behind him, tilting his head from side to side. "Oh, she said no."

I nod. "I said no. I don't need to be enlightened."

Salvageable . . . Please. They're all on some weird Kool-Aid.

"Then you have nothing to fear," Anders tells me.

"No," I state again.

Green Mask floats past me. "We're very good at turning a no into a yes."

. . . when you're rich, I'm sure.

But then I hear a familiar voice. "Knock it off."

I flash my eyes to my left, spotting Misha walking up. He glares at the Horsemen, pursing his lips as the ring glints in the light. His classmates pay him no mind.

Anders inches in. "Where are your friends?"

What?

"The guy and girl you arrived with?" he clarifies.

I glance to where Lyla was a few minutes ago, but she's not there now. I circle my eyes around the area. Riley Costigan drifts into my periphery, but I can't find Ten, either.

I swallow.

Jarek Anders' eyes shift upward, and I follow, seeing Lyla and Ten hanging thirty feet above our heads by their ankles.

I gasp. "Stop!"

I start for the ends of the rope, where a crew of guys holds each one on the other side of the bonfire, but Trey pulls me back.

"Let them go!" I shout.

I don't give a shit if this is a joke. Pranks go bad all the time.

But all I hear are chuckles behind the masks.

Goddammit!

"I said knock it off," Misha tells them again.

Anders lifts his eyes. "Careful, Misha. Your cousin keeps you safe, but four years is a long time to fucking push us without learning your lesson."

I pull away from Trey. He won't fucking do anything without backup.

"And you waited until he was *out of prison* to give me that lesson?" Misha taunts.

I hesitate. *Cousin . . . prison . . . huh?*

There are some things he hasn't told me, apparently.

I look up at my friends, their wrists tied and gags in their mouths. Ten thrashes, and I want to tell him to hold still. I could move on with my life if I lost Lyla, but I'd miss him.

"I'll make you a deal," Anders tells Misha. "You take her place."

"No." I jerk away when Trey tries to pull me back again. "I'll do it, but you win nothing. This night is far from over."

But Misha steps forward another step. "I'll do it."

I turn to him, seeing his eyes already on me. I shake my head. He doesn't have to do this. Why take my place? He doesn't know me. As far as he knows anyway.

Anders spins around, addressing the crowd. "Misha gets a minute head start! Whoever finds him . . . gets him in their tent all night long."

Laughter goes off, followed by excited coos, and I'm guessing there's some inside joke I don't know about.

I can tell Misha isn't friendly with the Horsemen, though. Getting him right where they want him sounds like a big deal to everyone.

"Does he have to put out?" a guy jokes.

"You get him in your tent," Anders replies. "The rest is up to you both."

Chuckles surround us, and I notice young women sharing whispers between them, eyeing my best friend in the world with a smile I don't like.

I turn to him. "Misha . . ."

But he stares at Anders instead. "Release her friends."

"As soon as you're gone," he assures him.

I turn my eyes on Misha, barely breathing. What happens when someone finds him? Sex was what the Horsemen were implying, but there are other possibilities. I don't like a single fucking one of them.

Misha steps, getting ready to take off, and I shake my head.

"Watch her," he tells someone, and I look to see his friend from earlier standing next to his sister.

I open my mouth to argue. Why would he need to watch Misha's sister? Is Misha planning on not being back for a while? What—

I turn to him. "Misha . . ."

"Ready?" Green Mask calls out.

Misha meets my worried eyes but looks away from me just as quickly.

"Set?" White Mask follows.

And then Silver Mask bellows, "Go!"

The crowd howls, screams rise into the sky, but . . .

Misha doesn't run.

Of course he doesn't run.

He walks.

One step, then another, as shouts go off around him, and I ball my fists, knowing he only has a minute to hide or do whatever it is he plans on doing.

Turning to face me, he backs away, holding my eyes.

"Run!" I whisper-yell.

Jesus, run!

But of course, Misha Lare never does what he's told. Twisting around, he walks, disappearing into the trees and the dark woods beyond.

Trey snakes a hand around my waist, pulling me. "Let's go."

Without Lyla and Ten? I shove his hand away and charge forward. "Cut them loose," I order Anders.

But he's still watching the black hole between the trees where Misha disappeared.

"Fuckin' piece of shit," Silver Mask says at his side. "I want to teach him a lesson."

"He's a legacy," Riley Costigan chimes in. "You can't touch him."

"You stay out of this," Anders tells him.

A legacy? Because of his cousin? Who's Misha's cousin?

"Grayson will cut off your heads," Costigan warns them.

Anders' mouth curves into a smile. "We'll see."

Lyla and Ten are lowered to the ground, their hands and feet unbound before they rip out the gags.

They run over to Trey and me. Ten grabs my arm. "Let's get out of here . . ."

But I spin around, watching everyone don masks, the Horsemen jumping up and down and getting pumped up as Jarek Anders watches the countdown on his phone.

"Ryen!" Ten blurts out. "Let's go!"

The music blares; people dig their shoes into the ground, getting ready to shoot off. Are they for real? What's going to happen when they catch him?

"All right!" Anders raises his hand and then brings it down, slicing through the air. "Go!" he shouts.

As I lock my jaw so hard it aches, the crowd fires off like a sea of baby spiders scurrying into the night at top speed.

I gulp. *No.*

Someone clutches the crook of my arm, and I almost yank away, but Riley Costigan gets in my face. "You want to save his ass?" he bites out. "Find him first."

And he shoves me toward the woods. I stumble as the urgency in his eyes makes my heart stop for a second. If he's scared, that's not a good sign. I don't know if they'll hurt Misha, but they'll make sure this isn't fun for him.

Whipping around, I bolt after everyone else, hearing Trey shout behind me, "Ryen, stop!"

But fire blazes in my legs, and it feels like they have a mind of their own. I fly through the woods.

Students scatter, shouts and howls filling the air as all the predators search for their prey, but after a few seconds, I slow to a stop.

Misha's not stupid. And he doesn't run from people.

Everyone around me disappears ahead, thinking he's on the move, because that would be smart.

He's not there. He's close.

"Misha!" I whisper, branches creaking over my head as I look around large boulders and thick trunks. "Misha, I'm not gonna make you have sex with me. Come out!"

If I find him, then he's mine. They'll leave him alone.

The light breeze chills my bare legs, and I push my hair out of my face. "Misha?" I yell in a whisper again, scanning the forest for any sign of movement.

He's near. I know he is. He's not giving them the satisfaction of making him run anywhere.

Howls echo all around.

They think they're predators.

I drift around in a circle, seeing the Ferris wheel past the glow of the bonfire.

I stop.

I remember the first time he mentioned the Cove, because it was the first time he mentioned a place I'd been to, as well. And he loved it even more once they condemned it.

I bite back my smile. He doubled back.

They're all going in the wrong direction.

I race back to the bonfire, staying hidden in the tree line, and jog into the parking lot, thankful my friends are still at the fire. They're probably waiting for me to come back.

I enter the old theme park, the deserted tents, rides, and booths rusty and tattered from years of being left open to the weather to rot. Fallen leaves whirl in baby cyclones around the steel steps leading up to the Tilt-A-Whirl, and I can't even hear the waves crash against the rocks off the nearby cliffs. Just the flap of the torn tents in the wind.

"Misha?" I call out, louder this time. "Misha, say something."

Calls and screams echo in the distance, and I spin around, making sure they're not heading here.

But before I can see anything, arms circle me and a hand covers my mouth. I scream, but it's muffled in his fingers as he drags us backward.

We enter a small booth. He draws the curtain and then releases me. I whip around, seeing Misha with his hands planted high on the walls at his sides.

He pinches his brow together. "How did you know I'd be here?"

He's not angry but definitely suspicious.

"Because you knew they were stupid," I tell him.

And I know my animal.

But I don't say that out loud.

He cocks a brow, looking like he doesn't believe me, but he doesn't argue. "We're not screwing."

Yeah, poor me. "I don't even have a tent," I gripe.

I came to find him as a favor to get him out of suffering any consequences. I don't chase guys for sex.

Dropping down to the little bench, I see the screen in front of me, realizing this is an old photo booth. Everything is dark, though. There's no electricity here anymore.

It's not a good hiding spot.

"What's your name?" he asks me.

I open my mouth but close it again. I'm not ready to tell him, but I don't want to lie, either.

"You know mine," he points out.

He's going to find out I'm me eventually, and he's going to think I played with him, so it's best to just deal with it now, but . . .

I'm not ready for our friendship to end. It might if he knows who I am.

He hangs his head, his eyes pressing into me from behind locks of hair. "Was that your boyfriend?" he asks.

"Who?"

"The one who looks like a date rapist."

I can't help it. I laugh. It's not at all funny, but it's a classic display of why Misha is my favorite person in the whole world. He's great at reading subtext.

I don't know if Trey would ever do something like that, but he's definitely the type to sleep with his friends' wives someday.

"No," I reply. "He's not my boyfriend."

A smile teases his lips. "He dresses really well."

I shake with another laugh. Coming from Misha, that's a huge insult. I'm good at reading subtext, too.

"He drinks protein shakes," I go on, grimacing. "And uses Snapchat and has, like, a concrete future."

He shakes his head, smiling.

But then his expression grows serious. "He wants to sleep with you."

I go still. How long was he watching us talk?

I know what Trey wants from me, but it hurts to hear someone else notice. Makes it more real, because I don't trust myself to resist him forever. I do dumb things, because how good it'll make me look to other people is more of a temptation sometimes than how it's going to make me feel.

That's why I can't lose Misha. I'm exactly who I want to be around him.

"Should we go?" I start to rise. "I found you. You're in the clear. They'll think you're with me tonight."

But he steps in. "I don't want go back to those fucking people yet."

He gazes down at me, and I stand there, my chest brushing his.

Sensation lights under my skin, and I don't want to go back, either. He may not feel like he fits in with those people any more than I feel like I fit in with the people at my school, but Thunder Bay boys have a reputation for being hard to resist, and I think he's more like them than he knows.

And I'm suddenly jealous, when I wasn't for all the years before now. No one else should've ever had him.

I hold his eyes. "Are you going to ask your friend about me?"

"Why?"

I pause. "I don't know."

Maybe I just want to know what he'd say about me.

"Why do they hate you?" I inquire instead, sitting back down.

He sighs, dropping his arms and leaning back against the wall. "Because I have a limited bullshit tolerance."

Yes, he does.

"And because I see through them," he tells me. "Because I know I'm going to die . . ."

My eyebrows rise.

"And you're going to die," he continues, "and everyone who knows us will eventually die . . ."

I hold my breath.

"And even if we create anything that lasts beyond our death, there will come a time when our names are forgotten," he says. "That in the trillions of years left in the universe, there may never be any evidence that we were ever here. That we ever existed."

My eyes burn.

He shakes his head, whispering, "Nothing they do is a valuable use of my time."

Tears fill my eyes, and I can't look away from him.

This is how he is. How he always is. A constant reminder of how lucky I am to be here. To be breathing.

And to know him.

"And right now?" I ask quietly.

Would he choose to be here with me?

He gazes at me, a light sweat cooling my neck as the breeze brushes my lips, and I stop breathing as if I no longer need air.

I only need him.

He dives down and scoops me up into his arms, and I gasp, wrapping my body around his. I circle my arms and legs around him, his mouth crashing down on mine. *Misha*.

His lips are mad, moving over mine in a frenzy as I moan and bite, flicking his lip ring with my tongue and feeling him between my teeth as I slide my fingers into his hair. I groan, his arm tightening around my waist like a steel band and my legs locking him hard, trying to get closer and closer.

I force my mouth off, our eyes meeting, but I can't stop. I kiss him again, breathless as the warmth of his tongue seeps into every inch of my body.

"Misha . . ." I breathe out.

"What the fuck is happening?" he begs, but he doesn't wait for an answer. He pulls off my top, and I work off his hoodie and T-shirt, his skin meeting mine and his hand peeling down my bra strap to kiss, suck, and bite my shoulder and my neck.

I kiss the tattoo over his collarbone that trails up his neck, the fire on his lips burning every inch of me he touches.

"We can't." I tilt my head to the side, almost in fucking pain with how good his lips feel on my neck. "We can't."

"Jesus Christ." He grips my hair at the back of my head and presses our foreheads together. "Who are you?"

I shake my head. What the hell am I going to do? We can't be friends now.

He pulls down my bra, staring into my eyes as he covers my breast with his hand.

"Please stop me," I whisper. "I'm bad news."

His other hand squeezes my thigh, a gleam hitting his eyes. "Oh, good."

And he kisses me deep and long, yanking my body in closer and harder so I feel the thick muscle in his jeans pressing between my legs.

I can't stop. I'm never stopping.

But just then, the curtain flies open.

We startle, our lips separating, and I cover my chest with my arms.

Jarek Anders grins, the other Horsemen standing behind him, still in their masks.

"Look at that," he coos. "He's a man, after all."

"Fuck off," Misha growls, and I'm glad I'm naked enough that he wants to shield me or else he'd be going after them.

"Your cousin would be proud," Anders says. "Taking back some of the Falcon's Well pussy."

Misha tenses in my arms, but one of Anders' friends grabs the curtain. "Come on, let's leave them alone," he says.

They shut the curtain, chuckles fading away as they leave. Did they know I'd find him? Did they follow me? Predator, prey, son of a bitch. I'm so confused.

I stare at the side of Misha's face as he glares at the closed curtain. My chest hurts.

Physical pain. I press my lips to his temple, caressing his face one last time.

He'll think none of this was real. He'll think I did this on purpose to toy with him.

Everything hurts.

"I should go," I murmur, trying to push against his chest.

But he keeps me pressed against the wall of the photo booth, my legs still wrapped around his waist.

He turns, his sharp eyes boring into me. "Who are you?"

I clamp my mouth shut.

His stare pierces me. "I won't ask her about you," he says.

Her. His friend in Falcon's Well.

Me.

My heart skips.

"She always tells me the truth." He pinches my chin, keeping me still. "Do I want to know the truth about you?"

I tremble but not from the cold.

Flexing my jaw, I push him away and grab my cheerleading top off the ground, pulling it back on. Swiping open the curtain, I see those assholes making their way out of the Cove and back to the bonfire. I don't want to want to run into them again. It won't be good.

I step out of the booth, but Misha takes my arm, pulling me back.

I plant my hands on his stomach as he hovers over my mouth. The ring on his lip is smooth against mine.

I don't want to leave him.

"Tomorrow's Halloween," he says in a low voice. "I'll be around."

I hold his eyes.

"Find me again," he whispers.

Please keep reading for Ryen's letter to Delilah.

Dear Delilah,

My name is Ryen Trevarrow. We were friends in fourth grade.

I'm sure you don't even remember me, but I remember you. In fact, you cross my mind quite a lot. And if you do remember me, then please keep reading, because there are a lot of things I'd like to say.

You're under no obligation to listen, but I would be grateful.

By now, I'm sure your life—like mine—has changed a lot. Your memories of me—if you have any—could range from resentful to so ambiguous that I barely register on your radar anymore. Maybe you haven't thought about me in years.

But just in case . . . I needed to do this. Maybe for you but especially for me. I have a lot of guilt, and I deserve it, but there are things that need to be said, and it's long past time.

You see, the image is still in my head. You standing against the wall on the playground, alone because I wouldn't be your friend anymore. I can't imagine what you were thinking that day and every day after, but I hope you know that what I did and what everyone else said or put you through was never your fault. It was mine, and you were simply there.

There's a secret I want to share with you. I haven't even told my best friend, Misha, because it was so embarrassing.

When I was nine I had a routine every Sunday night. At about six o'clock, after dinner, I would start to gather all of my hygiene products: shampoo, conditioner, soap, loofah, clippers, nail file . . . I'd line up everything on the windowsill above the bathtub, and for the next hour, I'd bathe.

That's right. I was in the bathroom, cleaning, scrubbing, and making sure every damn piece of hair smelled like a lily-scented brook in a mountain meadow for an hour. Then I'd finally emerge and begin the moisturizing and nail-cleaning process.

Good grief, right? But wait, there's more.

Then I spent ten minutes flossing and brushing, and even more time picking out my clothes, which of course had to be ironed and laid out for Monday morning. It was a new week, and it was a new me. I was going to have more friends. I was going to be with the popular girls. People would like me.

Because in my nine-year-old head, the bath washed away more than the daily grime. It washed away the old me, and somehow, because I polished up my appearance, my personality would magically be different, too.

This went on for about a year. More than fifty Sundays of high hopes, and more than fifty Mondays ending with not a damn thing different than it was the previous week. No amount of soap and water, perfect nails, or pretty hair could change what I hated about myself on the inside.

That I was timid. That I was uptight and never broke rules. That I felt so uncomfortable in large groups and couldn't talk easily with people. That my music and movie choices weren't like the average kid's.

Plain and simple: I didn't fit in.

I had nothing in common with other kids around me, and being limited to my small environment, I couldn't find anyone I did have things in common with. I constantly felt like I didn't belong. Like I was crashing a party and people were just waiting for me to get the hint and leave.

That was until I met you. We started hanging out and talked about everything. Every day at recess, we'd walk around the perimeter of the field and chat about stuff we had in common. You were kind and funny, you listened to me and didn't make me feel pressured or awkward. I was glad to finally have a friend.

Until I started wondering why I didn't have more.

We'd keep walking and talking, but sooner or later, my eyes would drift over to where everyone else was playing and laughing, and I'd start to feel left out again. What made them so special to be crowded with people? Why did they seem happier and a part of something better? What were they doing and how were they behaving that I wasn't?

I came to the conclusion that I needed to see myself as better before I could be better. And by better, I mean popular. In putting myself on a pedestal with whatever nasty behavior I could, I believed I was elevating myself. And in a way, I guess I was. Being mean got those friends I thought I wanted.

Now, there's nothing I can say that makes what I did to you all right. I know that. Even a kid knows how to be nice. But I wanted you to know that I'm sorry. I was wrong, and I regret what I did. It was the first act in a long line of acts that made me a very unhappy girl, and I see now how valuable one good friend truly is and how little those popular kids actually mean in the big, wide world.

I can't change the past, but I will do better in the future.

I'm sorry if I bothered you. If you're reading this and wondering why I dwelled on something that was perhaps so insignificant to you. Maybe you're surrounded by a great life and tons of happiness, and I'm not even a memory.

But if I hurt you, I'm sorry. I want you to know that.

You were a good friend, and you deserved better. Thank you for being there for me when I needed you. I wish I'd done the same.

Love,
Ryen

LYRICS

Punk 57

Anything goes when everyone knows
Where do you hide when their highs are your lows?
So much, so hard, so long, so tired,
Let them eat until you're ground into nothing.

Don't you worry your glossy little lips.
What they savor 'ventually loses its flavor.
I wanna lick, while you still taste like you.

Bookmark it, says the cheerleader
I promise we'll come back to this spot.
I have shit to do first. You won't wait a lot.

I can't make her stay,
And I can't watch her go.
I'll keep her hellfire heart,
And bookmark it 'fore it goes cold.

Fifty-seven times I didn't call
Fifty-seven letters I didn't send,
Fifty-seven stitches to breathe again, and then I fucking pretend.

Fifty-seven days to not need you
Fifty-seven times to give up on you
Fifty-seven steps away from you,
Fifty-seven nights of nothing but you.

I'm just the punk who passed the time,
Your bouncing board, your secret little thrill.
Something tells me you're close to breaking,
'Cause I need to be more to you than just time to fill.

Bookmark it, says the cheerleader
I promise we'll come back to this spot.
I have shit to do first. You won't wait a lot.

I can't make her stay,
And I can't watch her go.
I'll keep her hellfire heart,
And bookmark it ' fore it goes cold.

Pearls

A picture is worth a thousand words,
But my thousand words slice deeper.
What doesn't kill us makes us stronger,
Fuck that. I've become a hide and seeker.

Treat others how you want to be treated,
But what if tonight I want to be burned?
You told us it's better to be safe than sorry,
And little sister listened, but I was the one who learned.

Reap, reap, reap, you don't even know,
All you did suffer is what you did sow!
Necessitate, medicate, eradicate, resuscitate.
Swallow your pearls, but for me it was too late.
Alone, Empty, Fraud, Shame, Fear,
Close your eyes. There's nothing to see out here.

Do better, be more, too many, too much,
I'm about to fucking choke, I can't force it down.
So string up the little wisdoms and wrap them 'round my neck,
I'll strangle myself with your pearls of wisdom and die a wreck.

You told us to prepare now and play later,
But what's in here is better than what's out there.
I took an umbrella to save me from the rain,
But the lightning hit, and you didn't care.

Reap, reap, reap, you don't even know,
All you did suffer is what you did sow!
Necessitate, medicate, eradicate, resuscitate.
Swallow your pearls, but for me it was too late.
Alone, Empty, Fraud, Shame, Fear,
Close your eyes. There's nothing to see out here.

AUTHOR'S NOTE

If you're reading this, then hopefully that means you finished the book. And if that's the case, then I'm very glad.

Punk 57 was a different book to write, and a difficult one. We romance readers can be very hard on our heroines. We often see ourselves in those roles and compare their decisions to the decisions we would've made instead. We tend to judge them more harshly than we do the heroes, because we hold them to the same expectations we hold ourselves. This is why many heroines are often innocent, timid, and kind, with good hearts. Seeing those women find their power is a fun journey. They're easy to love.

Ryen, on the other hand, was not. Especially in the first few chapters.

Knowing this, of course I was very scared. I only hoped you'd stick with her long enough to see her come around and eventually be proud of her.

Ryen's need for recognition, adoration, and inclusion echoes with us all. We see it all the time. No kid wants to be different. They want to belong, they desire the approval of others, and they, most often, aren't yet mentally strong enough to be able to stand alone. As we get older, though, most of us develop that capability. We learn that nothing feels better than truly loving yourself, even if it means those around you do not. We joyously find that we just don't give a damn anymore.

And it feels pretty great.

But most of us have done things—unfair things—in the name of self-preservation. That's the story I wanted to tell. Ryen hating who she was, trying to be different and trying to find a way for people to finally see her, but then discovering that she hates herself even more. Lying to yourself never moves you forward.

Thank you for reading, and thank you for (hopefully) finishing the story. And to anyone out there who might've related to what some of the characters went through—just remember: it gets better, you are important, and you can't be replaced.

Hang on. You'll find your tribe.

Penelope Douglas

ACKNOWLEDGMENTS

First, to the readers—so many of you have been there, sharing your excitement and showing your support, day in and day out, and I am so grateful for your continued trust. Thank you. I know my adventures aren't always easy, but I love them, and I'm glad so many others do, too.

To my family—my husband and daughter put up with my crazy schedule, my candy wrappers, and my spacing off every time I think of a conversation, plot twist, or scene that just jumped into my head at the dinner table. You both really do put up with a lot, so thank you for loving me anyway.

To Jane Dystel, my agent at Dystel and Goderich Literary Management—there is absolutely no way I could ever give you up, so you're stuck with me.

To the House of PenDragon—you're my happy place. Well, you and Pinterest. Thanks for being the support system I need and always being positive.

To Vibeke Courtney—my indie editor who goes over every move I make with a fine-tooth comb. Thank you for teaching me how to write and laying it down straight.

To Kivrin Wilson—long live the quiet girls! We have the loudest minds.

To Ing Cruz at As the Pages Turn book blog—you support out of the goodness of your heart, and I can't repay you enough. Thank you for the release blitzes, blog tours, and being by my side since the beginning.

To Milasy Mugnolo—who reads, always giving me that vote of confidence I need, and makes sure I have at least one person to talk to at a signing.

To Lisa Pantano Kane—you challenge me with the hard questions.

To Lee Tenaglia—who makes such great art for the books and whose Pinterest boards are my crack! Thank you. Really, you need to go into business. We should talk.

To all of the bloggers—there are too many to name, but I know who you are. I see the posts and the tags, and all the hard work you do. You spend your free time reading, reviewing, and promoting, and you do it for free. You are the life's blood of the book world, and who knows what we would do without you. Thank you for your tireless efforts. You do it out of passion, which makes it all the more incredible.

To Samantha Young, who shocked me with a tweet about reading *Falling Away* when I didn't even know she knew who I was.

To Jay Crownover, who came up to me at a signing, introduced herself, and said she loved my books (I just stared at her).

To Abbi Glines, who gave her readers a list of books she'd read and loved, and one of them was mine.

To Tabatha Vargo and Komal Petersen, who were the first authors to message me after my first release to tell me how much they loved *Bully*.

To Tijan, Vi Keeland, Helena Hunting, Penelope Ward, and Penny Reid for being there when I need you.

To Eden Butler and N. Michaels, who are ready to read my books at the drop of a hat and give feedback.

To Natasha Preston, who backs me up.

To Amy Harmon for her encouragement, positivity, support, and courage to break the mold.

And to B.B. Reid for reading, sharing the ladies with me, and giving me a Calibre tutorial at twelve thirty in the morning. I'll be nicer when you start sharing your chocolate.

It's validating to be recognized by your peers. Positivity is contagious, so thank you to my fellow authors for spreading the love.

To every author and aspiring author—thank you for the stories you've shared, many of which have made me a happy reader in search of a wonderful escape and a better writer, trying to live up to your standards. Write and create, and don't ever stop. Your voice is important, and as long as it comes from your heart, it is right and good.

Copyright © Penelope Douglas

Penelope Douglas is a *New York Times*, *USA Today*, and *Wall Street Journal* bestselling author. Their books have been translated into twenty languages and include the Fall Away series, the Hellbent series, the Devil's Night series, and the stand-alones *Misconduct*, *Punk 57*, *Birthday Girl*, *Credence*, and *Tryst Six Venom*.